Mendallon

Lark Fitzgerald

Imryn River Press

Editing by Lacey Braziel at On The Page Editorial

Proofreading by Lindsey Hinkel at Ink Rebel Editing

Book Cover by Miblart https://miblart.com/

Map of Mendallon by Stardust Book services https://www.stardustbookservices.com/

First edition 2026

Author website: www.LarkulaAuthor.com

ISBN: 979-8-9941327-0-8 (ebook), 979-8-9941327-1-5 (print), 979-8-9941327-2-2 (hardcover)

Contents

For my boys. May you reach for the stars.

Prologue

Early spring
Year 242 After the Fall

Lieutenant Jaxson stared through his looking glass at the city below. Voluminous white sails billowed above the craft, catching the wind and giving direction as the ship soared over Mendallon. Magic thrummed through the warship. Deep vibrations emanated from the core's magic chamber, which kept the massive frigate aloft. Underneath, the wide, flat hull came to a gentle peak at the front of the ship to prevent rocking when sea landings were necessary.

This landing, however, would be on solid ground, so the crew prepared large iron legs to stabilize the ship's belly. Sailors in black pants and white billowy shirts trimmed the sails as the ship approached the landing site. Magic could steer the ship, but for stealth jobs like this, they used linen sails instead of magic. Thanks to the ship's shields, passersby below who might be sensitive to magic would look, only to be greeted with a reflection of the night sky and find themselves with a gentle urge to look away.

Jaxson smirked as he lowered his spyglass. The reports he had received were true. This land and city had no air defenses. He wasn't here to take advantage of that fact, since air battles were expensive, and he had his orders. They would try subterfuge first and integrate into this society to take what they wanted.

The ship landed outside Mendallon, in a field purchased by one of his brokers. Willowy trees enclosed the field. The moon cast the field in living shadows as the trees swayed in the breeze. Two of the shadows resolved into men dressed in dark robes. The men boarded the ship and came to attention in front of Jaxson, lowering their hoods. The man on the left was dark-haired and fair-skinned, while the other was brown-haired with sun-kissed skin. Both men were brown-eyed and clean-shaven, as was common in these parts.

"Report," Jaxson commanded, crossing his muscular arms. He held them tight to his chest to resist the urge to rub his newly shaven face. To his relief, he had been allowed to keep his mane of black hair—a mark of status with his people.

The man on the left spoke first. "Our city accommodations have been secured. Mages have confirmed that the main hosting site will support our projected numbers."

Jaxson nodded, shifting his gaze to the second man. "We have acquired several sites within the city in different districts. I have arranged meetings with three nobles who want to see a change in the current power structure."

"Very good. You will find the forces you requested below deck. I expect reports daily. Head out."

The two men bowed and moved to the lower deck. Moments later, soldiers wearing black leather armor, common to the local noble guards' attire, and dark cloaks departed in groups of twos and threes.

The next day, the first of the city's children disappeared.

Chapter 1

Market

Three weeks later

Kal narrowly avoided a fellow pedestrian as he expertly navigated the crowds of the wide street market, edged with booths and tents. His height gave him an advantage in choosing a path.

Kal inhaled as a cool spring breeze brought relief from the thick cloak he wore. He pulled the hood down, exposing his thin black locs and clean-shaven face. The sounds of hawkers selling their wares filled the air, and the thoroughfare was rich with the scent of roasting chicken, pork, and beef—some slathered with a variety of Kimora sauces and others spiced with seasonings brought into the city from the outer provinces of Cartusia. Some vendors catered to tastes from other countries, like the dwarven homeland of Faragrim or the elvish lands of Olander. As a child, Kal had wanted to visit those lands. Instead, he ended up the proprietor of Lily's Inn, where he collected tales of those faraway places instead.

Kal crossed into the shade from the city walls, which loomed nearby and were sectioned with watchtowers.

"Young man! Come try our famous Kebon sticks."

Kal nodded in greeting but continued toward his goal. The food smelled tasty, but Lily wanted him to buy from a butcher whose meats were so tender that visitors from across the realm considered them delectable.

Kal picked his way through the crowd. He had spent the last two years getting used to its rhythms, which had shifted in the previous few weeks as children started disappearing. Kal noticed children's hands clasped too tightly by parents and eyes darting around as people became more cautious of their surroundings.

Mendallon was a city filled with various peoples, most of whom were represented in this market. There were primarily humans, but he saw a few dwarves and even thought he glimpsed elven ears, rare in these parts. The Rim, which spread outside the city up to the gates, catered to those less fortunate or the dockworkers who serviced the bustling trade flow along the River Imryn. If he stayed on this road, he would eventually reach the city gates. All the Rim roads led to the city.

Kal approached a set of message boards and paused. Worried families had pinned images of over a dozen missing children to the board. People had taken to placing flowers near the signs spread throughout the city. Kal suspected the number was higher, since not all missing people got reported. He moved closer, studying their faces. Once he had committed them to memory, he moved back into the flowing crowds, searching for their faces.

Reaching his destination, Macellum's Meat Market, Kal entered the building. Display windows lined the sides with assorted cuts of meat, and a long line snaked through the store. With a heavy sigh, Kal waited.

When it was his turn, the young clerk's eyes sparked in recognition as she greeted him. "Young Master Kal. The usual?"

"Yes, please. Either Lily or I will come by tomorrow to pick it up," he said and paid her.

As he left the store, a painful prickle ran along his skin as tendrils of powerful magic billowed through a crowd of onlookers. His body ached with longing, which propelled him forward. His skin tingled, and he could feel the edge of memory rise within him.

Pain shot through his back, ending at the base of his skull. He felt every nerve ending crackle to life and had an intense urge to turn toward the magic.

It isn't your problem, something deep within his body whispered to him.

He paused and took stock, breathing through the discomfort. More often, he had been getting these debilitating symptoms, always when he was on the cusp of learning something new. Whatever it was, was right there, only a few steps away. Would he find answers if he pushed through the pain? A long moment passed before he decided to endure. He needed answers.

The street, lined with vendors and people, blurred, and his eyes throbbed with the sounds of a man screaming as though he were being branded by a hot iron. Kal blinked rapidly. The pressure behind his temples increased with each step. He tried to swallow, only to have his tongue stick to the roof of his mouth, the taste tinny and flat. He rubbed his temples to ease his headache.

Curled up in front of him was a woman with raven-colored hair. Her arms covered her head as though she were warding off blows. To her right lay a dark-haired adolescent girl, her brown skin covered in bruises and blood. He couldn't tell whether she was dead or just unconscious.

Off to the left stood several street-toughs, eyes wide, mouths agape as they stared down at their companion, who screamed, muscles taut with pain. Bystanders stood around with various looks of horror on their faces.

Kal's stomach twisted, and his vision flickered in and out. In one heartbeat, he could see cords of light joining the street-tough to the young woman curled in a ball, and the next, he could not. In strobing flashes, he made out a black corded thread of power flowing from the woman on the ground into the screaming man.

Kal's throat clenched and his stomach churned, mouth watering as the contents of his stomach searched for a way out. Without thought, he made a chopping motion with his hand, unaware that it created a blade that sliced through the life-threatening flows of magic she wielded. The man's screaming diminished as the magic no longer cut into him.

Kal approached them and looked down at the young woman's face. Though beautiful, her irises were wide and fixed, unseeing, her face taut. Blood dribbled from the side of her mouth. He saw the instant she came back from her trance, face twisting as she heard the screams—guttural gasps of a man whose voice shredded with each raw and wretched whimper.

She turned toward the commotion, a look of confusion on her face, but Kal's cloak blocked her line of sight.

The thugs came forward and gathered up their man, hurrying away as the crowd dispersed.

Kal squatted down in front of her. He knew he shouldn't intervene more than he already had, but something about her situation touched him. Lily would chide him for bringing home more strays, but these women were clearly not the instigators, so she would eventually understand.

"My name is Kal, and you must not kill with magic. I'll take you both somewhere safe before they regroup or the guard arrives, asking questions. It's best you two not be here to answer."

Her shoulders hunched, but she nodded agreement, and as he lifted her, she mumbled and reached out a hand for a green token on the ground surrounded by other coins. A token that, as they watched, changed color to the silver of a regular coin.

Her hand twitched, then fell slack as she sobbed in his arms.

Kal looked around, making eye contact with a young man. "You there. I'll pay you two crowns to carry the younger girl."

"Don't need your money. What they tried to do to those ladies was wrong," the young man said as he gently scooped up the bleeding girl and followed Kal.

Chapter 2

The Mage

K al settled the woman and the adolescent girl in separate rooms at the inn, leaving Lily and the staff in charge of their care. He had just returned from the attack site a second time to remove all traces of the ladies when bells rang behind him, announcing a new arrival to the inn's common room.

Kal turned to find a squat man standing there, his robes tight around the middle as it held in his girth. His hazel eyes changed color as he moved closer. The broad black band on his left arm bore the sun symbol of the mage guild surrounded by six stars.

The man walked up to Kal and stood studying him, before speaking. "Hekallion."

Kal furrowed his brow at the use of his full first name. "And you are?" Kal inquired.

"I am Master Evans." The man paused as if waiting for a response. Kal didn't know the name or the face.

"You are a mage?" Kal asked, wanting confirmation.

"I am."

Surprise roiled through Kal. He assumed there were no overweight mages, because the price of wielding burned up your resources. "I presume you are here for the young woman and the girl?"

Master Evans cleared his throat, tilting his head to the side as he reached into his pocket and withdrew a letter. "The young woman, when she awakens, give her this." He handed the letter to Kal, who took it from him, frowning. The letter was addressed to Jenna Sturmich.

"You will not be taking them with you?" Kal raised his eyebrows.

"Unfortunately not. The elder has other tasks to complete before she can return, and the younger girl... she should be here for now."

So they are both mages.

Confusion roiled through Kal as Master Evans reached into his coat and pulled out a large purse, which he also handed to Kal. "For their care."

"Wait, are you cutting them loose?" Kal asked. "I believe what happened was an act of self-defense."

"The Healers Guild has strict rules about using lethal magic against the nonmagical. It will bend them occasionally, but in this instance, a higher authority has intervened."

Kal frowned. It didn't make sense. Mages were precious and rare, especially after the blight came through, killing off so many of them.

Master Evans frowned. "They have not been entirely cut loose but have instead been tasked with a different role."

"Will they see it that way?" Kal crossed his arms.

Master Evans flinched, then lifted his head. "In time, they will see it was for the best." And with that, he turned and left.

Kal grimaced as the bells chimed once again. It had been his choice to rescue them; he would see it through.

K al made his way through the wide carpeted halls of the inn toward his room.

When he entered, the hair on the back of his neck stood up. He scanned the room. Based on the traps he set, he was confident that no one but him had entered the room since he last departed.

He walked the perimeter of the room, studying the details. His bed was on the left. To the right, he passed a small side table and a dirty clothes basket and ended up at a small desk near one of the windows. Stacks of well-used books crowded the surface, leaving little space for writing.

For a long moment, Kal stood there, studying the desk's surface. Something on the desk had changed since the last time he observed it. Subconsciously, Kal went up on the balls of his feet, as if preparing for an attack.

He placed his hand on his breast pocket, which contained the letter for the young mage. At least that remained unchanged. Kal chewed his lower lip in thought.

He breathed raggedly as he looked at the desk again. This time, he saw it. The cap was not on the inkwell. He reached out and closed the jar, then scanned the desk again. Now, he couldn't find anything out of order. He might have forgotten the cap, but he didn't believe so.

Kal relaxed back onto his feet. Hmm, what had he come here for? Ah, the money pouch. He went over to the rumpled double bed and knelt down, opening a rosewood panel on its side, which exposed a small black safe under his bed. He placed the coin purse Master Evans had given him inside. Closing it, he resealed the panel and studied the room again.

Returning to the desk, he shuffled through the pile of books until he found his journal. He flipped to the last page and added an entry for today's encounter with the two mages and the inkwell.

He flipped back through the pages. There were dozens of entries spanning the last six months. There was the time he followed a light, only to have it go out. It had taken him a candle mark to get back to the inn. Then there was the time Lily accused him of walking through a wall. He definitely didn't do that, but she had been so sure. Then there were more minor issues, like supplies he knew he'd ordered failing to arrive with no trace of an order, followed by a double order the time after that. It was as if somebody erased large swaths of his memory.

His mouth went dry as he recalled the time spent reconstructing his whereabouts. Now, Lily and he had mages to keep an eye on. He would have to lean on her more since he needed to figure out what was happening to him.

Kal grimaced.

Enough. He'd spun his wheels on this before. He would focus on this again after he delivered the letter.

Chapter 3

Jenna

Jenna awoke, blinking to clear her vision. The warm scent of her rescuer tickled her nose. Her bruised throat ached, and her breathing echoed loudly in the room. A round wooden bedside table sat beneath a small window to her right, and there was a white archway in the far wall. Jenna's eyes widened as they darted around the room. Where was her sister? She tried to sit up, but pain rose in her, drying her mouth. Last she had seen, Casi was bleeding in the street.

Her stomach rumbled, and her hands shook as a wave of dizziness struck her. In her panic, she'd used too much magic. Weariness washed over her. She needed to eat something to replenish some of what she'd lost.

She heard the soft murmur of a woman's voice. "Take these towels to the stag room. I'll handle things here."

Her door opened and a middle-aged woman came through the archway.

The woman wore a modest brown apron over a gray dress. Deep brown eyes sparkled in the meager light, and dark curly hair framed her face, hanging loosely below her shoulders. The woman opened the curtains to let more light in, revealing bronze-ringed fingers common to the working class as she turned toward Jenna.

"I'm glad you're awake. Are you thirsty?" the woman asked in a tone that reminded Jenna of her mother.

Jenna flinched at the additional light flowing into the room and nearly coughed, her eyes watering. She tried to ask where her sister was, but nothing came out.

Instead, she nodded to the woman, which set her head throbbing. The woman left the room and returned a few moments later with a jug. Jenna's eyes followed the woman as she poured the liquid into a cup and brought it to her.

Jenna sat up tentatively and reached for the water. Her body protested at her first real motion since waking. She groaned with the effort, and her hands started to shake again. The woman helped to steady the cup, and Jenna drained it twice before looking up at the woman, who smiled pleasantly, taking the cup.

She filled it again and set the cup on the side table. "My name is Lily. Can you tell me your name?

"J-Jen-na," she managed to croak.

"Jenna. That's a lovely name. I run this Inn. Kal found you and brought you here."

Jenna remembered Kal's words. *I'll take you both somewhere safe.*
"G-girl?"

"She is recovering in a different room."

Jenna sagged in relief. Her sister was alive. "H-how lo-ng?"

Lily paused, considering.

"Four candle marks."

Jenna's eyes went round. Pain spiked in her ribs as she reflexively reached into her empty pocket, looking for the token she knew had been lost in the street.

They would have come for me if they wanted, but they didn't. That means I have failed. Try as she might, she couldn't find a way to sugarcoat it, and tears streamed down her face.

"Jenna, what's wrong?"

"Th-they just l-left me there to die," she mumbled.

Jenna felt a warm touch as Lily placed her hand on her shoulder. "It's all right. We'll figure it out together."

But the words brought her no comfort.

L ily sat with her a little longer, holding her hand while she wept. She must have fallen asleep again, but she couldn't remember closing her eyes. When she sat up this time, Lily was gone, but the smell of food greeted her. A steaming bowl of stew sat beside her cup of water. Jenna's stomach growled at the smell of beef. Tears welled again in her eyes.

With trembling hands, Jenna mechanically ate the food Lily had brought her, not really tasting it.

She understood the school had strict codes against the use of magic on the nonmagical, but she had used it instinctively to save herself. Surely, they would let her explain.

She had watched as the green token representing her entrance into the Healers Guild had turned into a regular coin. It was lost to her. She examined her feelings. Would she have done anything differently? She didn't believe so. If left with no choice, she would act. Decisively. But she wanted to be a healer—only there would she be willing to dedicate herself to others.

Jenna wallowed in her loss, unsure of what she should do, before something tugged on her senses, gently pulling her free from herself and back into the outside world.

Someone approached. Someone with a unique semblance of magic, like an echo of what should be magic. It was so odd, Jenna was surprised she sensed it at all. Yet this magic appeared bright and shimmery, with hints of sadness and pain. It took a moment for Jenna to realize it contained the same magical signature she sensed after losing control in the Rim—the one that rescued her.

Kal stepped through the wall into the room.

The Three guide us! Only the strongest mages could do that, and it was never done so casually. This man was different. She couldn't come up with an explanation.

Jenna studied Kal as Lily gasped from the archway and stomped over to him. In her astonishment, she hadn't seen Lily enter. He gazed down at Lily, his face full of gentle concern despite her palpable anger.

"You came through the wall," Lily hissed.

A look of confusion transformed to certainty on Kal's face.

"No, I did not, Lily. I came through the door."

Confusion roared through Jenna. *Was he trying to keep it a secret?*

"Only mages can do what you just did. Are you in hiding?" Lily asked.

"No, I'm telling you, I came through the door."

Jenna focused on him—he had dark hair, beautiful brown eyes, and a trim physique. He appeared to be only a handful of years older than she—and unusually bright colors leaked from him. Usually, only new mages leaked colors. It showed a lack of control, but only masters could walk through walls. He was an anachronism.

He and Lily did not appear to be a couple, but his body language showed that he cared for her. Could they be related? Sadness gripped Jenna as she thought of her chance meeting with her sister, who had needed her. Jenna had helped her, but it had cost her everything she had worked for.

Lily turned away from him. "First, you bring us more mouths to feed, and now you lie to my face?" She turned back to him, glaring, before she threw up her hands and strode out of the room.

Jenna suppressed a groan. She and her sister were a burden. What should she do? Where would she go? She couldn't go home with her sister.

Kal stared wide-eyed as Lily stalked away from him. He started to follow her, but then stopped and turned toward Jenna.

He approached her as though she were a wild animal that might react unpredictably, and she nearly laughed. *She* hadn't just gone through a wall. Her heart fluttered as she stared up at his piercing brown eyes. He studied her for a long moment before reaching into his pocket and pulling out a letter.

"Master Evans stopped by. He left this for you."

Relief flooded Jenna. *They had come for her!* She wiped her eyes, and with trembling fingers, she took it.

Jenna straightened the single sheet of paper and read the words on it. She reread it and then read it again.

Jenna, you belong with the one who returns your token to you. That which you truly seek can only be found on this path.

Master Evans

She didn't understand, but relief poured through her. A chance still existed that she would be a healer.

Jenna smiled up at Kal, who stood staring at her. She inhaled his scent. Rosewood and ink. *What an odd combination*, she thought, *but not unpleasant.* "Thank you," she said, voice still rough.

Kal's eyes went wide for a moment. He nodded to her, then reached out his hand again, turning it over so its contents spilled onto the bedcover.

"These were all I could find." He gestured.

Jenna stared, and there, lying on the bed amongst several coins, lay the black token given to her on the morning of testing. She had received two tokens, a green one from the Healers Guild and a black one from a mysterious wizard she had met on the street. She had cared only for the green token, but that had lost its power. Somehow, the black one remained. *You belong to the one who returns your token to you.*

Glancing down at the black token, then up at the shimmering colors bleeding off the man. *That which you truly seek can only be found on this path.*

Young as he was compared to other masters she'd seen, she belonged with him now. He would be her teacher. She believed this represented her last chance. No matter what, she would not fail him. Jenna closed her eyes, and in a calm but gravelly voice, she spoke the ritual words of acceptance that generations of trainees have spoken to their masters.

"I, Questee Jenna Sturmich, humbly accept you as my master until the time of trial ends. In all things, I will honor my guild and my master."

Several heartbeats passed and nothing happened.

Is he rejecting me?

Uncertainty welled up in her, but then she sensed it. A trickle of magic slid around them both. A place opened in her mind where Kal existed. He had accepted her! She smiled up at him, practically moaning in relief and joy as the ritual magic took hold and bonded the two of them. She had a master now. She was no longer alone.

Then she took in his pained expression. She felt confusion and shock through the bond. The shimmering lights around him almost strobed through their colors. Then she felt pain. Kal's hands rose to his head, and he groaned before he doubled over the bed and disappeared.

Chapter 4

Safe House

Kal sank to his knees. His chest rattled as deep gasps of air whooshed in and out of his lungs, and he loosened his vice-like grip on his head as the pain began to ebb. Boisterous sounds bombarded his ears. And then a voice cut through the din. "Two pints of ale!"

He was near a bar. *What is that smell?* It was awful. His nostrils flared at the sharp stench of offal. Kal lowered his hands and opened his eyes.

He blinked. He was in an alley. The wall next to him was rough stone, not the painted walls of the inn. He was kneeling on cobblestones, and they were wet with... he wasn't sure he wanted to know with what...

To his right, someone lay passed out in refuse.

Music played nearby, and he could hear drunken singing. He knew this spot. He was around the corner from a safe house he had set up long ago. How had he gotten here? He never thought he would need it, but his mind had churned for weeks until he had relented and paid for one.

What happened? He was speaking with Jenna when pain lanced into his mind, sending a streak of red across his vision.

He retreated from the thought. This wasn't the place to figure it out. He needed to get out of the alley.

Stumbling to his feet, Kal hunched slightly since his back throbbed. He headed toward the safe house, gritting his teeth against the pain. Each step brought him more relief.

By the time he reached the tavern that held his room, he could more or less stand up straight.

He entered a large room filled with the pleasant smell of pipe weed. Though not full, most of the tables were occupied, and a companionable rumble of conversation filled the air. Kal made his way to the polished oak bar.

"What can I get you?" the grizzled barkeep said as he dried glasses, stacking them for future use.

"My name is Kal, and I have a reservation in the blue room."

The barkeep paused and stared intently at Kal, then resumed his drying. After placing the glass down, he called out, and an older woman with her hair tied back opened the door wide enough to peek around. "What is it?"

"Watch the bar for a moment. Guest for the blue room has arrived."

Her eyes darted to Kal, then back to the barkeep as he motioned for Kal to follow him up the side stairs.

Kal entered a small but clean room, which was lightly furnished with a bed, a table, and two chairs.

"How long will you be staying?" the barkeep asked.

Kal's head throbbed. "Don't know," he said, and his headache eased up.

"Food is not included with the room."

Kal paid for food for tonight and tomorrow morning, and the man gave him the key and left.

He did a quick inventory. He had enough money on him for just over a week. Surely that was enough time to figure this out?

Kal sat down on the bed and removed his shoes. He lay back, grimacing at a lump in the middle. The bed had seen better days, but the sheets smelled of lavender.

K al knew he was dreaming. He went through the previous day's events, feeling the death magic, hearing the man screaming, carrying Jenna to the inn, and her words. They kept repeating, only he couldn't quite make them out. *I, Questee Jenna*... then the rest would fade away under the pulsing in his head. It would restart, and he was back on the street, sensing death magic.

The sound of knocking woke Kal. Sweat trickled down his back, and his head throbbed. He sat up. How long had he slept?

"Coming," he said before he opened the door to reveal the barkeep with a tray of food and drink. Kal allowed the man to put the tray on the table, then closed the door behind him. The smell of braised lamb, herbed rice, and vegetables caused his mouth to water. As Kal sat down and ate, he remembered why he'd picked this place. *Good food.*

Rising, he placed the empty tray outside his door and stretched. His back and head still hurt. He would have to see about getting his clothes laundered. There must be a bath house near here. Kal yawned. He would think about that tomorrow.

The following day, Kal's headache had cleared, so he decided to return to the inn, and a shaft of pain lanced up his back, causing his temples to throb.

Okay, not the inn. He had to do something, so he left his room. The tray he had put outside the night before was gone. He made his way downstairs and came up beside the bar to find the bartender studying him.

"Where is the local doctor?" Kal asked.

Klaus gave him a once-over, taking in his pinched eyes and stiff shoulders. "The best doctor around these parts is over on Chauncey Street." Klaus gave Kal directions, and he headed out.

Like many buildings in the Rim, this one was run down. Kal grimaced. *Do I really want to go in there?* But after a few moments, the throbbing in his head propelled him forward. Kal opened the door to find a handful of benches filled with people and a brown-robed monk sitting at a desk. The interior was clean and as bright as the single window could make it. Kal approached the young man at the desk.

"Name and ailment?" the monk asked.

Kal gave his name and described his head and back aches as the young man took notes.

"Please have a seat. The doctor will see you shortly."

Kal found an empty bench and sat down. It was not a short wait. As the people ahead of him were called in, new people entered. Kal rubbed his temples, thinking about the meats he had ordered the day before. Someone needed to pick those up, but then he would have to return to the inn. A sharp pain lanced through his head at the thought of going back to the inn. *Why does it hurt when I think of returning?* He decided he would send a message to Lily after this, letting her know they were ready. The pressure in his head eased.

They called the last patient before him, and Kal studied the room to avoid thinking about the inn. A new patient entered and spoke softly to the young man at the desk. Kal closed his eyes for a long moment, letting his mind drift. His headache eased.

"Kal, the doctor will see you now."

Kal's eyes snapped open. His brief respite evaporated as his thoughts returned to the present. Kal rose and followed the monk's gesture into the room beyond.

A young man, roughly the same age as Kal, sat behind a desk. His gaunt features gave the impression of a man who didn't quite have enough to eat.

"You're a mage," Kal said, unsure why it hadn't occurred to him before. Most healers were mages.

The young man studied Kal and then said, "So are you."

Kal blinked as pain flooded his senses, sharp and piercing. Grinding his teeth, he managed to get out, "I am not a mage," before he felt the cool, comforting hands of the doctor on his face.

"Hold still," the doctor said.

The touch was so soothing that Kal couldn't imagine moving. Waves of tranquil force flooded him, releasing tension in his back and head as the doctor worked on Kal. After several long minutes, the young man stepped away, and the comforting presence of his hands went with him.

Kal blinked, taking in the concerned expression on the doctor's face. His facial features seemed familiar, but he couldn't place him. Maybe he had seen him around the market.

"What did you do?" Kal asked.

"I siphoned off an excess of nites."

Everyone and everything had nites. They were as essential to people as blood or a heart. The more nites one had, the more power they wielded. Nites meant power, as they were what allowed magic to happen. It was believed that nites were finite and moved from one being or place to another depending on what one ate or where one lived. Kal's stomach dropped. It didn't make sense.

"Why would I have an excess of nites? I'm no mage."

The doctor studied him. "It's true you don't feel like a mage, but you are gathering nites."

"Is that why my head hurts so much when I think of certain things?" Kal said.

"Things like what?" the doctor asked.

Kal hesitated, assessing himself. He didn't feel any pain, so he said, "When I think of magic, or people and places that remind me of magic."

The doctor frowned at him. "Show me your arms."

It was Kal's turn to frown. He lifted his sleeve on one and then the second arm, showing clear skin on both forearms. Kal knew what he was looking for. He was looking for the mark of a mage-born criminal. Such people were branded and had their magic suppressed.

"I am not a mage," Kal said, more for himself than for the doctor.

"Well, you have a unique problem. Magic seems to be welling up in you. Until we can find the cause, I will need you to visit me daily so I can siphon off some nites. It should help with your symptoms."

Relief flooded Kal. Coming every day would be a hassle, but at least he could function.

"I need you to keep track of what you are doing when you get headaches. Bring a list to each appointment." The doctor went to his desk and scribbled out a note. He handed it to Kal. "Bring that to the monk, and he will set up the appointments."

Kal looked at the note, unable to make out its words.

"Thank you," he said as he took the slip of paper and went to make the appointments.

Kal took the two stairs down and stepped into the morning crowd. The smell of fish assaulted him. Taking a quick left down a side street, he found himself outside the Couriers Guild, where he sent a messenger to Lily before he returned to the safe house. Several days passed, and he attended daily sessions with the doctor. In his spare time, he went to the bathhouses, had his clothes cleaned, and followed his daily exercise routine, which was a mixture of stretches for flexibility, muscle-building calisthenics, and meditation. He found the rhythm of movement soothing. His headaches were almost gone except when he tried to recall what Jenna had said to him. Oddly, he was sure he could sense her nearby, but focusing on that sensation too long always triggered a headache. Just thinking of returning to the inn set off waves of pain, but he had to return soon. He was almost out of money.

He came to a decision. He would go back to the inn, but he would go at night to avoid meeting anyone.

Chapter 5

Waiting

J enna awoke, panting heavily, hands grasping at her throat. Fear coursed through her as images of her attacker faded. *It was just a dream,* she reminded herself. *A dream.* "You're safe," she panted, and she had a master.

He didn't know about her past. Most people avoided her when they found out what she'd done. At some point, he would find out. How would he react then? Would he regret accepting her?

Jenna took a steadying breath, pushing those thoughts aside. Her sister was alive. Jenna hadn't told Lily that the other girl was her sister. She only asked to ensure she was okay. That was all that mattered.

She would wait for Kal's return. She thought of her last sight of him, doubled over in pain. He was okay, too. She knew this because the bond would be cut off if he died. For now, it was a softly throbbing presence. But he was in pain. She wasn't sure if this was natural, but it was all she had. When he returned, she would be the best student he'd ever had, and she would repay him or she would die trying.

As Jenna waited for Kal, her wounds began healing. Her arms still shook if she exerted herself, so she chose not to speed the process with magic, but allowed herself to heal naturally. After a week, she walked upright again, and her voice had returned to normal. Her skin, still mottled with bruises, was clearing. Unsure of how to pay Kal and Lily back for taking her in, Jenna stopped Lily in the halls.

"Do you need help around the inn?"

Lily frowned at her. "You're still recovering."

"I'm doing much better. Besides, I'm not used to just lying around. Surely there is something simple I could do to help you? You've been so kind to me."

Lily chewed her lip. "Well, one of my cleaning staff had to take a sudden leave, so I could use some help. I could put you on light duty. If you're sure."

"I'm sure. Thank you."

Lily took her to the kitchens and introduced her to the staff, where they assigned her light cooking and cleaning. Jenna threw herself into the tasks, going to bed that night with a satisfied smile.

As she lay there between wakefulness and sleep, she sensed Kal was in less pain. As she considered his absence, her throat tightened with worry. Why was he in pain? Eventually he would have to come back; she would ask then. Jenna yawned, and her eyes closed.

The next day, while Jenna was organizing the pantry, her thoughts turned to her sister. She longed to see her, but she feared it too. She had been avoiding her for years. Seeing her in the Rim had been a surprise. Pride had surged in her chest as her sister had stood up to the thugs who had set up a toll on the road, forcing people to pay.

Her pride had turned to horror when he had begun beating Casi. Jenna's body had moved on its own, inserting herself into the situation, where she too had been beaten. It was at that moment she lost control. She could have done any number of things to stop him, but all of her training had washed away, and she had simply wanted him to die. Just like that day two years ago, when she had last seen her sister.

Lily entered the room, breaking Jenna out of her introspection.

"Jenna?"

"Yes?" Jenna blinked away the memory.

Lily studied Jenna, then said, "You haven't asked, and I didn't want to push, but the young girl you helped, her name is Casimira. I think you should meet her now."

Jenna's cheeks flushed. Her insides twinged over not telling Lily earlier. She would find out eventually, and the longer she waited, the harder it would be to explain, so she might as well say it. "Casi is my sister."

Lily pursed her lips and looked away, something indecipherable flashing in her eyes. "Follow me," she said as she set off down one of the side hallways, stopping at the third doorway. The door had a stag symbol burned into the wood.

"Wait here a moment," Lily said as she knocked lightly and entered the room. "Casi, I've brought Jenna to see you."

The mattress squeaked, and Jenna heard Casi hiss in pain.

A little while later, Lily poked her head out of the door. "Come in."

Jenna stepped slowly into the room as Lily exited, closing the door behind her. Jenna had eyes only for her sister sitting up in bed. Her beating had been worse, and it showed. Her eyes were drained and sunken, bruises discolored her face, and her long hair was unkempt but tied back to keep it away from the many cuts on her skin. Her left arm was wrapped tightly and bound in a sling across her chest. Her right arm, on top of the blankets, was bruised. She had bandages around her torso. After a few moments, their eyes met. Casi had been studying her as well.

"Thank you... for saving me."

"You're welcome," Jenna mumbled, the words turning to dust in her mouth. Jenna hadn't thought about her sister's pain. She'd assumed she would be healed. But healers are expensive, and not many of the good ones come out to the Rim.

Jenna couldn't miss the hurt in her sister's voice as Casi said, "You never replied to my letters."

Shame burned through Jenna. "I could have killed you."

"But you didn't," her sister muttered.

"But I could have. You're better off without me."

"Really? Isn't that type of thinking that got us into this mess to begin with?"

Jenna flinched, unable to deny it, unwilling to forgive her brother.

"Rowen has been teaching me," Casi said.

Anger flowed through Jenna at the sound of her brother's name. "Teaching you what?"

"Magic. He says I'm a prodigy."

Jenna's face spasmed as she barely managed to contain a snort. Still angry at her brother, she cleared her throat. "Then why haven't you healed yourself?"

Casi's face fell. "I haven't learned that yet. I can only work on others, though he limits those."

"Why?" Jenna demanded.

Casi blushed and mumbled, "I tend to use too much power."

Jenna ground her teeth. *A prodigy, huh? Was he trying to make it up to her?* Jenna took a moment to master her anger. There was something she could do for her sister. "Here," Jenna said as she stepped forward and touched her sister's arm. Magic energies filled her as she healed the worst of her sister's wounds.

Casi gasped and leaned back on the bed. "Thank you," she said, eyes drooping.

"Sleep," Jenna said.

Casi nodded, closing her eyes, as Jenna turned and left the room. Lily was waiting for her.

"I could use your help in one of the suites. It's a foreign lady from Olander and her two guards."

Jenna nodded, grateful for any distraction.

Lily knocked and announced, "Cleaning time."

The door opened wide, filled with the frame of a large man with dark, close-cropped hair.

"New help?" he asked, eyes focused on Jenna.

"This is Jenna. She recently joined us."

The man studied her a moment too long, lingering on the residual bruising showing above her collar. "Come in," he said, moving out of the way and gesturing into the suite.

Lily led Jenna into the main room. It was the largest at Lily's Inn, with a small hallway that opened into a large central room with three doors, each leading to a private room.

"Jenna, you take the one on the right and this room. I'll go left and center."

Jenna nodded and headed in, gathering the linens and straightening up. She returned to the center room, and the large man had left. Jenna's shoulders relaxed, and she placed the bundle of linens near the exit and set to work cleaning. As she finished up, she sensed a pulse of power from Kal. Instinctively, she turned in his direction and pulled on her magic, trying to find him. The scent of rosewood came to her, and her heart beat faster.

"Looking for someone?" a voice said from behind her. Jenna jumped, losing hold of her magic, and turned to find an older woman standing behind her. The woman wore an ornate yellow hood, usually worn by well-off ladies who wanted to be discreet. The hood had a veil that was see-through from the inside only, obscuring the top part of her face. Realizing that using magic in someone's rooms could be misinterpreted, Jenna froze, thinking of what Lily would say.

"S-Sorry, I was looking for my master. He's..." She was going to say missing, but changed the word to "away."

The woman studied Jenna, taking in her bruises, and frowned.

"Are you a slave?"

"No, ma'am."

Softly, she asked, "Did your master do that to you?"

Jenna's hand went to her neck; seeing an image of her attacker, she paled.

Her words came out breathlessly. "No, he—"

"Lady Millaine, I hope Jenna is not inconveniencing you!" Lily interrupted.

The veiled woman turned towards Lily and back to Jenna, who still stood with her hand on her throat.

"No, dear, I was just curious."

Lily sighed. "Time to leave, Jenna."

"Yes, ma'am," Jenna said, gathering up the sheets as they left the room.

Later that day, Jenna had her arms up to her elbows in washing fluids as she worked through some of the inn's laundry. Lily folded clothes nearby. "Lily?"

"Yes?"

"Where is Kal?"

Lily closed her eyes. "I don't know, but he messaged that he is okay."

Jenna glanced down, knowing she pushed, but spoke anyway. "You know him, right?"

Lily paused. "Before last week, I would have said yes. Now? I don't know."

"Does he often disappear for this long?"

Lily stared at Jenna again.

"No. Kal lives here in one of the rooms. I haven't gone into his room, but as far as I can tell, he hasn't returned since you met with him."

Jenna started. "He lives here? Why didn't you say so?"

"Because it's not my place, girl. I may run this inn, but Kal is the proprietor. He will return when he is ready, so just leave it be until then."

Jenna bit back her words. Lily was, of course, right, and from the bond, she could tell he was alive and unharmed. Unfortunately, he wasn't responding to her attempts to call and speak with him through it. Having never had a bond like this before, she wasn't sure if Kal was ignoring her or if she was doing it right. Jenna sighed. Did he want her to wash bedding forever? Already, she was being ungrateful. She would do what was needed, even if it meant washing blankets till the end of time. Jenna went back to her scrubbing as Lily studied her, frowning.

Jenna awoke with a start when she sensed Kal arrive in the building, his magic ringing like discordant bells in the back of her mind. There was a wrongness to that magic she had never encountered before, and it worried her. She got up and started dressing to go to him when she felt him leave his room and head back toward the entrance. She finished dressing and followed him. Focusing on the bond, she pushed her magical senses outside their average radius to keep track of him.

Kal went down several streets and alleys, each lit only by the brightness of the nearly full moon. Jenna ghosted behind him, walking quickly to catch up. As he rounded a corner, she felt four men surround him. Fear flooded her as she came around the corner to witness all the men draw their swords. One of them stepped forward and swung his sword at Kal, which he barely dodged.

An image of the man Kal had saved her from flashed before her, causing her to quiver. This encounter was different; Kal wasn't her sister, but he was her master. Without fear and urgency to drive her, could she act to save him?

Jenna inhaled sharply, vowing she would not allow them to harm him. To her, these men were like the thugs the other day. She would not give them a chance to retaliate. Reaching out, she sent a lance-shaped flare of her powers into the neck of the man in front of her.

As he fell, the man in front of Kal raised his sword again, and Jenna sent another flare right into his armpit. He rocked back, falling to the ground. One of the men turned toward her as she sent a third shot into his head.

Drawing his dagger, Kal had turned toward her, eyes going wide.

"Don't kill with magic!" he shouted as the last man drove a knife into his back. Kal went down, leaving Jenna to face the man, who then turned to flee.

She sent another scalpel, but this time, she aimed for the leg. The man went down, hamstring cut.

Jenna raced over to Kal, who was struggling to sit upright.

"What are you doing here?"

She stared down into his face, dazzling colors appearing around him. They flickered in and out while rotating around his head and torso. She studied him cautiously, as she had never seen such an occurrence of magic and couldn't make sense of it. One thing was clear; her master was angry.

"I was following you, Master," she replied.

"Why?"

"Because you accepted."

He glared at her, mouth quivering in pain, then his shoulders slumped. "Look... Jenna," he said in frustration, words slurring.

Jenna could see the dazzling colors of his magic mute. Her eyes widened as she realized the dagger must have been poisoned.

Jenna moved to his back and pulled the dagger out.

Her master sighed, his breathing labored as blood ran down his back. She studied him through a film of her magic, where she recognized the dark mass of poison spreading. Jenna hissed through her teeth.

"Hold still, Master. That dagger was poisoned."

Holding her hand over the wound in his back, she grounded herself in her magic, viewed his injury through its veil, and dove into the wound.

Jenna set to work in a frenzy. She visualized the path of the poison through the lens of her magic and raced to stop its deadly spread.

Reinforce here. Divert there. Push. Twist. Pull.

Sweat broke out on her brow as she delicately gathered up the toxin and pulled it up and out through the small hole in his back. A round globule of poison rose and floated away from him. She flung it at the wall, where it splattered, black venom steaming. Kal moaned and started to move, but she held him still and went back in. She had removed the poison, but it had blazed a trail of damage through him. Her stomach rumbled as her body began cannibalizing itself for energy. Ignoring the cost, she rested her forehead against his back to help her synchronize her magical energies with him and began again.

Pull from fat, convert into energy, rebuild arteries, shore up weakened tissue, and replace fluids.

She moved carefully so as not to take too much essence from him, or the aftereffects would kill him almost as quickly as the poison. She came dangerously close to passing out herself. Something was off. There was an incongruous jangling against her senses that left her repulsed. This aura of throbbing blackness was the real source of his problem. It wasn't just the poison that was killing him. There was something embedded in his lower back, near his spine. She moved her hand from the newly forming skin around the puncture wound over to the spot above the object in his back.

"Kal?" Jenna said.

"Yes?"

"This is going to hurt," she warned.

Jenna used her magic to paralyze him. Then she covered her hand in magic and slowly reached into his back, carefully grabbed the black marker, and slowly—oh so slowly—pulled it out. As her hand left his back, she released him. Mobility came back to him, and he fell, flopping forward onto the ground, gasping for breath as if he had run a race.

Jenna stared down at the black marker in her hand, taking it in, seeing the markings etched onto its side. She clenched her fist tightly over it as a wave of dizziness hit her, bringing her to her knees before she crumpled sideways. Jenna gripped the black marker tightly, her mind whirling with possibilities as exhaustion claimed her.

Chapter 6

Awakening

Kal groaned, shivering as the pain in his back subsided. Visible colors burst around him in a brilliant kaleidoscope of shimmering magic.

More importantly, he recalled everything.

He remembered who he was, why he was here, what had been in his back, and who had put it there.

Awe surged through him as he caught sight of Jenna, crumpled on the cobbled streets beside him. He was free! Kal laughed out loud as magic coursed through him, growing with each heartbeat. He turned that magic towards Jenna, studying her. She had pushed herself to the limit and fallen into a deep slumber, but otherwise, she was fine. What she had done was fantastic! Few could do such a thing without killing the patient.

He speculated on who she was and how she came to be with him. No matter how coincidental it felt to have come upon her in a time of need, he couldn't get past the niggling feeling that his brother was somehow involved.

Kal used magic to rise to his feet. He hovered an inch off the ground as power rippled through him—warm and welcoming, full of possibilities. He basked in the sensations for a moment until a wave of exhaustion struck, causing him to release the flow and return to the ground. He gritted his teeth as a spasm ripped through his back. Realizing that the healing had taken a lot from him, he stood still until it passed. Beads of sweat covered his brow as he gazed over at the bodies around him. He went over to the one who had his hamstring cut. The man had managed to drag himself to the wall of a nearby building.

Was the king behind any of this? Or had someone else discovered where he was? Kal carefully leaned over the wide-eyed man and touched his forehead. He delved into the mind of the hired assassin and found a wall of nothing. Kal snorted. It would take more time and energy than he had to breach that wall. If Kal managed to break down the shields, it would trigger a failsafe, killing him. It was illegal to create such a shield on someone. Because of that, it was an expensive option few were willing to perform. Kal pulled on his magic, and the knife flew into his hand. He may not kill with magic, but he wasn't opposed to killing. Deciding he couldn't have this man reporting back, Kal cut the man's throat.

After cleaning the knife, he went to Jenna and hoisted her upon his shoulder. A wave of fatigue hit him as he walked back towards the inn. Jenna had used both of their resources to fight off the poison. Removing the maghin would have a price, as well.

By the time he reached the inn, Kal was stumbling. He ran into the door, bumping his head lightly as he fumbled with Jenna's weight. He couldn't reach his keys without dropping her, so he knocked. Gently, he pressed his forehead against the cold doorframe, resting his head there. Lily opened the door, startling him awake.

"Kal! Come in." Lily opened the door wide to let them pass. "What happened?"

"Later." Kal shook his head, and with Lily's assistance, carried Jenna to her room and flopped her onto the bed. He straightened his arm on the bed to keep from falling on top of her. If he laid down now, he wouldn't be able to rise.

Kal stumbled blindly out of the room, almost plowing into Lily as he headed back to his room. He opened the door and stumbled towards his bed, and Lily followed him in.

As she helped him into his bed, she asked, "Can you tell me what happened?"

"Jenna followed. Was attacked. She's fine. Danger. Need sleep. Explain later..." he mumbled as he passed out.

Kal snapped awake in a fog of loss, screaming, "No!" His chest was tight as he panted. The maghin was gone, and with it, its suppressing effect on his magic and memory. It was why he hadn't remembered being places and doing things.

Thinking back, he owed Lily an apology. He really had been entering rooms through the walls. For months, he had been leaking magic, and the maghin had been trying to suppress it and erase his memories of it. Unused magic accumulated over time. Since he had been suppressed for two years, it built up. Now that he was free, and he started using magic again, he wouldn't have enough to spare for that.

He had asked for one thing when they put in the maghin: Don't let him forget his crime. The new king had ignored his request. He had been merciful indeed.

Here in the dark, Kal silently cried himself back to sleep.

J enna blinked awake. She stared up at the ceiling, recalling the previous night's events. Her stomach gurgled in protest. She would need to eat soon, or she would start shaking.

What have I done? She took a deep breath.

I can't just do something. I have to overachieve.

Jenna took another deep breath, blowing it out to steady her nerves. She then lifted her hand, gazing at the small black disc she had somehow held onto. The disc was smooth and rounded, with slightly curved edges.

It was a maghin, otherwise known as a command seal. She recalled hearing about these from her magic teacher. They were often put in mage-born criminals. Maghins guaranteed that the container would follow specific rules, which manifested in many ways. Some formations were for communication and others for self-destruction. Whatever its intended purpose, it was a tool limited to the rich. To top it all off, this wasn't just any maghin. This one bore the purple crown of the Royal Seal.

Jenna's hand shook as she expected someone to break down the door, demanding retribution. She closed her fingers around the disc and lowered her hand. Was he a weapon, or had he been on a leash?

What would be the repercussions of removing the seal? She had not covered maghins in her training, as they were artifacts, and she studied the body. Perhaps it was the source of the colors swirling about him? The seeming of magic and not magic. Was that intentional, or was it damaged? Just who were those men hunting him?

Who is my master?

K al awoke to the sounds of someone quietly entering his room. In a panic, he flung a hand out toward the approaching person.

Kal and Lily both cried out. He in realization, and she as the tray of food and drink she carried slammed into her face. She flew several feet into the wall and stuck there as the tray and its contents fell to the floor.

Horrified, Kal let his magical hold on her go.

Lily fell to her knees, retching, and pulled a small knife from under her skirt, holding it up defensively.

Kal stumbled out of bed.

"Lily! I'm so—"

Lily inched away from him, plastering herself up against the wall with fear and defiance showing in her eyes.

The look on her face made Kal groan as several things about their past interactions clicked into place. Someone had harmed Lily. It wasn't the realization but the ashen cast to her face that stopped Kal in his tracks.

"Lily." Kal's voice softened, brows coming together. "I'm sorry." He started toward her again, more slowly now.

The tone of his voice brought Lily back. She held up her empty hand, and he stopped moving, giving her time to master her fear.

He was not injured, so he didn't know why she had chosen to enter his room. What if he had hurt her?

Lily inhaled and rose to her feet, fluidly slipping the knife back into her boot sheath.

She stared at Kal for a long moment, then exhaled, her features taking on a sad cast. Kal opened his mouth to speak—he had to explain—when the door burst open, and a patron, a burly man named Zach, entered.

"Miss Lily! Are you all right?" Behind him stood Jenna, Casi, and several of the cleaning staff.

"I'm fine. I... stumbled," Lily said as she glanced down at the broken dishes and food and made a face.

Casi, whose room was closest, stared in disbelief, and Jenna seemed skeptical. Casi opened her mouth but closed it at Lily's glare.

"I appreciate you all coming to my rescue, but it's unnecessary. Casi, I'll stop by once this mess is cleaned up."

Kal stepped forward, biting his lip.

"Are you all right?"

Lily gave him a bright smile. "I'm fine. Okay, everyone, back to work! Jenna, be a dear and bring me some rags and soapy water."

Eyes locked on Lily, Jenna nodded in relief and went off to do her task.

Kal bent to pick up the tray and added bits of broken glass and food. Lily walked to the door and shut it, turning around and leaning against the door.

Kal kept his head down as he continued cleaning up the mess.

"Who are you, Kal?"

"A murderer," he said before thinking. A memory flashed through Kal's head of a middle-aged man, features twisted with a look of surprise as his eyes glazed over in death.

"Bullshit."

His eyes snapped to her.

"I've met murderers, Kal. If you killed someone, they deserved it."

Kal blinked, his eyes tearing.

"Lily, people may come for me. They did last night, and Jenna was there. I will leave—"

"You will not," Lily said, voice full of steel. "Jenna is your pupil now?"

He nodded.

"I won't have you dragging her around the underbelly of the Rim. You both stay."

Kal rubbed his chin, then ran his hand over his face. Seeing her stare, he smoothed his features, removing all emotions and tells from it.

"Don't do that. Don't distance yourself."

Life returned to his face. "Sorry, it's something I learned as a child."

"Do you feel like you need it with me?"

"No," he said with surprise. "It's just..." *I can remember it now.* "Lily?"

"Yes."

"You probably don't want to come into my room without warning me."

Lily smiled, raising one eyebrow, and said, "I've already figured that out."

He paused, blushing. "Do you trust me?"

"I do," she said with a sigh.

"Here." He stepped in and brushed a hand across her forehead, sending a trickle of magic into her.

"What was that?" she asked.

"A key. I may need to set some traps. They will recognize you as a friend if you ever need to enter my room without me."

"Oh. So you are a Mage?"

"Something like that." He glanced away. "It's complicated."

"It's simple. Either you are or you aren't."

He stared at her. She had been with him for the better part of two years. She deserved honesty.

"I am," he admitted, "but I'm also something more." He stopped talking.

"Kal—"

"No, it's dangerous for you to know more."

"And Jenna? Will you tell her?" she asked softly, hurt showing in her eyes.

Kal paused for a moment, chewing his lip, and sighed.

"At some point, I will have no choice. No matter how Jenna got here or what state I was in when bonding, she is my apprentice."

K al knocked softly on the door across the hall from his room.

"Come in," came a muffled reply.

Casi's eyes widened when Kal entered, and then her expression shifted to one of caution. Kal studied her bruises. She seemed to be in her early teens, with unruly black hair and a lean build. She was sitting at a desk, writing a letter.

"You look like you are healing up."

"I am, thank you," Casi replied cautiously.

"I'm glad." Kal realized her first impression of him was seeing Lily looking like she'd been harmed.

"Last night," he began, "several men attacked me." Casi's eyes narrowed. "Jenna was with me." Kal listened to Casi's intake of breath as she started to speak, but Kal cut her off.

"She's fine, as you saw, but Lily came into my room this morning and woke me." He paused. "I reacted without thinking, and I could have hurt her. I've made my apologies."

Casi nodded, tension leaving her shoulders, and she chewed on her fingernail.

Kal studied her momentarily. "You are a bit young for an apprenticeship. Do you have somewhere to go? Are people looking for you?"

Casi glanced at the letter on the desk before replying. "Yes, I have somewhere to go."

"Are you safe there?"

Casi blinked, then smiled. "I am."

"That's good. Then Lily or I will escort you home when you are ready."

"What about Jenna?"

"She is my apprentice. She will stay here."

"Would there be an issue if I stopped by occasionally?"

"Of course not."

Casi glanced at the letter again and back to Kal. "Would you be able to help me deliver this when I am done?"

"Yes. Either Lily or I can help with that."

"Thank you." She smiled.

"I'll leave you to it, then."

Chapter 7

Price

A knock sounded on Jenna's door.

"Come in," she said. When Kal entered, they stared at each other. Jenna's heart constricted at the memory of the men trying to harm him. She wanted to touch him to make sure he was really okay. He was her master, and she needed to keep him safe, but she couldn't do it without answers. Kal opened his mouth to speak, and Jenna held up her hand, palm flat with the maghin showing.

Kal walked over to her, took it in his hands, and studied it. "Thank you," he said, finally looking at her.

"Why were those men trying to kill you?"

"I don't know. Why did you kill them?" Kal demanded.

"Because they were trying to eliminate you," she said through gritted teeth.

"So?"

"So?!" Jenna's stomach clenched. "Those men wanted you dead!"

"That's not good enough, Jenna."

"Not good enough!" Jenna checked herself, lowering her voice, and tried to be rational. "What was I supposed to do? Say, 'Excuse me, but would you mind not hacking up my master?' I am not so good as to be able to throw shields around objects other than myself. Do you have a death wish?"

He stared at her uncomfortably for a moment. "Do you?"

Jenna froze, and an unbidden image of her mother came to her mind. Before she spoke again, he cut her off.

"Do not ever kill for me, Jenna."

She opened her mouth to speak.

"Find another way," he said and left the room, taking the maghin and the answers with him.

J enna sat at the front desk at Lily's Inn. The staff had ushered the last of the people to their rooms for the night. Jenna leafed through a news flyer—more missing children.

Jenna sighed as she sat for the first time that evening. She stretched, releasing some of the tension in her back, and chewed on her lip. She felt troubled all day. Had she gone too far with those men trying to kill Kal? He thought so, but Jenna had grown up in the Rim. People like the thugs who had targeted her sister were not uncommon. They sought the weak to make themselves feel strong.

Jenna sighed. Could she have targeted nonlethal parts of Kal's attackers? Yes, she could have. The question that gnawed at her was, why hadn't she? Why did she always take things to the extreme? Deep in thought, Jenna chewed on one of her nails as a memory of her mother surfaced.

"Be smart, Jenna. Always avoid fighting if you can, but if you can't, be decisive. Do not leave them room to come after you. If you do, they will."

How long had it been since she'd thought of her mother? Her heart clenched as her finger unconsciously traced the plant design on her mother's necklace.

"I miss her, too."

Jenna jumped, meeting her sister's eyes. "How long have you been standing there?"

"Not long." Casi shrugged.

"How did you know I was thinking about Mom?"

Casi smirked. "That's her necklace."

Jenna stopped tracing, realizing it was what had given her away.

"Sometimes, I can't remember what she looked like," Casi said, then she smiled bravely.

Jenna flinched. Unlike her sister, Jenna could recall her mother's thick mane of hair and delicate features. "Oddly, it's her hands I remember the most. She was always doing something with them—grinding up medicinal herbs, kneading dough, holding my hand. She would have been proud of you."

Casi's eyes filled with tears, but her smile held firm.

"You've been through so much, yet you still smile."

Casi's smile faltered.

"So." Jenna held out her arms, and her sister ran into them. Jenna held her for a long while as she cried.

"I've missed you," Casi whispered, voice muffled in Jenna's shoulder. "When will you come home?"

Jenna clenched her sister tighter.

"Soon, Casimira," Jenna lied while stroking her hair.

Casi stiffened as if hearing the lie, then pulled away, looking up at her. Her young face, mature beyond her years. "I have to go back tomorrow. Lily is walking me home. Can we at least still see each other?" Casi said, voice quivering.

Jenna smiled softly down at her sister. "Of course. I will always be here for you."

The next several weeks were a blur. Jenna worked at the Inn and spent her free time with her sister. She only encountered Kal through brief glimpses in the bond, but that made her think of him constantly. She was sure she could spin around in a circle blindfolded and still locate him.

Lately, she found herself on the verge of tears for no apparent reason. Strange feelings pushed their way to the foreground, and for some reason, cookies kept coming to mind.

"Jenna, is that blood?" Lily asked as they walked toward the kitchen.

She removed her fingernail from her mouth. The salty taste confirmed that she had chewed it raw.

"Are you all right?" Lily asked, reaching for her hand.

"I'm fine." Jenna pulled away. "The cleaning soap must be bothering me. I'll heal it later if it gets too bad."

Lily frowned as she studied her.

Jenna hadn't been sleeping well lately. She was sure she had the dark circles under her eyes to prove it. There was something wrong with her bond to Kal. The closer she got to him, the worse it was.

At night, Jenna worked feverishly to build and maintain her shields to give herself some distance from him. Without that, she felt like she would disappear underneath the torrent of his presence. Jenna shook off the sensation of being in someone else's skin. She was just tired.

Lily looked like she was about to say something Jenna didn't want to hear. So, desperately, Jenna reached for something to distract her. "Do you mind if I bake some cookies?"

K al entered the kitchens a half candle mark after Jenna left.

"Just what is it with you two?" Lily asked.

"What do you mean?" Kal responded, shifting his attention to her.

"You look exhausted. Jenna looks exhausted. You're avoiding each other. Perfectly. It's like you're painfully aware of each other, both miserable and yet unwilling to meet. Those cookies you like to make? The little white ones?"

"Yes."

"She made them. She says she's never even seen them before. Seriously, even your mannerisms are becoming the same."

"Our mannerisms? Oh no. Lily, come with me."

Lily followed along as he hastily walked through the corridors of the inn.

He knocked at Jenna's door and entered the darkened room after hearing no reply. They found her in a corner, just sitting there with her eyes closed.

"Jenna? Come here," Kal commanded.

She opened her eyes and stared at him. Her shoulders slumped.

"How long?"

"Since that night," she replied, voice ragged.

The Three protect us.

"Jenna, listen to me. I need you to build a shield."

"I've tried! Ten layers deep. It makes no difference."

Ten layers? They declare you a master at eight. How could I not have realized my nites were attacking her?

"Jenna, listen to me. I am going to call those nites back to myself."

"Y-you can do that?" she asked hesitantly. Kal made out the hope filling her eyes.

No time for doubt.

"Yes, I can." He spoke calmly.

"Lily? Please stay close. If one of us passes out, pour water over us as fast as possible."

Lily pursed her lips. "Let me get water first."

Kal settled in, sitting on the edge of the bed. When Lily returned with a bucket of water, Kal spoke.

"Okay, Jenna. Do not take down your shields, got it?"

"All right." The relief in her voice was palpable.

"I will do all the work on this one." Kal closed his eyes, engaging his magic, and observed the patchwork shields she'd built around herself. He perceived all kinds of shapes and sizes, like she was experimenting with the best structures to fend off the attack. *Who the hell taught her that?* He stared around in disbelief. *Oh, wait.* Then he detected it.

Little swarms of nites settled over parts of her shields and worked to convert them to a different pattern. Nites are what could be considered unconscious magic. The more nites one had inside them, the more magic they could use. Nites responded to subconscious thoughts, but they also acted on their own in defense. To his horror, he recognized the pattern the nites were forging. They were trying to consume her and make her compatible with him. He reflected on his training and made a decision.

There were only two proven solutions to this problem, and he sure as hell wouldn't do the second one. Since they were modeling him, the nites would likely respond to him, so he would create a bridge and call them back to himself. The only problem was that after two weeks, they had multiplied several times. There was no telling how much damage they had already done to her.

He began to siphon the nites' magical signature from her, creating dams to prevent most of them from literally gushing into him. He took in as much as possible and shut off the flow. Reaching into her, he built a shield layer over hers to attract the remaining nites to it and act as a cage. He would have to go in and do regular maintenance, or they would subvert the pen and use it against her. *By The Three,* he swore. His consciousness backed out of her, and he came back to himself.

She stared at him with intense relief, awe, and something else.

"Thank you, Master."

With effort, he kept his face bright and nodded to her. How long could they maintain this? By saving him, she had virtually destroyed herself. *Will there be another life on my hands?* Not if he could help it.

"Come on, Jenna." He stood and then leaned down, grabbing her by the arm. "You probably haven't slept well in weeks. Let's get you to bed."

Lily stepped in and said dryly, "I think I'll take care of that part." Lily extricated Jenna from Kal and left him worried and deep in thought.

Chapter 8

Messenger

The next morning, Jenna woke refreshed, all thoughts and sensations about Kal muted. Jenna stretched her arms over her head, luxuriating in the feeling of being alone in her head again. She could still feel the bond with him, but she had to seek it. If the nites began pushing at her again she would know what to do. Jenna frowned. If only she had trusted and gone to him sooner.

It was her turn to watch the front desk, so she dressed and walked into the lobby of the inn, carrying a cup of tea she'd gotten from the kitchen. She set it down and retrieved a watering can from a small alcove and moved around the room, watering the various plants nurtured by light streaming in the large-pane windows on the far side of the room. She straightened chairs in several seating areas.

Jenna returned the watering can, moved behind the desk, and retrieved her tea, taking a sip. The peppermint tickled her nose. Jenna turned around from closing the inner door and found a man standing in the center of the room.

Her tea fell from her hands, crashing to the floor as she backed away.

She sensed magic all around him, densely packed and glowing, but her healer senses, the ones that could tell the difference between life and death, sensed nothing. To her senses, this man was devoid of life, which meant that what stood before her wasn't natural.

Visually, she detected him. He was of average build and wore a cloak with a Messengers Guild armband on the sleeve. His hair was short against his scalp. His brown eyes were wide, even welcoming, and focused on Jenna.

"I am sorry to have startled you," the man said in a slightly stilted cadence. He remained standing in the center of the room, arms at his side, cloak unnaturally still. "I am looking for a man who goes by the name Kal. Do you know where I can find him?"

Jenna stared at the man in shock, the peppermint of her tea permeating the room, her mind whirring in unease. Something like panic set in as she stood there, staring at that void overlaid with the man. Her mouth tried to form words that resulted in nothing but motion. She slowly backed away, but found herself up against the wall next to the inner door she had entered initially. Only the lobby desk was between them.

She stared at the apparition of a man with wide eyes as the inner door opened and Kal strode through, back straight and eyes alert. Lily came in on his heels and stopped next to Jenna. Lily was panting slightly, revealing they had run. Kal did not look at Jenna, but something about how he moved and where he stopped, placing himself between her and the figure, made it clear he was aware of her.

Oddly, the colors Jenna had associated with Kal's mind were missing. It was like he was a new man. This man did not have random bursts of color. This man was in control.

Relief flooded her. He had felt her alarm through the bond, and he had come to her.

Lily took in the ordinary-looking man in the messenger's garb and scurried around Kal, who stood tense and frozen.

"May I help you?" Lily asked, wedging herself just slightly in front of Kal, avoiding the broken teacup but far enough back she could quickly get out of the way.

The man did not move. He simply turned his gaze from Kal to Lily.

"Ah, you must be Miss Lily. Please pardon my intrusion. I did not intend to startle your maid. I am looking for a man by the name of Kal Torvald. Do you know where I can find him?"

Lily kept her eyes on the man before her, frowning slightly. Jenna noted how unnaturally still he was.

"May I know who is asking?" she queried.

"Of course. I am a messenger for Corvald Didymus," he said, eyes darting back to Kal. The messenger frowned slightly at the lack of response and turned his attention back to Lily.

"Kal hasn't been around in a while," Lily said. "If you want, I can give him a message when I see him."

The man paused a moment too long, dragging his eyes back to Kal. He spoke just as the hair rose on Jenna's arms and neck.

"Yes, please do. Tell Kal that Master Didymus would like to meet with him at the old church at his earliest convenience." Then he bowed. "Good day, Miss Lily. My apologies for startling the help."

The messenger turned, his cloak flaring out briefly, and exited through the door. The bells above the door did not jingle as he left.

After the man left, both women turned and stared at Kal, but he focused on Jenna.

"Are you all right?" he asked.

"Yes, Master," she replied automatically.

He clenched his jaw, frustrated with the term. She was right to use it, but he was too young to be a master. He turned to Lily, seeing his old sheltered life slipping away. She already stared at him like he were a stranger.

"Who was that man?" Lily asked.

He resolved to give her what answers he could without endangering her.

"That was a construct."

Understanding blossomed on Jenna's face, and she made an 'oh' of comprehension.

"What is a construct?" asked Lily after hearing Jenna's reaction.

He raised an eyebrow at Jenna, and she took her cue. She spoke as if reciting from a manual. "A construct is a magical illusion created to look like a person, except it has mandates to speak and act in a certain way. Only the highest-grade constructs can interact with the physical world." She stared at Kal to confirm her accuracy.

"Who sent it?" Lily asked.

Kal paused. "Master Corvald Didymus."

"Is that his real name?" Lily asked, brow arched.

"No," he replied with a slight smile.

Lily studied him briefly. "Do you know his real name?"

"Yes."

After a few moments, when he didn't share it, she tried again. "What does he want with you?"

"I don't know." Kal's brow furrowed at the possibilities.

"Was he responsible for the attacks on you?" Jenna asked.

He paused. "I don't know. It's possible."

"Will you meet with him?" Lily asked.

Kal mulled his options. "Yes."

"Will you take me with you?" Jenna's concern for him was clear in her voice.

He turned his attention back to her, considering. "No."

Kal wore formal attire expected of the great houses. He stood outside the ornately carved doors leading to what used to be the office of a large church dedicated to The Three. The church had declined over the last two hundred years after its three deities inexplicably disappeared from public view. The former cathedral had long ago been purchased and refurbished as an estate house for the man known as Corvald Didymus. Kal stared at the engraved doors, thinking about the possible outcomes of today's meeting. He took a deep breath and turned the knob.

Corvald Didymus glanced up as Kal entered the room. He was a heavyset man with strong muscled arms and a soft belly. His eyes were intelligent and piercing in their observations.

"You came," he sighed, sitting up straight and placing his ledgers aside.

"Yes." Kal nodded, closing the door behind him as they studied each other.

"I dreamed of you, you know," Corvald said. "I could feel your grief and knew you had finally awakened."

"I killed him," Kal said bluntly, his voice filled with anguish.

"Yes, you did," Corvald acknowledged, yielding under the force of Kal's sorrow.

"I killed him," Kal said again, more softly.

"You did an act of kindness. He was mad, or I should say, he was driven mad by the curse."

"What curse?" Kal asked sharply. Corvald's eyes drifted away.

"I have done a lot of research in the last two years, searching for clues. The closer I get, the more forgetful I become. I do not know if the search is the trigger or if it's just a factor of time and use of my brand of magic." He paused a moment, staring. "Kal?"

"Yes, my lord."

"I require your services," Corvald said formally.

Kal's eyebrows rose. "My services?"

"I may soon need you to do the same for me."

Kal stilled, his mind flashing with the image of the surprise on the dying man's face, and asked, "The same what?" eyes glaring in suspicion.

"I can no longer ignore the fact that I am having symptoms similar to his. I keep hearing the voices. I hear them almost all the time now. Every once in a while, they ask me to do things, and I find myself doing them before thinking. You know how bad he was in the end. At some point, I will need you to kill me."

"Absolutely not," Kal said.

"Have you had these symptoms?" Corvald asked him.

Kal paused several moments before quietly saying, "No."

"I believed that locking away your magic would protect you, and it seems I was right. As long as it is locked away, you will be safe."

"It is no longer locked away." Kal argued.

"Then, we must give you a new maghin."

"I will forget?" Hope seared through Kal.

"No. Not this time. You must remember if you are to do the task at hand."

"Kill you?" Disappointment, fear, and anguish made Kal's stomach churn as he choked the words out.

"Yes."

He wanted to say *I cannot kill you*, but instead, he chose to say, "I cannot kill you with the maghin in."

"You got it out before I could discreetly have you freed. You will need to get it out again."

Kal recalled the white-hot pain, and he considered Jenna's current state.

"She was not ready. The last time bound us too closely. Shielding myself is not enough. I have to shield her as well. She needs more training. Without it, she could lose herself at any moment."

"She is your pupil, is she not? Train her as a master should. I hear she is quite a prodigy, so she should learn quickly. Train her well, Kal, for all our lives depend on it."

"I cannot train her with the maghin."

Corvald sighed. "I know. It will have to wait."

"Is murdering you the only reason you wanted to see me?"

"No," Corvald said, gesturing towards the chairs. Kal took a seat, and the two men settled in. Corvald picked up a folder and opened it. "Have you seen the flyers for the missing children?" Corvald placed a folder in front of him.

Kal took it and flipped through it. Each page within held the likeness of a youth. "Yes, someone is kidnapping children."

"Yes, and people are turning to the crown for answers, but there are none to give. Kings who can't protect their people don't last long. There is already talk of a curfew."

Kal studied Corvald, trying to see through the magic that hid his face. "You want me to investigate the missing children?"

"I do."

"Officially or unofficially?"

"Officially."

Kal paled. He would have to take up his old life again. His old responsibilities. His gilded cage. "I'll need an appointment with the king..." *Which could take weeks.*

"Fortunately, I've already started the process. Be at the palace in two days at the eleventh morning bell." Corvald grinned.

Kal grunted. *Of course, he wouldn't have asked me to do this if he hadn't already set it up. He knew I couldn't turn him down.*

Chapter 9

Oath

"Why can't I do it?" Jenna growled, laying her hands flat against the square wooden table. Kal sat across from her, leaving two other chairs vacant. They worked in a small room at the inn that Kal had set aside for magic training. He had stayed up late last night, adding extra shields to prevent outsiders from sensing the use of magic in the room. With the extra nites he had gathered from Jenna, he reinforced the room's structure in case their magic work melted down or blew up in their faces. The additional layers would protect the rest of the inn.

Kal studied Jenna for a moment, realizing she was used to succeeding at magic. "It's because you are so good at complex things that your teachers overlooked the simpler ones. We're going to start with the basics. Visualize, puncture, siphon, merge, expel."

"That's not right," Jenna said, pouting.

He raised an eyebrow, and she blushed, then rushed to explain her statement.

"Well, my magic teacher taught us that in the wild lands, warders locate, not visualize, and don't merge at all."

"Really?" Kal asked. "Hm, well, that would explain it. Lower-level mages need to locate, but higher-level mages are naturally closer to the source and can pull directly from it after visualizing. As for merging, warders probably funnel it through raw, which works great when working with inanimate objects. I'm surprised you didn't learn this in healer training, but when working with another human, their system will naturally orient to you. Sometimes, it will act for you and assist you with the healing. Other times, the system may view you neutrally and let you do what you want without help or hindrance. As for the last option, it will see you as the enemy and attack you."

Jenna pursed her lips. "Can it start one way and then change in the middle?"

"Good question. The answer is yes."

Jenna's eyes widened slightly, and she inhaled deeply before blowing out.

"Let me guess, you didn't sense any resistance when working with the poison in me. Did you?"

"No," she said.

"My system recognized you as trying to help, or at least, as not the problem. When you worked with the maghin, it was different?"

"Very."

"Some of that could be the maghin itself. Its design allows for removal after certain steps. You just reached in and grabbed it, right?"

"Basically, yes," she said.

"Unfortunately, when you grabbed it, because you didn't give the secret handshake, the act triggered some sort of attack, causing my system to change its orientation toward you. You see, higher-level magicians can absorb the magic draw and make it their own. Much like what I do when absorbing my nites from you."

"Isn't that more dangerous, though?"

"Depends on how you isolate and convert it. This process essentially removes all positive or negative inclinations from it and makes it neutral so your system can use it for anything."

"That takes time," she said. "Time a patient may not have."

He nodded. "Healers or any profession that works with other complex magical systems have to deal with this problem. Even when you use it properly, there is a price. If you do it wrong, you can damage or even cripple yourself using it. Take, for instance, this bond between us," he said.

Jenna flinched.

"When the maghin triggered a negative reaction, my system didn't see the maghin as an invader and assist you in removing it. Instead, it took you as a threat and tried to expel you. It's still trying to expel you, either that, or fix the errors it finds. It does this by either killing off your cells or by rewriting what it finds into what it sees as the correct state."

"How does it determine state?" Jenna asked.

"Your innate magic is always circulating and passing information about its surroundings. Its state is what it perceives to be true right before an attack occurs. You would have prevented or at least blocked the attack if you had merged, which would have been like giving the all-clear sign. However, to be honest, even that may not have worked in the case of the maghin. Merging could have triggered a whole different set of issues." He sighed. "I don't know, since it depends on the creation of the maghin."

Jenna grimaced. "So now we know what went wrong, but how do we stop it?"

He stared at her. "We have two choices. I have been working to siphon off my magical signature from you, so the effects are even less. It took a lot of power to do what you did—drained you nearly dry. There is more of my signature floating around in you than there is yours, and because of that, it converts your new energy almost as fast as you make it. You were very close to death. To truly fix it, I would have to drain you again almost to death, getting every last nite with my signature out, and if anything went wrong, you would be dead."

She winced. "Option two?"

"The other option is to try to do a post-merge of your magic with mine. That one is trickier, since it's not really under my control any-more. The longer I am away from it, the more I diverge, the less control I have over it. It only sees you as not me. It will ultimately either try to destroy you or isolate your consciousness from your body. Neither of which is survivable. For us to merge, well, we would need to get a lot more, uh, personal."

"More personal?"

"Yes, as in, completely share our pasts, hopes, and dreams. It's sup-posed to be more like reliving each other's lives. When it's complete, both people are perfectly in sync until they have different experiences. Experiencing another person at that level changes you. You would understand me in a way that the nites would recognize, and you would no longer be considered a threat. You and I would be able to call on each other's magical training, memories, and powers at will. For a while, we would become extensions of each other."

Jenna blushed furiously.

"Oh yeah, we wouldn't be able to hide anything," he said.

"Nothing?" she said.

"Nope."

"Hm, I see the issue."

"Yes, you see why I've been going with option one."

"Why not just let me die?"

Anger coursed through him. "That's not an option. You are too important."

"You're not the first person to say that to me, you know," Jenna said, and Kal frowned, about to ask her to elaborate when she continued. "Just what makes me so important?"

"Everyone is important, Jenna," he said softly. "You are stronger than you know in magic, and in your sense of self, or you would never have held off as long as you did before showing symptoms of nites rewriting your memories. You have a keen mind, and more importantly, you are," he paused, looking for the right words, "my trainee." Kal shifted in his seat. "When I was in the haze of the maghin, it was your voice that drew me out."

Jenna looked like she wanted to say something, but he pushed on. "Everything you do reflects on me and vice versa."

"Oh," she said, looking down. "I think, well, I *know* you saved me, too."

As the day moved on, Jenna was getting the hang of things. She could call and dismiss her magic in the shape of a glowing orb at will. She had mastered the basics and agreed with Kal's assessment. *He was lucky. I really could have fried his brain.* She snorted.

"Hm? You have a question?"

"No, Master," she said automatically.

He frowned, and she recalled he did not like it when she called him master. It reminded him of his training with his father and brother. She shouldn't perceive things like that about him, but she did. Even with the extra sessions they had been having to remove nites, images and feelings made her feel familiar with places she had never been, and thoughts of foods or people brought out memories of food she had never tasted or people she had never met. It was strange at first, but one thing it taught her was that he wasn't just a good master, but he was a good person. She should be afraid of losing herself, but she wasn't. Instead, resolve hardened in her.

I will not fail. I will be a good pupil and defend him when needed. I will make him proud, and he will recognize me as a good person, too. Someone worthy of... worthy of what, exactly?

Just what did she want from Kal? What did she want for herself?

"Again," Kal said gruffly.

Shaking off the thoughts, Jenna began again, relearning how to access her magic quickly and efficiently. He had her repeat the process until she could do it flawlessly, even when he startled her.

They stopped for a food break.

"Who trained you to use healing magic?" Kal asked.

"Well, I had the basics and theory in class, but I was mostly just feeling my way."

"See, I am lucky you didn't paralyze me."

"I'm not that bad." She laughed.

"No, but I don't think you realize how dangerous or rare what you did was."

"Well, I had tried something once before," she said, uneasy, recalling the circumstances.

"Tell me."

"That man who attacked me." Her voice went hoarse.

"The one from the market?"

"Yes, I knew I wasn't allowed to do something flashy, but I thought, what if I attack him from the inside? I tried to make his organs grow old. I kept pulling wave after wave of magic and attacking his..."

Kal went unnaturally still, then turned away from her.

"Master?"

His face was ashen.

"What? I wasn't going to kill him, Master. I'm sorry."

"Jenna." He turned back to her to ensure he had her attention. "What you did is known as death magic. It would have killed him."

"No," she said, but she knew, at the time, she had wanted him to die.

"Yes, Jenna. Very slowly and very painfully. Once you degrade the body, it doesn't recover."

"Oh," she said, her voice quivering.

He frowned at her, eyes taking on a dark cast.

"You must swear to me."

"Yes, Master, anything." *Please don't break our bond*, she pleaded with her eyes.

"Swear never again to take a life with magic."

"I swear, Master."

"No, Jenna. It must be a binding oath."

She paused. If she did this, she would give up her primary defense against anyone seeking to harm her or others she loved. She struggled momentarily.

"Jenna?"

"Yes, of course, Master."

"Now, Jenna!"

"I-I, Jenna Sturmich, swear never again to take a life with magic." The binding soaked into her skin and took hold of her. A small diamond pattern appeared on her left wrist, representing the bond. A mirror image appeared on Kal's.

In that instant, their bond intensified, and Jenna trembled as she keenly sensed his anger at her for killing with magic.

"Lesson's over for today."

"Yes, M-master." She fled the room. *What will happen when he finds out about my past?*

Kal resisted the urge to go after her. Instead, he sat there for a long time, recalling his father and the sensation of his life snuffing out. Corvald had called it a mercy killing. He was hard on her by making it a binding instead of a sworn oath, but he wouldn't risk it. He would not kill or allow her to kill by magic. No matter what the king wanted.

He sat and wept. *Will my beliefs condemn me to unimaginable torment?*

Chapter 10

Jenivieve Sturmich

"Did something happen between you and Jenna?" Lily said as she approached Kal.

"Why?" His stomach clenched as he thought about the oath.

"She seemed upset when I saw her, and now I can't find her."

He paused and opened his mind. He sensed Jenna deep in the Rim, near the shanties, farthest from the walls protecting the city. The Rim was dangerous during the day, but it was night, and even a mage had to be cautious...

"Fool girl," he growled. "I'll go after her."

"Wait," said Lily. "One of the other innkeepers, Valem, saw her on an errand with me and asked about her today." She paused, her face creased with concern. "Do you remember the night you and I met?"

Kal frowned, thinking back to that night. Two years was a long time, and during that period, he had moved around to different inns in the Rim, searching for something that suited his long-term needs. It was the proprietor of the Golden Lantern tavern, Valem, who had introduced them. Thinking back on it, he had been about eighteen, probably Jenna's age now.

Living on his own with the maghin had aged him in ways he couldn't articulate. He'd received a regular stipend, but under the influence of the maghin, he hadn't contemplated questioning it. How many other things had he not asked?

"Yes, why?" he replied.

"Well, a few days before that, there was a Choosing in the Rim, where possible candidates are reviewed for potential and selected. According to Valem, Jenna was the one chosen."

His brow wrinkled as he reflected further, recalling the news. The taverns had been alive with the tale. Usually, parents brought their children to the wardens on Choosing Day, hoping that they would be selected, but sometimes, something happened which triggered a child early. That year, it happened. A traumatic event activated a girl, and it took three masters to pull her down and take her away before she did more harm to others.

His eyes went wide. "She's *that* girl?!"

Lily nodded.

He hurried out of the inn.

Why her? Why then? That was the same day I received the maghin and began looking for an inn. A few days before that was when father...

He stopped. Sweat beaded his brow.

When I killed him.

He forced the thought away. What he knew for sure was that he needed to find Jenna and find out what had activated her two years ago.

He located her again. Concentrating, he felt wind on her face and the openness of the sky. She must be on one of the roofs, so he vaulted up, sending enough magic through his legs and feet to propel him upward. His foot connected with the roof's edge, and he ran onwards, his fears pushing him closer to the controversial beacon he had come to perceive as Jenna.

He found her scrunched up in the shadows of an overhang, staring out at the city lights. A warm summer breeze blew, cleansing the city as the stars glistened in a cloudless sky.

Kal studied the visible side of her face. From his vantage point, she appeared so young, but her actual age was closer to his twenty years. How odd it was that, knowing nothing about her, he had already planned her training and future decision to stay with him even when the bond was released. She was his pupil, not his slave, and plans rarely survived first contact.

"Jenna?" he called softly, even though he was sure she was aware of him.

"Yes, Master?"

"I am sorry."

Silence met him as she stared at him, watchful.

"I will not take back the oath, but I need you to understand why."

He had never told anyone except his brother about the death of his father. He needed to know whether they would work well together.

"My father was a very influential man, and for most of his life, he was a driven and loving man." He stopped, eyes roving Jenna's face, looking for doubts. She simply stared back at him, expression unchanged.

"But he was being influenced by what my brother and I have come to call... the voice. This voice has plagued our family for generations, and it seems to want us to find it." Kal trailed off.

"Find it? How?" Jenna nudged gently, cutting through his reverie.

"It wants us to dig. Many have been able to ignore it for a while, but over time, they start to lose track of things, lose track of time, and, in the end, lose track of themselves. Each generation is being affected by it earlier. When I killed my father," he stumbled over the words, "it was for self-preservation." This was the first time Kal had allowed himself the benefit of the doubt.

"My father was no longer there. He was just raving. He wanted to dig day and night. He no longer ate or focused his powers. When left untied, he would dig until his fingers bled. Nothing else mattered. That thing in him had completely taken over."

He recalled the sensation of it pushing against his shields, repeatedly trying to jump from his father into him. Kal broke into a cold sweat.

"One day, I went to see him." He paused, his eyes going unfocused in memory. "He seemed lucid, and when I spoke, he nodded as if listening. To the boy who wanted his father, it meant the world." He paused again. "And then he asked me if I would untie him." Kal clenched his jaw, recalling the decision.

"You untied him?"

"I did." Kal took a ragged breath. "He attacked me, grabbing me by the throat, while he—no, not him—that thing inside of him started pushing on my shields. All my life, I was taught to kill only to protect, and I loved my father." His voice broke, but he continued. "But he had been gone for so long, and I was dying. He was killing me." His voice quieted further.

"My shields fell, and I, and we both screamed as I stopped his heart."

For the briefest moment, Kal sat perfectly still.

"I felt him then, my real father, full of relief and love, but I also felt the other one. It lunged for me, and I closed my eyes, opening them when I felt it recoil, bouncing off. The voice was surprised, and then they were both gone." He gathered himself.

"The guards came in and found us; Father sprawled on top of me."

Kal's shoulders hunched. "I was devastated. I barely slept or ate." A tear slid quietly down Kal's face. "I lost track of time for a while, but eventually, my brother took over, and my father's death was ruled an accident. But still, I killed my father." He shrugged and laughed harshly, remembering. "The maghin was a kindness."

Kal wiped his face. "He was a great man, and he was also gone before I killed him, his mind lost in the voices. But in my heart of hearts, I believe I should have been able to save him."

As Jenna listened to the story, little pieces of him fell into place. Disjointed dreams she had begun having of him, primarily sensations and impressions—his sadness and feelings of being betrayed, coupled with his own betrayal.

"Jenna?"

She came back to the present. "Yes?"

"I was trained younger than most, but you are my first pupil, and with everything going on, I've been pretty self-absorbed. The point is, I haven't gotten to know you. Would you tell me about yourself?"

Jenna looked down, sighing. "What do you want to know?"

"Well, let's start simple. Tell me your name."

My name. She stilled, staring out over the Rim. *It's been so long.*

"Jenivieve," she breathed. "My name is Jenivieve May Sturmich."

"That is a very nice name. May I call you Jenivieve?"

"No." Her tone was harsh and distant, causing him to flinch a little. Her voice became hollow as she said, "That person died two years ago."

Kal drew in a deep breath. *That would be right around the time of the Choosing.*

"Will you share that story with me, Jenna?" He spoke softly, afraid she would balk. She sat still for several long moments. Kal was beginning to lose hope when she got up.

"It's better if I show you." She turned and launched herself off the side of the building, feet and legs glowing with magic as she glided down to the slums below.

Kal admired her graceful landing and then, pushing magic into his feet and legs, he launched himself after her.

She wound her way through the Rim toward a cleaner section of the city, closer to the city walls. Streetlights lit the way, and guards patrolled the streets. She came to a side street and surveyed the houses lining the left side. When Kal reached her, she pointed to a home. It was a modest house for this area, likely a three-bedroom flat.

"Jenivieve and her family lived here. They were very happy. One day, her mother, who was a healer, got assigned to leave the city with a war band sent to protect the borderlands. Jenivieve's mother promised she wouldn't be gone long, but she never returned. Instead, what came back was a box with some of her belongings." Jenna reached into the collar of her shirt and pulled out a small pendant, holding it reverently. "Apparently, she died defending the healer's tent when they were overrun."

Kal studied her as she stood holding the locket. Feelings of pride and sadness filtered through the bond. Just as he was sure she wouldn't continue, she spoke. "The light went out of Father's eyes that day. I mean, we were all devastated, but I didn't realize what it meant." She took a deep breath. "Father was still here. He moved and spoke, but really, he died when he heard the news of her. Only his body lived. He did what he could to bring food and shelter, but the depression and drinking started, and he couldn't be the father we needed."

A choking grief filled the bond.

"Jenivieve and her sister took up the chores, cooking, and cleaning. Her brothers tried to help by doing odd jobs in and out of the house, earning extra money to help pay for food. Her second older brother, Rowen, knew enough about healing that he started taking on some of Mother's clients, but the oldest brother, Justin, was angry all the time.

"He started going out at all hours of the night and even started hanging around with thugs. Jenivieve overheard the younger brother confront him one night. They fought and Justin left, saying he was searching for the group that had killed mother. Justin never came back." She laughed bitterly. "Their father barely noticed. He began staying out all hours of the night, drinking and gambling. One day, city men came to claim the house. Father had lost it gambling, so they threw them out. Father never returned. They gathered what they could carry and left."

Kal twitched at the loss coming through the bond.

She turned then and leaped to a nearby roof, hesitating until Kal followed after her. She wound her way through the streets of the Rim, pausing at a dark side street before turning down it. Mounds he identified as people were asleep in the gutters or huddled in doorways. The air smelled strongly of garbage and waste. Some of the piles coughed or mumbled. Jenna did not balk at their presence, so he continued behind, walking along in her wake. At the end of the alley was a small boarded-up door. Someone could have entered it, but no one did, as if they believed it was far preferable to sleep on the street. Jenna pried the boards away from the doorframe and opened the door to the dusty room beyond. On the other side of the road, Kal sensed the eyes of one of the homeless on them.

They entered the room, and she shut the door behind them. Kal visualized the outline of her green aura before him. She had gotten better at controlling it. After entering, she created a series of small lights and positioned them around the room.

"After that, Jenivieve and her family lived here," she said, her skin pale in the light.

She showed him a single-room dwelling with a small cooking area.

"Rowen took it hard. He was always the happy one and the smart one. After Justin left, even he became depressed. Jenivieve tried to cheer him up, but he started glowering at her and Casi in a way that made them uncomfortable. Jenivieve tried to send Casi on errands and keep them apart, and for a while, it helped. They settled into their new parent-free life with Rowen in charge, and he eventually started talking and joking again."

Longing rose in the bond.

She turned and walked out of the dwelling. The sad little lights followed after her. Kal closed the door and followed her back out of the alley and into what, by day, would be the marketplace. Several of the homeless were watching her, but he sensed no ill will from them. A couple followed behind them, staring at the lights in awe. One in particular caught his eye. Something about his movements seemed almost militant.

Jenna turned and started walking. Kal, the lights, and the homeless man ghosted solemnly behind her. When they reached the far end of the market, she continued her tale.

"One day, Rowen came home and smiled at them as if he had solved a problem for one of his customers. It was a busy time of year, and the market was always lively during Choosing. Even after what had happened, Casi always wanted to go to the markets. That day, Rowen promised to take her and buy her a gift. I—Jenivieve thought things were looking up," she said bitterly.

The bond flashed cold.

"Jenivieve asked if she could go with them and could tell he was pleased when he agreed to it. Later that day, Rowen took Jenivieve and Casi to the market.

"For a while, it was wonderful, all the sights and sounds. Jenivieve loved the smells most of all. Little lights twinkled everywhere, and there were even magicians," she said with a half-smile, knowing those were not real mages. "Over the day, we wound our way through the market and ended up near the sellers of people. Casi asked to leave since she wanted to go to a play, but Rowen said he had a patient to meet.

"The man, when he came, was slender and moved like he couldn't stand still. He made them all nervous.

"He greeted Rowen, reaching for his wallet as if to pay him, but instead, he gave a signal to a man, and suddenly we were surrounded by slavers.

"He demanded Rowen hand us over and he could go free.

"Rowen said, 'That wasn't part of our deal,' but the slaver laughed and said he was changing the deal."

"That's when it struck her," she said bitterly. "Rowen had brought us there to get rid of us."

Kal stared at her in horror, the bond flooding with bitterness, anxiety, and abandonment. Even the homeless listeners shifted uncomfortably.

Jenna shrugged. "Oddly, I have always wondered how much we were worth," she continued. "Before Jenivieve realized what was happening, the slavers had come up and grabbed them. Casi started to cry. Jenivieve... well, something broke in Jenivieve.

"People became too loud, and the world was both bigger and smaller all at once. She could feel the energy all around her, and she struck out blindly, pulling power from anywhere she could find it. Once Jenivieve was full of energy, she just balled it all up and threw it at all of them, Rowen included. Fortunately, or unfortunately, Jenivieve had no real skill, just raw anger. Most of the energy just dissipated before hitting them, so she kept doing it over and over again until something hit her."

The bond roiled with shame and fear.

She was quiet for a few moments. Then, she shook her head as if coming back to herself.

"I woke up at the Warders Guild two weeks later and was informed the slavers had died. Rowen and my sister were gravely injured, but I could not see my family until I could control my powers." She paused, running a hand over her face. "They said I sucked all the life energy from them. Jenivieve died that day, and the burnt-out husk of her was left." She shrugged. "Just me."

81

Kal walked up to her and wrapped his arms around her. She stood there, arms at her sides. When he started to step away, she wrapped her arms around him, as if she were afraid to lose the warmth and nearness of him. All at once, a dam broke within her, and she cried. Not the streaming tears from before, but deep, shuddering sobs. They stood like that with Kal rubbing her back and hair for a very long time, the little lights bobbing mournfully around them.

K al stood there, offering Jenna what comfort he could. While she told her tale, he felt the anguish, abandonment, and fear through the bond. The truth of what he had done to her with this binding started to sink in. She didn't take the binding because she considered it the right thing to do. She did it so he wouldn't throw her away as her brother had done. She seemed to need him in an almost visceral way.

Kal leaned his chin down on the top of her head and whispered, "I am sorry, Jenna. I did not know." Jenna's only response was to hold him tighter.

He was honored and humbled, and then the fear began. *What happens if she tries to kill with the binding on?* He believed it wouldn't be intentional, but she could slip up. The binding wouldn't allow her to kill someone, but it wouldn't leave her unscathed in the process. The energy she used to kill would turn back on her, causing excruciating pain depending on her intent. What if he removed it, but because she hadn't mastered her fear, she killed again?

His arms tightened on her. *I need to make sure she never feels that way again.*

Once Jenna had cried herself out, Kal used a dry patch of his shirt to wipe her face, which set her to giggling. His breath caught at how resilient she was, and he could finally admit it, she was beautiful.

"Come on," he said, voice husky as he wrapped his arm around her. "Let's go home."

As they turned to leave, his eyes settled on one of the nearby homeless people who had been sitting vigil with them.

"Just a minute," he whispered to Jenna.

Kal approached one of the men he noticed following them earlier and tears shined on his face.

He bent over him, studying his features.

"You are one of her brothers," he said.

The man nodded.

Seeing him in this state would do Jenna no good, so Kal took a gamble and gave the man one of the inn's business cards.

"My name is Kal. Clean yourself up and come find us there," he said, straightening.

He headed back to Jenna, took her by the hand, and led her home.

When they returned to the inn, Lily, seeing their hands still clasped, arched a brow at Kal and hurried Jenna off to her room.

A short while later, Lily returned and eyed him skeptically. "I thought she was your pupil?" she asked.

Kal grimaced. "She is, and yes, I know any relationship outside of master-trainee would be grounds to break the bond. Nothing is going on."

Lily still looked skeptical, so he changed the subject.

"A homeless man may stop by."

She glared at him.

"If he does, please take him in."

She frowned.

"He may also ask about Jenna." He hesitated momentarily. "If he does, it is okay to tell him she is safe here."

Her eyebrows shot up.

"Also, he may not want you to tell Jenna about him, and if so, please respect his wishes within reason."

Lily opened her mouth to speak.

"He is her brother."

With that, Kal turned on his heel and left the room. He had to prepare for a meeting with the king.

Chapter 11

Casi

The next morning, Jenna stared at the inn's door, willing it to open. Her sister, who had been coming by for short visits the last few weeks, had stopped coming. Jenna treasured those visits, though she wouldn't let on to her sister.

Where was Casi?

Lily came into the room and sat beside her, pulling out a sheet of paper. "This is the schedule for the next week. Are you sure you want to work so much? Everyone should have some time off."

Jenna studied the schedule, frowning as Casi popped back into her mind. She chewed on her nail. "I could use some time off," she said.

"Oh? Are you and Casi going to do something together?" Lily asked.

Jenna flinched. Had Casi been waiting for her to suggest something? Is that why she hadn't been by? Guilt flooded through her.

Almost casually, Lily asked, "Did you and Casi fight?"

Jenna stared at her. "No."

"Have you considered going to see her instead of waiting around for her to come to you?"

Jenna's skin flushed. She had spent so much of the last two years avoiding her sister and not replying to her letters. Grimacing, she admitted, "I don't know where she lives."

"Ah. It's a good thing I'm the one who walked her home, then."

Lily reached into her pocket and pulled out one of the inn's business cards and wrote an address on the back. With shaking fingers, Jenna took the card.

Jenna made her way through the Rim toward the address on the card. She ignored the crowd as her thoughts wandered back to last night. She didn't know where things stood with Kal. They had shared something important last night. She smiled. She didn't blame him for killing his father. She would have chosen the same if she had been in a similar situation.

Their bond had been alive with emotions as he told his story. Fear of acceptance, dread, and heartbreak. She wondered what the bond had said about her when she told hers?

Jenna rounded the corner and stopped. There, just ahead of her, was her brother Rowen. He was hanging up a flyer on a board. Jenna waited, studying him. She felt no rage or fear—just emptiness. He had bags under his eyes, and his shoulders were hunched. He finished hanging his flyer and went further down the street. Once he rounded the corner, Jenna moved to the bulletin board. On it was a likeness of Casi, and under her picture was the word "missing" with contact information matching the address she was headed toward. Jenna stood staring at the picture for a long while, muscles tense. She felt her hands move of their own accord as she gingerly took the flyer down, holding it close to her chest as she stumbled back to the inn.

K al paced back and forth as Jenna made her way back to the inn. Normally, Jenna was a calm, balanced presence in the back of his mind. Yesterday, when she'd told him her tale, she was hot flashes of anguish, abandonment, and fear. But what he felt now was even more alarming. The bell jingled as a wide-eyed Jenna entered the building.

Kal took in her blank stare. Now that she was closer, he felt the roiling emotions inside her.

"Jenna?" Kal spoke softly, trying not to startle her.

She stared, not seeing him.

"Jenna, what happened?"

He wasn't sure she'd heard, but then she gave him the flyer.

Kal's eyes widened as he read it. It was Casi, the girl she had rescued, her sister.

Children were going missing all over the city—children just like Casi.

Kal closed his eyes a moment, breathing deeply to clear his mind. Kal felt the last two years of his life flash past. This was a comfortable life, but he couldn't sit here and do nothing, especially since he was uniquely suited for this. Not only did Corvald want this, he owed Jenna far more than he wanted to admit for freeing him from the maghin. Decision made, he opened his eyes.

"Jenna, do you trust me?"

"Yes."

"I will find your sister."

That got a reaction. Her eyes locked onto Kal's, and his heart lurched at the trust and hope he saw and felt mirrored in the bond. He didn't know how or in what condition, but he would find Jenna's sister.

Chapter 12

Shadow Weaver

Kal's carriage entered the sprawling palace grounds. Two years had passed since he'd last been there, his training as a Shadow Weaver complete. This time, his father wouldn't be there to greet him. His shoulders hunched, and he steadied his breathing. From what he had learned, his brother needed him.

The carriage pulled up to the palace proper, and he went in for his appointment.

Kal entered the chamber where the king awaited. King Corindanthanus Mendathalon sat surrounded by his guards, drinking tea. Kal bowed to the king, who gestured he rise.

"Please, have a seat."

Kal sat in the seat opposite the king and found himself studying his brother. At only a couple of years older than Kal, he was surprised to see the stress lines on his face, the purse of his lips, and the slump of his shoulders. Kal's inner voice cried out. What had happened while he was away?

The manservant brought Kal tea, and he took a sip before placing his cup back down.

"You wanted to meet with me?" the king asked.

"Sire, I would like to take up my old position as Shadow Weaver."

Corin blinked at him, and his expression shuddered briefly, as if in relief, before becoming neutral.

Corin sipped his tea before asking, "Why?"

"You have a problem, and I think I can do something to help."

"Oh," he said almost hesitantly. "And which problem do you refer to?"

"The one involving the missing children."

"Ah." A look flitted across Corin's face, but he didn't continue, so Kal took that as acceptance.

"Is my old team still intact?" Kal asked.

"We lost Gerald to the blight, but the others were uninfected."

"Is Master Harram still available?"

"I can make him so."

"Good, I need him also. What of Lord Sandoval?"

"I can request his presence."

"Even better." Kal grinned.

"Kal, he is getting older, and he lost all of his heirs during the blight. He could refuse the honor."

Kal grunted. "I'll convince him."

"What are you planning?"

"I plan to find the person, or persons, behind this and bring them to justice," Kal said. "If there is treason, I'll find it."

"Okay, I will send the requests over tomorrow. I presume you will want to meet in the old halls?"

"Yes, they can be secured and are more or less central. I'll need a copy of the missing children's files and any commentary made so far."

Corin nodded. "I will have Captain Abasi provide the information to you."

"Oh, one more thing," Kal said. "I'd like access to the archives for both my apprentice and me."

"I will add that to the list. Anything else?"

"No, sire," he said.

"Then you are dismissed."

Kal rose to his feet, and just as he was about to leave, Corin said, "Kal?"

At the door, Kal turned back. "Yes?"

"Glad to have you back." The corner of his mouth quirked into a smile.

"It's good to see you again, brother," Kal said.

"And just so you know, Mother is at the Kimora Temple." And with that information, Kal bowed and left.

Chapter 13

Missing Children

"No!" Kal jerked up in bed. The feel of his father's life snuffing out washed over him. He panted and sweat trickled down his back. He had experienced this nightmare every night since Jenna had removed the maghin. Somehow, this one felt more visceral. *This is just first-day jitters.* Kal rubbed his face. *I can do this. I have to do this.*

He had a meeting in a few hours with the captain of the guard and his lieutenants to get an overview of the missing children.

The image of Jenna's grief-stricken face came to mind. He needed to find Casi.

The first glimmer of light came through his window. It was early, but he knew he wasn't going back to sleep. Hoping for clarity, Kal rose and set about his daily exercise routine. It often helped calm him. He would take it one day at a time.

K al waited in the Guard Hall on the main floor of the palace. It was a large room with a round table and red carpets. Portraits of former Royal Guard captains covered the walls. The door opened, and Captain Abasi, followed by two Lieutenants, one female and the other male, walked in. They all seated themselves at the table.

"Lord Mendathalon." Captain Abasi bowed.

"Please, just call me Kal."

"These are Lieutenants Vithuriel and Dohanson," Captain Abasi said as he gestured to the lieutenants. "The king has requested we give over leadership to you on the missing children's case." He frowned. "You have been unavailable for the last two years, so it may take you some time to come up to speed on procedural and court changes."

Kal shifted in his seat, not sensing any overt hostility but still uncomfortable. In the coming days, he would encounter people who knew he killed his father and, though deemed blameless, would judge him. He had to get used to it.

"In the last ten days, roughly twenty youths have disappeared. All the missing are under the age of sixteen."

Lieutenant Dohanson unrolled a map on the table in front of Kal, then pointed. "The red markers indicate known locations of child abductions."

The red markers were spread across the city and surrounding lands. Kal frowned as he could not find a distinguishable pattern.

Captain Abasi continued. "Two youths disappeared at different ends of the market. Several more while working in the fields. One even disappeared from a pantry. We checked for hidden doors and back panels but found nothing." Abasi shifted in his seat. "These events happen at different times of the day. Some happened at nearly the same time and have been happening so fast that parents turn around to find their children have vanished." Kal studied the map as unease flowed through him.

"So far, we have found three missing children, but only one was alive—a young boy named Patrick Turner, age eleven. Unfortunately, the lad had no recollection of what had happened, which is likely trauma, but medical findings show that something is off about the boy. The healers have diagnosed that a vital part of him is missing. He has since slipped into a coma."

Lieutenant Vithuriel spoke. "When we do find the children, they are in places they shouldn't be. One was found in a tree, while another was on a small rock island in the middle of a rapid river. The one alive was in an alcove on the edge of a cliff face."

The captain sat up a little straighter, then said, "There is no way these children got there themselves. Someone or something had to put them there."

In the grim silence, Kal arranged his thoughts. He would start with the basics. "Did the bodies have any markings?"

"None, my Lord," said Lieutenant Vithuriel.

"Any family connections?"

"None so far," Abasi replied.

"Time of day?"

"Random."

"What were the children wearing when they were taken?"

"Local dyers' browns, blues, yellows, or reds."

"What about when they were found? The same clothing?"

"Good question. We will have to get back to you on that one," Abasi said.

"Where have you not checked?" Kal asked.

There was no reply.

"Let me rephrase the question. What areas have, so far, been off-limits?"

Kal stared as Lieutenant Dohanson opened his mouth and closed it. While everyone else in the room gave him speculative looks, he tried a different tack. "Are all the children bright ones?"

A longer pause. Lieutenant Vithuriel answered, "No, not all the children are mage-born, though it is skewed that way."

"Were any of the found children bright ones?"

"No," Abasi said.

A hush settled throughout the room. Kal gazed around the table.

"Mendallon is built on mages. Its artisans and guilds are powered by them, not to mention the military. Removal of these children represents a threat to the crown, yes?" Silence greeted him. Kal plunged ahead. "So, who currently benefits the most from undermining the throne?" The question brought silence. "In recent months, have there been other threats to the king or the bright ones?"

This time, the silence was almost brittle. The two lieutenants stared at the table, but Captain Abasi's gaze turned predatory, as though he were going to speak. Kal continued. "I myself have recently been attacked by assassins."

Kal's voice cut through the silent room like a knife, drawing everyone's eyes. "Who else is in line to inherit the throne if something were to happen to the king and me?" Kal asked.

This question brought a response from the captain. "There is no one with direct lineage. They all died of the blight last year."

Kal blinked, dropping the map. He had heard tales of the disease known as the blight ravaging the mages and nobility. Most in the city's rim, where the inn was located, were unaffected. Then, a horrible realization struck. "What? You mean all of my cousins are dead?"

Captain Abasi nodded, studying Kal like a hawk.

Kal's stomach twisted. "That means I am the only one in line to inherit?" Kal asked, rubbing his hands on his knees under the table. "And someone is trying to kill me."

Captain Abasi said nothing.

"Well, that is not good." An ache formed in Kal's temples. "With no one alive to inherit the throne, it would be up for grabs amongst the nobles. Any of them could be behind this." Kal gritted his teeth at the enormity of the issue. He closed his eyes, breathed deeply, and fell back on his training. He opened his eyes and said, "Okay. One problem at a time. Tell me again about the first children taken, and I would like to inspect this pantry."

Chapter 14

Roolia

The door to the magic training room rippled. Kal frowned as it caught his attention. Lily knew not to disturb him when he was training Jenna.

"Please hold, Jenna."

Kal released the seal on the warded room and opened the door.

Lieutenant Dohanson stood outside the door.

"Sir, we've had a report."

"Just a minute." Kal turned back to Jenna. "Continue going through the basic forms. I will test you when I return. If I'm not back by lunchtime, check in with Lily."

Kal almost smirked at the flinch Jenna tried to hide. She definitely struggled with the simple things. Complex actions she excelled at.

Kal shut the door behind him. "What seems to be the problem, Lieutenant?"

"Lord Braydon has urgently requested the arbiter of the missing children's case."

"Lead the way."

Lieutenant Dohanson and his guards escorted Kal to the Noble Quarter. Each wore black clothes with silver trim and purple armbands denoting them as Royal Guards. The lieutenant, whom the others deferred to, spoke as they rode in their carriage.

"Lord Mendathalon—"

"Please, call me Kal."

Doha nodded. "Kal, please call me Doha. I will be your guide." He reached out a hand, and Kal shook it. "I have been given the following instructions regarding this case. As part of your investigation, you can go about the city and speak to whomever you deem necessary. You must submit daily reports to Captain Abasi. They can be done in person or through me. You will provide weekly updates in person to the king. You have one restriction. Per the king, you may visit his quarters by invitation only. All other venues are open. Also, while working on the case, you will have five guards assigned to you. All guard assignments will go through me."

When they reached Lord Braydon's, Doha positioned his guards—two outside the door and two inside the room—while he stayed with Kal.

Upon entering Braydon's sitting room, Kal observed Lady Emilia Deleon down on her knees, weeping, with Braydon standing over her. Anger radiated from him like a shroud, filling the room.

Kal stood regarding him a moment. "Lord Braydon, I see you still have a temper."

Braydon's eyes turned on him, flashing with bitterness before returning to the lady. "Tell him, or I will," Braydon said through gritted teeth.

Lady Deleon's mouth worked a couple of times silently before she replied in husky tones. "He wasn't supposed to die. He knew not to interfere with them." She opened her mouth to say more when Braydon interrupted.

"They were your children."

Lady Deleon flinched and started crying again. "They weren't supposed to take *our* children," she wailed.

"Who died?" Kal interrupted, his voice soft and commanding.

The lady wept harder. It was Braydon who spat out, "Lord Aaron Deleon."

"When did he die?" Kal asked.

"Sometime in the night," Braydon answered.

Kal turned to the lieutenant. "Were you aware of this?"

"No, my lord."

"Send someone over there to secure the site. I would like to see the scene before it gets cleaned up."

Doha signaled, and one of the guards departed.

Lady Deleon sobbed. "Sir Gavin said they would only take Bright Ones."

Kal glanced at Doha, and he spoke without further prompting.

"Sir Gavin is affiliated with House Cardinas and is rarely seen about without Sir Roland or Sir Farrel, also of House Cardinas."

"Bring me Sirs Gavin, Roland, and Farrel," said Kal.

Doha signaled to the remaining guard, who, as she left, sent in one of the outside guards to take up her post.

It had been two years, so Kal had to ask, "What is the main source of income for House Deleon?"

"Commerce," Braydon said. "The Deleon family has its hands in nearly all trade in the city."

"What about Cardinas?"

"Banking and treasury," Doha confirmed.

Well, at least that hasn't changed.

Kal turned back to the woman, still on her knees, her dress crumpled around her. He held out his hand. Tentatively, she took it, and he helped her to her feet, leading her to a chair. Pulling a handkerchief from his pocket, he handed it to her, and she dabbed her eyes. Once she was composed, Kal spoke. "Now, let's start at the beginning."

Her voice quivered. "About a month ago, Aaron was approached by an odd man. He looked like he was from Mendallon, but his accent was unusual. He played along, introducing him to Sirs Gavin, Roland, and Farrel."

She blew her nose. "Aaron and the others grew suspicious of the man and had him followed. Of the three men Aaron sent, only one returned, and he died shortly after." She wrung her hands. "I don't know what Aaron learned, but last night he was adamant that he had to go to the king."

Fresh tears slid down her face. "This morning, my children were gone, and Aaron was..." Her face crumpled.

"You think this man took your children?"

"I don't know." She wailed. "But who else could it be?"

"And what brought you here? Why didn't you go to the king?"

She hunched down, dress shifting around her. "Braydon and Aaron have never been close, but he and I were—" She hesitated. "Childhood friends." Braydon crossed his arms, grimacing at the implications.

"And the king, well, he hasn't been himself lately. I didn't know where else to go."

"What do you mean, he hasn't been himself?" Kal's stomach dropped.

She flinched as if realizing who she was talking to. "Rumor has it he is becoming," she paused, looking down at her hands, "unreliable."

Kal's stomach churned. *Unreliable?* Was he getting to be like their father? To secure the throne for his brother, he needed to solve this—and soon.

Kal reviewed the bloody massacre in Lord Deleon's inner chambers. Unfortunately, the cleaning crew had gotten there before his order.

Kal kicked everyone out of the tampered scene and walked deliberately through it, avoiding bloody areas. The body lay in repose on the large four-poster bed, all wounds cleaned. Kal inspected the body. It wasn't clear what had killed him, but he had several puncture wounds on his neck and jagged gashes on his arms and torso.

A platter of food was on the table, holding treats. All the sweet-meats were gone, leaving the fruits scattered behind like an afterthought. He went over to the bedside and squatted down, reaching out to the edge of the table and picking a tuft of fur off the side of the furniture before standing.

Kal rolled it between his fingers, smelled it, and then rolled it again.

As Kal studied the hair between his fingers, he realized there was a familiarity to it he couldn't place. Maybe he had read about it somewhere? There were lots of wild, untamed animals in the borderlands. Some were even rumored to think and speak like humans, but no one had ever seen any so far inland. Kal shrugged, bringing himself back to more practical thoughts.

"Do the Deleons have any pets? Where was the body found? And what time was Lord Deleon last seen?" Kal asked.

"I'll find out," said Doha, stepping into the hall. He returned several moments later. "He was last seen a candle mark past midnight. He was found on the floor by the bed, and no, they do not have pets."

"Can you find out what type of sweetmeats were served on the platter? I want a sample if they have any," Kal asked.

Doha eyed him skeptically, but went back out to check.

Kal continued to study the scene, looking for signs of magic. Not finding any, he walked over to a large mahogany desk, took a small sheet of paper, and folded it into a pouch, placing the fur inside. He put it in his pocket.

Doha came back with a small wrapped package, handing it to Kal. "They are Kebon meats."

"Like the kind the street vendors sell?" Kal asked.

"Yes." Doha nodded.

Kal put the package in his cloak pocket, resting against his chest, just as one of the guards returned. "Sirs Gavin and Farrel never came home last night. We have guards out looking. Sir Roland is dead."

Kal sighed. *Of course he is.*

"We made sure the cleaning crew knows to wait," said the guard.

"Good job," Kal said, dismissing the guard. Turning, he spotted the head butler and nodded to Doha. "Let's view the children's rooms now."

The head butler escorted them. The rooms were side by side, and each room was spotless. Both had a set of double doors, which stood open, leading to small private balconies. The curtains billowed gently in the morning breeze. The only difference between the two rooms was the decor.

"Are those doors kept open all night?" Kal asked.

"No, sir. The doors are closed and locked, but the windows are open at night."

Kal studied the broad windows, peering down to the private garden below. It was difficult to reach the windows from the balcony.

"Thank you, sir," Kal said, and the butler escorted them back to the main room.

Kal turned to Doha. "I've found out all I can for now. Have an investigative team continue looking for clues."

"They are already on the way," said Doha.

"Good, let's go."

One of Kal's guards led the way out to their waiting coach. They made their way through the Noble Quarter to the Cardinas' estate. City watch guards were positioned along the street. Once they reached the main house, they were escorted to a secluded part of the third floor. A guard stood at the end of the hall. After a brief nod to the lieutenant, they were allowed into Sir Roland's chambers.

This scene had not been tampered with, as the remains of Sir Roland were visible all over the room. There was even blood on the high vaulted ceiling and streaks along the bedcovering to the right. Red droplets clouded the otherwise picturesque view of the River Imryn seen through the windows on the left. On its side lay one of two blue chairs in front of a cold, ash-strewn fireplace. In front of that was the body.

Kal stared at the remains as a wave of nausea washed through him. He had seen death before, even gory killings, but he had never seen slaughter like this. His stomach churned as he mastered his senses and took in the sight with an investigator's eye. He considered his mentor's words. *Look beyond the scene to what's missing*. Kal did that, scanning the room with magic, and he again found no buildup of nites. He frowned. Magic wasn't used in this killing, or someone had thoroughly cleaned up. Something was off about the scene. But what was he missing?

He studied the blood marks on the floor, the walls, and the ceiling, and it clicked. There were no footprints anywhere on the floor where the body parts were lying. In fact, there were no footprints anywhere.

A scream rang out through the halls. Everyone ran towards the noise, Kal in the lead, even though he was on the other side of the room when the screaming started. They ran through the dining area and into a dimly lit corridor when Kal stopped.

The fur, the missing footprints, the savagery.

It couldn't be, but just in case, he said, "Do not move, and no matter what happens, do not show fear."

Kal took two steps down the wide corridor and paused, making out a faint form in the distance. *Is it what I think it is?* He took a deep breath. He would have missed it if he hadn't been looking for it. There it was, a faint scent similar to the fur he had found.

From the far end of the corridor, an enormous multi-legged animal loped towards him. Kal dredged his memory for all he knew about the beast and internally repeated the words he had just said to the men. *Do not show fear*. Doha stepped forward and drew his sword in a high stance.

The creature crouched.

"I said do not move!" Kal barked, fear threatening to show. Kal mastered himself.

The lieutenant relaxed his stance but did not retreat. His body was poised on the edge of motion, and his eyes locked on the beast as it took him in and dismissed him.

The creature started forward, this time more slowly. Six black orbs twinkled, taking in the room and its occupants. It had two large tufted ears that swiveled inquisitively, large canine teeth, and a broad, well-muscled back. The creature had a covering of silky black fur that would make it nearly impossible to find in the dark. Its most alarming feature was its six large legs ending in padded feet. Its muscles bunched and released in an almost feline gait as it moved closer. Its back was thicker than its front, padded with extra muscles for balance. The beast slowly approached Kal and leaned its broad, flat snout into his chest, inhaling with deep, huffing noises. Kal did not move, just stared at the creature, and after a second, it leaned back from him and spoke.

"Alpha?"

Relief flowed through Kal, which he covered by nodding. "Call me Kal."

The creature sat back on its haunches as Kal reached forward into his pocket and withdrew the sweetmeats. Unwrapping the package, he offered it to the beast.

"Treat!" The creature lunged forward, jamming its monstrous head into Kal's hand and licking up the meat.

Kal's face broke out into a broad, boyish grin, and Doha's sword dipped to the ground in surprise.

"Good girl!" Kal said, patting her furry head and scratching her neck.

"Yummy! Want more! Want more!"

Kal laughed. "I'll see what I can do."

Doha sheathed his sword and stepped back to speak with his men. Kal listened to him instruct them to seal off the area so no one else stumbled onto the creature. Two of the soldiers rushed out of the room while the other two stood guard. Kal felt their eyes on his back as he rubbed the beast, still grinning like a little boy.

Doha, standing to Kal's left, cleared his throat.

Kal turned his grin up at him.

"I never thought I would see one of these." Kal spoke with delight.

"One of these?"

"A Lycanide. Though some refer to them as spider wolves. They are usually found in the borderlands. I've never heard of one coming this far inland."

"Is it dangerous?" Doha asked.

Kal grinned. "She, and yes."

"Why is she here?"

"Good question." Kal flashed Doha a warning glance.

Doha pursed his lips, then followed his lead. "What do we call her?"

Kal raised his brows, opening and then closing his mouth. He turned back to the Lycanide and asked, "What are you called, young one?"

"Roolia." She shook out her fur and bowed her head.

"It's a pleasure to meet you, Roolia," Doha said.

Roolia sniffed at Doha. "Is pack?" she asked Kal.

He considered. "He's on trial."

Roolia's gaze settled on Doha, whose eyes widened as he took in just how intimidating she was. She leaned in to get his scent and asked, "What you called?"

"Doha." He looked to Kal, nervously but he did not move a muscle.

She made a soft, barking noise. "Is funny."

She paused, locking all six eyes on Doha.

"Roolia watch out for you—until trial done."

Kal stared at Roolia, ignoring Doha's curious glance. "Roolia, do you know who killed in this house last night?"

"Roolia does not know. Was returning children."

"Roolia. Where are the children?" Kal asked.

"I save ones I can."

"From who?" Kal asked softly.

"From stupid."

"Stupid?" Doha interjected.

"Pack Yugraph, cousin stupid."

"What pack are you?" Doha asked.

Roolia put one of her front paws on his face and pushed gently.

"This one," she pronounced proudly.

"Sorry, wrong question," he said, voice muffled through the sandpaper roughness of her paws.

Doha reached up and gently moved her paw from his face to his shoulder.

"Which pack were you in before this?"

Roolia paused. "No pack."

Kal reached out and rubbed the soft fur across her back.

"The children. Where are they?"

"Roolia has one here. Come!"

They followed as she turned and trotted back down the hall, which opened into a large chamber. Roolia bounded up the sidewall into a corner opening near the ceiling.

Kal's legs shimmered, and he leaped into the air after her.

The lieutenant turned.

"Someone bring me a rope!"

K al entered the crevice behind Roolia. The openings, functioning as vents, cooled the halls in the summer. The short tunnel widened into a small triangular-shaped room. Kal stood to the side as Roolia worked to unravel the threads holding the child-sized bundle up. Doha arrived just as she freed, then lowered, the child down to them. They laid the bundle on the floor. Doha reached for his knife, but Kal stayed his hand.

"It will be easier to move this way, and awakening the child here could be disconcerting. Can you arrange transport to the Healerie?"

"Yes, of course."

Kal glanced at Roolia. "Is this the only one?"

"No, Roolia saved more."

By the end of the day, they had gathered four of the missing children. All were in a coma-like state. When Doha asked why they weren't awake, Roolia said, "Prey sleep. Less squirming." The lieutenant paled, then flushed at the chittering laughter directed at him.

Kal arrived back at the Healerie sometime after the evening bell with Doha and Roolia in tow. The guards escorted them through a series of empty hallways until Roolia growled low in her throat.

Sweat broke out on Kal's back. He had been accepted as alpha, but packs always have challengers.

"Smell death."

Members of their escort glanced around and frowned. The attendant, a tall woman with her hair pulled up in a no-nonsense bun, glided over to a door at the end of the hall, opened it, and led them into the room. Four children were in small beds at various points in the brightly lit room. Beside the last bed, closest to the wall, was an old woman who sat stiffly in her seat, eyes on them as they entered. After everyone was in the room, she spoke.

"Lord Mendathalon." Her voice rustled like dried parchment.

Kal flinched. "Please call me Kal. Matron Langley, it is a pleasure to see you again. You are a hard woman to reach."

"Well, truth be told, the healers are a bit overprotective." The twinkle in her eyes gave the impression that they were speaking with a much younger woman.

Kal returned the smile. "But it wasn't me you wanted to meet, now was it?" He was confident that news of the creature was blowing through the city like a breeze.

"Perceptive of you, Kal."

Matron Langley turned towards Roolia.

"Lady Roolia," she said and gave a small seated bow.

"I see you pack mother."

Kal's eyebrow rose.

Roolia surprised them all by scuttling over to the matron and sniffing her before licking the back of her hand three times with her rough tongue.

Langley let out a breath as if her pain vanished. She relaxed in the seat, eyes wide, mouth open as she inhaled deeply and slowly exhaled.

"Thank you, Roolia," she said a little breathlessly. "That was a gift."

The matron stood up slowly with a delighted expression on her face.

She held her hands out in front of her, studying them.

"How long will the pain be gone?" she asked with awe in her voice.

Roolia sniffed and growled low.

"Not long," she said with a tinge of sadness.

Langley nodded. "Then to business. I am old, and I do not wish to miss this." She turned to Kal and Doha. "Lieutenant, welcome."

"Matron." Doha's eyes were glassy as he bowed.

She studied him for a moment and nodded.

"Kal, I hear you can wake the children?"

"Not I, Matron, but Lady Roolia can."

Matron Langley stared down at Roolia and smiled.

"Indeed."

Kal smiled to himself as she grinned like a little girl. He knew the feeling.

Matron Langley turned to ring a bell hanging from a cord, and four healer assistants came in. They huddled around the matron, chattering to themselves until she shooed them towards the children.

She signaled Roolia to begin.

Before Roolia went to the children, she spoke. "Only half candle mark. Children must sleep again." Matron Langley nodded her understanding.

Roolia went over to the first child, a small boy, sniffing his scent. She leaned over him and bit down on his leg, slowly injecting him with her antivenom. When the color returned to his cheeks, she removed her fangs and repeated the process with the other children.

When she finished with the last child, she returned to the matron, sitting in a chair, and put her head in her lap. She focused all six of her eyes on her. "Soon."

Matron Langley slowly reached out a hand and rubbed Roolia's head, eyes glistening in pleasure.

Within a few minutes, the first child stirred.

The children awoke slowly, confused, and unable to stay focused. They kept sliding back into an unhealthy stillness as if they couldn't stay motivated. A slight blue tinge colored their lips.

The few bits of consistent information they extracted came down to bright lights, no socks or shoes, their feet submerged in a pool of water, intense pain, and a girl who was strong and carried the load of several children.

They described her, and Doha brought in an artist to draw a composite. None of them recognized her, but something about her struck Kal. Her features reminded him of Jenna. This had to be Casi.

Chapter 15

The Archives

The next day, Jenna awoke to find a note slid under her door. Her stomach dipped, and her fingers shook opening the seal. Kal must have come home late last night because she hadn't sensed him nearby before she went to bed. She felt for him and found him off in the distance, deep in the city. Her eyes shifted back to the note. He expected her at the royal library.

The library was under the palace, a place where few commoners ever went. Jenna opened her door to find a package. She undid its bindings to find official apprentice garb for mages—black slacks, a tan overcoat with black buttons, complete with an armband the color of her guild, black, royal black, just like the maghin she had removed from Kal. The King's Guild was reserved for those who reported directly to the king. She dressed quickly and studied herself in the mirror. All of her bruising had healed. She looked older than her eighteen years. A smile appeared, and her brown eyes twinkled. She was going to the palace. She lifted the last piece out of the package—a travel satchel. In it, she found the documents that would grant her access to the archives. She donned the satchel and went in search of breakfast.

J enna exited the carriage at the entrance to the royal library, which sat in a secure location on the castle's ground floor. Several guards stood around the massive iron gates. A young boy in royal livery approached Jenna upon entry.

"May I be of service?" the boy asked.

"I am here to see the archivist. I have an appointment."

The boy brought her over to the main desk. "And you are?"

Jenna gave her name, sweating as he searched the list.

"Ah, here you are." He checked her name off in the register. "You are expected. Right this way, ma'am."

The boy led Jenna through a hallway and down some stairs. Mage light—which burned bright but didn't give off heat—lit the stairwell and railings.

A massive power source must be nearby to keep so many mage lights lit.

At the bottom of the stairs, the room opened up into an expansive hall with hundreds of rows of books, most of which were only reachable with ladders. Jenna stopped, eyes wide. She had never seen so many books. She couldn't believe the sheer wealth of knowledge they represented. Her mouth snapped shut as her guide moved further ahead, and she hurried after him.

At the far end of the hall was a series of small rooms, some of which held people reading. Her guide led her to the last door on the left, knocking softly twice before opening the door.

Jenna followed the boy into a surprisingly broad room. A large desk dominated the room and two small chairs were in front of it. To the right sat two more comfortable-looking chairs, and in one of those lounged a man Jenna assumed to be the archivist. Behind him were shelves filled with books of all sizes and shapes. The steady glow of mage light lit the room.

The archivist, a middle-aged man with a muscular upper body, sat reading.

He must carry a lot of books.

The archivist glanced up at her briefly, then back down. "Please be seated." He spoke in a deep voice.

Jenna sat opposite him, and another long moment passed while the archivist finished his paperwork and put it aside.

"Have you ever been to the Royal Library?"

"No."

The archivist nodded.

"Books do not leave the palace grounds. Magic is suppressed in the library, though mage lights do work. Each section has common areas where you may read the books you find. When done, you may leave the books there, and the staff will reshelve them at the end of each day." He then went into how the indexes worked for finding books before reaching into his drawer and pulling out a small lacquered box. He turned the little box around and opened it. It contained a ring made up of what seemed to be three types of metal braided together.

"Put this on," the archivist said, handing her the box. "Register with one of the assistant archivists each day you come in. They will recharge the ring. The magic it uses to track and store your information is costly. The ring is a chameleon and acts as a key, giving you access to the Royal Reading Room when it touches the handle, so do wear the ring on the hand you use to open the door." He paused, and Jenna cleared her throat.

"Why is the ring a chameleon?"

"To prevent someone from cutting it off. And before you ask, yes, it has happened, so to prevent that, it blends in with your hand."

He must have seen the confusion on her face because he continued.

"Only the bearer of the ring can enter the Royal Archives, which houses not only rare books but priceless treasures and artifacts that many would kill to get their hands on. Once you put it on, you must wait for the charge to dissipate before you remove it."

He gestured toward the box. "Here, put it on."

Jenna paused. She had no illusions. If someone wanted this ring, they would cycle through each finger until they found the right one. Jenna sighed. *Fortunately, people rarely mess with mages.*

She slowly picked up the braided ring and studied it. It was quite lovely. Neither too masculine nor too feminine. Jenna considered which hand she would use for the door handle and moved the ring to the selected finger, which then resized itself as she slipped it on.

A tingle spread through her hand and into her body as a binding settled into her. She couldn't speak about what she learned with anyone due to the binding. She just hoped that this was the only thing it required of her. Why had Kal summoned her here?

When the tingling stopped, she glanced down at her hand. The ring had disappeared.

"Now that you have the key, I will explain how to get to the Royal Archives."

Jenna raised an eyebrow and held back surprise, having figured she was in them.

J enna stepped into a comfortable-looking room and stopped. Some of the tension drained out of her as she took in her surroundings. She had not expected this room when the archivist gave her directions to the royal archives. Small but cozy, it was well-lit with a plush, crushed velvet wingback chair and two matching side tables. The wall to her left held a simple desk with a straight-backed chair in front of it. The side tables and the desk held beautiful dried and fresh flower arrangements. A painting hung from each wall, but rather than sober portraits of past royals, these were beautiful historical scenes. The room appeared to be well-used. Relieved, Jenna smiled. Contrary to the rumors, not every room the royals used was gilded.

Jenna's smile faltered. Her sister would have loved this. With shoulders slumping, she got back to business.

The instructions said to leave her bag by the desk, then go to the painting to the right of the wingback chair. She did so and studied it. It depicted a rendering of The Three—mythical beings who were said to protect the world. One showed a woman, Lora'lillian, with pointed ears, but face shadowed, holding balanced scales. To her left was a man with wings, Drakothadam, who held a book, and to the right was another man, Gilgamesh, holding up a hawk with a large wildcat at his side. The whole image shimmered.

As instructed, Jenna reached up and placed her key against the left scale. She almost removed her hand as the wall began to waver, taking on a quality similar to The Three in the painting. She found herself enthralled as the wall became translucent and then disappeared, revealing an enclosure that would fit two people comfortably.

Removing her hand, she stepped inside and turned around just as the wall shimmered back into place. Gentle light cascaded down from above, and she sensed herself moving, though she couldn't tell in which direction. Soft padded leather with inlaid buttons covered the walls. Fresh air flowed into the room from above. The wall shimmered again and then turned translucent. Once it disappeared, her breath caught, mouth dropping open.

She stood staring into the most extraordinary room, brightly lit by a series of small, high-placed windows. Everything was gilded or plush. Sculptures of dragons—some massive, some small—dotted the room. Books were everywhere: on shelves, on the room's desks, in piles. A fire roared in a fireplace to her right. As she stepped into the room, mouth still agape, Jenna's head swiveled around, taking it all in.

"This way, Mage Sturmich," said a manservant.

Jenna managed to snap her mouth shut and not trip as she followed after the servant to an area of the room previously overlooked, a corner with shelves that held rows upon rows of books. Past this stood a small arched doorway, which became opaque after she followed the man through it. Jenna almost plowed into him while looking back at it.

The servant kept his expression neutral as he spoke. "The king has set this area aside for Kal and your work. I assume the archivist explained the ring?"

Jenna nodded, not trusting herself to speak. The servant continued.

"The shelves on the left contain family history. The ones on the right contain current information from the last hundred years or so." As he continued, Jenna studied the room. There was an ornate desk to the right with a high-backed chair behind it. A door was at the far left corner, next to some dangling knotted cords on the right.

The manservant reviewed most of what the archivist explained earlier, but she learned about a small alcove at the back left of the room in case she needed to relieve herself, and the function of a pull rope string on her right to be tugged when hungry or thirsty.

The manservant pointed out the menu with markers—one tug for an emergency, two for drink or food. A staff member answers after two tugs, and you can make food or drink choices. Jenna marveled at the sheer scope of this. There was even more to running a castle than she imagined.

Could we apply the pull rope to the infirmary?

After the manservant left, Jenna glanced around the room again and snorted. *Out with cozy, in with... gilded.* Jenna went over to the chair, a high-backed piece with arching arms that tapered into claws. Purple crushed velvet covered the cushions on the back and seat of the chair. *Ha! More like a piece of art that resembled a chair.* When she made contact with it, however, she tingled, and she considered briefly what magic the chair held before sitting down in it. She quickly found out as the chair molded itself around her.

Tension in her back, which she wasn't aware of, went away and a small sigh escaped her. *Now this I could get used to. I wonder if I can consciously change it?* Jenna went through a simple mental technique used by mages where she reached out with her senses, enveloping the chair, and then she created an image of what she wanted. The chair changed underneath her.

The chair was still just as comfortable as before, but when Jenna pushed the chair away from the desk, it rolled with her. She carefully turned left, and the chair rotated with her. Jenna's eyes crinkled in a smile as she gave a more substantial push and spun around in circles, knees up to prevent her feet from slowing her down.

"Well, I see you are settling in nicely," a dry voice stated, surprising Jenna. In the second it took her to stop the spinning chair, all the color drained from her face. His youthful likeness was posted all over the city. The king and one of his guards stood in the doorway. The king's face twitched, and the guard stood in an imposing stance, staring sternly down at her, but he couldn't hide the twinkle in his eyes. Turning to face them, Jenna squeaked. "S-sire."

The heat of embarrassment rose in her face, and she launched herself up out of the chair in an unconscious attempt to distance herself from her perceived crimes, which caused the chair to shoot backward and slam into a wall and made the mounted picture shudder and slide sideways. Jenna's eyes turned into saucers as she lunged back, grabbing the picture before it managed to dislodge from the wall completely.

Corin burst out laughing, the guard joining in as well.

Jenna stood holding the painting and stared in mortification.

Chapter 16

The King's Study

Jenna stared in horror while the king snorted, his lean, angular face smiling, tears dripping from of the corners of his eyes. As he brought himself back under control, he said, "I don't know what was funnier, the spinning, the stuttering, or the lunge to save the picture!" His eyes danced with amusement as he spoke again, almost to himself. "I haven't laughed like that in a long time."

Jenna moaned. She stood stiffly a few feet from the desk, face aflame with embarrassment.

King Corindanthanus marched right past her to the chair, which he said aloud, "had already been proven to be of *sound design*," and sat down, giving himself a small spin. His face lit up. The guard positioned himself by the door, but Jenna caught the occasional twitch, as if he replayed the events in his mind.

Jenna blinked, took a breath, and allowed herself to relax slightly. She focused on the king. All that laughter took years off of him. He was probably only five to seven years older than her. Even though the laughter was at her expense, she found herself curious about him. He had a genuine quality to him she supposed not many people got to see.

As she studied the monarch, Jenna went stiff again, which brought the guard to full alert.

"Sire, may I ask why there is blood on the arm of your robe?"

"Oh, that." He waved his hand dismissively.

"May I?" Jenna asked indicating she would like him to give her his hand.

His Eminence glanced at her briefly and nodded, features turning aloof. Jenna almost flinched at the loss of humanity and reminded herself not to get too personal with nobility. It's dangerous. Jenna ensured she had her healer face firmly locked into place as she knelt by the king and gently rolled up his sleeve.

His arm had a gash about three inches long, but not very deep. It seemed likely to scar. Jenna visualized what she wanted as her magic slid into the wound. First, she applied pressure to the sides to bring the edges together and then placed layers of flexible webbing inside the wound to hold it in place. After that, she added a layer on top to prevent it from getting infected but still allow air in, and finally, she stimulated the king's immune system to send in its own warriors to fight any infection and circulate blood. Once she was sure everything was in place, she gave it a last boost to speed the process along. The wound closed up without a trace. The layers of magical webbing she wove rose out of the king's skin and returned to Jenna.

The king gazed at her. "That was efficient."

Surprised at the word choice, Jenna asked, "You study magic, sire?"

The king hesitated, then said, "It's a bit of a hobby."

Jenna sensed that there was more to it, but did not push. "Does this type of injury happen often, my Lord?" The guard shifted behind her, and she quickly added, "If so, I really shouldn't leave my bag behind."

Some of the warmth came back to the king's eyes. "Filled with little treats, huh?"

Jenna grinned. "Absolutely," she said, as her stomach growled at the need to replace spent energy.

"Well, let me show my appreciation, then." The king launched his chair toward the pull cord, gliding across the room. When he caught it, he gave the cord two tugs, and a staff member's voice flowed magically into the room. He ordered food and drink for two.

They ate a pleasant meal where they discussed the merits of the chair. By the end of lunch, they talked about how these chairs could be used for the elderly or those injured in war. Jenna even brought up whether bedridden patients could use the pulls to summon help. Jenna agreed some patients would recover better at home. If patients had a summoning spell, traveling doctors could make house calls if something urgent happened.

Kal entered the room as they finished.

"Sorry I'm late. Something came up."

Jenna's eyes flashed to Kal. His coiled hair was pulled back, and he wore the official crown colors. His head was cocked, taking in her and the king. She frowned at the similarities. Her eyes flicked back and forth between them. They didn't share the same looks. The king had more lines around his eyes and forehead. But then Corindanthanus spoke. "Oh? What happened?"

Jenna's eyes went wide. These two were related. She thought back to Kal's description of his father and his brother. Kal spoke as conviction rippled through her.

"Yesterday, while investigating the death of Lord Deleon and a missing knight, I met a Lycanide who led me to some of the missing children."

Jenna tried to focus on the words, putting the revelation aside for the future. What had he said? Ah, wait. "A Lycanide?" she asked.

"Cross between a wolf and a spider," Kal said as Jenna shuddered at the image of a giant spider.

"Wait till I introduce you." He grinned.

Her stomach churned at the thought until she took in the expression of joy on Kal's face, mirroring the king's earlier display. *Definitely brothers*, she thought.

"How many missing children?" Corindanthanus asked, gaze sharpening. Hope flared in Jenna. *Was one of them Casi?*

"Four." Kal filled them in on the afternoon's findings, handing the drawing to the king.

"This is a picture of Casi, Jenna's missing sister," said Kal.

Jenna caught sight of it and froze.

He looked at Jenna. "Some of the returned children identified her."

"Where is she?" Jenna said.

Kal grimaced. "We don't know, but we know she is alive."

Jenna's eyes closed, and she inhaled. Opening her eyes, she smiled at Kal. They would find her.

A carriage deposited Kal and Jenna back at the inn. "Jenna, I have someone I want you to meet," Kal said as they exited the coach.

"Who?" she asked.

Kal grinned. "Roolia, the Lycanide. Whatever happens, don't show fear."

Jenna raised an eyebrow.

"Come on." Kal led her first to the kitchens, where he picked out some sweetmeats from a platter and handed them to her on a small plate. "This way," he said, leading her to the inn's central garden. They came to a stop in the middle of the courtyard.

"Roolia!" Kal called.

Jenna stared, mouth agape, as an enormous wolf-like beast glided down from one of the roofs into the garden and hurtled toward them on six legs. Jenna started to inch back.

"Steady, and remember, no fear."

Jenna snapped her mouth shut and straightened her back as the creature stopped in front of Kal.

"Alpha," Roolia said. Jenna's eyes widened at the throaty growl of a voice with a clear feminine cast.

"Roolia, I'd like you to meet Jenna. She is my apprentice."

"Ap-prentice?" she repeated, cocking her head in Jenna's direction. Jenna tried not to squirm as six predatory orbs locked onto her.

"Yes, I'm training her to be like me."

"Ah! Future mate."

Wait, what? Heat rose in Jenna's face, and she turned to see Kal's eyes widen.

"No, not mate. Like Doha."

"On trial?"

"No, accepted."

"Future alpha?" she said slowly. "You die?"

"No..."

She huffed. "Can be only one alpha. Train female, train mate."

Kal raised both brows as he deciphered her meaning.

"Jenna, apprentice." He tried again.

"Jenna lead pack?" Roolia asked.

"No, she's learning magic. Not pack."

"Jenna, mate," Roolia declared, staring at Kal.

"No," Kal said, clearly at a loss. Jenna couldn't help but grin. It was rare to see him so perplexed.

"Jenna, not mate, not pack. Why meet?" growled Roolia.

Kal stared at Roolia, his features taking on an alarmed cast.

"Jenna is a... friend." He tried the word tentatively.

Roolia's head swiveled back to Jenna, so she offered the plate.

"Friends?" Jenna asked.

"Alpha, friend," said Roolia, "is rare. Think future mate." Jenna blushed while Roolia ate the sweetmeats off the plate.

Chapter 17

Two Auras

A week later, Kal's shoulders popped as he yawned and stretched at his desk in the Royal Library. He had spent the last week digging for more clues in the murders. He had tasked Doha and Roolia with searching for more missing children, and with Jenna's help, he had spent the last few days reviewing old documents and medical histories. First, so he could learn all he could about the Lycanides to avoid further misunderstandings with Roolia, and second, to review his family history. There must be some clues as to why only his family succumbed to this "voice."

He'd spent time charting and graphing symptom progression from family members for the last five generations. He had a good handle on the stages of what seemed to be a disease afflicting the royal line. Unfortunately, with each generation, the symptoms appeared earlier, almost as if they were being bred into their family. That didn't make sense, as each generation married people from various backgrounds. The only thing everyone appeared to have in common was that they lived here in the castle. He absentmindedly chewed his nails as it occurred to him that there was one possible exception: himself. Why had he been able to repel the attack as his father died?

Kal turned back to ponder his grim figures. If his estimates were correct, the king's condition should be far more advanced than it seemed to be. That meant either his calculations were off or Corin was good at hiding things from him and the general population.

Kal triple-checked his findings, then sighed.

Well, he wouldn't get anywhere until he met with Corin again.

Jenna had mentioned healing the cut on the king's arm. Where had he gotten it from?

Frustrated, he decided to stretch his legs.

Kal wandered around the palace grounds, rolling the disease parameters around in his head. It frustrated him that it seemed to manifest the same way for each victim. They all masked it in slightly different ways, but ultimately, they ended up on their hands and knees, clawing at the earth. Thanks to previous royal physicians, he knew they never dug in the same location. It was like they each lost something irreplaceable, and the need to find it drove them to dig.

Why did they all believe it was buried somewhere? Maybe I should get a map, pin the locations, and check for a pattern. Who knows, maybe something is calling out to them.

Kal snorted. He would follow up on that later. If he were immune, it would make all the difference in the world. He would have to get some signature crystals to store a map of his and Corin's magical imprints. The signatures would give him a snapshot of their current state for future study. That way, he could map any changes. He was curious as to how the king's magical signature manifested.

Kal scratched the back of his neck. His hair was standing up, and his stomach dropped. Something was wrong. He shivered at the sharp tang of magic building up—a lot of magic—and it was close.

Kal stared across the courtyard at a group of men surrounding the king as he walked toward him. Each man had the cloth bands of the Royal Guard displayed on their arms. A large magical signature was gathering among those men. As they got closer, he sensed it coming from the king, who also appeared to be ranting. The hairs on his arms swayed in warning as the king got closer.

"We need to stop them now," the king said.

"You stay out of this. I'll stop them," the king replied.

"But it is my duty," the king said.

Kal's chest tightened. Not only was the king arguing with himself, but he was holding onto an awful lot of power while doing it.

The king and his guards moved closer. The soldiers had their hands on their swords, eyes darting around, searching for trouble. Corin was acting, well, he was acting crazy, but his guards were searching for trouble elsewhere.

"The Three protect us," Kal murmured as he perceived a battle taking place in his brother. They pushed against each other like titans vying for the same space. The invader, who appeared black, was massive, but the king's majestic red aura was crisp and clear and moved quickly in his defense.

Almost as if the king sensed his presence, the group slowed and stopped in front of Kal. The guards spread out around them. Kal continued studying their battle for control, unsure if intervening would help or hinder.

129

As the black aura gained the upper hand, the king spoke, "They are trying to kill you. They have hidden up ahead." The red aura took control. "I feel it too, but I will deal with it." The black aura ascended. "It is my duty." The red swirled on top. "Duty! Are you my subject? If you were, you would leave me be!"

Kal stared, mouth ajar. It wasn't clear to him whether this was an alternate personality or another being entirely, since their energy signature matched so closely. He ignored their words, studying the flow of the battle. If he were going to intervene, then he would have to time things perfectly. Just as he began interpreting their pattern, a new wave of magic rushed at him from behind.

Reflexively, Kal spun and threw up a shield big enough to surround them. Yellow sparks flared against the shield, followed by white, and coalesced into a solid blossom of blue. Kal stood with his arms slightly forward, palms up, as more attacks came, and the men huddled closer to him as the shield shrank. Two years of magic build-up under the maghin gave him a buffer, but he was burning through it.

Sweat broke out on his brow. Power poured out, starting to sputter as he fought to keep up such a large flow. The shield shrank again and hairline cracks appeared throughout. His heart pulsed erratically. The shield would shatter, or he would burn out. Either one would mean death.

Just before he lost control, two hands came to rest on his shoulders and a fresh exchange of energy poured into him. He wasted none of it and sent most of it to the shield while using the rest for farsight.

With farsight enabled, Kal gained sight from a vantage point above the shield with a telescopic view. He searched around and found the attackers. Four of them stood in a diamond pattern, all sharing energy, with the lead man acting as the flow's focal point. The men wore nondescript black clothing favored by the houses but without the colors or markings of any particular house. They were of similar height and build, with no distinguishing marks. Even their hair was the same color. They poured power into the attack.

One guards came over to Kal. "Can you let some of us out?"

Kal nodded while keeping his attention on the attackers and the shield. "There is something you need to see first."

Kal pulled one hand away from the shield and placed his hand on the man's forehead, giving him a view of what he saw. The guard went rigid and then relaxed taking in the scene. Once done, he nodded, and Kal opened an archway in the back of the shield.

The guard signaled, and half of the troop left with him.

Kal resealed and shrank the shield to conserve energy. Several long heartbeats passed with no let up on the assault. Sweat poured from Kal as heat residue from the attack started to build. The pounding on the shields throbbed through him, giving him a sense of deja vu, the image of the being banging on his shields. Kal tensed, and after what felt like candle marks, everything stopped.

The shield's thickness flared as it solidified from the lack of attack. Without the pounding on the shield, the colors brightened until the shield became translucent again. Some distance away, they could make out the King's Guard signaling the all-clear. With a sigh of relief, Kal released the shield.

From behind him, Kal heard a chuckle from a voice he recognized.

"He will do," the voice said.

Kal turned as the king's hands fell away from his shoulders.

"On this, at least, we can agree," the king replied.

131

Kal understood then that the auras of two people had shared energy with him to keep the shield up. The king gazed at him as if he were a lifeline. Heat rose in Kal's face. As Kal studied the king, the black aura flickered and was gone.

Kal escorted his brother off the exposed palace grounds into the palace, his eyes roving for threats until they made it into the king's private office. Corin sat in one of the padded chairs, exhaling as Kal poured him a glass of wine. Handing it to him, he asked, "Are you okay?"

Corin shrugged, as if this were an everyday occurrence, then took a sip of the wine, exposing a bruise just above his wrist.

"Does that happen often?" Kal tried again, hair raising on his neck as he tried not to stare at the bruise.

Corin frowned. "The assassination attempt or the voice?"

"Either. Both." Kal quivered with the need to fix everything.

"Someone is always trying to assassinate me, but it's rarely done with magic. I think that's what woke the voice."

Kal parsed that statement. *Someone is always trying to kill me*. He frowned, mind snagging on the second part, about the voice. "So you remember it? In the past, father didn't remember."

"Usually I don't remember, but if I feel him coming, I can fight him. When that happens, I remember," Corin said.

"How often does this occur?"

Corin flinched. "Often enough."

That answered his earlier question. Kal decided to change the topic. "Do you know who could be behind this attempt?"

Corin grimaced. "No. I don't believe I've offended anyone lately."

Kal clenched his fists as Corin took another sip of wine.

"You stay focused on the missing children. The guards will investigate this attempt, but you should know that assassins hide their tracks well."

Anger welled up in Kal. He opened his mouth to argue that this was just as important.

"Enough, Kal. I'm tired. Stay the course."

Kal gave a short-clipped nod as his stomach growled. He had expended a lot of energy earlier. Grimacing, he said, "I need to replenish my strength and check on the other things under my care, but I need to ensure you will be fine."

"Yes, I have my guard," said his brother.

Noting they were nearby, he bowed and left. The sight of the second aura weighed heavily on his mind. Not only did he have to find the missing children, but he needed to be more available to his brother in case of attacks. He rubbed his temples, scowling. First, he would track down the other two missing knights. Kal's stomach rumbled again.

Correction. First, he would go back to the inn and eat.

Chapter 18

Relentless

The next morning, Kal sat at the desk in his room. A man named Lent sat across from him, staring back placidly. Lent's hair was cut short, and his skin had the weathered cast of someone who had recently spent time on the river. He was wiry and surprisingly fit for someone pretending to be homeless.

"Jenna doesn't have a brother named Lent," Kal said.

"My real name is Justin."

Kal shifted in his seat to hide his surprise. "Where have you been the last few years?" Kal asked.

"Like Jenivieve said, I went to find the ones who killed my mother."

"And did you?"

Lent grinned wolfishly. "I did. It's where the name Lent came from."

Kal's eyes widened. Many tales had been told at the inn, but several months ago, before children began disappearing, he recalled one about a man named Lent. That man had joined the army and relentlessly hunted the individuals who had killed his mother. It was said to have taken more than two years of careful planning, but he had done it.

Lent stared at Kal, giving away none of his thoughts.

Kal glanced at the folder of materials before him on the missing children and then back at Lent. He needed a man like him. He decided to test the rumors. "Are you free from duty?"

"Yes, I have retired from service."

"Do you still have underground ties in the city?"

"I do."

Kal slid the folder toward Lent. "You have skills I'm looking for."

Lent picked up the folder and leafed through it, pausing on one particular picture.

"What happened to these children?" Lent asked, shifting in his seat.

"Someone has taken them," Kal said. "I am working to identify the culprits. I need someone with your, um, patience to join the team."

"What exactly is it you want me to do?" He spoke quietly.

"I need two things. First, I need you to track down Sirs Gavin and Farrel." Kal gave him pictures of the two missing knights. "Second, I want you to work for the captain of the search team."

"Why?"

"Those men in the pictures are the only link we have to the missing children. All others associated with the case have been found dead. Since they haven't turned up yet, they are either dead or in hiding. I'm betting they are in hiding. As for the team, well, this paperwork only goes so far. What I want is real eyes on what's happening. I want facts and insights, and if possible, I want someone on the recovery team."

Lent placed the picture of Casi on the desk in front of Kal.

"I'll do it."

A surge of triumph rushed through Kal. He'd figured that would get him, but he'd had to be sure.

"Of course. But it's time to bring Jenna in."

Lent stared at him for a few long moments before nodding in agreement.

Kal called for Jenna through the bond. "This shouldn't be an issue for you, given your past, but I will give you a sword test, which you must pass before I can recommend you to the guard."

"Of course," Lent said.

Kal was putting the pictures back in the folder when Jenna knocked on the door.

"Come," Kal called, and she entered. Lent turned his face away from her and sat still.

"Have a seat," Kal said, indicating the open chair next to Lent.

Jenna sat down, fidgeting with her skirt. She turned to look at their companion, and her eyes widened in recognition.

"Justin?" She grabbed his shoulder and turned him towards her.

He nodded, eyes filling with tears.

"Jenivieve." His voice was raspy. "I'm so sorry."

Tears clouded her eyes as she launched herself into his arms.

Nodding to himself, Kal gathered his files and left them to reconnect.

Later that afternoon, Kal returned to his room to find Jenna and Justin still there. When he came in, she stood up and greeted him.

"Kal, thank you," Jenna said.

Kal's eyes widened at the warmth in her gaze. It took him a moment to recall himself. Kal nodded, then gestured towards Lent.

"Did he explain why I'm hiring him?"

"Yes." Her face clouded with worry. "He said you hired him to work on one of the teams."

"I did, and I have a job for you as well."

Her eyes cleared, all business.

"I am putting together another team, and you are uniquely positioned to infiltrate the courts."

"I thought you were working for the courts?"

"I am working for the crown. The courts, you will come to learn, are an entirely different thing. You figured out who I am, right?"

She stared at him, thinking back to the sound of their voices. "You're the king's brother," she said.

"I am," Kal said. "One of the jobs I was trained for since childhood was to be a Shadow Weaver, whose purpose is to gather information used to protect the crown."

"Okay, so you want me to spy?"

"Essentially, yes." Kal seated himself behind the desk. "There is at least one house that wants the king dead. You are going to help find out which one."

Jenna laughed. "None of them are going to talk to the likes of me." She waved her hand over her scullery apron.

"You would be surprised what the help hears, but for the information I'm looking for, the parties involved probably do not talk to the help." Kal studied her. "But believe me, Jenna, you'll fit in."

Jenna blushed.

"You look just like her," Kal said.

"Like who?" Jenna's brows furrowed.

"Lady Abigail Sandoval, an expelled heir to House Sandoval."

Justin cleared his throat, and Kal froze, realizing he had forgotten he was there. *That's quite a skill.*

"How much danger will she be in?" Justin asked.

Kal straightened. "Not much, but there is always an element of risk when spying. I have a curriculum prepared for both of you that should help you fit in. There are also techniques and training that you can use for misdirection and escape. If all that fails, Jenna can use her bond to call me, and I will come. You, however, will have to carry a copy of my seal."

Kal gestured toward Jenna. "I will host Jenna with one of the families hit hardest by the blight, posing as Lady Abigail's cousin's daughter. You will have a coming-out ball and meet everyone at court. As for backstory, you will have come from the Rim, so it will be okay that you are unfamiliar with courtly ways. After the blight killed most mageborn nobles, more than one house has had to pull family in from the farming portions of the Rim, or the countryside, as they like to call it."

"When does it start?"

"Training? Right now."

Kal took them to the small training room he used to teach Jenna magic.

"Both of you. Watch my face," he said.

Kal added lines under his eyes, age spots, and wizened hair.

Jenna breathed in sharply, eyes wide.

He then held up his hands, adding veins and wrinkles followed by a slight tremor.

"Jenna," he said in an old man's voice. "Did you see what I did?"

She nodded.

"Good. Try it on yourself."

It took her several attempts, but she eventually achieved a good likeness of an older man on her face.

"Good," Kal said in his own voice.

Using Jenna as his model, he pointed out how to identify a person wearing a Seeming to Lent.

"Always look to the moving parts. That's where it becomes most obvious that it doesn't flow like skin or move like muscle. If you are not sure, keep them talking. The more motion, the more likely you are to see the imperfection.

"Good, you can take it off now," he said, letting his natural facial features return. "You need to build up a repertoire of Seemings that you can pull up at a moment's notice."

"What about clothes?" Jenna asked.

"Those you should prepare in advance."

"Can I make the clothes out of magic also?"

"You can, but you'll have the same problem as with faces. Creating natural movement takes years of practice. Any unnatural movement will draw attention. If you don't want to risk it, use real fabrics.

"I would recommend that you keep it simple at first and just change your hair color or add a mole. I will make sure you have boots of different heights so you can be more in character. Tomorrow, we will see about your outfits."

The next morning, Jenna trailed behind Kal and Lent as he brought them cloaks and took them through the crowds of people milling around the shrines of the missing children to an upscale clothier located in the Noble Quarter near the palace for a fitting.

Jenna appreciated the cloaks they wore as the garb of the people around them grew more elegant. Even with the robe covering her well-used attire, she glanced around, looking for people staring at her shoddy work shoes, ready to point and call her a fraud, but they ignored her, like she was invisible.

When they arrived at Marsaltz Clothing Boutique, she stared in awe at the colors and quality of fabrics on display. They entered a private room with several changing stalls, and she and Lent were provided several changes of clothes. The third time Jenna changed, she came out and stood on a platform in front of a large mirror, studying her makeover.

The clothier had done a fantastic job of turning Jenna into a captivating woman. Lent stared at her, stunned at her transformation. Even Kal's eyes held an appreciation she had never seen in them before. Jenna couldn't believe the difference a dress made. No illusion she could have ever come up with would have given her these results. She turned and stared at her brother in his crisp guard uniform. As a child, he was always her hero, and now he looked the part. He stared at her with a mixture of shock and adoration. Jenna glanced at Kal and observed a flash of something before it was gone. She blushed, trying to hide it with a curtsy, and almost fell over.

The clothier smoothly held his hand out to stabilize her and escorted her down off the platform, her dress making faint rustling noises as she walked. Kal reached out an arm, and she transferred to it with a firm grip, as though he were a lifeline. Kal raised an eyebrow and suppressed the upward turn of his mouth. Lent came over, smiling broadly. "You look lovely."

Jenna grinned. "If I'd known this is what it would take to get a compliment, I would have insisted we do this sooner."

This time, Kal smiled. Then he excused himself and went to speak with and pay the clothier privately. He came back carrying several packages.

"Come on, now the real training begins." Dressed in their new finery, he escorted them to their next destination.

"Jenna, Lent, this is Courtier DeFluer. He will be training you on how to behave in court. I have some other things to attend to, but I will be back to pick you up later this afternoon."

Kal hurried toward the meeting with his old team. It had taken a while to get them all to agree and coordinate schedules.

Kal entered the meeting room. Seated around the table were Master Evans, a high mage at the Arcanum Mage Guild; Lord Sandoval, head of the Warrior and Healer Guilds; Master Harram, Kal's master in the arts of Shadow Weaving and advisor to the king; Sir Quinn, who managed everything going into and out of the docks; and Lady Freya Emelda, Shadow Weaver and gatherer of social commentary. If something significant happened in Mendallon, she knew about it.

Kal allowed himself a slight smile as he beheld his fellow spies. He had missed them. It took him a moment to realize they would not look him in the eyes. Kal's smile faltered. He thought back to the last time he had seen them all. It was just before he killed the king. His mouth went dry.

Bracing himself, he said, "Ask," into the stony silence.

After a long pause, Freya spoke. "Why did you kill the king? And are you planning to do it again?"

Kal blinked at the bald questions. She was never one to pull punches. Licking his lips, he studied them. Haltingly, he retold what had happened between him and his father. "Killing him was an act of self-preservation. I'd take it back if I could."

"The current king suffers from the same affliction?" Quinn asked.

"You tell me," he said. "I've been under the influence of a maghin for the last two years."

They all exchanged glances as if pieces of a puzzle were settling into place. No one spoke, but it was confirmation enough.

"If you are immune, should it not make sense—"

"No." Kal felt the weight of their gazes—the unspoken words.

"As for doing it again..." Kal thought about the two auras he felt in his brother and what that could mean in the long term. "I wholeheartedly pray that never happens, and if I have any say in the matter, it won't happen. I don't want the throne. I want my brother to flourish. That's why I asked the king to call you all here today. I'm sure you've all figured this out, but someone's been undermining him by taking Bright Ones, and I need your help to find out who it is and stop them. Are you with me?"

One by one, their eyes locked with his, and they nodded.

Kal had his team.

Chapter 19

Teamwork

"We will practice here each morning," Kal said, leading Lent into the inner courtyard of Lily's Inn. The inn was a two story courtyard house, which was structured like a large square, with rooms along the outside of the quad wrapped around an inner courtyard.

The hooded foreign woman, Lady Millaine, and her two guards were seated at a table on the other side of the enclosure. They were far enough away so he couldn't make out their faces. Kal hoped they weren't offended by his plans, as Lady Millaine had been with them for several months. She hadn't caused trouble and always paid in advance. He didn't want her to leave.

"What about Jenna?" Lent asked.

"I will train her separately for now, as her situation is somewhat unique," he said. "But eventually, she will join us."

He gave Lent a practice sword, keeping one for himself, then walked him through the warm-ups. Lent followed along with a fluid form, comfortable with the movements. Once done, he supervised Lent in basic moves, offering minimal corrections as they went.

Kal and Lent then went through simple exchanges, starting slowly. After a few minutes, their synchronized movements were almost a blur. Lent was deep in concentration, and Kal breathed evenly, joy washing through him at the movements. It had been a while since he had danced with a blade. After a few more exchanges, Kal stepped back, signaling an end.

"Good, you'll pass the exams." He slapped Lent on the back.

Lent nodded, appraising Kal. It was clear Kal had surprised him. Few lords knew the sword as well as Kal, but he was the second son, and he had always liked the adversity of it. Even while under the influence of the maghin, he had done his daily calisthenics routine. Keeping himself in peak condition.

Lily came over, carrying a tray with two water cups.

Kal was collecting the training sword from Lent when the guards from the other side of the enclosure approached. "Mind if I have a go?" said a masculine voice.

Kal turned, appraising the two guards. The man had short dark hair, was well built, and had a sword on his belt, while the female guard had close-cropped blond hair, which was unusual in this area. Kal didn't want to offend the guards, and he needed the practice—since people were trying to kill him. He didn't know these guards well, but they hadn't been any trouble, unlike other guests. Besides, these were his practice swords. There were no hidden traps that could harm him.

The woman spoke. "You seem like you know your way around the edge of a sword, and Donovan is getting tired of losing to me."

Donovan grimaced.

Kal nodded. "Sure. I'll walk him through his paces if you want. My name is Kal." He threw the training blade to Donovan who caught it, and they clasped hands.

"This here is Kelly," Donovan said. She, too, clasped hands with Kal, and then Lent.

"He's a little rough around the edges. Just needs more practice," Kelly said.

Kal nodded. "It's been a couple of years since I was in the ring, but I'll do what I can."

"I appreciate that," she said.

Kal and Donovan squared off in the center of the courtyard.

Donovan charged him. Kal deflected and immediately flowed into a series of combination moves, which Donovan deflected. They circled, trying each other's defenses. Kelly studied them, gaze sharp.

Again, Donovan tried to break through Kal's defenses and was turned away, but this time, Kal identified an opening as Donovan backed away from a blocked attack. Kal maneuvered them back into the same series of movements, and Donovan went for his side again. Kal blocked and there—the same gap! Kal slipped his blade in and wrenched the practice sword from Donovan's hand, sending it clattering a few feet away, then stepped back, lowering his practice sword.

Donovan cursed under his breath, rubbing his hand.

"Your left arm drops slightly when you back away from a side attack. Have you ever used Dawson's stance?" Kal said.

"Yes," he said.

"If you follow his form when you pull back, it forces you to keep your arms up. Try it again."

Smiling, Donovan picked up the blade, and they went through the moves again. This time, when he pulled back, there was no gap.

Kal backed off.

"Good job. Do you feel the difference?"

Donovan nodded in agreement.

Kelly stepped in. "Do you think you could go another round? This time with me?"

Kal stared at her. She was tall, almost the same height as him, and lean. He nodded in agreement.

Kelly took the practice sword from Donovan, who walked over to Lent, where they greeted each other and turned back to the pending battle.

Kelly and Kal squared off.

Both stood studying each other for several long moments, and then they erupted into a blur of motion. Blades knocked together in rapid succession. They glided through stances and flowing transitions, bodies always in motion. Kal and Kelly were caught up by the movements as they danced around the courtyard. Kelly had her back to the railing when they paused, both breathing deeply. She removed one of her hands from the sword and made a fighter's hand gesture meaning arena—with limited magic.

His eyes widened as he took in the invitation behind the sign. They would not be able to attack each other with magic, but could use it on themselves. Again, he assessed. If she had asked for full magic, he would have declined. If she wanted him dead, this would be the place to do it. He could tell from her moves that she was classically trained, and one rule always enforced was, *your word is your bond*. She would not try to kill him, but she would try to beat him beyond a shadow of doubt. Kal grinned in acceptance.

Kelly flashed a signal to Lady Millaine, who nodded, got up, and approached the wall edging the courtyard.

Lady Millaine held out her hand, palm facing down. Vibrant, shimmering magic erupted all around her. The magic flowed, morphing into a bright dome-shaped shield that rose around the borders of the courtyard, forming an arena and trapping Kelly and Kal inside. The veiled woman changed her hand direction, and both Kal and Kelly rose a few feet off the ground. The shield filled in underneath them, so its spherical structure floated off the ground with Kal and Kelly in its courtyard-sized center.

At opposing sides of the sphere, Kal and Kelly took up fighting stances explicitly designed for untethered combat.

Donovan gave the open-palmed chopping sign used to indicate they should begin, and Kelly launched herself at Kal. He blocked, pushing her back, but she came hurtling toward him again. He reached out, grabbed her by the arm, and spun, throwing her towards the shield wall.

Kelly reacted immediately by controlling her spin, landing in a squat, and immediately launching herself back at Kal. He was ready this time and met her sword with his. They held their positions and traded increasingly powerful blows, both using magic to strengthen their practice swords to stand up to the impacts. Five blows, eleven, twenty-one. They twirled in the air, using the residual magic of their strikes to power the next one, their blows sending them to the shield walls for leverage. Kal turned to land first and noticed Kelly grimacing on the landing. She launched herself at Kal, and they exchanged blows before going to the sides of the sphere. Kal watched again as she landed. There was a moment's pause as she heaved herself from the wall, this time slower. He pushed to meet her.

They danced through the air—tumbled and rolled—using the sides of the shield to control their attacks. Since they were strengthening their swords, their impacts charged the staves up so they began to spark on impact. The swords had a slight halo effect when held apart, growing brighter with each impact.

Both Kal and Kelly were sweating freely now. They closed for another round, and in a blur of movement, Kal blocked a swing that sent him back into the shield in front of Lent. Kal squatted down, coiling himself for launch. The bottoms of Kal's feet glowed, and when he launched himself at Kelly, aided by magic, cracking noises came from the shield as the force of his push caused the shield wall to fracture. This time, it was Kelly who slid back, her right leg hitting the shield wall awkwardly, causing her face to blanch.

Kal left her no room to maneuver before knocking the practice sword from her hands and pinning her to the wall. The light from Kelly's practice sword died as it went through the shield and hit the ground. Kal pushed back, and he and Kelly sank slowly down to the earth as the shield weakened and dissipated.

Kal and Kelly stood facing each other, eyes locked.

"So, Master Kal," she said with a soft smile, "what did I do wrong?"

He smiled broadly, bowing to her over his sword, which he held stave down on the ground, and replied, "Master Kelly, you have an old injury in your right leg. You have excellent balance and strength to compensate, but over time, it becomes slightly more pronounced, causing you to overbalance. If it wasn't for that, this could have ended differently." He paused. "I know of a battle healer that may be able to help with that, if you are so inclined."

She nodded. "I will take you up on that offer."

They turned and walked together towards the others.

Kal gave Kelly the information for the doctor, then collected the practice swords and excused himself, leading Lent back toward their rooms.

Lent reached into his pocket.

"What's this?" Kal asked as Lent handed him a piece of paper.

"This is where the knights are staying."

Kal unfolded the paper, frowning at the location. "Are you sure?"

"As I can be. I have people keeping watch, so if they move, we'll know."

"That's good," Kal said, trailing off in thought.

"What will you do now?" Lent asked.

"Now we'll build an extraction team."

"I have one request," Lent said.

Kal waited for Lent to speak.

"Please keep Jenna out of this."

Kal hadn't planned to include her as she was learning to be a lady. "Agreed."

Several days later, Kal knocked on the door at the inn where Lady Millaine was staying. After a few moments, it opened, and Donovan's wide frame filled the doorway.

"Kal! Good to see you again." Donovan grinned broadly, and Kal smiled back.

"You too, Donovan. Is Kelly here?"

"Sure, come in."

Kal entered their suite.

"Have a seat. She'll be out in a minute."

Donovan moved to a side table.

Kal sat on one of the chairs facing the exit, leaving one door at his back and the other two off to his sides. Donovan brought out some tea.

"Have you been keeping up with the stance I gave you?" Kal queried.

Donovan smiled and spoke excitedly. "Yes, it's been helping."

"Good," Kal replied as the door to the left opened, and Kelly stepped out, closing the door behind her. She walked over and took one of the two remaining seats. Donovan poured her a cup of tea.

"Kal," she greeted him.

"Kelly," he replied, but before he continued, she spoke again.

"That doctor you recommended was great."

"Oh good, you went. I'm glad."

"We've only had one session, but I already feel the difference. I should heal up in no time."

"That's good to hear," Kal's voice trailed off.

Kelly tilted her head, studying him. "But that's not what you wanted to talk about, is it? What brings you here?"

"I was wondering if I could buy your services."

Kelly's gaze sharpened and she frowned. "For what?"

"Are you aware that children have been disappearing in the city?"

Kelly and Donovan nodded.

"Yes, you can't go anywhere without running into the guard these days," Donovan said.

"I am following up on a lead and expect to encounter some resistance."

"Isn't the search for the children under the crown's authority?" Kelly asked.

"It is," Kal replied.

"Then why don't you use their manpower?" she asked.

Kal put down his teacup.

"To find this lead, I had to go outside normal circles." He paused.

"You think there is a mole?" Donovan interjected.

Kal grimaced. "Likely more than one. I am putting together a team of outside agents only."

Kelly chewed her lip as Donovan's eyes flicked from Kal over his shoulder to the room beyond.

Kal stiffened at the presence behind him that he had not heard.

Kal rose slowly and turned, giving a brief bow. Behind him stood Lady Millaine, wearing a long cloak and a hat with a yellow veil that completely hid her features. She was his height and slender.

"My lady," Kal said.

"That was very perceptive of you," she said in a clear but firm voice. Her head dipped and rose as she studied Kal. "You wish to hire away my bodyguards?"

He raised his hands placatingly, realizing his mistake. "Just temporarily, though it could be dangerous."

"Give me your hand," she commanded.

Kal bit down on the questions that popped into his head and reached forward with his left hand.

She cupped it in hers. His palm took on a pulsing glow as power radiated from her hands and into him. Her magic flowed up his arm and into his body. His magic responded instinctively, rising and unfurling around him like wings. It was rare for him to show his full powers. He wasn't sure what she had done, but his powers stretched and spread out as if basking in sunlight.

She tilted her head up, her golden-hued eyes locked on his through the veil.

"Have you ever had the blight?" she asked.

"No."

"Good." She released his hand, and Kal had to stop his fingers from reflexively reaching for her as his magic retracted, folding back into him. He set his jaw and let the feeling pass. He couldn't read her, but it was clear she was more powerful than he.

Is she part of the Arcanum? Why was she here?

"Do you have anyone or anything that you wish to protect?" she asked.

He thought of his brother and Jenna. "I do."

"Do you have the power to keep them safe?"

Kal blinked slowly, thinking of how his father had died and the fact that his brother was having symptoms. He contemplated Jenna, her barriers crumbling under the slow onslaught of his rogue nites, and then he considered Casi and the other missing children. "I do not."

"I will give you power and let you borrow my bodyguards on one condition."

Kal frowned, questioning who she was to give power as his magic quivered within him, wanting the return of sunlight.

"What condition?" He pulled himself back into the moment, still fighting the urge to reach for her hand.

"The girl you brought to the inn," she said almost casually.

"Jenna?" he said in surprise.

"Yes, Jenna. I want her."

All urges to reach out and touch the cloaked woman vanished. Kal took a step back, skirting the table.

He angled himself towards Kelly and Donovan while keeping the veiled woman in view. "It looks as though I will not require your services, after all."

He turned his full attention to the woman and pulled his magic back into him, ready to fight if needed. "Jenna is not a slave to be given away."

The woman's cloak rustled. "But she is yours."

"She is mine until her training is complete. She belongs to herself." The words were harsh and clipped as he recalled her story.

Kal turned to leave the room when the woman started laughing. Ignoring it, he kept walking towards the door. He was almost there when she said, "You will do. It is rare to find one who would not trade others for power when they themselves feel powerless."

Kal reached the door, placing his hand on the knob.

"Wait, Lord Mendathalon."

Kal froze. His hand clenched tightly on the doorknob as the words reverberated through him. Mendathalon was his house name. When his brother became King, Kal became Lord of House Mendathalon, though it was symbolic, as the king also held sway over the house.

Nonetheless, he was technically the head of the house. If he chose to, he could have a seat on the council. *How could she know?*

"Come, sit. I do not require your Jenna. I just wanted to see what kind of man you are."

The woman sat in the chair Kal had vacated. Kal weighed leaving, but curiosity won out—barely. Compromising, he turned around but did not step away from the door. "Who are you, really?"

"You already know my name."

Kal doubted that was her real name.

"How did you know?" he asked.

"Your name?" She gave a small laugh. "You look just like your father, and the arena fight confirmed it. You carry his magical signature."

Several questions came to mind. *How did you know my father? Who are you?* But he settled on the most important one. "What is it you want from me?" Kal asked in soft, measured tones.

She paused for a moment. "I wish to give you power."

Kal snorted. "A true gift has no strings attached."

"Let me rephrase, then. I wish to trade."

"What is it you want?" he said flatly, causing Donovan to shift.

"Have you ever heard of Skybrium?" she asked.

Kal raised an eyebrow. "It's a mythical stone said to store the power of the sun. One piece of Skybrium the size of my hand could power a city this size for a year." Kal stopped talking, wishing he could make out her face. One of the biggest secrets held by the royal family was that the castle itself got its magic from a piece of Skybrium the size of a coin.

The woman continued. "Very good. Have you heard of Mendai?"

The muscles along his back tightened.

He had heard of Mendai, but if she knew who he was, she already knew the answer. Mendai was the signature ore mined by his family. It was a base material used to combine more than one type of metal. "I have."

"I wish to purchase a gram of it."

Relaxing, Kal said, "You can get that at the market."

"It must be black."

Kal kept his features bland. Mendai came in many colors. White was the easiest to work with; it was plentiful and, as such, sold in the market. Black was notoriously tricky and required specialists, but when worked properly, it created the most stable structures. His house color was black for Mendai Black. It was precious, closely guarded, and rarely sold. The crown was made of Mendai Black and trimmed with gold. The purest gems representing each house color were worked into the crown's peaks and set in silver. A gram was a small fraction of what went into the crown. When he was a child, his father would take him and his brother down into the secret mines, and they always came back with a sample to add to their collections. Last he checked, his was in a storage box in his room at the palace.

"Why?" Kal asked.

"That is none of your concern." This time she spoke flatly.

His eyes flicked to Kelly and Donovan. Neither had readable expressions on their faces. He glanced back at the woman.

"And what is it you offer in return for the black Mendai?"

Without any motion, her magic flared to life, unfurling much like Kal's had, but her wingspan almost reached both doors.

Kal stared in awe at the display of power. He had never seen anyone close to this level.

"I will train you," she said.

Kal nodded in acceptance.

Chapter 20

Missing Knights

K al had been training with Lady Millaine as well as his potential teammates for over a week and was making steady progress with both.

Lady Millaine had him memorizing dozens of patterns found on nites and the purpose of each of them. There were ones for enhanced power, sight, sound, smell, and one that—oddly enough—destroyed metal. She even let him link to some to see how they felt.

Taking his newfound knowledge, he created a batch of yanzu wax and fed hearing nites with his magic into it, which would allow a person to place yanzu into their ears and speak to and hear other people with the same batch of yanzu.

As for the extraction team, he cut the group down to five—Lent, Donovan and Kelly as well as Gabe and Wyn, who were recommended through Lent. Kal was careful to ensure everyone could think on their feet, yet still take orders. It should be a snatch and grab but plans always fell through, so he wanted to be sure.

While they made ready, they kept eyes on Gavin and Farrel's location continuously. Kal had informed Corin that they had located their quarry, and he and his crew would bring them in.

Kal and his team approached the Canticle Inn located on the eastern part of the Rim on foot, having hired a carriage to wait a couple of blocks away. They stood by the roadside, and Kal studied the inn, taking in its structure as a large falcon flew overhead, landing on an adjacent rooftop.

A few moments later, a group of youths came around the corner, approaching them. As the teens passed, one boy bumped into Lent, whispering into his ear before apologizing loudly and rushing to catch up with his friends. Lent turned to the team and spoke.

"They entered yesterday evening and have not left all day."

Kal shaded his eyes from the setting sun and studied his surroundings. At this time of day, foot traffic thinned as people went inside to eat. Kal nodded to Lent and turned his attention to the rest of the group. He had provided them all with maps of the area covering the inn and had given them yanzu to give them a means of talking to each other that would last the night. During training, and for this mission, Kal wore a Seeming. He appeared slightly older, fit, but balding with freckles. Kal made eye contact with each member before speaking.

"Gabe and Wyn, you are team one. You have the south entrance. Kelly and Donovan, you are team two. Take the north entrance. Lent, you're with me. If something happens to me, Lent is in charge. Next in line is Kelly. We will meet at the designated location on the map. You've all had time to study the pictures of the men. Keep your eyes open and report anything unusual."

Kal waited for foot traffic to thin before speaking again.

"Team one, go." Gabe and Wyn disappeared around the corner.

"Team two, go." Kelly and Donovan headed for the other corner.

Kal and Lent waited until they reached their locations before entering the front doors. The entrance to the inn was large, clean, and well-lit. Lent went to the main desk, speaking briefly to the woman behind the desk. She gave him a set of keys. "As requested, the second floor is empty. The room you want is on the third floor, and I have given all nonessential staff the night off."

"Very good." He handed her a pouch. Lent walked back to Kal, and the two men started up the stairs.

"Team leader, this is team one."

Kal listened to the call from Gabe. "What's your status, team one?"

"We just passed two men in unusual clothing that looked like they've been in a recent fight."

Kal checked the location of team one using the yanzu. They were still close to the exit.

"Understood. Team one, split. One member stays on those men. One stays by the exit. Teams two and three will stay on task," said Kal.

"Understood."

Kal and Lent arrived at the door to the third-floor suite as Kelly and Donovan came around the corner.

With a soft jangle of keys, Lent opened the door. Near the entrance of the room, two robes hung on pegs. The garments called to Kal's magic. He reached out, touching them. The inside lining of the cloth contained symbols used by mages to prevent magesight. They must have been wearing these when they went out into the city, preventing people from locating them with magic.

Lent and Kal went down a short hall into the main room. They stopped silently, hands dropping to weapons, eyes darting around the room.

The two knights were strung up by their wrists from the central beam. Bruises covered them, and fresh blood dripped from the men. Lent approached and checked them over. "This one appears to be conscious," he said.

Kelly and Donovan arrived, taking up guard positions just inside the doorway as Kal moved towards Lent.

Sir Gavin opened his eyes.

"Who did this to you?" Kal asked, stepping forward.

"The C-compact. Drugged," he said before passing out.

Compact? Kal wasn't aware of any organizations going by that name. At least they wouldn't have to worry about the knights using magic to escape.

"Let's cut them down," Kal said.

Lent reached up, hands shimmering as he lifted Sir Gavin. Both men froze as a popping noise, followed by a sizzle, swelled and pulled in the ambient magic around them. Someone had rigged a magical explosive. The longer the hiss, the more ambient magic it drew in, and the bigger the explosion. Kal began a silent count in his head.

Two.

He spoke out loud.

"Team two, get everyone out of the building." Kelly and Donovan dashed off. "Lent, cut them down and get them out of the building. You're in command."

Three.

Lent slit the ropes holding the men up and yanked them, none too gingerly, behind Kal. As Lent cut the second line, there was another popping noise followed by a sizzle.

Four.

Lent dove behind Kal as he threw a shield up around the beam, encasing the growing pull of magic. If it blew, it would take down the whole building. Lent used magic to pull the men from the room. Kal disabled his connection to the team.

Five.

Sweat broke out on Kal's brow as he built shield after shield around the pending explosion. He needed a layer for each count. The typical count was ten, but there were two of them, so the first likely had a shorter fuse.

Six.

He was just finishing the sixth shield wall when it blew. The room flared white, momentarily blinding him. Kal's shields were ripped down layer by layer. He had tied them off as he built them, so it didn't physically hurt him. He sensed Jenna reaching out to him through the bond, but didn't have time to answer.

Seven.

Power bled from him as he frantically added more layers. He pulled from the ambient magic in the surrounding area, but it wasn't enough. The second explosion would feed on the force of the first explosion. He had contained it, but he hadn't dissipated it. With all that energy, the second explosion would be even more massive.

Eight.

He didn't have time to build enough shields. Kal reflected on the lessons he had been having with Lady Millaine and focused on his nites, searching for ones with the right colors. Finding one, he pushed his magic into it, forming an acute link with it. He pulled. Magic flared from the main nite to the surrounding nites, each one synchronizing with the lead. Power of a level he had never sensed before poured out of him, beating back the light of the explosive forces he was holding back. Kal then considered Jenna and her shield structures.

Nine.

He funneled all of his new power and then some into crystalline formations, completely encasing the glowing sphere in a massive rock-like structure. Magic poured out of him in waves. Sharp slices of pain flared up all over his body as nites began burning out. He gritted his teeth and continued through the pain.

Ten.

The second bomb exploded.

Jenna sensed a concussive force through the bond. Then her senses blazed as she felt Kal screaming.

She ran out of Lily's Inn, locating Kal. Jenna sent power to her legs and leaped onto the nearest rooftop, running in a straight line instead of following the streets. The second concussive force struck a few blocks later. Glass broke in nearby buildings, and people screamed in the distance. Panic coursed through her, and she continued forward, moving even faster. Jenna stayed on the roofs until she neared the building.

As she got to the building closest to the shattered inn, she coiled her magic around her and leaped, propelling herself through the husk of a window on the second floor. She landed awkwardly, falling to the floor before regaining her footing and heading out of the room towards the nearest stairwell.

Jenna rushed up the stairs and came to the third floor. Everything had blown off the walls, and debris was everywhere. She carefully picked her way until she came to a room with the door missing, pieces of it splayed out across the hall.

She stepped through the doorway and went down the hall. As she came around the corner, Kal came into sight. He lay face down on the floor. There was no debris within a three-foot radius of him, but the rest of the room was in shambles, with furniture pushed up against the walls. The windows were giant holes with no framing or glass. The support beam at the top of the room was gone, and the building made creaking noises.

Jenna scanned him with her magic. Finding nothing broken, she cradled his head, gently rolling him over. His skin had a grayish cast, and his lips were blue as if he couldn't get air. Jenna pursed her lips, thinking furiously as his initial scan had been clear. After a few moments, Jenna carefully delved into him, checking each system individually. She shivered when she finally recognized what she was seeing. Jenna continued to check each system, wanting to be sure.

Kal was in the throes of nite depletion.

He had used a great deal of energy, which didn't necessarily remove or destroy nites unless you took shortcuts while pulling on your magic. Whatever he had done, he didn't have time to pull everything from the environment, so instead, he had removed them from himself, destroying most of his nites in the process. Without nites, Kal would die.

Her mind raced through a list of options, coming up blank. She needed nites; she needed...

"Jenna!" Lent shouted as he entered the room.

Jenna ignored him and began to laugh. Then she started to glow.

"Wait!" Lent yelled. "You'll die!" He took a step forward, hand outstretched towards his sister as she flared brighter.

Jenna opened a channel between her and Kal, bringing them closer together. It took a moment, but most of the nites attacking her internal shield walls still recognized his signature over hers. One by one, nites flowed into Kal. She dropped her outer shield wall. Some of the nites moved to attack her inner shield while most others turned, heading for Kal. She repeated the process on two more layers, sweat building on her brow as more of the resistant nites attacked her shields. She ground her teeth through the pain and brought down the next layer and the next.

The magic around Jenna began pulsing like a heart. Her flows encased Kal, circulating through each of his systems in a wave-like pattern. After a long pause, Kal began pulsing in the same cadence. It was subtle at first, but after a few minutes, it became stronger. The gray color left his skin, and he seemed to breathe more easily. Jenna blinked in relief as Kal opened his eyes, the last of the blue fading from his lips.

Kal's eyes met Jenna's.

"Hello," he rasped.

"Hi," she replied. A lopsided grin took over. They were so close. If she leaned over a bit more, she could kiss his forehead.

He cleared his throat. "You seem to have a habit of saving me."

Jenna laughed. "I believe this puts me ahead of you."

"You're keeping track? Does bringing you your brother count?" he asked, sounding hopeful.

Jenna's smile was quickly replaced with a frown. She sighed. "Fine, we're even, but I would appreciate it if you would take better care of yourself."

Kal smiled and opened his mouth to say more, but Lent cleared his throat, breaking the spell.

"Team one, team two, Kal is alive. I repeat, Kal is alive."

L ent and Jenna supported Kal as they made their way out of the inn. Jenna had forbidden him from using magic for two days, so his real face was exposed as they entered the alley. The teams came over, taking in his real features.

"Team one, report."

Wyn spoke. "I followed them into the fur district when they must have made me, because they split up. I reported in, chose a target, and followed, but I lost him near winery row."

Gabe took up the thread.

"As I approached Wyn's location, I found the second target doubling back to attack Wyn. I stopped him, but he slashed me and got away."

"Team two?" Kal said.

Kelly took up the report. "We found Gabe and Wyn, but no signs of the targets."

"Lent, report."

"Assassins tried to attack the knights as I was bringing them to the carriage, injuring one of them, but then some creature attacked the assassins, taking them out in moments."

Kal grinned. "That would be Roolia. I asked her to keep an eye out. I will introduce you later. Kelly, are you injured?"

"No."

"Please retrieve the carriage. We need to leave before the city guard arrives. Jenna, please take care of the teams' injuries."

Chapter 21

Answers

K al wrote a report of the raid's results for Corin and Abasi. His team had brought the two knights to the highest-security portion of the Royal Dungeons for safekeeping. Kal rested for the two days prescribed by Jenna and could now hold a Seeming for protection from assassins.

He hadn't just rested. The captain of the guard had given him piles of paperwork to fill out about the explosion at the Canticle Inn. Fortunately, they had cleared the building in advance, so there wasn't a loss of life, just livelihood. It would be months before the inn could take customers again.

Kal reached over to the box that had been delivered from his Shadow Weaver mentor, Master Harram. With it, they could pass messages instantaneously. You wrote a note or letter, then sprinkled Aellar dust onto both sides of the letter. When you put the letter into the box, it would be transported to the matching box in Master Harram's office. Instead of sending missives that could be intercepted, he would pass on any info learned from the knights this way. He didn't know what he would find, but the knights were being hunted after the death of Lord Deleon, and he needed to know why.

Kal pulled a note from the box and opened it. It was an updated list of names. At least twelve more children had been abducted since he had accepted the lead role in the case. His stomach churned as he recalled he had promised to find Casi and the other missing children.

Amongst the missives, Kal found a box and a short note from his brother.

Don't forget to see Mother.

Kal put the note aside, then opened the box. It contained several unrefined Mendai rocks. He pocketed one and put the box in the safe. He would be heading over to the dungeons soon to question the knights. He was just waiting for the lieutenant. A knock sounded on his door. Kal smiled at the man's promptness. You could set a clock by him.

They journeyed through the tiers of the city to the palace. Kal did not catch sight of Roolia, but she had orders to stay nearby.

They entered the secure area of the dungeon. Kal's Seeming dissolved as the dungeon's blocking effect on magic took hold. The guard escorting them glanced back and smiled faintly before his eyes caught on Roolia. He turned back, proceeding. He led them to a door. The locks here took combinations of keys to open. The door glided open on well-oiled hinges. Behind the door was a wide, well-lit hall with barred doors on either side.

"Sir Gavin is here," the guard said as he pointed to the first door on the left. "Sir Farrel is there," he pointed across the hall, "though he hasn't regained consciousness yet. He's been in a healing trance and should awaken soon."

Kal nodded. Both men had been tortured, but Sir Farrel had taken the brunt. He was also the knight the assassin had further injured before Roolia had killed them.

Doha and Kal entered Sir Gavin's cell, leaving Roolia in the hall, out of sight. The cell had a mattress, a lidded chamber pot, a chair, and a table. The last three were bolted to the floor. Sir Gavin sat on the bed, leaning against the wall.

Doha took up a guard's stance by the door, but Kal sat in the chair. The guard left, closing the door.

Kal studied Sir Gavin for a long moment, making sure he saw the royal band on his arm. "Glad to see you are doing better," he said. "My name is Kal. It was my team that pulled you out of the Canticle Inn. Tell me about the Compact."

Sir Gavin's eyes, trained on Doha's sword, snapped to Kal. His muscular frame shifted on the mattress toward Kal.

"They will come for me," Sir Gavin said, voice rusty with disuse.

"Why? What did you discover?"

Sir Gavin licked his lips. "They are taking children of magical descent." His eyebrows bunched when he realized Kal wasn't surprised.

"Do you know why?" Kal asked.

"No," he said too quickly.

"Do you know how they are finding these children?"

Sir Gavin started to shake his head and then said, "They have creatures with them. Creatures that scale walls and hide in remarkable places."

Kal motioned to Doha, who opened the door.

"Creatures like this?" Kal asked as Roolia entered the room, head down, nostrils flared.

Sir Gavin froze, eyes wide, mouth open.

"This is Roolia," Kal said. "She is a Lycanide."

A slight noise escaped Sir Gavin.

"I'll ask again. Why are they taking the children?"

Sir Gavin panted. "I don't know," he said as if his lungs had finally remembered to draw air.

"What do you suspect?"

Roolia stepped closer. The knight flinched back, sputtering. "I thought it was to destabilize the crown, but now I'm not so sure."

"Continue."

"From what I overheard, they want the children for something specific. Not just to undermine the crown. They mentioned something about harvesting them."

Harvesting? Kal thought about the children Roolia rescued. The healers said they had been missing something vital, as if their energy had been drained.

"Is there anything else you overheard?" Kal asked.

"They are also looking for old artifacts, ones from at least two hundred years ago."

"Artifacts of the mage wars?"

"Yes."

Kal knew from reading in the Royal Archives as a child that the war was more extensive than mages. It was said there was a portal to another world, valiantly shut by the heroes of old with the aid of dragons. Back then, The Three, still worshiped today, were active in the world. No one had seen dragons or The Three since. It was as if they had gone through the portal or, even worse, died. People still spoke of The Three and dragons reverently, but they had become myths.

"The Compact. Where did you find them?" Kal asked.

"We trailed them to Winery Row. The Magic Brew House."

Kal sighed. His team had been so close the other night. They had triggered the trap at the Inn, so the Compact probably thought we were dead. If he were lucky, they would still be there.

"Did you report any of this to your lord?"

"I left a coded message but didn't hear a response."

Either Lord Cardinas didn't get the message, or he left his knight to die. That didn't necessarily make him a traitor, but it did make him a person of interest.

Roolia growled as the guard came up behind her.

"My lord," the guard said. "Sir Farrel is awake."

"He's alive?" asked Sir Gavin. "What about Sir Roland?"

"Unfortunately, he didn't make it," Kal said, standing.

"What about me?" asked Sir Gavin.

"For now, you are a guest of the crown. Your safety is our utmost priority." Kal left the cell. A resigned knight sat staring at his back.

After locking the door, the guard led them to the chamber across from Sir Gavin's. They entered a similar cell, but this time, the knight sat propped up on his mattress. His face was ashen, and his fingers were in splints.

They took up similar positions as before.

Kal introduced himself. "Tell me about the Compact."

"What would you like to know?"

"Who are they?"

"I don't know. They hide themselves well, but they are foreigners."

Kal's shoulders tensed. "From where?"

"I don't know. I've never heard their accent before." The knight yawned.

"What do they want?"

"They are looking for allies amongst the nobles."

"To do what?"

"I don't know." The knight's shoulders slumped.

Kal suppressed a grimace. "How did you find them?"

"We followed two of Lord Deleon's knights to a meeting in Winery Row."

"Which winery?" Kal asked.

"The Magic Brew House."

"What did you find?"

"The knights went into a private room for a meeting. Sir Gavin kept watch while I went to the office."

The knight paused, prompting Kal to ask again, "What did you find?"

"I found deeds of sale to the brew house and several other properties in the city."

"Can you list those properties?

"I can," he said, head drooping before he righted himself.

Kal nodded to Doha, who stepped out momentarily, coming back a few minutes later with paper and ink. The knight listed several addresses in the Rim as well as places of business similar to the winery in the city proper, and Doha wrote them down. Kal realized they were all places where information flowed. He would have the Shadow Weavers investigate.

"What happened next?"

"Sir Roland came in and said it was time to go. We all snuck out while an argument raged in the private room. As we got clear, soldiers descended on the winery and killed Lord Deleon's men. We decided to leave, but someone must have followed us. Not wanting to lead them to our lord, we hid."

Kal didn't believe him, though he was hard-pressed to know the lie.

"Can you describe any of the Compact soldiers they met with?"

He blinked several times, as if trying to stay focused. "Yes. Hm, well, no, I didn't really see them clearly." Farrel backtracked as a bead of sweat rolled down the side of his face.

"What were they arguing about?" Kal asked.

"I'm sorry?"

"In the room. When you left, you said they were arguing. What were they arguing about?"

"Ah, well, it sounded like they were arguing about the children."

"What children?" Kal played dumb.

"Th-the young Deleon children. They were missing."

"And why would that come up here?"

"I don't know," he said, eyelids drooping.

"Is there anything else you can tell me about the Compact or the children?" Kal asked.

"No," he said, eyes fluttering closed.

"Well, if you do, just tell the guards, and I will come back," Kal said, standing.

As they were leaving the dungeons, Kal left strict instructions that the two men were not allowed to interact. He would speak with them again, cross-referencing their stories. For now, he had another appointment to keep.

Kal dropped his Seeming as he knocked on Lady Millaine's door. Donovan answered, letting him in. "She is waiting for you."

Lady Millaine sat in one of the cushioned chairs, wearing her customary veiled hat. Donovan left them alone and went into his room.

Kal walked over to the couch and sat down. Reaching into his pocket, he pulled out a pouch containing a gram of Mendai Black. After removing it from the pouch, he laid it on top and slid it over to her.

Lady Millaine picked up the Mendai, rotating it in her hand, its rough surfaces unrefined. He felt a short pulse of magic, which he would have missed if he hadn't been looking for it.

"This will do," she said. "Tell me what you know about shields and zones of awareness."

Kal shifted in his seat, gathering his thoughts. "There are two types of shields. Hard, or rigid shields, which are the quickest and easiest shields to make, do not bend. They will shatter if hit by more force than the magic used to create them. Soft, or flexible shields, take more effort but can take on much more force as they bend, spreading out the force of the hit."

Kal wove his fingers together.

"The zone of awareness is the dome extending outward around you that you use to create a shield."

"What if I told you there is a third type of shield? One that is more like a web you can extend even farther from yourself?"

"For what purpose?" Kal asked.

Lady Millaine smiled.

"You can use it to extend your senses. Determine when someone is coming close. Identify an arrow strike." Lady Millaine paused, but it was clear she had more to say. "Protect others."

Kal's eyes widened. The easiest way to kill a mage was with an arrow. If you could sense the arrow coming, you could step out of its path or knock it aside. "How does one cast this web?" he asked.

"Watch." She drew nites to her, then plucked nites with gray markings and consumed them, forming a ball of power. She spun it into a web of dense lines all over her body. Then she pushed energy into it, and it expanded around her into a dome. "The distance you can expand is personal to each mage, but the more you learn about power, the wider your net. You've memorized the nite designs I gave you?"

Kal thought back to the Canticle Inn explosion. He had used some of those nites to help him contain the explosion. "Yes," he said.

"Good. Did you see what I did?"

"Yes."

"Now you try it. Keep it small for now."

Kal started to cast, but instead of solidifying the shield, he expanded it outward a few feet. He could feel Lady Millaine at the edge of his web.

"Good, now make it as large as this room."

Kal expanded it again, feeling some part of his perception go with it. Oddly, it wasn't as tiring as a traditional shield, since it was webbed and the energy was still tied to him. But it was distracting as new sensations demanded his attention.

Lady Millaine shifted inside the web. A tingling awareness of her washed over him, then faded. He knew exactly where she was. He could find her with his eyes closed.

"Good. Now try expanding further. Do it slowly, as it will start to drain you."

Kal expanded again. He felt Kelly and then Donovan come into his sphere of awareness. Then, someone walked by in the hall outside.

"Now try making the spaces between the web larger and thinner."

Slowly, Kal thinned out the web. It became like gossamer. Kal felt lighter. "How thin can it be before you miss an arrow?"

"It should be no wider than the fletching on the arrow. It has to touch the net on the way by for you to notice it."

Kal adjusted the webbing. "Like this?"

"Yes. Very good. Now bring it back in a bit."

He shrank the shield.

"I want you to practice always having this web around you. Learn to wear it like a second skin."

"Won't that be tiring?" he asked.

"Use the nites around you as they pass through your shields. Find the ones that give you energy and absorb them. Save your personal energy as much as you can for secondary spells."

Kal found one and absorbed it. A small burst of energy went through him, and he realized he wasn't hungry.

"Does this mean I won't need to eat immediately after using magic?" Kal asked, thinking of Master Evans. All the upper Arcanum mages had some girth to them. He wondered if this was how they did it.

"Not if you do it right," she said.

"Is there a limit? It seems like one could do anything," Kal said.

"There is a price, if that is what you're asking."

Kal lost control of his net. It collapsed into him like a physical blow, stinging his eyes. "What price?"

"There is a range where you can use this power without repercussions. However, if you grow too powerful, you may gain the notice of Guardian's minion, the Oraswick. If he notices you, he will test you."

Oraswick? This was straight out of the old religious texts. According to the old doctrine, there was a being who prevented people from growing too strong for the sake of the world. It had been a long time since he had read the old texts. He'd have to read up on it when he had time. *How did she know this? Was she a religious scholar?* Not for the first time, Kal wondered what she looked like under that hood.

"And if I fail this test?" he asked.

"You will die."

"What if I pass this test?"

"You will be bound by unbreakable oaths."

"What kind of oaths?"

"I cannot say, and it isn't a concern for you. The amount of power I am introducing you to is no more than your Arcanum masters would wield. Like them, if you do this and eat delicacies, you will gain weight."

Kal considered her words. How did she know all this? Was she bound? He couldn't see if there were binding oath marks on her skin under her robes. If he could do this much, he should be able to protect Corin and Jenna.

Kal reestablished his net. "This will take some getting used to."

Lady Millaine exhaled as if in relief. "Practice it," she said. "Come back when you can hold it for at least four candle marks, and we will move on to the next lesson."

Kal nodded and stood. He'd been dismissed.

Kal headed back to his room, his senses tingling with information. He could see solid walls, but he could also sense people beyond them, in their rooms as he moved through the halls. It was an odd sort of double vision. Under his door was a series of letters. His senses flickered as he bent down to pick them up, so he adjusted the power level of his shield and shut the door.

Going to his desk, he went through the mail, where he found a thick one in the familiar handwriting of Master Harram. His eyes trailed over to the box. He still needed to send an update on what he'd learned from the knights.

If it had been urgent, Master Harram wouldn't have mailed it but used the box. He put aside the thick envelope and wrote a letter recounting what he had learned from the knights. Sealing it, he coated the envelope lightly with the Aellar powder and placed it in the transferal box, closing the lid. A moment later, he opened the lid to an empty box.

His eyes teared up, and he realized his net had fallen. He rebuilt it and picked up the thick envelope from Master Harram. He broke the seal and read, a frown blooming on his face.

Here are the plans for the subterranean levels under the castle. Kal took them out of the package and spread them out on the desk. *There are many unmapped catacombs beneath. I want you to build a model and identify any chambers large enough to hold fifty or more people.*

Kal thought back to when he was a student. Master Harram would always give him tasks that came through the guilds or were related to the crown in some way, along with his regular assignments. If given a choice, Kal would have been a builder. He loved creating things, but that wasn't practical for the king's son. Master Harram knew this and used the tasks as rewards. Kal had learned they stabilized his emotions when he worked on them when he got stuck on his other work.

How he longed for that simplicity. All he'd had to do for the last two years was make sure the Inn had what it needed. Kal flinched as his web dropped again. Rebuilding it, he muttered, "I can't afford any more distractions. This task has to wait," as he put the package aside.

Unfortunately, he had a lot of problems to work on right now. He had to find the missing children, find the Compact, figure out what they were doing, and who they were doing it with. He had to help his brother with the voice. He still had to hide from the assassins, siphon nites from Jenna regularly while training her, and learn from Lady Millaine.

He had found precious little on Lycanides in the archives. He needed to learn more about Lycanides, or he wouldn't be alpha for long. He then took up pen and paper to request more information on Lycanides from the borderlands. They must have more current information.

He tore open the following letter, read it, and swore as he felt the sting of his net collapsing. He would get the hang of this. He opened the next letter and the next. It was only on the last letter that he managed to maintain his hold. Sighing, Kal took up his pen to send out responses, his net crumbling around him.

Chapter 22

Magic Brew House

Kal took Wyn and Gabe to the Magic Brew House. They dressed the part of day workers looking for a night out. Kal added calluses to his hands and wore a weathered face. He needed to follow up on the lead from the knights.

As they approached the building, Kal frowned as he saw an under new management sign on the gate. *Maybe we can find out where they went?* Upon entering, the gated structure opened up to outdoor seating. They settled onto benches surrounding a wooden table near the door as a waitress came by with a menu.

"How long has this place been under new management?" Kal asked.

"About a week," she said. "The new manager also owns the Tasty Brew."

"Oh, I like the Tasty Brew's food," said Gabe, "but I preferred their previous owner's casks. Will they use new casks here or the casks that the previous owners used?"

"For now, the casks from the previous owners, but I'm sure they will switch it up."

"Do you know what else the old management owned?" Wyn asked. "Maybe we can check out their casks as well."

"Not sure. They didn't own the place for long, but I think they picked up a new place on Cedar Street."

"Oh, really? What's it called?"

"The Flying Gull," she said.

"Thanks, we'll check it out. What do you recommend on the menu?" Gabe asked.

The waitress launched into the specials for the day. They ordered and settled in for the evening.

Kal nursed a hangover the following day. Gabe wasn't kidding about the casks. They were full-bodied and flavorful. Hardly the drink his brother would like, but one he had grown accustomed to over the last couple of years.

Kal sat at his desk, going through missives. He, Gabe, and Wyn would go to the Flying Gull for show, but he would have the Shadow Weavers spy on the places on the list.

Kal had already handed off the other addresses Sir Farrel provided. According to the missive in his hands, each property, a combination of residences and commercial properties, had been purchased anonymously via auction. Each place had workers and activity, but none were open to the public. Master Evans was sending in some mages disguised as workers to investigate.

Kal wrote a note back to them to add the new property, then got up to start his day.

"**M**aster, where are we going?" Jenna asked, walking with more grace now that she had grown accustomed to court attire.

"We are going to go see Master Corvald Didymus."

Jenna recalled the messenger, her muscles giving an involuntary shiver.

He brought her to an upscale part of the Rim. It was as close to the inner city as you could be without actually being inside. They entered through a side gate obscured by ivy.

Jenna studied the guards stationed by the entrance as they walked through the enclosed courtyard. Being in the Rim had made her more attuned to her surroundings. She sent out a pulse of magic, easily detectable by other mages, and was shocked by the number of guards scattered throughout the residence. Kal raised an eyebrow at her. What she had done would be considered rude at the least, and an attack in some places. She sheepishly restrained her magic as a doorman allowed them entry into the house and escorted them to a small sitting room.

Moments later, the butler brought them through another door and into a large inner courtyard. There, sitting near a fountain, a paintbrush in hand, flowing against canvas, was a man.

Their guide seated them. It was clear they were to wait here until acknowledged. During that time, Jenna studied the figure she presumed to be Corvald as he painted. He was a middle-aged man with a bald spot forming at the top of his head. His hair was sun-kissed, his skin weathered, and his eyes blue. He was thickening in the middle, but fit. As she studied him, she could tell that something was wrong with him, something in the eyes and the face.

Kal shifted in his chair, and she realized he was studying her, waiting for her to figure it out. Jenna looked again and inhaled sharply when she saw it.

Jenna stared in awe. This man was wearing a Seeming, but it was far more complicated than what Kal had taught her. She studied him. Many parts of his face were constructed and anchored at specific points. Overlaying his face was an outer set of muscles, jaw, bone, and eyes. She then checked along his body. There were anchor points all over. So many that he likely appeared nothing like this.

"Are you through?" Corvald asked, his voice clear and commanding.

Jenna startled, concluding the safest answer was best.

"Yes, thank you, sir."

He flawlessly moved an eyebrow, and she couldn't help but be fascinated by its fluidity. *A master must have done this.* Then, to her delight, he stood up and walked over to them, seating himself across from them. Jenna leaned forward, riveted by the labyrinth of overlapping magic as it moved in time with him. Some of them added the illusion of color, and others of length or width. There were no seams in the Seeming. It was a fantastic piece of work, and she itched to ask if he was wearing real clothes. Amusement rippled through her bond with Kal.

Eyebrows up, she looked at Kal but he just smiled. Was that fondness in his eyes? She jerked her attention back to Corvald as Kal spoke.

"Master Didymus, you asked us to come?"

After a moment, the "us" sank in, and her eyes sharpened. Corvald went from an object of awe to one of danger.

He turned and pouted, the Seeming rippling realistically.

"You've ruined my fun, Kal."

Kal just raised an eyebrow.

Master Didymus slumped in his chair before straightening.

"How much longer?" Didymus asked.

"Six months," Kal replied.

"Make it three," Didymus countered.

Anger flared in her bond. Jenna's attention snapped back and forth between the two men. She didn't understand what they were talking about but knew better than to ask.

"Too dangerous." Kal's eyes glinted. He leaned forward, and Jenna felt a ripple in their bond. Kal was using magic. The flow stopped, and Kal leaned back. He looked relaxed, but she could feel the fear through the bond.

"Five," Kal softly conceded.

Corvald gave a brief nod. He stood up and went back over to his painting supplies, rummaging through them.

"Ah, here it is." He threw a small object over to Kal, who caught it with one hand.

"It's everything I have gathered so far. I am not sure it will help."

Jenna kept her face smooth, even though she was burning with curiosity. Kal appeared to be both afraid for and of Corvald. It occurred to her that these two had known each other for a very long time. Corvald obviously wanted something from Kal, and Kal was afraid to give it to him, and yet scared not to.

Kal studied the object.

Corvald walked over to her and handed her a small purse.

"My lord?" she asked.

"You will need to travel in larger circles soon. Use it for supplies."

Kal gave no indication of intervening, so she accepted the pouch.

Corvald went back to his easel and started painting again.

They were clearly dismissed.

K al dropped Jenna off at the inn, then made his way into the city. The coach swayed as he approached the Sandoval estate. Green banners hung outside with the Sandoval crest of a sword crossed with a medicinal herb.

The carriage came to a stop, and he got out. The doorman escorted him into the house, bringing him to the parlor where he served Kal tea.

Seated, Kal sipped his tea as he went through a mental list of arguments to support Lord Sandoval taking Jenna on as a temporary heir.

Lord Sandoval entered and seated himself opposite Kal. His gaze never left Kal's face. "What brings you here, Kal?"

"You have need of an heir, and I need information that can only be obtained at court."

"No," Sandoval growled. "I already have a narrowed list of candidates."

Kal had expected that. "She's a mage, trained to be a healer," he said.

Sandoval blinked, and Kal knew he was at least interested. "She's smart and invested in the missing children's case."

"Who is she to you?"

"My apprentice."

Sandoval's eyebrows rose. "You have an apprentice?"

"I do, and I think you would find her uniquely qualified."

"How so?" Sandoval crossed his arms.

Kal sipped his tea before speaking. This last bit of information would either cinch the deal or break it off entirely.

"Her resemblance to your daughter is uncanny."

Sandoval's eyes narrowed, and Kal could feel the anger simmering underneath.

"Is that supposed to make me take her?" Sandoval asked.

Kal suppressed a wince. He didn't know the lord's disagreement with his daughter, but maybe this wasn't the selling point he thought it was. "Of course not. I only ask that you meet her and judge for yourself."

Sandoval grimaced, uncrossing his arms, and leaned back in his seat, face contemplative.

Kal waited as the older man sat in silence.

Sandoval's hands spasmed. "Fine. I'll meet your candidate, but I decide if she's worthy, not you."

Kal bowed his head. "Understood."

Chapter 23

Heirs

"Are you sure you want to do this?" Kal spoke with Lord Sandoval in his private study. While speaking, he stared at an elaborate painting of the late Lady Sandoval. Her eyes, the line of her neck, and even her hands spoke of a similarity that skirted the edge of coincidence.

Kal had brought Jenna and Lent with him after a shopping and tutoring session. He had wanted to introduce Jenna to her possible cover story, and Lent had insisted on coming along.

"Yes, yes, consider me warned. If she's to be my heir, then some resemblance is good. Let's get this over with. I need to get back to my mentee." Lord Sandoval huffed and straightened his jacket while seated behind his office desk. "You went through all this trouble to get me on board, but now you're balking? Just how close can the resemblance be?" Lord Sandoval waved a hand dismissively.

Kal rose, handing the picture back to Lord Sandoval, and left the room. A short while later, he returned, escorting Jenna. She walked gracefully in the shoes and wore a gown of forest green silk with silver flowers stitched along the edges. The dress cinched at the waist, showing off her figure. She was adorned simply with dangling flower earrings and a simple flower necklace shaped in silver. Her hair was in a loose bun with strands hanging on either side of her face.

Lord Sandoval froze.

Jenna glanced at Kal, but he shook his head at her, and she waited.

"Who was your mother?" Lord Sandoval managed to ask with some dignity a few moments later.

"My mother's name was Abigail Mackenzie Sturmich."

Kal watched in alarm as Lord Sandoval closed his eyes, took several deep breaths, and opened them. Then he got up from the desk and walked around it, all business.

"And your father?"

"Finian Nathan Sturmich."

"What did your parents do for a living?"

"Father was a dockworker. Mother was a healer."

"What kind of healer was she?" he asked

"Body and mind. I studied the body, but my brother studied the mind."

"Your brother?" he asked, surprised.

"I have"—she frowned, fidgeting with her dress—"two brothers and one sister."

Lord Sandoval quivered as he sat on the edge of his desk.

"What happened to your siblings?" he asked softly.

"My eldest brother and I have recently been reunited." Her eyes did not flick towards Kal. "My sister is one of the missing children, and my other brother lives in the Rim," she said, thinking about how forlorn he looked hanging the missing person's picture of Casi. She shrugged, then cringed at the unladylike motion.

Sandoval pursed his lips.

"Would his name happen to be Rowen?"

Her head shot up, eyes round.

She said nothing, but the answer was in her eyes.

"The Rowen I know heals the mind. I've been mentoring him. He, too, bears a strong resemblance to my daughter."

She nodded, thinking of her brother.

"Shall I show the eldest brother in?" Kal said.

"He's here?" Sandoval said, eyebrows raised.

"Yes."

"Then, yes, please do so." A small smile came to his lips.

Kal went to the door and waved. Lent came in wearing formal guard attire and bowed to Lord Sandoval. They made introductions as the Lord showed him to the seat next to Jenna.

"Were you born with the name Lent?" Sandoval asked.

"No," he said in his quiet way. "I was born Justin McCabe Sturmich."

Sandoval perched himself on the edge of his desk again.

"Why are you here?"

They both said, almost as one, "To find our sister."

"What will you do once you find her?" he countered.

"Take care of her," said Lent. "I have some money saved up. As long as we don't live too extravagantly, we should be able to start new lives."

Sandoval studied Lent.

"What is it you do for a living?"

Something moved behind Lent's eyes before he spoke. "Whatever needs doing," he said with finality, causing Jenna to frown.

"Have you been trained as a warrior?"

"I make do," he said, tone grim.

Sandoval nodded and turned to Jenna. "And you? What is it you do for a living?"

Jenna shuffled through several answers, avoiding glancing at Kal.

"I am a trainee to Kal Torvald. I do what I am asked to do."

Lent frowned, not liking the answer.

Sandoval frowned, too, nodding again more slowly, then shot a glare at Kal and turned back.

"Just a moment." Lord Sandoval stood and headed towards the door, leaving. Soon, Lord Sandoval returned to the room followed by Rowen.

As Rowen entered Lord Sandoval's private study, Lent and Jenna froze. Kal also went still. This was the doctor who had treated him in the Rim. Rowen's medical bag dropped to the floor unnoticed, and his mouth moved, but no sound came out.

"Why would you trust slavers with our sisters, Rowen?" Justin lunged at Rowen, pushing him back and slamming him against the wall.

"J-Justin?" Rowen watched his brother, uncertainty on his face.

"Why?" Justin demanded.

Rowen shook his head back and forth.

Jenna stood up and took a step closer.

Rowen's eyes snapped to her as force rippled out of him.

Surprised, Justin lost his grip and slid back a few steps before stopping.

Jenna took one step back before putting up a hand and stopping the force of his push.

Neither Kal nor Sandoval moved at all, but the desk and chairs all shifted away from Rowen, whose eyes were locked on Jenna.

"I—" Rowen paused. "I didn't know.' He stopped again and licked his lips. "I thought taking you there was the right thing to do."

Justin took an imposing step toward Rowen, brushing past his push. Rowen's face shifted from fear to anger.

"I was trying to put food on the table. I took over Mother's patients, or as many as I could handle. I was trying to save Father. He was like a baby. I was sixteen!" He pleaded for understanding, with despair in his voice.

He stared Justin in the eyes, anger flaring. "You left us!" Lent stopped moving one step away from Rowen, struck by the words. "You left me," Rowen said more quietly.

Lent went still.

"I needed you." Rowen slouched, anguished tears streaking his face. "I needed him!" he yelled, looking beseechingly toward Jenna. "I needed him to be the way he was before Mother was killed." Rowen barked a bitter laugh, then turned to Jenna.

"I didn't know what he would do. It was supposed to be temporary. He said you would be paid wages for work. Rent was due, and he promised to pay in advance—"

"And you believed him?" Jenna snorted. Rowen's eyes filled with fresh tears.

Yes, he had believed him, she thought.

"Father is dead," she said. "Killed himself, or at least that's what they told me."

"And the ones who killed Mother?" Rowen demanded of Lent.

"Dead," he answered tightly, but he didn't seem victorious, just sad, hands twitching like he wanted to kill them again.

Lent stepped away from Rowen and went back to his seat. His angry presence folded away, submerging itself deep within him. Kal followed the process with wariness, unsure if he could ever tell when a man like Lent would strike.

Jenna sat down, too, hands straightening the gown she wore.

Kal unclenched his fists, straining at the effort he'd had to put forth to prevent himself from interfering. His eyes met Sandoval's, and he nodded that it was over.

Sandoval got a chair for Rowen.

"There is something you should know," Rowen said as sadness rose again. "Casi is missing."

The room paused. Rowen didn't know that they knew. "Kal"—Lent waved a hand in his direction—"has brought us into his investigation for the missing children. I am joining the guard responsible for searching, and Jenna is seeking nobles who may know more about them."

Rowen turned towards Kal, studying him. "You're the man who came to me in the Rim."

"I am. As you suspected, I bore a maghin, and your sister removed it. The king has tasked me with finding the missing children." Kal pulled out the seal given to him by the king as proof of his authority.

Rowen frowned, taking in the words and the seal.

Sandoval spoke. "Perhaps it would help if you all told me your stories."

Jenna started first, telling him of their mother's passing, the slavers, waking, and being told that Rowen and her sister were gravely injured and that she would not be allowed near them until she could control her powers. Spending the last two years as a ward in training. She talked of Choosing Day and how she ended up with Kal.

When she paused, Lent picked up the thread.

"I left to find the ones who killed Mom. I joined the military, doing whatever needed to be done. I changed my name and became a thug, a sailor, a hatchet man, and a military spy, waiting patiently to identify the unit that did the deed. They didn't respect support personnel and were proud of the deaths in the Healerie. One by one, I brought them to the attention of the military as targets. With approval, I picked them off. My journey ended six months ago when I got close enough to kill the last of them."

"Did they know why?" Rowen asked with a bloodthirsty edge to his voice.

"I made sure of it," Lent replied with a grim smile before picking up the thread again.

"Two months ago, I completed my contract with the military and took a ship back to Mendallon only to find our house lived in by some other family. I followed the trail to the new house in the Rim. Word on the street was that the house was cursed. I camped with the homeless, watching and waiting until one night, Jenna and Kal came. I listened as she told her story and felt like I couldn't break the spell. It was Kal who recognized that I was different from the other homeless and gave me a way to reach her."

Everyone turned to Rowen, who told of how he had been rescued and brought to the Healerie. "It didn't take them long to realize that I knew what I was doing, so they apprenticed me, and Casi stayed with me," he said hollowly.

"What is your birth name?" Sandoval asked Rowen.

"Rowen Oswen Sturmich."

Lord Sandoval blinked several times as if to hold back tears.

He took a moment to gather his thoughts. "Now that everyone has caught up, let's continue where we left off. Rowen, you already know this." He glanced at Lent and Jenna. "Kal mentioned that I have no heirs?"

They all nodded.

"From this point onward, consider yourselves my heirs. I will arrange a coming-out ball and introductions to the court for you all as lords and ladies. Appropriate attire and attendance are required. Our house will provide everything you need." He turned to Lent. "As for you," he started, as Lent held up his hand.

"Your pardon, Lord Sandoval, but I have to pass," Lent said in his quiet way.

"Why is that?" Lord Sandoval asked almost sharply.

"Kal has already given me a job as a guard looking for Casi. I mean to be there when they find her."

Sandoval frowned and gave a slight bow.

"I can work with you later."

Lent blinked several times and shifted in his seat. Rowen also raised his hand.

"I am working with patients who require the utmost secrecy. It would be better if I did nothing to bring attention to myself." Sandoval went stiff.

He addressed all of them. "I know your stories, so it is only fair that you know mine." Sandoval frowned, gathering his thoughts.

"I had three children—all healthy, strong, and intelligent. One died in a sporting accident. One I disowned and disinherited. The last one died with his wife and children during the blight a year ago."

He detected the question in their eyes.

"The name of my disinherited child was Madeline Abigail Sandoval, but everyone called her Abigail. She was a healer trained in mind and body, as most of our family have been." He stared at them, and they stared back at him in surprise.

"My wife's name was Jenivieve Casimira Sandoval. She died in childbirth." Into the stunned silence, he said, "My name is Oswen McCabe Sandoval, and whether the timing is convenient or not, you are my heirs. Anything you need to get Casi back is yours for the asking."

The silence was deafening.

Three sets of eyes stared at Lord Sandoval.

"Why did you disinherit your daughter?" Jenna asked.

Sandoval took a deep breath and blew it out. "There are rules to nobility. We, each house that is, watch over a part of society. Our mandate is to protect, discipline, and grow that which we hold."

"What does this house watch over?" asked Lent.

"This house patrons healers and warriors, which may seem odd at first, but they are two sides of the same coin. Almost all healers of note have gone through training designed by this house. Nearly all guards have been trained, at some point, by someone of House Sandoval.

"Your mother was a brilliant healer and a good warrior. She met your father when she healed him after a brawl. He had been testing his latest theories on shields and their nature. His theory needed more work," he explained. "Your father was a driven man. Some considered him brilliant as well."

"So, what was the problem?" Jenna asked.

"He was without family or means. He was not driven to attain means but had his head buried in the clouds of his theories."

Jenna, Rowen, and Justin all shifted uncomfortably, recalling what he was like before.

"Father would give us complex shapes and designs to puzzle over. I build my shields with the shapes he taught us."

Rowen nodded. "Depending on the type of attack, different shapes shield better than others."

"For me," Lent added, "the different shapes break apart energy, preventing magic from holding you. The rest can be absorbed and reused."

Jenna reflected on Lent walking up to Rowen through the force of his push.

"I forbade them from seeing each other," Sandoval explained.

Lent snickered. "Mom was a force of nature."

"As you say," Sandoval responded, as if recalling their many fights. "She knew what she was doing. She made her choice and left. When she did, she forced me to make mine."

"You never looked for her?" Jenna asked.

"No." He paused.

"You expected her to come back to you," Rowen surmised.

He nodded to Rowen.

"She never did," said Lent.

"Pride runs strongly in us," Sandoval replied. "Welcome to House Sandoval."

Chapter 24

Inversion

K al sat at a table across from Rowen. He'd done his research, and Rowen really was the best person for the job.

"What can I do for you?" Rowen asked.

"You work with nobility on magical and mind issues?"

"That is correct."

"I have a highly secretive patient I'd like you to see."

"Can you tell me about the patient?" Rowen asked.

"Not here. I'll have to bring you to the archives and show you."

Rowen tensed, and Kal realized his mistake. Only the king's records were kept in the archives.

"I'll need you to clear your schedule for a couple of days," Kal said.

"Of course."

A few days later, Kal sat with Jenna and Rowen in the Royal Archives, going over all they had found on the mind issues plaguing his family. The two siblings sat stiffly at first as Jenna described instance after instance in the royal family where symptoms had occurred.

Rowen bombarded her with questions, and though he felt irritation in the bond, she answered each of them thoroughly. Rowen turned to Kal. "So you think there is a difference between you two?"

Kal grimaced, and Jenna said, "Yes, something that blocks the voice."

"Have you been able to test this theory?" Rowen asked.

"Only once," Kal said.

"Do you have a theory, Jenna?" Rowen asked.

Jenna shifted in her seat, eyes down. "Not without more information." She hesitated a moment, then said, "Also, I don't specialize in the mind."

"I trust your instincts," Rowen said, turning to Kal as Jenna gaped at him.

"Okay, I'll have to do some scans on the two of you for comparison. Then I should be able to determine the differences and we can go from there."

Relief flooded through Kal. "I'll set up a meeting."

Kal pulled his hood up, covering his Seeming. He wore shoes with different heel sizes to give him an uneven gait. The smell of alcohol and horse dung coming off of him made Kal's eyes water.

Hobbling, he made his way through the Rim toward one of the addresses on the list he'd received from Sir Farrel.

His team of Shadow Weavers had planted three spies at this location, and one of them had signalled they had something to report.

Kal moved to the designated location next to the entrance to find a one-legged beggar mumbling to himself. Kal squatted down next to him and pulled out a bottle of spirits, taking a swallow before wiping his mouth with a dirt-encrusted hand.

The beggar eyed the almost full bottle with undisguised desire.

"Want some?" Kal asked.

The man's eyes focused on Kal. "What's your price?"

"Already paid." Kal used the code phrase, and the man's eyes went back to the bottle.

"Two men entered wearing black cloaks." The beggar licked his yellow teeth. "I only caught a glimpse, but underneath was blue."

"Which house?" Kal asked. Several houses used blue. He needed to narrow it down.

The beggar hunched down. "Dunno, it was dark, though."

"What kind of shoes?" Kal asked.

His face took on a faraway look. "Fine leather, brown."

Kal took another sip from the bottle, put the cap back on, then handed it to the beggar, who took it with shaking hands.

Kal leaned back against the wall, listening to the sounds of the city. Three major houses had dark blue in their banners. He would put watches on each of their estates. Hopefully, they all didn't have matching brown leather boots.

Three days later, Kal and Corin sat side by side in a pair of chairs Kal had set up in the king's office. Rowen gave them a series of exotic fruits to eat that, when ingested, were known to spread throughout the lymphatic system. Once consumed, Rowen sent steady streams of magic through them to gather metrics. He directed nites into two three-dimensional displays. The markers from the fruits shimmered in the air, rendering an outline of their lymphatic systems. He set them to have different colors and overlaid them on top of each other. Many sections showed differences, which he highlighted in orange.

"Here it is," Rowen said, picking a particular section and making it larger.

"How can you tell?" Kal asked, staring at the mass of lines.

Rowen smiled. "Well, I'm not one hundred percent sure yet, but of the differences I've looked through so far, this is most likely the reason you never showed symptoms."

He pointed to the spot of comparison.

"Your lymph system is similar to the king's, except for this area here. If you look closely"—he blew the image up further—"Corin's system is inverted." He circled the spot on both images, and a reddish line surrounded the area.

"I'll need to review all the differences and make sure I haven't missed anything, so that will take me some time, but I think I can come up with a solution that will work from this. I have all the scans I can think of, but if I need more, I will reach out to you."

The two men nodded as Rowen gathered up his supplies.

K al led Jenna into the heart of the city. He had decided to take their training out in the field. They both wore simple brown cloaks over plain clothes.

"Okay, see that couple over there?" They were older and holding hands as they strolled through the market. The woman had crow's feet around her eyes and a slight limp. "When we get around the corner, I want you to become her. And remember, I'm going to try to distract you."

Jenna nodded and studied the older woman, committing her to memory. As they rounded the corner, Jenna's back hunched, and her features changed into a likeness of the woman, complete with crow's feet.

Kal smiled down at her with the face of the older man, then he held out his hand.

She stumbled a bit, but he stabilized her. Her Seeming wavered.

"Remember, Jenna, you must stay calm and in character no matter what is thrown at you."

She glared at him, and he hid a grin as her Seeming stabilized.

Kal threaded his fingers with hers, enjoying the slight widening of her eyes. She turned away from him, studying a cart selling trinkets.

Kal followed her lead as she led him to the cart. Her transformed hand ran over the items, lingering on a wrought-iron cloak pin.

"How much for the cloak pin?" Kal asked in an older man's voice.

"Two copper," said the mustached vendor.

"That's okay, dear. I don't need it," Jenna said with a quaver in her voice, her hand moving away from the cloak pin.

Kal reached into his pocket and handed the man the money. Then he picked`up the pin and gently fastened her cloak together. Jenna looked away from him as he worked.

Kal leaned forward and put his lips to her ear. What he wanted to say was, "Maybe you'll think of me when you wear it," but he couldn't. He was already skirting the line of propriety. He was her teacher, and she his student. They could never be together.

Jenna's Seeming shivered, and he felt heat through the bond.

"Good job," he said gruffly in the old man's voice before pulling away. The word *coward* echoed in his mind.

A long moment passed before Jenna's Seeming solidified.

Awkwardly, he took her hand and pulled her back into the crowd.

The next morning, Kal sat at his desk, reviewing messages sent to him from fellow Shadow Weavers. Each location designated by Sir Farrel was being watched. Some of the information had led them to new locations, but so far, each operation was exactly what they seemed to be—well-run gathering places like bars, teahouses, and wineries for various class levels. Places to gain information and gossip. Just what were they looking for?

As for the children, he'd been sent a list of places they were not at. So far, they were not being shipped out of the city as part of a slave ring, they were not being made into free labor in the city, and the only children found so far were weak mages. Gabe and Wyn joined in monitoring the sites, while Kelly and Donovan had returned to Lady Millaine. If he needed them again, he would call on them.

A knock sounded at his door.

Kal opened it to find Doha, white webbing in his hair and on his arms.

"Come in. Are you okay?" Kal gestured to the webbing, which extended down Doha's back, as he closed the door.

Doha grimaced. "I'm fine. Roolia keeps hijacking me on the way to breakfast. I'm getting better at spotting the webbing, but now she's using it as a diversion and ambushing me. This morning, she hung me upside down from the rafters until I could explain what I did wrong."

"Has she said why she's doing this?"

"She calls it training games for pups."

Kal reached out a hand to the webbing on Doha's sleeve.

"Don't, or you'll get stuck to me. It's causing quite a stir in the laundry room." He grimaced again.

"How do they get off?" Kal asked.

"They said it dissolves after a day or two, so I've had to order more uniforms."

Kal grimaced, and Doha continued. "Roolia found another child. He's in the Healerie. She woke him, but we didn't find out anything new. I came by to make sure you knew before I went to clean up."

"Good job," Kal said. "And thanks for dealing with Roolia's training."

Doha grinned. "It's oddly invigorating."

Kal pictured himself being wrapped in Roolia's webbing and hung upside down. Invigorating wasn't the word he would choose.

A week passed before Rowen reached out to Kal that he had double-checked his analysis. Rowen, Jenna, and Kal met in the shielded magic room at the inn.

"If you look here, you'll see the differences," Rowen said.

Jenna peered at the list and compared them to the image Rowen displayed above.

She frowned in concentration, then pointed. "It looks like this area here is the biggest difference."

"Correct, and what do you think the treatment should be?"

Jenna chewed her lip. "Perhaps some sort of inverter?"

Rowen nodded. "Exactly my thought."

"What is an inverter?" Kal asked.

Rowen grimaced. "It comes in several forms, but it's a magical device that inverts the flow of magic."

"So if I can get my hands on one, it will solve our problem?" Kal asked.

The room went silent. "That's the theory," Rowen said.

Kal added it to his mental list of things to research.

K al walked through the bowels of the archives, searching for symbols that matched the work of builder Aldquist. He spotted the first set of matching symbols and turned down the aisle. Looking up, Kal found several intriguing items on dissolving metal.

Does it use one of the nites Lady Millaine had me memorize? Kal shook his head. *No distractions*, he chided himself as he went back to reviewing the original shelf.

After a few moments, he sighed. Nothing matched what he was looking for. He flagged down one of the young archive runners and showed her the symbols from Rowen's notes.

"That's in the restricted section," she replied. "Do you have access to the Royal Archives or just the archives proper?"

"The Royal Archives."

"Okay, follow me then."

The young girl led him through several sections and down to another level, where they entered a part of the archives he had never been in. The room was bright, and the air crisp and dry. As they walked, he recognized some of the symbols on the signs.

She brought him to a small gate and gestured for him to open the door. He was careful to reach with his ringed hand. The gate clicked on contact and then rotated, letting him enter the room. When he got in, the runner reached out and opened the gate. It turned again, and she came through after him. She gestured for him to follow and led him through to the center of the room, which held tables placed in a large circle that curved around the outer portion of the center, with extra seats and tables in the middle. The seating was arranged for maximum security and as a space for sharing information.

"How long have you worked in the archives?"

"This is my first year," she said, smiling tentatively up at him, then spread her hands, launching into her description. "This is the center of the Royal Section. The aisles and sections are similar to the ones above. Books in this area cannot leave the gateway we just entered. Once we find your book, you can bring it here to read."

He nodded and placed his satchel on the table. Kal grinned to himself. She didn't know who he was. It was refreshing.

The runner then brought him over to the matching section and aisle, pointing out the hefty tome. Kal gingerly pulled the book from its place and followed her back to the table section.

"If there's nothing else?"

"Ah, no. Thank you. You've been very helpful."

She gave a small bow and left the gated royal section.

Several hours passed as Kal searched through the massive tome, whose index had led him to a page dedicated to inversion spells. From what he had learned, people were like receivers, each tuned to a slightly different frequency. Some frequencies everyone picked up, and others only a subset discerned. Corin acted as a receiver, but Kal, who listened to almost all the same frequencies, was not able to listen to this crucial one. An inverter, if tuned right, should act as a shield on Corin, preventing him from receiving; at least, that was the theory.

There, this design should do. Now, he needed to test the theory. He had to work with a builder to get the mold and weight right on the device. Kal took a magical imprint of the design and materials list, which he stored in the ring he wore. Only someone of similar clearance would be able to view it. After putting the tome back on its shelf, Kal went to find out about getting access to the royal builders.

Chapter 25

Lords

K al sat up panting, awakened from his now too-familiar nightmare of his father's last moments. His whole body was tight, his hands balled into fists. It took effort to unclench his jaw. He took slow, even breaths to calm himself.

He had been summoned before the Council of Lords, representing all guilds, today. He took it as a good sign that the surveillance was getting closer to whomever was responsible for the missing children, since the Lords were taking offense to both Roolia and his investigation. Someone must be getting nervous.

Kal got out of bed and began his exercises. The movement left a sheen of sweat over his skin, flushing out his worries and calming him. He finished and went to the shared washroom in the Inn. On the way back, he found a plate next to his door. Bending down, he retrieved the note.

Master, for your nightmares.

Kal grimaced. He couldn't control the bond when he was sleeping. His fear and terror had probably woken her, though there were some nights when it was her nightmares that woke him. They took turns bringing each other comfort food. Jenna liked peaches, but she always brought him cookies. He carried the plate of cookies into his room, popping one into his mouth. A small sigh escaped him as he chewed.

As Kal walked through the enclosed garden section of the palace to his meeting with the nobles, the hair on the back of his neck went up. Expanding his net, he felt Roolia nearby. She was stalking him like prey.

"What is it, Roolia?" He spoke calmly, with authority.

She dropped down from the ceiling and approached. Her fur was sticking up, and she was chittering.

"Doha reassigned. Can't train. You fix."

Kal realized he hadn't seen Doha at his last briefing. Captain Abasi could reassign Doha wherever he wanted. It was his right as the captain, but Kal didn't have time for this. He was going to be late.

"No," Kal said.

Roolia's chittering became softer, and she began to growl.

Panic rose in Kal. He resisted taking up a defensive stance and instead reasoned with her. "Roolia is in charge of pup. Roolia fix." The moment the words were out of his mouth, he wished he could take them back.

The growling stopped. Kal's eyes widened a bit at the silence, unsure of what it meant. Then, her hair lay flat.

"Yes, alpha," she said, almost whining, then leaped away. Kal exhaled a sigh of relief, wondering if he had time to warn Abasi she was coming.

He was lucky Roolia didn't seem to want to become alpha. The Royal Library just had some fables about Lycanides, and he was still waiting for word from the border. He would make do until then.

K al grimaced. He had avoided the council meetings for as long as he could. He had too many things on his plate and couldn't be tied down in hours of politically driven debate.

As unhappy as it made him, he paid close attention as they raised issue with Roolia, who had taken up stalking Lieutenant Doha on off hours, so much so that he had to be on hand to answer questions about it. Kal observed quietly from the side of the room as voices got heated.

"Surely you understand that having this... spider-wolf, roam about unchained is concerning to the nobles and staff," Lord Erick Andrade said.

His was one of six houses designated as councilors representing city interests in today's meeting with the king.

Lord Beltine, whose house dealt with regulations and mediation, spoke. "She has broken no rules, and as such, I will not approve any actions against her."

Lord Stephen Deleon, whose focus was commerce, was the newest member of the council. He took over after Aaron Deleon died in his chambers. "What if she's the one who took the children?"

Lord Cardinas and Lord Navarro, who ran the judiciary processes, silently followed the byplay.

"Sandoval? What do you think?" asked Lord Deleon.

Lord Andrade snorted. "He's too happy to have heirs to care about something like this."

Sandoval had a self-satisfied air as he spoke. "Yes, I'm happy to have heirs, and because of that, I want to keep them safe." He nodded to Lord Deleon. "But I think they are safer with the spider wolf roaming free to intercept any more attacks." Deleon clenched his jaw, and Andrade glanced down, pursing his lips.

The king stared at Cardinas and Navarro in turn.

Cardinas said, "Though I agree with Sandoval, I think she makes people uncomfortable. It would be good to defuse that."

Navarro spoke firmly. "Until she breaks the law, I do not condone imprisoning her."

"What-ifs aside, Deleon, how do you stand?" the king asked.

"Leash her," he said with a grimace.

Kal studied the new head of House Deleon. *Just what type of man is he? Will there be trouble going forward?* He was young for the councilor's position, only in his thirties, but was well-known and had performed effectively on house-led ventures up till now. Kal hoped that once this was all resolved, House Deleon would be able to move past the events that removed the former head and proceed forward. Long term, he didn't believe it would be an issue, as the city consisted of many different cultures, and one rarely observed strong bias from those in commerce, unless something interfered with making money.

"And you, Cardinas?" the king asked.

"Leave her," he said.

The king spoke. "That's four to two. She stays free. I will point out that Kal already leashes Lady Roolia."

Kal flinched at the words as the king continued.

"Plus, he is doing the job set before him. So long as you or your guilds had nothing to do with the missing children, there is no cause for concern. We will not interfere with either Kal or Lady Roolia without just cause. Next order of business?"

Kal rose and a hush descended. He gave his report on the current standing of the missing children.

"So you have found no more missing children?" said Lord Beltine.

"Only one," Kal replied.

"Do you have additional leads?" asked Lord Cardinas.

Kal grimaced. "Not at this time," he said, and saw something flash in Cardinas's eyes. Was that satisfaction? Did he want to see Kal fail so badly? Or was there something more? There was blue in his house colors.

"How many children have disappeared so far?" asked Lord Navarro.

Kal hesitated. "Eighty-seven, though we believe additional children haven't been reported. Our current estimate is closer to one hundred children."

"A gathering of citizens was dispersed in the Rim near one of the sites dedicated to the missing children," said Lord Deleon.

"I am aware. Reports indicate it was peaceful." Kal couldn't deny that tensions were rising in the city. There had also been reports of vandalism on Crown-owned properties. He needed to solve this soon.

The king cleared his throat. "Is there anything else anyone wants to address?" There was a long moment of silence. "Very well, this meeting is adjourned."

Chapter 26

Expectations

Jenna hunched into herself as she ate breakfast with Lord Sandoval. Justin was at the barracks, and Rowen was working. Jenna sat beside her grandfather at a large table.

"In preparation for the ball, you will have a series of dinners and lunches to acclimate to your new peers."

"Okay." *That makes sense.*

"This rotation will start today."

Jenna blinked. "Who do I meet first?"

"Whom, and you meet with the Andrades for lunch." He leaned over and pulled a stack of papers from his carrying case. "The Andrade house deals primarily with city infrastructure. They are not one of the wealthiest houses, but they are one of the most influential and, as such, hold a lot of sway over the proposals that reach the king's ears. Established houses are responsible for working with the guilds and the king to further the interests of Mendallon. These are the dossiers on each member. Please read them carefully. I will meet with you before they arrive to answer any questions."

Jenna stared at the pile, conflicting emotions warring within her. She moved her lips a couple of times, but nothing came out. She should be thrilled, but somehow she just felt trapped. She shook herself; her sister came first.

"I was informed that you could read," Oswen said.

"Yes, of course I can," she said a little breathlessly while picking up the first page.

Cornelius Andrade, age twenty-nine, heir apparent to the Andrade fortune. A small hand-drawn likeness was included. He had short hair and doe-like eyes. *He's handsome.* She flipped to the next one.

Victor Andrade, eighteen, second heir. She flipped again.

Arianna Andrade, age sixteen, third heir.

Jenna cleared her throat. "Just what is it that the Andrades do?"

"They cover infrastructure and buildings," he said.

"So they're architects?"

"Some of them. The Andrades work closely with builders and manage the licensing for the creation of new estates. If a structure was built in the last two hundred years, the Andrade family likely had a hand in it."

"Are they all coming to lunch, or can we distill this list?"

He smiled. "They are all invited, but usually only the young are free on such short notice—or the ones searching for a suitable marriage partner."

"Marriage?" she said, eyes wide.

"Don't be so surprised. You are now an heir. Many will seek your hand, or at least your good graces, in the hope of gaining alliances."

Jenna reflected on Kal and his effortless grace and sighed.

"How much choice will I have?" Tears welled in her eyes as she considered her mother.

Oswen stared at her. "There are some requirements. I, of course, have preferences, but I have also learned some things from your mother. Plus, there are four of you. I would have you be happy."

Jenna nodded tightly, considering what would make her happy. She sighed, realizing she was no longer hungry, and leafed through the rest of the dossiers, wondering why she wasn't pleased.

Jenna had been relatively happy since she had found a master. He needed her, and she had planned to go undercover and prove her worth. In her mind, she would help find the bad people and then return victorious to her previous life of learning with Kal.

Now, these dossiers in her hand represented her true life. Yes, she was going undercover, but even if she succeeded, things wouldn't return to what they were before. Horror washed through her as she compared her future to that of a marionette going through a dance. She would be ensconced with these people she couldn't relate to or talk to, doing things she wasn't interested in for, well, ever. Her eyes teared up again.

Oswen patted the back of her hand, and she almost lost it. At least she wouldn't be doing it alone.

Jenna stared in alarm at Arianna Andrade. Her skin was pale, and she wasn't eating. The healer in Jenna just couldn't leave her alone. "Arianna?"

"Yes?" The girl looked up listlessly.

"What do you do for fun?"

Young Lord Cornelius, heir of house Andrade. It sounded like he was reciting from one of the dossiers. "Arianna can play string instruments. She can sing, read, write, and recite *The Tale of The Three*. She can cross sti—"

"Yes, but Arianna, what do you do for *fun*?"

Cornelius frowned, clearly not used to being interrupted.

Arianna stared at her and blinked, not entirely taking her in. "Oh, I like to read."

"Ah, what are your favorites?" Jenna asked.

She paused again and glanced down. "Cooking."

"I'm not sure how that is of importance." Cornelius scowled.

Jenna fought the urge to spill her drink on him. "Do they let you cook?" Jenna asked, genuinely curious.

Arianna frowned. "Sometimes, I'm allowed to help in the kitchens, but they told me I should be running the kitchen, not behaving like the help."

"As well you should be," said Cornelius, looking down his nose at Arianna, who wilted.

"If you like, you can come here, and we can make cookies together."

Arianna's eyes focused on Jenna for what she was sure was the first time.

"I'd like that," she said hesitantly.

"Great, I'll have my people reach out to your people," Jenna said with a smile.

A kernel of life flooded back into Arianna's eyes.

After the luncheon, Lord Sandoval approached Jenna in the sitting room. "That was nicely done with the niece."

"Is she ill?" she asked.

"Not physically. What does the dossier say about her?"

Jenna blinked. "Um, it says that she's roughly my age and plays music beautifully."

"Was the information correct?"

"Seems that way, but she's miserable. Do you know why?"

"I suspect it has to do with her brother, Victor. Like you, they are both recent additions at court. She is under a lot of pressure to meet expectations. What she does reflects on her brother and vice versa. Her brother was recently caught in a compromising position with the help."

"Oh." Jenna pursed her lips.

"These things happen. Speaking of." Oswen handed her the next pile of dossiers.

"These are on the Navarros, who will be here for dinner." He patted her on the shoulder. "I'll leave you to it. Come see me with questions."

As he walked off, Jenna stared down at the next pile and groaned.

Jenna quietly entered the circular room at the Sandoval estate, where she and Kal had been meeting. The room had large windows on one side. Lavender plants, used to reduce inflammation, sat in front of each window, soaking in the sunlight. Kal sat on one of the curved seats that surrounded the room.

Kal didn't move, so she took some time to study him. His eyes were closed, and the feel of magic emanated from him. His brow creased in concentration, and shadows clung to his eyes as if he hadn't slept well.

Concern swelled inside her. She concentrated on their bond, and in a rare unguarded moment, could feel the weight of his burdens. His nites attacking her had taught her that Kal was a deeply conflicted man. He was ruthless in his own way, but he had a good heart. She knew from the binding oath he couldn't abide killing unless it was a last resort, and even then, it weighed on him. He didn't have a large family, but once he accepted someone, he would do what he could to take care of them as though they were family.

Jenna watched Kal's chest move with his breathing and fought off the urge to touch him, lips pursing with the struggle. She didn't know when it had started, but he was never far from her thoughts. At first, Jenna thought it was the nites eating away at her shields, but at this moment, as she watched the sunlight dance across his features, causing her breath to quicken, she could admit it was something else. She reached into her bag and drew out the sweets she had brought for him. He would grumble that they weren't necessary, but she knew from the nites that he enjoyed them, especially when stressed. It was all she could do for him, these little tokens. Carefully, she arranged them on the large round table in front of him. When she finished, she glanced up at him to find him staring at her.

She smiled to hide her surprise.

"I've brought you some meringues." She gestured at the table.

"You really shouldn't have," he grumbled.

This time, she hid her smile. "You will try one, won't you?"

Kal sighed deeply and leaned forward to take one.

"What would you have me do today?" she queried.

"Learn," he said. "You've clearly been practicing, since I didn't notice you when you entered. You've been suppressing your magic when you're not using it?"

Jenna smiled. "I have."

"Good, that will make it harder for other mages to identify you. Now, see if you can match me. I'll wear a persona for five seconds. You replicate it. Then, I'll switch to the next one."

Her smile faltered.

"You need to be able to pick a face out of the crowd and duplicate it at a moment's notice. Let's begin."

Sweat trickled down Jenna's back as she concentrated. They had been practicing for what felt like hours. As quickly as she could, she painted a picture with her magic, tilting eyes, adjusting skin tone, and filling or thinning lips. As soon as she had a viable semblance, Kal would shift to a new face. She couldn't believe the number of faces he had on reserve.

Jenna's shoulders sagged and her concentration was lagging, causing the Seeming Kal wore to frown.

"Enough." Kal's face became his own.

She breathed out a sigh, releasing her hold on the Seeming.

"Good job. Now let's talk about dealing with unexpected situations."

She nodded.

"What do you do if someone catches you listening outside a door?"

"Give them a lie mixed with truth."

"For example?" Kal ate a meringue.

"Tell them I was passing by but couldn't help overhearing, then give them a misunderstood version of what they were talking about so they think I didn't hear them."

Kal grunted. "Okay, how do you know when you should act or retreat?"

"If you believe you can get away unnoticed or with little trouble, then proceed, but the second your retreat can be blocked, step away. Better to leave early than never leave."

"Good." The questions continued, and she answered them to the best of her ability.

When Kal finally wound down, she noticed the shadows under his eyes were even more pronounced.

"Kal?" she prompted, eying him critically.

"Yes?"

"Get some sleep."

She could tell he wanted to argue, but a jaw-cracking yawn took over. He chuckled, took another meringue, and stood up. "We will meet here again tomorrow at the same time."

"Okay." She nodded.

"What's the number one rule?" he asked.

She grinned at him. "Don't give yourself away. Remember your training."

With a nod, Kal took her hand and kissed it. "Good night, Jenna." Then he strode out of the room.

Chapter 27

Andrade Ball

Several weeks passed and Jenna had been presented to all the major houses. Under her grandfather's direction, she had more or less memorized the dossiers on all the key players and had met with Arianna several times. Jenna liked how uncomplicated Arianna was. She also had an infectious laugh. She was the first person in a long time that Jenna thought could be a true friend.

Tonight was her first big outing. The Andrade's had invited her to a formal ball at their estate in the city's Noble Quarter. This ball was a prelude to the upcoming King's Vow holiday. All the significant houses would be present, as well as some portion of the minor noble houses, mages of various standings, guild leaders, and notable artisans affiliated with the Andrade house.

Kal, who would not be attending, had given her a task for the ball. Use her newfound skills to learn something new about the Andrade family—something not in the dossiers.

Jenna stared at herself in the mirror. Her maid fussed with the hem of her floor-length dress, which was a shimmering house green mixed with silver to denote nobility.

"Back straight, milady."

Jenna straightened, then blushed a bit at how its V-shaped bodice, done entirely in silver, fit her, and how her months in training made her look in her off-the-shoulders sleeves.

The maid pulled out a pair of matching green gloves with silver stitching.

Jenna shook her head, and the maid put the gloves back, then scrutinized her. "I suppose with all the brocade and jewels stitched into the dress, you don't really need the gloves, but your neck can't be bare."

The maid went to the jewelry box and pulled out the necklace her grandfather had given her for tonight. Its diamonds, separated with silver leaves, glinted in the late afternoon sun.

Jenna shifted her silver-slippered feet, bending slightly to allow the maid access as she secured the necklace around her throat. The maid stepped away, and Jenna studied her reflection once more.

Her hair was pulled up and away from her face in an artistic bun with glass beads spread throughout her hair. Tear-shaped crystals of house green hung from her ears, backed with silver links. In front of her bun was a small diadem encrusted with clear gems arching up to a little peak that encompassed an emerald gem.

"Milady, are you sure you know what to do?"

In response, Jenna sent a small burst of magic into the dress. The beadwork on the dress, diadem, and necklace lit up. They twinkled lightly, calling attention to the shape of her waist, the upper sleeves, the dip of her bodice, as well as the diadem on her head. Each was made of Galatian glass, which held magical charges.

Jenna reached up and the maid gently grabbed her hand. "You'll smear your makeup," she said, then quickly let go, as if she had broken a rule in touching her.

Jenna glanced back in the mirror. Her makeup was done in a clean, almost nonexistent way, but it brought out the depth of her eyes, sculpted her jaw into a thing of beauty, and enhanced her lips. No matter what angle she turned to view herself, the person in the mirror was someone else.

"Thank you. You are dismissed," Jenna said, self-conscious of the words. She watched the maid's retreating back. A few months ago, that could have been her. Now, she was Lady Sandoval.

Jenna suppressed a shudder as she fidgeted with one of the beads. She withdrew the magic charge, and the shimmering effect was reduced to refracted light, catching only at the right angles. She closed her eyes and reminded herself that she was more than this image in the mirror. Even with its constraints, it would be so easy to fall in love with being a noble. She had been too nervous to eat, and her stomach ached. She still didn't know where she fit in this new world. A dress and jewels didn't change who she was.

She breathed out, thinking of her sister held captive somewhere, of Justin, away on assignment, and of Kal, who had spent just as much time with her as her grandfather training her. Tonight was her first solo mission. All that studying, practicing, and primping would be brought to bear at this event to find clues about the missing children. Jenna took a deep breath, exhaled, and left the room. The scent of lilies wafted behind her.

Jenna took a deep breath and descended the stairs.

"You look lovely," said Lord Sandoval.

"Thank you, Grandfather, as do you."

He wore a formal black suit and a shirt in forest green with silver leaves embossed into the coat sleeves. His hair, thinning as it was, was drawn back away from his face. On his right hand, he wore an ornate emerald ring encased in burnished silver. The ring radiated magic. Nestled in his left hand was the hilt of a cane. She had never seen him use one, so she was sure it was for show. The grip was of a shiny black material shot through with green and silver.

"Come. This way," he said, leading her out the door and to the stagecoach.

Jenna stared into the open door of the ornately decorated carriage. The base color was a deep forest green, overlaid with silvery-white leaves. Tentatively, Jenna stepped into the carriage.

The interior was plush. The green motif went up the walls, but the ceiling was covered entirely in a gossamer silver material that gave off light. Jenna sat on one of the benches, spreading her dress artfully around her. Lord Sandoval followed her into the carriage. After he settled in, he pulled a lever, and the carriage began to move.

Jenna stared out the window as they trundled through the city. They didn't have far to go, as all the notable families had a place in the Noble Quarter. Still, she enjoyed people watching. The crowd was thicker than she expected. Clumps of pedestrians with signs silently watched the carriage go by. One read *Where are our children?* A lump formed in Jenna's throat as she thought of Casi. Another sign read *How long do we have to wait?* She wasn't the only one suffering. These people must be the family and friends of the missing. If they couldn't find the children soon, more people would join them. Eventually, they would take action. Kal owned the missing children's search, so he was at the center of this.

Determination flowed through her. She would do her best not to let them down.

Their carriage joined the queue as they arrived at their destination. Jenna glanced at her grandfather and found him watching her with a slight smile on his face.

"What?" she said.

"You remind me of your mother at this age." Her grandfather's voice was soft and nostalgic.

"Do you think..." She trailed off, unable to complete the question.

The Lord of the Sandoval estate smiled at her and said, "I do. Your mother would be very proud of you."

Jenna's eyes misted over, and Oswen leaned forward and patted her hand. "Just promise me one thing," he said, brow bunched.

She stared up at him. "What?"

"Be careful tonight. You're a quick study, and I've given you the most current information I could gather." He paused. "But not everyone is who they seem."

She considered and nodded. She would accomplish her task.

"I will be careful." She wasn't sure what Oswen saw in her expression, but he nodded and settled back into his seat, staring out the window as they made their way to the grand carriage entrance.

The carriage door opened and her grandfather, as Lord, exited the carriage first. A slight breeze entered the carriage, bringing with it the smell of artisan foods; the soft trill of music flowed in the distance. Jenna rose and, as majestically as she could, descended the carriage steps, hand resting on the carriage man's outstretched arm to steady her. When she reached the bottom, she hooked her arm around her grandfather's, straightened her back, and they walked the short, carpeted path into the Andrade estate.

Jenna had visited Arianna here before, so she had seen some of the main floor. Evergreens and an array of red camellias decorated the entryway. To one side of the entrance, people stood, glasses clinking, and there was laughter. A wide staircase led up from the main entrance and split, looping back to give access to either side of the upstairs hall. A young page dressed all in black with a ruby red overcoat denoting House Andrade bowed to them.

"This way, my lord." He turned to Jenna. "My lady."

They followed him to the left of the stairs, through a set of doors that opened into a large mahogany-paneled receiving room with red carpeting.

In the room was the entire Andrade family, lined up in reverse order of ranking to greet the guests. Each member of the family wore some variation of house red, mixed with black and silver. Arianna was in line with her brother Victor and a young man Jenna had not met before.

Jenna's grandfather greeted Arianna. Arianna was elegant in a split floor-length burgundy satin gown. Unlike Jenna, Arianna had chosen to wear gloves, which were also red satin. Her hair was upswept on one side and held in place by a silver hair comb encrusted with pearls and rubies. The rest of her hair fell in loose spirals, covering her shoulders and flowing down the middle of her back. The burgundy of her lips made her appear more mature. To Jenna, Arianna was beautiful. It must have shown in her eyes, because Arianna leaned forward and hugged Jenna as Lord Sandoval continued down the line.

"You look beautiful," Arianna said, still hugging her.

"So do you," Jenna said. They separated, and the young man standing on Arianna's left nudged her. Arianna flashed him a quick grin.

"Lady Jenna Sandoval, this is my cousin, Beltran Andrade."

Beltran was slightly taller than Jenna, but appeared younger. Arianna had mentioned to Jenna that her cousin would be arriving. His adoption into the house was forthcoming. Beltran stared at her wide-eyed and kissed the back of her hand. Jenna blushed at the expression in his eyes. She was relieved when the next person came up, allowing her to remove her hand and move to the next person in line.

Jenna came face to face with Arianna's brother, Victor. He resembled Arianna, but where Arianna was sleek, Victor was elegant. There were dark circles under his eyes. Maybe his maid troubles were still going on. Victor kissed the back of her hand. "Arianna has come out of her shell since meeting you."

"She's a wonderful person, and I'm lucky to have met her."

Some warmth trickled into his eyes, and he gave her a genuine smile before returning her hand. Jenna continued up the line and came face to face with Cornelius Andrade, heir presumptive of House Andrade.

Cornelius was short and wiry. He was handsome in his house colors and stood at ease amid the crowd. However, when their eyes met, a cold chill ran down her spine. There was no smile in his eyes. So, he hadn't liked being ignored.

He took her hand, holding it too tightly.

"You are becoming quite close with Arianna?"

Jenna didn't like the way he said her name.

"I am," she said, not wanting to give him more than that.

"How are you finding House Sandoval?" he sneered.

"Delightful." Again, she kept it short, not giving him anything to take offense at. He stared at her a moment longer before lightly brushing the back of her hand with his lips. Jenna suppressed a chill and moved on to Lady Vivianne Andrade.

Lady Vivianne was a short woman with sharp eyes and a harsh cast to her mouth. Her hair, pulled away from her face, was shown off by a diadem encrusted with rubies. She studied Jenna as if sizing her up for an auction before greeting her.

"Welcome to House Andrade, daughter of Abigail." The greeting surprised Jenna. This woman knew her mother, but she wasn't sure if that was a good thing or not.

Jenna curtsied. "Thank you, Lady Andrade." After a brief pause, she added, "You knew my mother? Were you friends?"

Lady Vivianne studied Jenna a moment too long. "No."

Jenna flushed uncomfortably. "I-I see." Unsure of how to recover from that, Jenna curtsied and moved on to Lord Erick Andrade, head of House Andrade.

Lord Andrade was of average height, with some gray showing at the temples. His formalwear accentuated his athletic build, and his dossier said he liked dueling. Most houses sponsored fighters for the arena, including House Sandoval, but few were willing to put themselves in harm's way. Lord Andrade was an exception and had made quite a name for himself.

"Lady Jenna," he greeted her, eyes roving over her flushed face.

"Lord Andrade," she managed to say.

He took her hand. "You truly are her daughter." A sad smile played over his face. "Your mother has been missed. I was sorry to learn of your loss."

His words were heartfelt, but she questioned the way he said "your loss." Jenna relaxed a bit and was about to reply when she sensed the stare. She bowed her head, glancing to her left to take in the flare of emotion on Lady Vivianne's face.

Hmm, I need to discuss those dossiers with grandfather.

Jenna's eyes went back to Lord Andrade, who was either pointedly ignoring his wife's stare or was unaware of her stance on the matter.

Jenna smiled awkwardly. "Thank you, Lord Andrade. That is very kind of you."

He nodded, releasing her hand. "Please be welcome in our home."

"Thank you."

Jenna moved away from the receiving line, trying not to run. She walked toward the doorway leading out of the reception hall, where her grandfather waited.

Jenna gave her grandfather a sidelong expression, and he smiled knowingly at her as she nestled her arm back through his.

"Grandfather?" Jenna asked with an edge.

"Yes?" he smirked.

"About those dossiers."

"Um-hum," he replied.

"There seems to be a few things missing." Jenna briefly wondered if this satisfied Kal's requirements, but decided not.

Lord Sandoval patted the back of her hand while another page motioned them forward.

"Some things are best learned on one's own," he said as they walked through the doorway.

Jenna opened her mouth to make a retort, but snapped it shut. Jenna and her grandfather were standing at the grand entrance to the ballroom. The room was two stories. Many windows and balconies lined the upper walls, which would have brought in bright light during the day, but for this evening event, a series of enormous chandeliers powered by magic globes were alight. Dispersed around the room were red-clothed tables as well as green swags at the base of the window frames, denoting the coming holiday. High tables for standing were off to the sides with votive candles, and the back of the room held large tables covered in foods of all types. Not only was the room full of people, but all of them had stopped talking, their eyes on them. On her left, the master of ceremonies called out, "Lord Oswen Sandoval and Lady Jenna Sandoval."

Jenna shot a quick glare at her grandfather, who had a broad, proud smile on his face. She plastered on a smile of her own and sent a small flare of magic into her dress, setting it aglow as they walked into a sea of waiting nobles.

Chapter 28

Tour

"Can you not control yourself?" The harshness of the voice made Jenna turn her head. She was on her way to the terrace, weaving through the crowds of people talking around tables filled with finger foods. The ball was in full swing, and the main floor was full of people dancing to the orchestra. Jenna had dodged no less than three well-meaning attempts by lesser nobles to ensnare her in a conversation her grandfather had encouraged her to avoid.

Jenna spotted Lady Arianna speaking with a group of young men at the arched entrance. As she passed through the crowd, she overheard parts of many conversations, but this one made her pause and listen.

"I endeavor to do better," came a soft reply.

"That's what you always say. I want results, not pretty words." Her ears focused on the sharp voice of an older man.

"Yes, Father."

"You're useless."

Jenna flinched. The ball was loud, but people nearby were shifting uncomfortably at the too loud words. She moved closer to put faces to the speakers. It was Lord Navarro and his second son, Darren. Darren stood just over six feet in height. He was handsome, with well-crafted features made more alluring by the natural darkening of one who exercises in the sun. Darren was a few years older than Jenna, and his dossier said he had ambition. When Jenna met him during her string of introductory dinners, he had been quiet and reserved. Jenna changed course and came up beside Darren.

She casually wove her arm through Darren's, hand brushing lightly against his.

"Lord Navarro," she said with her brightest smile.

Lord Navarro's eyes darted back and forth between Jenna and Darren as a faint smile appeared on his face.

"Lady Sandoval." Lord Navarro nodded to her.

She turned to gaze up at Darren, who was staring at her as if seeing something else entirely. "I believe you owe me a dance."

Darren stammered as Jenna pulled him away from his father through the crowd and onto the dance floor. He bit his lip in concentration as their hands met and parted in the dance. Once they had the rhythm of it, he said, "Thank you."

"You're welcome. Are you okay? You had a strange expression on your face when I first looked at you."

His eyes went distant again, and he lost the flow of the dance. Jenna covered for him.

"Sorry. You just startled me."

"I didn't mean to intrude. I just thought you might have wanted to escape for a bit."

Darren gave her a lopsided grin. "I very much wanted that."

Jenna smiled back. When the dance ended, they left the floor on the opposite side from his father and walked right into a small mob of girls who surrounded Darren, neatly cutting Jenna out.

"Darren, you never dance. I want to dance with you, too," said one, clearly pouting. There were similar remarks from the other girls. Darren's eyes pleaded with her, but Jenna smiled and shook her head. Seeing he wasn't in any real danger, she left him to the dance and moved through an arched doorway onto the terrace.

A cool breeze washed over Jenna, pulling a sigh of contentment from her. Her hands rested on the railing of the balcony. She listened to the music playing behind her as she stretched her neck upward to expose more of her skin to the breeze. A frown crossed her face. She had enjoyed the whirlwind of introductions, the quick exchange of dancing partners, and the food. Several of her dancing partners would make advantageous alliances. That wasn't what made her frown. An image of Kal, brow wrinkled in frustration, kept popping into her mind. He was nearby. Jenna sighed. Because what she wanted was to dance with him. She imagined the grip of his hands as he held her and the twirling of skirts as they spun. *Enough of that,* she thought.

She considered her training on infiltration and of the Andrade estate. Jenna was sure answers about the missing children were somewhere. She just needed the time and opportunity. Jenna paused as she sensed someone else step onto the balcony behind her.

"L-Lady Sandoval?" a familiar voice asked hesitantly. Jenna opened her eyes and turned, her dress swishing. In front of her stood Arianna's cousin, Beltran.

Since he had been formal, she chose to follow suit.

"Lord Andrade."

He flushed a bit, raising his hands. "Please call me Beltran. This whole lord thing is a bit strange."

Jenna smiled at him. "I know the feeling. When did you arrive?"

"Yesterday. I heard you are new to this as well." Beltran's voice trailed off. She nodded, so he continued. "They weren't going to let me attend, but Arianna said she would keep watch over me."

Jenna leaned to one side to glance behind him and arched an eyebrow. "I don't see Arianna."

He smiled, eyes twinkling as she righted herself. "Would you like to dance?"

An image of Kal flashed in her mind and she grimaced. Seeing her expression, he plunged ahead.

"Or we could just take a walk. Have you ever had a tour?"

Over the last few weeks, Jenna had spent time with Arianna, becoming familiar with some of the house. She hadn't toured it all. Besides, she needed to search for clues. "I have not."

He smiled, then, surprising her, he gave a decent courtly bow and asked, "Would milady accompany me on a tour of the house?"

Jenna smiled and curtsied. "I would be delighted, my lord."

They both giggled. Hesitantly, Beltran extended his arm, and Jenna stepped forward and took it.

Beltran led Jenna back through the ballroom and into the reception room. He led her to the right, and they stopped at the first set of wide-open doors.

"This is the drawing room," he said, leading her in. It was large and beautifully decorated, with statues and paintings spread artfully throughout. The room had a massive fireplace on the right with a large picture above it, showing men fighting in the arena. A few people milled about, talking and lounging on or around various sofas and chairs. Serving staff went through with hors d'oeuvres and drinks. The people in this room were older than the ballroom crowd. In the far corner, her grandfather spoke with the newest Lord Deleon.

Beltran brought her further into the drawing room toward the left, where a set of double doors stood open. Jenna overheard the conversation next to them.

"I hear the king's brother has returned to court."

"You mean the King Killer?" a stern voice replied.

"He was cleared of that," the first voice said.

"Then why was he gone for so long?"

"Who knows? Will he be joining us tonight?"

"This is the conservatory," Beltran said, drawing Jenna's attention back to him. She ground her teeth as she forced herself to move away and followed Beltran's gesture. Jenna drew in a quick breath and found herself practically pulling Beltran through the doors. Glass made up most of the far wall. The sun had set, and the light from the stars peeked through. Plants with red flowers hung throughout the room. Jenna contemplated Sandoval's house green, racking her brain for flowers that would work for their conservatory. The last gardener to care for it had died in the blight, and almost all the plants in their conservatory and garden were medicinal. Her fingers twitched, thinking of the soil. Beltran stared at her.

"You like flowers?" He smiled at her.

"Is it that obvious?" Jenna said, blushing.

"Only a little. Would you like to stay longer?"

She stared back out the windows into the red flower-filled garden beyond, then around the room at the people having intimate conversations in the internal garden, and sighed.

"Let's continue."

Beltran led her down the hall to a room with two large doors. He pushed the doors open to reveal wall-to-wall books. This room was decorated in dark brown wood and had a spiral staircase leading to a second level. Reading chairs and lamps were spread throughout the space. A large table with religious inlays in the shape of a triangle took up space near the stairs.

This time, she managed to keep her face in check, though she did reach out and brush her hand against the volumes closest to her, which appeared to be on structural reinforcements. The Sandoval estate also had a massive library that skewed heavily toward medicines, treatments, and historical battles.

Beltran led her past several alcoves, through the dining room with its crystal candelabra, and into the breakfast room. Though similar in size to the breakfast room at the Sandoval estate, it had a different feel with its antique tables and floral-patterned chairs done in Andrade house colors.

Beltran didn't take her down into the kitchen and serving areas, but up a servant's staircase. They stopped on the second floor while the stairs continued upward. She recognized where they were when they opened the door and stepped into the hall. Across the passage was Victor's room, and Arianna's apartment was just beyond it. He led her across the hall to Victor's room, where the door was ajar.

"Victor?" Beltran knocked.

The door swung open, and the sitting portion of the room became visible. A servant's overdress and hair cap lay draped on the far chair. Apparently, his maid troubles *were* still ongoing.

"We should skip this room," she said.

"This room has some of the best views of the city at night, but it's not like him to leave his door open. Maybe he went to the sitting room. Let's go look there."

He pointed out Arianna's room on the way to the doorway of his room, which was at the top of the grand staircase leading down into the foyer. Jenna did not go inside but complimented him on the four-poster bed, which seemed to make him happy. They continued to the sitting room.

Like the drawing room, it was full of comfortable couches and chairs. Unlike the drawing room, it was empty. It had big stained-glass windows and stairs that led to what must have been small, comfortable nooks. This room had paintings of Lord and Lady Andrade and several of the Lord Heir Cornelius. It also had an enormous sculpture with three sides. Each side represented a different person. One was a warrior, one was a woman holding scales, and the third was a man holding a book. The plaque on the bottom said 'The Three' with a small triangular symbol after it. After she studied the sculpture, Beltran brought her out and to the other wing. They did not enter the rooms, but he pointed out which room belonged to Cornelius and which to the Lord and Lady of House Andrade.

"This door leads to the servant's corridor. It connects the Lord's rooms directly to the sitting room and his inner sanctum."

"Is this the only entrance?" Jenna asked, trying to be casual.

"Oh, you can also reach it through the Lord's chambers."

"The servant's stairs we came up looked to keep going. Is there another floor above this one?"

Beltran's eyes widened. "No, there is no third floor."

Jenna furrowed her brow, clearly recalling the stairs, but said nothing.

"Come on, let's head back toward the sitting room," Beltran said, raising his arm.

She wrapped her arm through his, and he led her down the hall. When they reached the end, a loud voice came from one of the rooms.

"You will do what I tell you, or I will make her life a living hell."

Jenna couldn't make out the response.

Beltran frowned.

"Cornelius and Victor are at it again. Let me escort you back to the ball." He started to lead her to the grand staircase when there was a crashing noise. Their eyes met.

"On second thought, please go on without me. I will find you later." He turned and hurried off to Cornelius's room.

Jenna entered the sitting room, but instead of going down the main staircase, she turned and went back down the hall. She quietly entered Victor's bedchamber and took the maid's clothing. Jenna pulled the magic from her dress, and its twinkle stopped. She pulled the overdress on top of her clothes and went to the mirror.

The overdress bulged with her clothes underneath it. *It will have to do.*

Jenna carefully fitted the cap over her upswept hair and removed her earrings, putting them in a small hidden pocket of her dress. Then, as Kal taught her, she began adding illusions on top of herself. Jenna became older. Wearing two dresses covered her figure, so she enhanced it to make her shape more matronly.

The front of her gown peeked out around the overdress, so she changed its colors and texture to match house colors. Jenna couldn't quite get the sleeves to match, so she tucked them under the overdress and added another layer of illusion around her arms. That illusion wouldn't move like the rest of her dress, but it would have to do. Checking herself over one last time, she turned to leave. A bottle of wine and two glasses caught her eye. She picked up the bottle, holding it like she was delivering it and left the room.

Jenna headed for the servant's staircase. There was indeed a staircase leading up to a third floor. She made her way up the stairs and came to a door. Leaning forward, she listened for a moment, hearing nothing. She straightened her posture and opened the door. Jenna entered a long hallway, which she presumed mirrored the floor below. She turned left and headed toward the location above Lord Andrade's rooms.

Jenna found the door that should be over the servant's hall. Light seeped from under the door, but she heard no sounds. Quietly, she opened the door. No one was in the room.

The room held shelves filled with books and a large desk with a chair. Logs burned in a small fireplace. A red banner hung on the wall with the same triangular symbol from the statue, with what appeared to be a sword emerging from the center.

Holding the wine in front of her like a shield, she entered and moved toward a side table near a door on the far side of the room. As she got closer to the door, she could hear muffled voices.

"Where is he now?" asked a low, gravelly voice. She didn't recognize it.

"Unknown. He is no longer at Lily's Inn," said a self-assured voice.

"What about the agreements?" the gravelly voice asked.

"I have drawn up documents and all parties have signed. The latest caravan came through without a hitch," said the self-assured voice.

Jenna heard shuffling noises.

"Jaxson, here is your copy of the documents," said the self-assured voice.

She heard crinkling noises as Jaxson presumably put away the documents.

"What of the king?" This voice she recognized as Lord Andrade's.

Jenna leaned closer.

"Leave him be," said the gravelly voice. "Nothing he does will change the outcome."

"I suppose you're right," Lord Andrade agreed, sounding relieved.

"Now, onto current business," said the gravelly voice. "I have need of the Inanis rod."

"The rod of The Three?" asked Lord Andrade.

"If that is what you call it now," said the gravelly voice.

"Why do you want the rod?" Andrade asked.

"I am a collector of rare artifacts, and I wish to add it to my collection," said the gravelly voice.

"If you collect artifacts, you should see the box they keep it in. It's exquisite," said Andrade.

"Is it?" said the gravelly voice.

"It is. Which rod are you looking for? There are two rods that I am aware of. The original is kept by the Church of The Three and the copy by the mages."

"What are they used for?" asked the self-assured voice.

"Their true purpose is lost to history, but there are ancient texts available to those who donate generously to the church which say The Three used them to travel worlds."

"That makes them even more valuable to a collector like myself. I require an introduction to a church member and mage that has access to their rods," said the gravelly voice.

"I can arrange a meeting, but I don't think either of them will part with the rods," said Lord Andrade.

The fire made a loud pop, causing Jenna to jerk silently. Deciding that was her cue, she turned and hurried away from the door, still holding the bottle of wine. Quietly, she let herself out of the room and walked quickly back down the hall and into the stairwell. She rested her back against the door briefly before going down the stairs. When she reached the bottom, a man dressed in servant's garb greeted her.

Jenna froze. She tried to speak, but her throat went dry. She opened her mouth, but the man spoke first.

"Hurry, Jenna." He gestured to the doorway leading to the hall. "When you opened the upstairs door, you set off the alarms. I am suppressing it, but I don't know how much longer I can hold them off."

Jenna's eyes widened. The voice coming out of the male servant was Kal's. Jenna ran to the door and yanked it open. She peered down the hall. Seeing no one, she walked to Victor's room and heard the hall door close behind her.

She reached for the handle, but the door was no longer open. She put her hand on the knob and turned. It was locked. Jenna started to panic. She turned back towards the entryway, realizing Kal would be of no help. She closed her eyes and considered the servants at House Sandoval. They didn't all carry around a key; those were stored at specific locations. Jenna opened her eyes and went back to the door. Searching the frame, she found an enclosure. On the right side was an alcove. *What if it's locked?* Sweat beaded her brow. Jenna placed her hand on the alcove door, and two small threads of magic reached out to her cap and overdress. It must have found what it wanted, because the alcove opened. Jenna sighed with relief as she extracted the key.

She returned to Victor's room and let herself in.

She heard no sounds. Jenna hoped Victor wasn't in the bedchamber. She did a quick scan, not seeing him, then went into the changing area.

Jenna returned the overdress and cap to the chair, then removed the layers of illusion. She dug her earrings out of her pocket and put them on. Jenna did not charge her dress, as she didn't want to do any magic near the stairwell.

She hurried back to the door and opened it, only to see Lord Darren Navarro, second heir of House Navarro, who was mid-knock.

Covering her surprise, she recalled where she was and spoke first to divert attention.

"Lord Navarro, what brings you here?" She arched her brow in an attempt to take control of the situation. He blushed and stammered.

"I thought I felt something."

He turned toward the servant's stairs. Jenna stepped out of the room and shut the door behind her, hearing the lock click. She still had the key.

"Felt what?" she asked while walking toward the stairs.

She reached for the servant's door handle with her left hand to hide her rehanging of the key with her right. Just as she congratulated herself on rehanging the key and closing the alcove, Darren yanked her around, bringing her face-to-face with him.

"I'm sorry. Forgive me," he said, releasing her. "I just, well, please don't open that stairwell door." His voice hitched, and his skin was pale.

Jenna had no intention of opening that door. She glanced up at Darren, who was standing very close. Using the barest hint of her magic, she viewed him, and her eyes widened at the incandescent purple light she saw around him. She'd learned about that shade of light in school, when they had lectured on people who could read emotions.

"You're a Sensitive."

His embarrassment turned into a frown, but he nodded. "I am, and whatever is going on in that stairwell, someone wants you far away from it."

Jenna turned back towards the door, fear building up in her for Kal.

Unconsciously, she reached for the handle, but again, Darren reached out and grabbed her arm.

She stared at him. His face held an expression of pain. "Please."

She checked the bond with Kal, and he was deep in concentration but fine. So she nodded.

Darren practically dragged her down the hall. When they reached the sitting room area, she yanked her hand from his and sent a brief trickle of magic into the dress, causing it to twinkle to remind him of who and what he was dealing with.

Even with the reminder, he seemed like he would reach out for her hand again, and Jenna recalled that Sensitives were sometimes controlled by what they perceived. If the emotion was strong enough, they would act. They sometimes read truths and lies, and because of this, they tended to have judicial jobs. Unfortunately, they didn't always have control over their powers.

One thing she recalled was that contact enhanced it. She had brushed against him, if only briefly, then they had danced. She reflected on the odd expression on his face, curious what compelled him to come for her.

"This is why you struggled during the dance. How many people know you are a Sensitive?" she asked.

Darren ground his teeth. "Few, and I would like to keep it that way, my lady."

She considered what the dossiers said about him: humanitarian, sportsman, a staunch supporter of his family, and a royalist.

"What brought you up here?" she asked, unable to keep the tension out of her voice.

He chewed his lip, then shrugged. "Since we recently touched, I'm keyed to you. I sensed your alarm. So, I came to see if you were okay."

Tension eased from her shoulders at the sincerity she read on his face. *How noble*, she thought, studying him. "Thank you."

"You're welcome," he said, shoulders still tense.

He thinks I'll tell, she thought.

"I will keep your secret, but in exchange, if someone asks, you found me here, at the top of the stairs. Deal?"

He glanced down the hall as if realizing where they were and whose room she had exited. The sudden realization hit him as he made a false assumption, but an assumption any woman of standing would not want public.

The tension left his shoulders, making her aware of his answer before he said it.

"Deal."

Jenna held out her arm. "Walk with me, Lord Navarro."

He reached out his arm, and she took it, careful to avoid his skin. They descended the stairs into the grand foyer and returned to the ball, folding seamlessly into the dance.

Chapter 29

Outcome

J enna rose as a knock sounded on the door of her bedroom. A half candle mark had passed since her grandfather had brought her home from the ball. She opened the door to find Kal standing outside. He still had on the manservant's clothes from the Andrade estate, but his face was his own. She had long since changed into more comfortable clothing.

"You're safe." His statement was one of relief.

"I am. Come in," Jenna said, opening the door for him.

Kal entered, and she ushered him over to a chair. Dark circles marred the skin beneath his eyes, and he sat with a heavy sigh. She poured him a glass of water from the pitcher on her sideboard.

"Drink this," she said, offering it to him.

Kal took the glass, gratefully gulping the liquid. She took the glass back from him and refilled it. When she returned, he was staring at her strangely. Jenna put the glass on the table next to him, sure he would lecture her about being more careful. "When you looked at the servant's stairs, what did you see?"

She shrugged, eyebrows rising involuntarily. "Stairs just like the ones going down. It's funny, though, Beltran seemed to think there were no stairs at all."

"That is what you should have seen also. Were you wearing any heirloom jewelry or something your grandfather gave you?"

She gestured toward her makeup table, and he glanced over at it. He pulled himself up off the chair and went over to the table, picking up the diadem she had worn in her hair.

"This is likely the reason. It has enhancements to cut through magic."

He gently placed it back on the table and returned to his seat.

"Where did you get your clothes?" he asked.

She pursed her lips.

"I borrowed them from Victor's room."

Kal leaned forward. "Did anyone see you?"

"Darren Navarro, but he will keep my secret." He frowned, and she continued. "He and I have made a mutual arrangement."

Kal's frown deepened.

She held up her hands. "I can't go into it, but it will hold."

He nodded. "What did you see up there?"

Jenna told him of the room and what she overheard through the door.

Kal went silent, thinking.

"Kal?"

"Hmm."

"Are you still staying at Lily's Inn?"

His eyes captured hers for a long moment. "No."

Jenna started to pace, nostrils flaring as she reflected on the attack on Kal the night she removed the maghin from his back.

Kal reached out and grabbed her hand, stopping her. She stared down at him, and a twinge of desire rolled through her as her anger drained away. She didn't know what he saw in her, but he opened his mouth and then closed it. His hand fell away from hers, and she missed its presence. Kal stood. She had not moved, so he was close, staring down into her eyes. Jenna was breathless as he reached up and pushed a wayward strand of her hair aside.

"You did well tonight, Jenna. I'm glad you're okay. Did you have fun at the ball?" he asked, voice slightly husky.

Jenna considered what she'd enjoyed about the ball. It had been fun, but when she stared at him, what she actually wanted was to wrap her arms around him. Jenna shuddered, restraining the urge. "Yes," she said in a breathy voice.

Kal nodded and turned towards the door. Panicked that he was leaving, Jenna blurted, "There was one thing I didn't get to do."

Kal turned back to her.

She bowed her head, unable to meet his eyes, and moved her body into a dance pose only used when the women formally invited the men to dance.

Kal did not move, so Jenna waited. Still, he didn't move. She was about to glance up at him when the sound of his steps came to her. He passed her, pushing the chair out of the way, and returned, taking up the stance of acceptance. Jenna wasn't sure how long they danced, but it was long enough for the stiff formality to wear off. Warmth suffused their bodies as they moved, filling her with a sense of joy. The same joy she had felt before moving into the Sandoval estate. Even Kal relaxed enough to give a small smile. Their bodies moved in a fluid motion, sending a wave of warmth through her. Jenna smiled brightly, and Kal's hand twitched. The dance moved on. When it ended, they were both winded. Kal gave her a perfect bow and left.

K al added a Seeming to his features before leaving the Sandoval estate. He was always careful to conceal his true face and height when he went out.

His body was flushed with heat from the dance with Jenna, and he restrained the faint smile that threatened to emerge. He'd come so close to saying no to the dance, but he'd seen her on the dance floor and had wanted to dance with her all night. He was her teacher and mentor. His job was to keep her safe and nurture her, not to dance with her. Kal sighed. He didn't even know why she was on his mind when he had so much to do.

He climbed into his carriage and set off for the palace, and his mind shifted toward his brother. So far, the king recognized him more often than not. He was sure to hand in a false report when he didn't. His brows furrowed as he thought of the ramifications of the king having a split personality. Everyone around Corin walked on eggshells, wondering which king they would get. His jaw opened wide as a yawn overtook him.

He rubbed his eyes. At least information from his spy network was flowing. After tonight, he would recruit more people at the Andrade estate. He wished Jenna had recognized the two other voices in the room. He knew there would be more than one house behind such a large operation. Whoever it was had done an excellent job of remaining discreet. He spent all his time tonight dealing with the magical alarms at the estate. When he finally escaped, the lead servant cornered him and lectured for being late, so he couldn't watch the stairs to see who descended.

The carriage hit a rut in the road, and his mind shifted again. *How was Justin doing?* He should be settling into the guard by now with Lieutenant Doha. He didn't know what Roolia had done, but Abasi had reassigned Doha back to his regular duties. When he asked Roolia about it, she chittered with laughter. Captain Abasi had gone tight-lipped and a little gray. Kal rubbed his temples. He needed more sleep. Wearing a Seeming was second nature to him, but adding the net to it drained him. More nites were not always available. His stomach rumbled. Fortunately, there was always something available to eat at the palace. The carriage rolled onward.

Kal arrived at the palace and went up to his rooms. He removed letters from his box and read through reports from his Shadow Weavers. They found nothing at the docks. He wrote letters for the coming days to make sure they would be near the Inanis rods mentioned by Jenna. A yawn rippled through him, turning into a stretch. As tired as he was, he wasn't ready to sleep yet. The children were still missing. Kal rummaged through his outstanding items and found the package from Master Harram on the caverns.

He grinned as he decided to build a map.

I t had been several weeks since the ball at the Andrade house. Jenna was now getting to the point where she could decline invitations without offending. Her own grand ball was still several weeks away. In the meantime, she had a smaller gathering planned with some of the other young nobility she had become acquainted with. It would be her first time throwing a party, and she wanted it to be perfect. Arianna promised to come over later to do a practice run on some food they hadn't tried before.

She still met with Kal regularly, sometimes late at night or early in the morning. The way they interacted did not change. It was as if the dance had never happened.

She wasn't sure when he slept, but he was always the same steadfast beacon that guided her. They did maintenance on her shields and siphoned the nites regularly. She had taught him some of the designs she had learned from her father, and he had incorporated them into their lessons and shield maintenance. She did almost all the exercises assigned to her in less than the minimum time allotted.

He had also helped fill in some missing information about Lord and Lady Andrade from the dossiers. In their youth, there had been a love triangle between her mother and them. Her mother had ultimately walked away from Andrade for reasons that were never made clear. Jenna was starting to gain confidence in her new life, but her time with Kal was like the stillness amid a storm.

Jenna turned toward the doorway, sensing Kal before he arrived. As tired as fighting off his nites made her, she was always aware of his general direction. Sometimes, Jenna was aware of whom he spoke to, but only if he exhibited a strong emotion. When that happened, they performed repairs on her shields as it signified she was losing her battle against the nites.

"Lady Jenna," Kal said formally, bowing his head.

"Kal," she greeted him with a warm smile. Her grandfather had gotten her to stop calling him Master. Kal returned her smile, causing her knees to wobble. "Will you join me in the sitting area?" she asked.

He nodded, and they moved to the room.

"You have new instructions for me?"

"Yes. See if you can direct the general conversation toward new trade agreements or hidden storage facilities."

Jenna chewed her lip. How could she work these into conversations?

"You want to know if they are using the caverns for storing or transferring goods?"

He nodded.

"Same drill? You'll be nearby monitoring the situation?"

He smiled. "You felt me last time, didn't you?"

A wave of exhaustion hit her. Since she had lowered most of her shields to feed him nites when he lay dying at the inn, she had been reduced to only four inner layers of shields. The most resistant nites had accumulated there, trying to get through. She always maintained her inner shields against the nites while doing other things. It took little power, but it was a constant drain, slowly wearing her down. The closer they got to her core, the more she felt him. "Always," she said with a soft smile.

His smile faded. "Let's work on those shields."

The next day, Kal found Jenna on the stairs of the Sandoval estate, staring at a large portrait of her mother. Lord Sandoval must have brought the picture out of storage. Lady Abigail wore a green dress, much like the one Jenna wore now. Jenna frowned, and longing showed on her face. Kal's hand twitched as he suppressed the urge to reach out and touch her hair. Instead, Kal moved to stand next to her.

"I'm sure she would be proud of you," Kal said.

Jenna grunted as if he had kicked her. She rubbed a hand along her temple, then turned toward him.

"What of you? What happened to your mother? You never said."

Kal had been avoiding this for weeks. He was far beyond the limits of propriety. It had been long enough that he was sure even *she* knew he had returned.

Kal's stomach dropped as a memory awoke in him. When he had killed his father, his mother blamed him. It was she who had been holding the kingdom together. When Corin took over, he sent her to the temple to give her time to mourn. She was still there. Part of him wanted to see her, but he avoided it. He had to train Jenna, find the missing children, and free his brother. Bile rose in his throat—all excuses. Kal took a deep breath. He would face this.

Kal turned to Jenna to see the concern in her eyes. It was better that he show her.

"You have the clothes I arranged for you?" he asked. "Pick something suitable for the temple and meet me at the stagecoach."

Jenna opened, then closed her mouth before nodding and going to do as told.

They rode in silence. Kal ignored Jenna's stare. His stomach twisted as they moved inexorably toward their destination. Kal's jaw clenched as the spires of the Kimora Temple came into view.

A few minutes later, the carriage stopped. Kal led Jenna inside, where a robed clergyman greeted them.

"Where might I find Lady Mendathalon?" he inquired.

"At this time of day, she is usually in the gardens."

Kal escorted Jenna to a large enclosure surrounded by climbing roses. Benches and small tables dotted the site. The enclosure sat under a two-story glass canopy that provided natural light, and acolytes walked past the balconies above, going about their business.

His mother sat alone near a large flowering Azelianus plant, its petals a soft pink. She looked older to him, with a few gray hairs showing in the light, but she was still beautiful. She wore simple black robes, indicating her house. His shoulders released their tension as memories of happier times flooded him, where he sat on her lap at an event, or she read to him.

He became aware of Jenna studying him.

"This way," he said.

Kal moved through the garden toward his mother. He knew the moment she recognized him because her beautiful features darkened and her body tensed.

"Hello, Mother."

"So they freed you," she said.

"Corin needed me."

"He's got you looking for the missing children?"

"Yes."

She looked over Kal's shoulder, not quite looking at him. "Then he's doomed."

Kal heard Jenna's shocked intake of breath.

"I don't want his crown. I never have."

His mother snorted. "Then why did you kill your father?" she demanded.

Kal's eyes widened, but he had expected this much from her. "It was self-defense. That thing in father was trying to get into me."

His mother looked down at him from her seat. "Better you than your brother."

Kal flinched. He couldn't help it. But she was right. It would have been better for the kingdom if he had just let it happen.

What about me? cried his inner voice.

Scrambling, he said, "I think I've found a way to help him."

"So you are wasting time that should go to finding the missing children? Without those children, Corin will fall, and you will take over."

Kal reeled back as though she had slapped him. "No."

"It's what you've always—"

"It's not." Jenna interrupted the queen. Kal's mother focused on her for the first time. "He is doing his best."

Kal's mother laughed, a bitter sound. "Too little, too late."

"No real mother would say these things to her child. Does he not deserve the right to live?" Jenna said.

Kal stood, his heart pounding in his ears, his insides numb.

If the blow landed, Lady Mendathalon did not indicate it.

Jenna grabbed Kal's hand and pulled him away from his mother's bitter anger. She pulled him out of the garden's light and into the cool shadows of the temple halls.

Only then did he notice her burning anger through the bond.

She dragged him out of the temple and to the carriage, waiting to return them to the Sandoval estate.

Against propriety, Jenna sat next to him, her hands clenched into fists in the folds of her dress.

"Thank you," he said.

She turned to look at him and reached a hand up to his face. "You did nothing wrong," she snarled at him.

Her ferocity reminded him of Roolia for a moment, and he couldn't help but smile. Unsure of what to say, he nodded.

She lowered her hand. Her face colored as she realized what she had done, and the rage he felt coming from her cooled.

Kal wanted to grab hold of her hand again. His face tingled where she had touched it, but he was her teacher. This was the one thing they could never have. For some reason he didn't quite understand, that hurt more than his mother hating him.

Kal turned to watch the city go by as the carriage trundled on.

Chapter 30

Threat to the Crown

K al put aside his work mapping the caverns below the city for Master Harram as he furtively studied the king. He had a stern but proud face, which, at the moment, had a furrowed brow. Kal had convinced his brother to allow him into his personal office. Since the attack, Corin had further relaxed around him, or maybe it was the other way around. Kal had sensed the dual approval from both of the King's auras. From what he felt, there were two distinct personalities at play in Corin. The king's and the other entity's—for lack of a better word. *It definitely felt like a whole person.* After the attack, Kal had Corin assessed by the Royal Healer, which led to his diagnosis of him being a strong and healthy individual. Kal couldn't prove it wasn't an alternate personality, but he couldn't disprove it, either. Kal was still working with Rowen on the inverter.

"So, I heard you finally went to see Mother," Corin said.

Kal flinched as he met his brother's eyes.

"You know it's not your fault, what happened with father. No matter what she says, you're free of blame."

Kal looked away.

"Mother was impressed with Jenna," he said. "Says she has a spine."

Kal opened his mouth when a knock sounded on the door.

"Come," said Corin.

A messenger came in and handed the king a gold envelope. He dismissed the messenger and opened it. While he was reading its contents, Kal sensed more than saw the change in the king.

There was a burst of magic from him, and he appeared to expand and then contract. Kal enabled his magesight to look more closely. The aura appeared more like the secondary one Kal had seen during the attack. But there did not seem to be a battle for control. Kal could sense Corin's aura beneath the other.

Kal had witnessed the transformation multiple times. He stayed still, indirectly studying the king. Kal made out the differences now that he understood what to watch for—the way this king cocked his head, held his posture, the way he walked, and in some of the terms he used when speaking.

Kal was under orders from Corin to go along with the king when he sensed the change, but not to interfere or give away the fact that he was aware there was a difference. The other persona of the king had accepted Kal's presence without complaint.

Frowning, the king got up and headed for the door. His posture was subtly different. He was always commanding, but there was an air of sharpness to him. His movements were precise, as if he was focused on his actions. Kal, senses flaring, rose and followed along in his wake.

As they walked, the guards followed them. The king led them through the halls to the council chambers. When they arrived, the doors were closed and locked, which meant that a session with the king was in progress.

Kal sensed a buildup of magic in the king. With that much power, he would blow the doors off.

Kal stepped forward. "May I?"

The buildup stopped but did not disperse. The entity glanced at him. "As the *Scieldan* wishes."

Kal paused. "I am not familiar with that word—*Scieldan*. What does it mean?"

The king grimaced. "I suppose it is an old word. It means you are my shield, or more specifically, my shieldsman."

Kal considered the attack and his reflexive shield, then stepped forward and with a gesture, surgically cut through the wooden bar holding the door shut.

Several guards came forward as the king pushed the doors open. The doors crashed into the walls, echoing through the corridor. Kal followed, eyes on the king as he strode into the room and moved to stand off to the side and observe.

The king, occupied by the entity, looked each of the six council members in the eye, judging them. His eyes flicked to Lord Erick Andrade, who was seated in the chair reserved for the king.

"Sire." Andrade jumped up from the seat, bowing.

"My invitation appears to have been delayed and the doors locked before I could arrive. I'm unclear on the topic under discussion, but we're all here now. Shall we proceed?"

Some of the councilmen nervously shifted in their seats while Cardinas averted his gaze. Kal thought Sandoval and Deleon seemed relieved, though Navarro had the unusually neutral expression he wore when judging a trial.

"My apologies. There is no need, sire. This was nothing but a brief meeting. We had just finished up," Andrade said.

"Oh? Then please, do summarize for me."

Andrade cleared his throat. "We discussed treaties with Liang, upcoming caravans to the south, as well as a few other minor trivialities."

The king stared at Andrade, then spoke in a deceptively calm voice.

"Treaties are under the sole purview of the Crown."

"We meant no offense, sire. It came up concerning the caravans due in before King's Vow."

"Does anyone here have something else to add to the list?" the king asked the room.

Sandoval cleared his throat.

Andrade paled.

"Nothing else of import, sire," Cardinas said.

The king stared at Cardinas as if hearing the lie before turning his attention back to Andrade.

"I see, so this was all a terrible misunderstanding?" The king spoke blandly.

"Yes, sire," Andrade said

"It's good we've cleared that up, but I *will* have an invitation to any future meetings, no matter how trivial the agenda, or I will try you for treason."

"Yes, sire." Andrade bowed again.

The councilors visibly relaxed, but then the king continued as if recalling an insignificant fact. "There is one more thing, though." Andrade froze, as if sensing the trap. "Updates to the arena are complete. I require your presence—all of you—to review it."

No one in the room missed the word "require."

"This way, gentlemen." He waved his hand toward the open doors and exited the room, signaling the guards who poured in, escorting the councilors out.

Again, Kal followed, observing the king as he exited the coach and walked in his precise yet steady gait, leading them to the arena, which Kal had not been to since he had been in training. As they entered one set of large double doors, an enormous room spread out before them. Dozens of men practiced grappling and dueled in various portions of the main floor. The far end of the room had railings around it. They approached the guardrail and stared down into a spherical open space.

Kal sensed the energy coming off the shields, which made up the boundaries of the sphere. He studied the entity, who surveyed the stadium. Beyond him, the other councilmen were doing the same.

"Lord Andrade." The king spoke.

"Sire."

"Would you do me the honor of a match?"

Andrade frowned. No one dueled the king. No one.

"Sire, perhaps one of the—"

"No, I wish it to be you."

"As my lord wishes." He bowed stiffly.

Kal knew Andrade was an accomplished duelist. He was known to be ruthless in the ring. The king, to Kal's knowledge, had never entered the arena. As a noble, Andrade was oath-sworn never, through thought or deed, to harm the king. Andrade broke the first by holding the secret meeting, and the king could call him on it. Instead, the entity was forcing him into a situation where he could break the second. Depending on how badly he injured the king, he would be killed. His family destitute, stripped of their lands and title. All he had to do was swallow his pride and lose. Sweat beaded on Andrade's brow.

They suited up in padded armor that was standard for the arena. Kal stared as Andrade entered the sphere from the opposite side, angling himself to the center of the ring before coming smoothly to a stop on an island. Once inside the sphere, there was little to no weight. Combatants needed to use their own momentum and handholds to navigate. The swords used during the duel were short but not blunted and could cut through the padding. Andrade was not a mage, so this bout would be limited to nonmagical attacks. The entity moved toward the entrance, and Kal intercepted him.

"Sire," he whispered so only the entity would hear. "I cannot shield you in there."

"You cannot," he acknowledged.

Kal studied the king's face, searching for fear. Finding none, he said, "Do not die."

The entity smiled. "As my *Scieldan* commands."

He then turned and pushed off at the entrance, gliding weightlessly into the arena and landing on an island near Andrade, grabbing the handholds to stop his forward momentum.

The councilors sat in the royal viewing booth. The spaces around the arena began to fill with people as word spread of the unexpected bout. Kal stayed by the gate in case he needed to get in there quickly. Per the rules, bouts were best two out of three. Each turn went until contact or yield. Because of the limited gravity in the arena, the combatants would use the islands, anchored in place with various levels by magic, to push off of and maneuver around. After each round, the sphere reconfigured itself and shrank, leaving less space to maneuver within its clear shell. The third round, if needed, would be compact enough that it would not have stationary islands at all.

"Round one," the announcer called. There were a series of three flashes, with the final one signaling the start of the match. On the last flare, both men drew their swords and leaped toward each other. The king met Andrade's strikes blow for blow. The force of the impacts pushed them apart, towards the small islands. Weightless, they propelled themselves against the islands from any orientation. Andrade pushed off of one, coming at the king, who met the attack. Oddly, it wasn't the entity that went backward but Andrade, who had underestimated the power behind the king's blow.

Andrade smiled broadly, realizing he didn't have to hold back. The entity returned the smile. Kal's grip on the railing tightened, knowing the battle would begin in earnest.

The two men leaped from island to island, repositioning themselves to gain the high ground, then launched themselves at each other, swords flashing as they made contact, only to be pushed back again toward a different island. The next time they met, their swords clanged together. The king switched to a one-handed grip and caught hold of Andrade by the padding, slightly changing their trajectory. Andrade swung his sword, forcing the entity to release him and block the blow. They both spun out of control, each trying to locate an island and correct their spins. Andrade landed first, pushing toward the king with a smirk. Andrade's approach was faster than the king's descent toward the island.

From Kal's angle, it seemed like they would land at almost the same time. The entity landed first, but instead of pushing back at Andrade, he absorbed the remaining force, coming to a stop. Andrade's sword whooshed by over the king's head before the entity struck. Andrade's eyes went wide as he tried to pull back. The king's sword smashed into Andrade's side. His pads absorbed most of the blow, but it knocked the air out of him and sent Andrade careening into the island.

"Round one goes to the king," the announcer said. The crowd erupted in cheers and shouts.

Once the two men returned to their separate gates on opposite sides of the arena, it flared and reformed into a new pattern and size. When the king arrived, a water boy handed him a cup.

Kal scanned the king's body while he drank water, but he appeared the same. "How are you doing?"

The entity smiled at him, eyes twinkling, breath calming. "He is a worthy opponent."

Kal scowled, and the entity laughed.

"Round two," the announcer called.

Andrade and the king came together in a clash of swords, using the surrounding islands to expertly converge before bouncing back toward new islands. As far as Kal could tell, Andrade wasn't holding back at all anymore. Their path brought them to the shield wall, and Andrade used it as though it were an island running a few steps across its surface before leaping backward to collide with the king, which caused him to spiral and slam into the island instead of landing softly.

The king managed to grab the edge of the floating island to stop his momentum. He got up in time to brace himself for Andrade's next strike. Andrade was pushed back by his own force, and the entity used the edge of the island to launch himself after Andrade, who curled up into a ball to protect his legs as the entity overtook him. Andrade positioned his sword to block the king's strike. The king had more thrust, and Andrade was at an awkward angle. The blow sent Andrade tumbling out of control. His head clipped an island with enough force to daze him before bouncing toward a new island.

A warning buzzer rang, but Andrade signaled the all-clear. Since the king did not directly make the injury, it wasn't an automatic win, but Andrade could yield if the wound were severe. The king reoriented at the next island and angled to intercept. Andrade had blood running down the side of his face. He glanced up and caught sight of the king coming directly at him. Andrade, teeth gritted, rose to meet him. The king's next strike pushed Andrade's blade back into his shoulder, opening a self-inflicted wound and sending Andrade tumbling.

Again, the warning buzzer went off as Andrade careened out of control, leaving a trail of blood behind. Andrade's padding showed red welling up where the sword had landed and blood slowly ran down the side of his face where he had clipped the island. The king waited. There was a pause as the crowd waited in anticipation, but still, Andrade signaled the all-clear. The still-growing crowd erupted.

The entity bounced back, landing on an island, sighted Andrade, and pushed off to meet him.

Andrade landed awkwardly but maneuvered to another island. His next landing was good, but he was clearly at a disadvantage. Andrade grimaced as he angled his upcoming launch at the king. Their swords connected, but Andrade's injured shoulder balked. This time, it was the king's sword that hit him.

"Round two goes to the king." The cheers from the now massive crowd were deafening as sound rolled through the hall.

Kal, sighing in relief, unclenched his fists and entered the arena as soon as the round ended, launching himself toward the king and

Andrade. Both men glided to the bottom of the sphere, pulled by the arena's magic. As Kal came closer, the entity approached Andrade, sword still at the ready. Andrade was kneeling, holding his shoulder. Blood still leaked from the wound on his head. Kal landed nearby and jogged over in time to hear the entity say, "Consider this a warning. If you or any of your henchmen try to usurp my powers again, I will kill you. Do you understand me?"

Andrade stared up at the king, eyes widening, but he said nothing.

"Do you understand me?" The king enunciated each word with deadly calm.

Andrade, eyes locked on the king, could tell that his life was on the line. Knowing he had lost, he said, "Yes, sire."

"We will not speak of this again," the entity said as he sheathed his sword, turned, and walked away as the healers arrived.

Kal followed the entity as he approached the councilmen. Some had expressions of respect, others of fear. The king dismissed the councilors, who clearly understood the underlying message in the bout, and exited swiftly. Once they were gone, the king turned to Kal. He gave him a brief half-smile, and then his aura flared again, ballooning outward before coming back in. What Kal perceived chilled him. The entity's presence left, and Corin's familiar pressure emerged.

"What?" Corin asked before going to a knee. "What happened? I feel like I've been in a battle."

Kal went to him, scanning for injuries. Besides a small gash on his head, Corin had large-scale bruises on his back from impacting the island, but otherwise only minor scrapes on his hands. Kal waved for the healers, who came over to help. Corin tried to catch Kal's eyes as they worked. Kal avoided him. Once the healers were done and Kal and Corin were alone, Corin asked, "It happened again, didn't it?"

"Yes. What's the last thing you remember?"

Corin thought for a moment. "I was at my desk reading a message, though I don't recall what the message said."

Kal stared thoughtfully at the Corin. From the files, it was clear that he never recalled events when suppressed, though when the two auras were present, like in the attack, he recalled most of what happened. Kal's mind churned as he considered possibilities for what he had witnessed.

Corin cleared his throat.

Kal told him everything that happened as he escorted Corin back to the palace proper. By the time they had arrived, Corin was pale. Kal noticed a slight tremor in his hands.

Frowning, Kal escorted Corin to his chambers before returning to his own.

A candle mark later, someone knocked on his door. Kal opened the door to find the Royal Seneschal outside.

"Lord Mendathalon, your presence is required in the king's private chambers."

Kal frowned. No one went into the king's private chambers. Kal thought about the quaver in the king's hands. "What is wrong?"

"His Majesty is asking for you."

Kal followed the seneschal as he led him to the king's rooms. The seneschal opened the door and led him through an elaborate set of rooms to what Kal thought was a closet. He stopped and gestured for Kal to proceed.

Kal entered a small reinforced safe room filled with soil. His brother was on his knees digging with his bare hands.

All the hairs on Kal's neck rose, and his stomach clenched as the past flashed before his eyes. Memories of his father digging as the voice consumed him.

No! Not him, too. This can't be happening.

"I must find him," Corin mumbled over and over again as he dug.

Kal closed his eyes against the horror of it. He would not kill his brother. He *could* not kill his brother. There had to be a cure. He was so close. He wouldn't give up yet. Kal took a deep breath, opened his eyes, and entered the room.

"Corin? You called for me?"

Corin kept digging at the floor. His short nails were black.

Kal put his hand on the king's shoulder, and Corin looked up at him, his eyes slowly focusing. "Kal?"

Kal knelt down in front of him, aware of the seneschal in the doorway. "Yes, I'm here."

"I need you—" Corin began.

"You need me to help you find him?"

Corin blinked before frowning.

Kal took his brother's dirt-covered hands in his own and helped him rise. "We will look for him tomorrow, after you've had a good night's rest," he said gently as he pulled Corin from the room.

"But—" Corin said, eyes still unfocused.

"I know what you want, Corin. I'll do everything I can to help you," Kal interrupted again, heart beating loudly in his chest. Kal prayed his brother wouldn't challenge him as he led Corin to his bedchamber, then nodded to the seneschal, who began getting Corin ready for bed.

He stayed until his brother's hands had been washed and he was in bed. The confusion on the king's face slowly cleared until his gaze turned almost sharp, assessing.

"Remember our deal," Corin said.

Kal bowed and left the room. He had to go faster.

Chapter 31

The Rod

Kal yawned as he presented his model of the caverns to Master Harram. He hadn't gotten much sleep last night since he was up late working on a design he'd found in the archives for something that could help his brother.

Kal thought back to the bruising he had seen on the king, then of his arena fight. The king must have been training for months to pull off that bout. This revelation went a long way in explaining the bruising and injury Jenna had healed for him.

Master Harram cleared his throat, and Kal wrenched his thoughts back to the present.

The model hovered in the air in miniature, with beige lights showing an outline of the caverns below the castle. Kal moved his hands apart, and the scale increased, filling the space over the desk. He made a gesture, and six caverns filled in with a bluish color.

"The rooms highlighted in blue all meet the original criteria you sent to me."

Master Harram studied the model for a moment and pointed. "This cavern. It's by the eastern wall, right?"

Kal updated the model to denote directions. "Yes."

"Good. Now update your model to remove all caverns against the walls."

Kal focused, and two of the lights went out.

"Let's expand them, one by one."

Kal expanded the first cavern so it opened up above them, giving them an in-cavern view of their surroundings.

"How did you decide on the texture?"

"*Strata and Rock Minerals* by Homer Willow."

"Is this human scale?"

"Yes."

"Go to the next cavern."

Kal changed the view, which showed a little walking space within the rock formations.

"May I see your calculations?"

"For this room, or all of them?"

Master Harram smiled. "Let's start with this room."

Kal made a motion, and the calculation showed up underneath the model.

"Huh," Master Harram said. "Look at the base calculation."

Kal focused on it.

"You chose Gram's model instead of Plumber."

"It seemed appropriate with the sea level."

Master Harram leaned forward. "Try swapping them out."

Kal took several minutes to make the changes.

He pushed the diagram off the desk, and it disappeared from view.

He then put his hands together and spread them, showing a new diagram inside. He expanded it and re-highlighted the rooms. He went back into the cavern, and they observed a simple open cavern with what appeared to be pillars holding it up.

He glanced at Master Harram. "You knew."

"I suspected."

Kal panned around the room. "Wow."

"Yes. Let's go through them all."

Kal selected each room and changed the calculations. When finished, they were standing in an underground city. Of the four caverns, only two were suitable for caging people, with only one opening to guard.

Kal was sweating from the exertion of maintaining the complex model.

Master Harram nodded and pointed. "You've included possible entrances to the caverns?"

"Yes." He motioned, and the points lit up in red.

"Good. You can dismiss the model."

Kal sighed in relief as he released it. "We've got to send a Shadow Weaver in there."

"Talk to Master Evans. He has people who specialize in caverns. He's likely to have someone he can spare."

"I plan to see him later today."

"Is it time for the Compact meeting at the church of The Three?"

"Yes, we've blocked Andrade's meeting request for as long as we could to plan. I meet with the bishop after this to get situated, and I've got several teams assigned to tail him. Master Evans will tempt Jaxson with seeing the second rod."

"You're going in yourself?"

Kal nodded. "I want to look him in the eyes."

"Do not give yourself away. Remember your training."

"Yes, Master Harram." Kal smiled as he gave him a little bow. He was pretty sure he had said something similar to Jenna recently.

Kal studied the Threefold Bishop Skander, the highest-ranking official in the Church of The Three and the titular Guardian of the East. He wore resplendent gray robes with the symbols of The Three cross-stitched into the fabric—a sword and shield, scales, and a book.

Kal would pretend to be the bishop's primary attendant today. He wore similar robes and the face of Attendant Denelly.

"It is your job to retrieve the rod from the box," said the bishop, gesturing toward a rather plain-looking box.

Kal frowned. He had heard tales of the beauty of the ornate box that held the rod. This was not it. "Where is the box of Inanis?"

"We recently received a large donation so we could have it restored. This is a temporary box."

Disappointment flashed through him, then was gone. He would have liked to see it, but it was secondary to his true purpose.

"How shall I retrieve the rod?" he asked.

"Gloves must be worn when handling the rod." He gestured to a smaller box. "Which you will find in there."

"May I practice?" Kal asked.

"Of course."

Kal stood, stooping as he had seen the aide do before he had been dismissed. With quivering hands, he opened the small box and put on the gloves. Then, fumbling with the latches, he opened the larger box containing the rod.

The rod was short, about the length of his forearm, and seemed to be made of silver. Kal knew from reports that the metal never tarnished, so likely not silver. It was said that touching it made people uncomfortable at best. Some had even passed out.

Kal reached in and pulled out the rod, reverently cupping it in both hands. He turned to the table where a metal stand sat. Gently, back arched to simulate age, he placed the rod on the stand, then turned back to the bishop, who stared at him, mouth parted.

"Was that alright?" Kal asked.

The bishop's mouth snapped closed. "Yes, that will do."

Kal retrieved the rod, moved cautiously back to the desk, and placed it back in the box. He closed the latches, removed the gloves, and put them away. Gingerly, he sat back down.

A knock sounded at the door.

"Remember," the bishop said, "Do not talk and keep your face passive."

Kal nodded, rising to position himself at the bishop's left shoulder.

"Come in," commanded the bishop.

The door opened, and in walked a monk, followed by Master Evans and a well-built man with hair tied away from his clean-shaven face and penetrating green eyes.

"Your Grace, Master Evans and Baron Jaxson."

Kal studied Jaxson as he glided into the room.

With that stance, he was definitely a fighter, Kal thought. He struggled to keep from shifting his position into a fighter's stance as well. Kal shifted to magesight, but the Rod of Inanis glowed white-hot. All the nites in the room rotated around it. He shifted back, blinking. He couldn't tell if Jaxson was a mage with all that interference.

"Please be seated." The bishop gestured to the empty chairs at his desk. "Master Evans, it is a pleasure seeing you again. When shall I see you at service?"

Master Evans shifted in his seat. "I shall make every attempt to be there this weekend."

"I look forward to seeing you."

"Your Holiness," said Master Evans. "This is the newly anointed Baron Jaxson. His family trades in antiquities as well as unusual spices."

"Your Grace," said Jaxson in a gravelly voice. "It is a pleasure to meet you."

"I understand you've come to see the Rod of Inanis. Since you trade in antiquities, I must warn you that the rod is not for sale," said the bishop.

Jaxson's face took on a disappointed cast. "It would be an honor just to hold such a well-known antiquity."

"Maybe Master Evans will show you his?" said the bishop.

Master Evans froze as Jaxson's gaze fell on him.

"You have a Rod of Inanis?" he asked, eyes wide and calculating.

Master Evans cleared his throat, glaring at the bishop. "Ah, yes, well, we have a replica of the rod, but it, too, is not for sale."

"May I see it?" Jaxson asked, voice pleading.

"Hm, yes, that can be arranged. Perhaps—"

"After this meeting?" Jaxson interrupted, eyes glinting. "The rods are artifacts of The Three. Since I cannot purchase one, I would love to see both on the same day. Not too many people can make that claim."

"Hm, yes. I can spare a little time right after this meeting, but no more than a candle mark."

"Of course, Master Evans," Jaxson said, smiling broadly.

"Alright, then, Your Grace, if you wouldn't mind," said Master Evans.

"Please." The bishop held out his arm for the others to follow him.

They moved to the far side of the viewing table with the stand and box of gloves, and the bishop nodded to Kal, who repeated his earlier performance without fumbling on the locks. Kal gently placed the rod on the stand and stood back. Jaxson's entire posture shifted into one of intense scrutiny. He gave the impression of an antiquities dealer as he reached into his coat and pulled out a pair of white gloves. He put them on and gestured to the rod. "May I?"

The bishop nodded as Kal tensed.

Jaxson carefully lifted the rod with two hands. He rotated it, leaning in close to study its surface. "Is it true it doesn't tarnish?"

"It is true," the bishop said as Jaxson placed a hand in the center of the rod and rolled it across his gloved palm.

"It's heavier than I thought it would be. Any thoughts as to what it's made of?"

"The ores used are currently unknown," said the bishop. "That is what makes it invaluable."

Jaxson rolled it around his other hand, inspecting the entire length of the rod while asking, "Master Evans, how did you replicate it if the ores are unknown?"

Master Evans cleared his throat. "That would be a trade secret."

Jaxson held it by the edges again and carefully placed it back on the stand, putting his gloves away.

"It's exquisite. If you ever change your mind and wish to sell, please keep me in mind."

The bishop smiled. "I'll do so." He signaled Kal, and he deposited the rod back into the box, closing the lid.

"If that is all?" the bishop said.

"Yes. Thank you for the opportunity to hold the rod, Your Grace, and thank you for the introduction, Master Evans."

"Good day," said the bishop.

"Good day," said Jaxson and Master Evans as they left the room.

The door shut, and Kal straightened to his full height and released the Seeming. He had memorized the baron's features and mannerisms. He could pick him out of a crowd or become him if needed. Jaxson must have purchased the right to be a baron. It was not an uncommon practice, used to create limited mobility in the lower classes, and was not directly overseen by the king. He would look into recent awards. Maybe he could find out who sponsored him.

"So, what did you think of him?" Kal asked the bishop.

"He seemed like a fine young lad, and the reverence wasn't feigned as far as I could tell."

Kal frowned. He was right, his reactions seemed genuine.

"I hope I have been of service to the king?"

"You have. Thank you for your time. I'll take my leave now. We will supplement your security in case someone tries to steal the rod. Be sure to report if you find someone snooping around."

The bishop nodded.

Kal changed and headed over to the Arcanum. He should just miss Baron Jaxson. He wanted to get Master Evans's impression right away.

The Arcanum was an old building, almost as old as the palace, with beautiful spires and arches. A young mage escorted Kal to Master Evans's office. Evans sat behind his desk, scowling.

"What happened with Jaxson?"

"Nothing. He was a perfect antiquities dealer," Master Evans grumbled.

"Then what's wrong?" Kal asked.

"Are you sure we should have given him access to both rods on the same day?" Master Evans said. "It's common knowledge that there are two rods, but I wasn't expecting the bishop to bring up the Arcanum's rod."

"Ah, I didn't ask him to mention it. I'm guessing he just wanted to be helpful. But you can ask him about it at services this weekend." Kal smirked.

Master Evans shot him a dark look at being reminded of his commitment.

"Any other thoughts on Jaxson?" Kal asked.

"Other than he was clearly a fighter, which many barons are, I wouldn't have been the least bit suspicious of him."

"That was my impression, also."

"You are having him followed?"

"Yes. Do you know who nominated him as a baron?"

"I believe he said Lord Andrade, which was how I was introduced to him."

"What did Lord Andrade offer you to get you to introduce Jaxson to the bishop?"

"Clearance to build an Arcanum branch in the Rim," Evans said.

Kal grimaced at the clear bribery. "Well, at least something good came out of it."

"Is this all you needed?"

"Ah, no. I wanted to show you something." Kal displayed his map of the underground caverns. Master Evans's eyes went wide at the implications. "I was wondering if you could spare someone to take a look?"

A candle mark later, Kal met with Master Evans and Edward, one of his apprentices at the Arcanum. Kal displayed the map and his findings, and the young man's eyes twinkled.

"There are buildings under the city? This fits with my thesis that the great magical library of Drakothadam is buried around here."

"The Orbis Arcanum?" Kal said, recalling tales of the great library.

"One and the same. When can I go?" Edward asked Master Evans.

Kal suppressed a grin at his enthusiasm.

"Have you finished your assignment on mage stones?"

"Yes, Master Evans."

"What about your mentoring the young ones?"

"Erickson can sub for me, sir."

Master Evans sighed. "All right, but I'm sending two guards with you."

"Yes, sir." Edward grinned.

"Give me a couple of days to get everything set up," Master Evans said as a knock sounded on the door. "Come in."

A messenger appeared, bearing an envelope from the church. Master Evans dismissed Edward and broke the seal on the envelope, face going pale as he read.

"What's happened?" Kal asked.

"The Rod of Inanis is missing."

"What? What about your rod?" Kal asked.

"Come with me." Master Evans took Kal to a secured area at the top of one of the towers. In its case, sat the imitation rod called Trellium. Master Evans sealed up the room, replacing its wards.

"Let's head over to the church," Kal said.

They were escorted to the bishop's office. He sat tight-lipped, his jaw clenched.

"What happened?" Kal asked.

"I was in my office all afternoon with only a brief leave to go to the restroom. The door was locked, and as far as I can tell, no one entered the room but me. The evening ceremonies were about to start, so I sent my aide to retrieve the rod, but it wasn't there."

Kal ruminated over the information. He was the last person to touch the rod. He had placed it in the box, but now the box was empty. Suspicion wormed its way through Kal. "May we examine the box?" Kal asked.

The bishop gestured.

Kal opened the rod's container. It was indeed empty. He sent his senses towards the case and found nothing amiss.

"Master Evans?" Kal asked.

Master Evans shook his head. "I sense no trace of magic in the room or in the box. May I take the container for further investigation?"

The bishop nodded. "We need a rod."

Master Evans pursed his lips. "Once I am done here, I will send our rod over as a temporary replacement until we can find the original. I would request that no one but you and your aide handle the rod until further notice."

The bishop nodded, and they left.

Chapter 32

Medallion

K al was on his third attempt at getting the design right. Since his brother's episode, he had been working with builder Worthings, and he sincerely hoped that this one would pass his inspection. He stood at his desk in the king's office and reread the note before putting it aside and opening the box that had accompanied it.

Inside the box, lined with silk, was a signet-shaped medallion. Kal picked it up to test its heft. It was firm and feather-light, but not frail. Its size and lightness would give him several options for placement. He gently twisted the top, and it separated into two thin, flat pieces. He flipped each one over and inspected their edges, then ran his fingers around the seams, searching for jagged pieces. Finding none, he locked them back together and separated them three more times until he was satisfied. This time, he gently put the medallion back together and placed it back into its box. He sealed it with a multilayered tamper spell and placed it on a small shelf behind the desk and out of sight of the door.

Kal settled in to do a final review of things that might go wrong and his mitigation options.

Kal and Rowen sat side by side in Corin's office. Corin stared down at Kal.

It was Corin who spoke first. "Let me get this straight. You want to put a maghin in me?"

Kal considered the medallion. It wasn't precisely a maghin, but it was similar. "More or less," Kal said with amusement tinging his words.

Corin's expression deepened into a frown.

Kal, however, burst into laughter, startling Rowen, who stared back and forth between Kal and the king. "Your turn," Kal said through gasps of air.

"Your Majesty, in his defense, this maghin does not hold any commands. It does, however, have an imperative, and that is to invert one flow of your magical sequence."

"How will that affect my magic?" Corin asked.

"It shouldn't affect it at all, though the feel of it may change. It will essentially make you deaf on a certain frequency and allow you to hear on a different one."

"So it will make me more like Kal?"

"Yes, and he will tutor you if needed." Rowen glanced toward Kal for confirmation, and he nodded, still wiping the tears from his eyes.

"That's why I had both of you clear your schedules for the next few days," Rowen said. "It will give you time to acclimate to the changes," he told the king. To Kal, he said, "And will give you time to mentor him if needed. This maghin is designed to sit just under the skin. It will leave you with a raised Royal insignia."

"Can it be damaged in a fall? Or stop working?" Corin asked.

"No. Once the seal is in place, it should change your magic in such a way as to protect itself from outside interference. Consider it a second imperative which was put into place to prevent"—he cleared his throat—"tampering."

"What if it doesn't work or has a negative effect?" Corin asked.

"It can be disabled." Rowen handed the key to Corin. It looked like a smaller version of what was going into Corin.

"Since Kal is naturally immune, he will have the key. I will implant it in him before implanting the other half into you."

Corin smiled. "Oh, so he gets one, too?"

Kal frowned.

"Again, this one has no commands. Its only purpose is to deactivate the seal in you."

"How close do they have to be to work?" Corin asked.

"The fact that it's inside Kal will prevent it from working. Kal tied his key to his will, and only he can remove it. It will perceive external attempts to remove it as an attack, and it will act to protect itself and Kal."

Rowen turned to Kal. "Once you choose to remove it, simply place your key over the skin of Corin's seal to remove it." Rowen held the seals over one another. "Anything I missed?"

"What if Kal wants to be king?" Corin asked.

Rowen glanced between the two brothers. "If we do nothing, he will be."

"What if Kal dies?" Corin asked.

Rowen shifted uncomfortably. "Without the power of Kal's magic to drive it, the seal will go dormant. Someone could remove it then, hence one of the reasons we are keeping this quiet."

Corin shook his head. "So if this doesn't work and that thing influencing me decides to kill Kal..."

Silence descended.

"It is a risk," Rowen conceded.

After a few moments, Kal pulled his shirt off. "Better than being king. Let's get this over with."

"Lie back," Rowen instructed Kal. Rowen placed the smaller key on Kal's chest while reaching out with his magic to activate it. The key glowed softly and sank into Kal's chest. Kal gasped a bit at the coldness of the metal, then relaxed as it warmed up to body temperature. The key showed as a raised indent on Kal's chest. Its edges left the impression of the Royal Seal.

"Try to remove it," Rowen said.

Kal put his left hand on the seal, and it came away onto his hand.

"Good. Now put it back."

Placing his hand on his chest, he willed it back in.

"Good, your turn." He turned to Corin.

Corin cringed, but removed his shirt.

Rowen laid the seal over Corin's chest, and it sank just beneath the skin.

Corin's aura shifted. "Please, you must free me; the world is in dang—"

Corin slumped forward. Rowen grabbed him and laid him down. Then, Rowen staggered back a step and went to his knees, shimmering as external energy seeped into his shields.

"Rowen, are you all right?" Kal asked.

"I," Rowen stuttered. "H-he needs help," he said, wrapping his arms around himself.

Kal was by his side, holding him up.

Rowen stared at Kal, horror and fear on his face. "We are in danger. We must free him." Kal stared at Rowen in alarm as he continued. "We must find him. We must—" Rowen's eyes rolled up in his head, and he slid to the floor.

Kal laid Rowen on one of the couches in the king's office and went to check on Corin. He was deeply asleep. Kal rolled his chair over to the other couch and transferred Corin there, the two men's feet almost touching. It was evening, and Corin had issued orders that no one was to disturb them. Kal sat down to wait.

Corin sat up, looking around the room. Kal went over to his brother, who relaxed the moment he came into view. Corin opened his hand and created a light, and then a large smile broke out across his features.

"Kal, you've done it! I'm free."

Kal did not smile back.

"What happened?" Corin asked.

"It's in Rowen now."

Corin stared at Rowen, eyes widening.

"How is that possible?"

"Are the Sandovals linked to the royal line?" Kal asked.

"At some point or another, all the noble houses are linked. There is just nothing recent." Corin stood, pacing the length of his office. "How am I going to tell Oswen?"

Kal twitched. *How am I going to tell Jenna?*

Chapter 33

Party

Jenna focused as she squared off with her opponent, sword held at the ready. Her house championed healers and warriors, so some training was required with both. She was up against a third-tier adversary—out of ten tiers—having bested foes in the lower tiers in the previous two months. Jenna instinctively read them, and she understood how to respond, but sometimes her body wasn't up to the task. The swordmaster had seen this and had given her strength and conditioning routines to extend her stamina and range of motion. As her fitness improved, her skills with the sword improved, or as he put it, emerged as if she were relearning them.

Jenna and her opponent circled the ring, each searching for an opening.

There.

She found a gap and went for it. Her opponent countered, and Jenna parried, backing away. They circled again, and this time, her opponent came at her lightning-fast. Jenna responded in kind, sword meeting sword until they broke apart, sizing each other up.

"Halt," called the swordmaster at the side of the ring.

They both stopped but didn't move away from each other.

He entered the arena and walked around them, studying their forms and general states.

"You still claim no master?" he said to Jenna.

"I have never held a sword before your class," she said.

He nodded sharply.

"Yet, you know all the forms."

Jenna frowned in frustration, thinking of Kal.

"You may leave, Jenna."

She released her stance and backed away from her partner. She gave a bow to the swordmaster and left the arena. Seeing her grandfather entering the room, she nodded to him as well. He nodded back and went to speak with the swordmaster.

Jenna cleaned up after practice and started getting ready for her party. Arianna would be over soon to help with the final round of cooking. Jenna had hoped these visits would bring her out of her shell, and so far, they had. As she was coming down the stairs, Rowen was going up, trailed by two Royal Guards.

Jenna raised an eyebrow at him.

"What did you do?" she asked, unable to hide the accusation in her tone.

His eyes focused on her, then lost focus and focused again.

"Are you drunk?" she asked, eyebrows climbing.

"No. Need Grandfather."

Jenna twitched at the stunted way he spoke. "He's at the arena."

Rowen turned around and headed for the arena, shadowed by the guards. Jenna followed.

Jenna studied Rowen as he found Oswen still speaking with the swordmaster. Rowen walked up and bowed. Swordmaster Rennard nodded back, never taking his eyes off Rowen. Rowen opened his mouth to speak, but was interrupted by Rennard.

"Would you humor me a moment?"

Rowen stared at him and nodded.

"Have you had any swords training?"

"No," Rowen answered. "Only the mandatory training."

Jenna stood next to her grandfather as the swordmaster got two practice staves. He threw one to Rowen and then flowed into a stance. Rowen took up a different position, but a fighting stance nonetheless.

Rennard's mouth clenched, and he moved forward to attack.

Rowen moved with him, sword flowing through defensive stances and shifting to offensive ones when an opening presented itself—five, ten, fifteen minutes passed as Rowen fought Rennard to a standstill. The only difference was that Rennard was barely winded, and Rowen was panting heavily. The similarities between this and Jenna's first battle were too hard to dismiss.

Rennard gave the sign to stop the fight, and Rowen bowed.

Rennard glanced at Oswen, who stood staring in shock.

Rowen turned to Oswen. "Grandfather, I need to speak with you." He gestured to the Royal Guards who stood observing. Each had a hand on his hilt, having followed the battle with interest.

"Indeed," he said and led Rowen up to his office.

Jenna and the guards followed Rowen into the office. One guard stepped forward and handed Oswen a letter bearing the Royal Seal. Rowen stood there, fidgeting with the buttons on his shirt. While Oswen read, the color drained from his face.

Oswen turned to him. "You found the reason for the king's ailment?"

"I did."

"He has been cured?"

"Yes."

"Only that ailment has now moved into you?"

"Correct."

"Is this why you fight so well?"

"Probably."

Oswen's eyes flicked to Jenna, who grimaced.

"You have been put under house arrest. Two Royal Guardsmen have been assigned to you until the ban is lifted."

Jenna blinked as something in Rowen's aura shifted.

"I must have access to the king."

Oswen flinched. "No, Rowen, that's the one thing you won't have."

Jenna studied Rowen as his aura shifted back, and Rowen's face turned confused for a moment, and he spoke softly. "I'm guessing I can't see patients?"

"Unfortunately, no."

"What should I do with myself?" he exclaimed, eyes wide.

"What would you like to do?"

Rowen started to shake. "I want to free him. I want to dig."

L ater that night, Jenna settled down into one of the chairs arranged near the musicians. No one had left yet, so she took that as a sign everyone was enjoying themselves. It was good to take some of the weight off her feet, and she was surprised to find that she liked the music they played, which was different from ballroom music, more subtle. One of the Cardinas boys had helped her pick the music. She would follow up with him later to map song names to the tunes.

Beltran Andrade came over and sat by her, which was the third time tonight he had managed to get her alone. It was as if he wanted to say something to her, but couldn't quite bring himself to do it. Every time he got close, Darren Navarro would appear.

"Congratulations on your party," he said, and she smiled brightly at him.

"I had a lot of help." She gestured to Arianna, who was speaking with several girls on the other side of the room, and one of the Cardinas brothers, who was speaking with the musicians during their break.

"Ah, you're like The Three then," he said wistfully.

"The Three as in 'by The Three'?" It was a widespread phrase in the Rim referring to the three beings who guarded the world. She recognized the phrase from the streets and had never scrutinized it beyond that. She had seen many references to The Three at the Andrade estate during her tour.

"Yes, The Three. Have you ever heard those tales?"

She shook her head. Her parents never mentioned The Three, but she had to admit she was curious.

"The Three are holy watchers. Their domains were split between morning, afternoon, and night as they took turns guarding the world against destruction at the behest of Guardian, one of the original caretakers of the world." He paused, making sure she was listening, then continued. "One of them fed on souls, one could fly, and the third was an elf."

Someone snorted.

Jenna turned. Others in the room had drifted over to listen. Surprisingly, the one who snorted was Rowen. She searched for and found his two guards.

"Is that what remains of The Three?" Rowen asked imperiously, not sounding like himself.

"If you don't like it, why don't you tell the story?"

Rowen blinked, and to her surprise, agreed.

He put his hands together and, using his magic, formed a small man of light. "One was a man of great prowess; he was ruthless and of great cunning. He communed better with animals than with people." As he spoke, the figure moved, playing out the part, and various animals came into view, walking and running with the man.

The room went silent, and those who had not yet joined their conversation moved closer to listen.

"He fought in many wars, and from all trials, emerged victorious." The figure battled other light foes, hacking and slashing them down with acrobatic ease.

"One day, he approached Guardian, the protector of Seed, who created all magic in the world, and in exchange for his vow, was given the power to destroy the world." The light figure approached an orb of light, and power streamed from the sphere onto the man, making him sparkle like a rainbow.

"Many pestered him to use his powers to their advantage, for no one could stand against him. He had used his powers with great care. But one day, after decades of avoiding the machinations of kings and men trying to manipulate him into using his power for their benefit, one of them kidnapped his love, who died trying to escape. On learning of this, he broke, and in a moment of grief and weakness, he called on his powers—all of them." Lights of all colors of the rainbow came out of the man, rising into the air and raining down on the world with flashes on impact.

"Power in measure heals. Power in force kills. People in the city died in droves. The guilty, the innocent—his grief knew no bounds. Different colors of the rainbow killed in different ways, making some grow old while others had growths inside and died. Some were forever changed, tied to him in a form of bondage.

"The presence of all powers was too much and caused great destruction. When his powers ran out, few remained alive, and he was the only unchanged man remaining. From that day forward, he was known as the destroyer of worlds."

The light man faded, and a woman appeared. "One was a woman of scholarly renown. She was a voracious reader and remembered all she read. She already had so much knowledge, but wanted to know everything." The figure carried a book, and many lined up to listen to her wisdom.

"She, too, approached Guardian, and for her vow, she came away with the knowledge of worlds at her fingertips." The light woman peered through a tool, and a new world blossomed on the other side. As she looked into that new world, yet another one bloomed.

"She manipulates animals and people, looking to breed the perfect human. The cost of her research has created many amazing and horrible creatures." His display showed flying creatures from legend, large land-bound animals, and fantastic water creatures.

"She still spawns and tracks new experiments today in her endless quest for knowledge. She became known as the weaver of fates."

The woman's figure faded away, replaced by a tall individual of neither male nor female persuasion. "The last was a fool," he said bitterly. "Being unique in self, and androgynous in nature, ze sought to save everything of uniqueness. Ze was a great hoarder of items and an expert in their protection." Rowen showed vast riches and items, statues, and gems.

"Ze sought Guardian and requested to have the largest repository of items. In exchange for a vow, Guardian granted zir great riches and items of power, which ze hoarded, never sharing knowledge or wealth with the world." Rowen showed doors closing over gates and walls that were cavernous.

"Ze was alone and never really noticed. This one was called the Keeper." The light person walked and then was joined by each of the other two.

"The Guardian called each of them to him and gave them the first command. 'Watch over the world and keep it safe from harm.'" The Guardian light figure sent discs, which reminded Jenna of maghins, to enter the bodies of The Three.

"Each of The Three strives to fulfill this command in their own way, sometimes working together, other times clashing."

The lights faded away, and Rowen stood staring at the place they used to fill, eyes glistening before turning and leaving the room amid cheers and applause.

Unease rose in Jenna. How did her brother know the story of The Three?

Chapter 34

Dinner

"**G**randfather? About Rowen..." She trailed off.

Oswen focused on Jenna. "What happened?" he asked.

"Last night, at the party, he told the most amazing story about The Three. He used magic the way the old storytellers used to and showed the story in the air. I thought it was a lost art."

Oswen shifted in his seat. "It's been gone for a hundred years."

Jenna nodded and continued.

"After the story, he looked so upset and immediately left the party. I, well, I'm pretty sure he was crying."

Jenna reflected on her relationship with Rowen. She was still angry at him, but the last time she had seen him cry was when they buried their mother. However, she recalled hearing him crying some nights after Justin had left. She sighed, conflicted. "Either way, I'm pretty sure he's the talk of the noble circle right now, because I received five inquiries this morning about his, ah, availability." Jenna rolled her eyes. He may be struggling, but her brother could manage his own love life.

"When I went to speak with him about it this morning, he said he doesn't remember it. On top of that, his back was all dirty. Apparently, he couldn't sleep indoors and said the walls were caving in on him."

Oswen closed his eyes briefly, then opened them.

"You know everything I know. He is not himself right now."

"When will he be himself?" she asked, irritated.

"I don't know if he will ever be himself again."

Jenna snorted, then frowned, thinking of all the research she'd done with Kal and Rowen on the royal family. *The king's ailment has moved into Rowen.* Her stomach clenched.

"This is something he got from the king?" she asked, seeking confirmation.

"Yes, it appears there was more to the king's condition than was previously thought."

"How so?" she asked.

"Whatever has been plaguing the king and causing his irrational behavior is now in Rowen."

Jenna's palms began to sweat. *What if Rowen also has the same pathways as the king? If that were the case, then it's not limited to the royal family as we first thought.*

Jenna couldn't reveal the king's specifics, so she couldn't tell her grandfather, but she knew how to cure her brother. It would take time, though. She would have to make him an inverter, and where would the voice go then? Into Grandfather? Justin? Herself?

Jenna rubbed her temples. "So until then, Royal Guards?"

"Yes, Royal Guards."

L ater that afternoon, Oswen entered the parlor.

"Lady Arianna, will you be staying for dinner?"

"Oh, yes, please do stay."

"If it's no trouble." Arianna nodded.

"Good," said Oswen. "We will have a special guest tonight. Please remember your manners."

Jenna frowned. She had made great strides, so it wasn't like him to remind her anymore. It must be a significant guest.

"I believe you and Lady Arianna are roughly the same size?"

They nodded.

"Good. Elegant attire, please."

Jenna's eyebrows rose. There had been many gowns made for her when she arrived. She had worn a good many more than she had ever believed possible, but they reserved elegant attire for important events. *Just who was coming for dinner?* She was still learning about her grandfather, but she understood that if he'd wanted to tell her, he would have said.

"Yes, Grandfather," she said, bowing her head. "Come on, Arianna, let's go see what works." Jenna practiced her elegant walk as they went up the stairs to her room. Arianna burst out laughing. Jenna smiled at her, took her by the arm, and they ran the rest of the way. Jenna glanced back to see Oswen smiling.

Kal and Corin entered the main hall at the Sandoval estate to find Rowen standing by the fireplace, trying to loosen his collar and looking lost. Rowen turned towards them and raised his brows, eyes roving over the king. Kal tensed when Rowen invoked magesight, but then Rowen broke into a broad grin.

"It worked," Rowen said.

"It did." Corin gave a small but genuine smile.

"Side effects?"

"Magic feels a little different, like you said, but Kal has been helping me."

Rowen started, eyes going wide.

"Sorry." Rowen apologized as he bowed to them both belatedly.

"No formalities required tonight," said Corin, holding up a hand. Rowen nodded, relief written on his face.

They entered and were just settling in when Jenna and Arianna glided into the room.

Kal glanced over and paused, appreciatively staring at the two beautiful women. Arianna was pretty, but Jenna looked lovely in her shimmering green dress.

Kal glanced at Corin, who stood transfixed. So far, he had spent his entire life determined not to marry and pass the voice down to his descendants, but now that the voice was gone, possibilities existed for him again. Kal's stomach clenched at the thought of Corin and Jenna together.

Jenna took in the room's occupants and then focused on them individually. Rowen appeared more relaxed than she had seen him since the house arrest, though he was staring at Arianna with his mouth open in a way that made Jenna quietly giggle to herself. She turned to study Kal, who was breathtaking in his dark coat, thick hair braided back and held in a simple clasp. He gazed back at her, eyes bright, and her heart quickened, recalling the dance.

She tore her eyes from him and found King Corindanthanus on his right. The king also wore a dark coat, but he had the royal emblem over his heart and had gold threading at the edges. Though it was not her first time meeting the king, she could hardly say they knew each other well. Jenna managed to keep the surprise off her face, as well as her irritation at her grandfather for not telling her who their guests were.

She continued to study the king. He was in his mid-twenties but seemed older, as if being king had aged him, but his eyes were bright as he studied Arianna. His raven hair was coiled and hanging loosely down, framing his face. He was shorter than Kal. Both men had strong eyebrows and long lashes, but that was where the resemblance ended. The king's features were chiseled and hard, whereas Kal's were softer or unfinished. They were both quite handsome, but in different ways. Out of the corner of her eye, she caught Arianna's curtsy and hurried to do the same.

"Your Majesty," they both said.

It was Oswen who put an end to all the gaping and made the introductions.

They were seated with Rowen on one end as the firstborn Sandoval heir present, the king and Arianna on either side of him as eldest present from their houses. Jenna sat next to the king, and across from her was Kal. Oswen was at the other end of the table opposite Rowen. The conversation was intentionally light to start. Jenna stared pointedly at Oswen. She would have liked to see a dossier on tonight's guests. It would have helped direct the conversation, and to make matters worse, Oswen was oddly silent. It was Arianna who saved them.

"Lord Rowen told the most amazing story the other day about The Three." She stared at him longingly. "Could you tell it again?"

Rowen cleared his throat.

Something shifted behind his eyes. Jenna sensed a flare of magic expand from and contract back into Rowen, but then it was gone. "No, most gracious lady, but I can tell you another tale."

Jenna frowned, his words not agreeing with what he had told her earlier. She shifted her gaze to a magical one and took in what seemed to be a cloud overlaying Rowen's normal tones. She glanced around the table. She wasn't the only one who perceived it. Oswen had gone still, and Kal and the king had tense shoulders. Only Arianna smiled, staring at him, enthralled.

Rowen wove light and started to speak.

"At the heart of the night sky lies a being of great power." The lights wove a two-dimensional oval-shaped view that had a large dark space in the middle.

"One day, this being became pregnant and gave birth." The lights became three-dimensional, where the dark center became a sphere and then burst apart, yielding globules of dark, which scattered the lights.

"One of those babes was flung far away from its parent, its cry echoing through the realm. The call reached out through the expanse, summoning different types of magical forces to it, and these elementals surrounded the babe, shielding it from sight." The lights showed lots of smaller rocks and gases surrounding the babe, forming a protective coating around it.

"Still, it cried, and more elements came to it. When its shell was deep enough to hide it, the being within grew tired and fell into a deep sleep, letting the currents pull it along." The lights showed the orb being pulled into and out of orbit of numerous stars until it settled into a stable flow around a single star.

"The child of enormous power began to dream, and from those dreams grew life, small and large." The lights showed familiar and unfamiliar creatures. Some Jenna recognized, and others, like the dragons, came from legend.

"One day, an Elden ship landed, spilling out new creatures." The lights showed an enormous ship approaching the world, shrinking in scale to a small dot as it matched the planet's speed. It then arced down for a landing.

"These creatures were builders of new and unique items." The lights showed farmers and people building buildings.

"The babe sent its dreams to speak with the new creatures, but the Elden did not understand and either killed them or ran them off." The lights showed clashes and battles between beasts and creatures.

"Then, the Elden did something unexpected. They built a portal." Rowen showed a pool of light beneath a gateway.

"Many more creatures came through the gate. Among them were those who would later become The Three." Rowen showed people, supplies, and machinery spilling from the portal.

"The Elden dispersed over the world, making new cities."

He showed the points of expansion. "The dreamer called into existence two of its most powerful creations, Guardian and Seed. They could communicate with both the dreams and the Elden. Using Guardian and Seed, the dreamer warned the Elden that one day, she would awaken, and when she did, this world would not survive its hatching. She was young yet, so there was time, but anyone other than the dreams would need to find a way to another world. The dreamer tasked Guardian and Seed to help prepare the creatures for that time." Rowen showed the dreams and creatures meeting with Guardian and Seed.

"Many years passed, and The Three had grown in power and knowledge under the tutelage of Guardian and Seed and were making their way in the world. Wars had broken out on other worlds, and several battles had spilled through the gate, devastating the city around it." Rowen showed massive scale battles with beasts and machines traveling through and defending the gate.

"The last to return before shutting the gate down was one of The Three, as the other two had returned earlier. To protect their world, they shut down the portal." He showed one of The Three and his team battling the invaders to hold the gate followed by them shutting down the world gate.

"At the request of the Elden, Guardian buried the world gate." Rowen showed the earth opening up and swallowing the portal and surrounding lands and buildings.

"Eventually, one of The Three was assigned the task of watching over the old city and its portal. A new city grew on top of the old, and knowledge of the portal faded away." Rowen showed the ebb and flow of a new city growing over the old. Jenna's breath caught. That city looked a lot like Mendallon, at least how she had come to perceive it.

"The one assigned to watch over the portal was betrayed and has been trapped in a dream ever since. While ze lies trapped, others have come to this world and work to build a new world gate, opening the world up once again to war and conquest."

The table was hushed as the lights faded from the air.

A brief pulse of magic flared from Rowen as he closed his eyes. He opened them, reaching for a glass of water. The cloud over his essence was gone.

"What would ze do if ze was set free?" Arianna asked.

Rowen glanced up at her in surprise. "Pardon? Who is ze?"

Arianna opened her mouth, but Kal put his hand on top of hers, shaking his head. She blushed at the contact, but stayed silent.

Jenna stared at Kal's hand as if it were on fire. She opened her mouth to speak when a servant entered and passed a message to Kal. He removed the offending hand to take the message and read it. Kal then turned to Oswen and bowed.

"My apologies. Something urgent has come up."

He turned, staring at the king, who nodded approval, then he bowed to the others and left.

Jenna frowned hollowly as she tracked him leaving the building. She opened her mouth again, and a different selection of words came out. "Arianna, perhaps after dinner, you could play something for us?" Arianna blushed and nodded. Oswen signaled, and the servers came in with the first course.

Chapter 35

Missives

As Kal left the Sandoval estate, a breeze brought an odd sound to his ears. It faded as he entered the carriage for the short ride back. When the carriage turned onto the main road, the sound got louder. Mendallon's streets were clogged with people holding signs or chanting, "Find the children." Kal's skin crawled at the charged air. All it would take is a spark.

He didn't have much time left before the crowds erupted.

His leads on the missing children had turned up nothing new. Andrade was clearly involved, as well as Baron Jaxson, but he needed to find out who the third person in the room was.

He was sure the Rod of Inanis was related to the missing children, but he didn't know how they triggered it. He was unsure of where to find the children. The caverns seemed a likely possibility, but could he trust a fantastical tale told by the entity that had been cursing his family? They had sent Edward into the caverns with a team. He should hear anytime now.

Kal rubbed his temples in thought as the carriage slowly navigated the throng as it returned to the palace.

T hree urgent missives had arrived for him. Curiosity got the better of him, and Kal opened the parcel from the border first. It contained a small handwritten journal. Kal flipped through it.

Never show weakness in front of a Lycanide. They can, however, be baited and trapped. Find out what they want and set the trap. It's keeping them that's difficult. Be prepared for a fight. Beware their webs, needles, darts, and venom. They have also been known to throw sticky balls.

He flipped ahead a few more pages.

Most Lycanide are simple and direct. They have no qualms over killing. One Lycanide can wipe out a small village in one night. They are loyal to their pack. The female Lycanides train their young, while the males take over after the trial period. Survival rates under the males are unknown.

He flipped to the end.

It is not known what makes Lycanides challenge their alpha. Their social structure is an enigma. Under no circumstances declare yourself alpha. If you find yourself in such a position, be prepared to die. Expect to be challenged, especially by the males. Killing a Lycanide is difficult and requires skill and luck. You must limit their range to prevent distance attacks and stop them from grappling with you with their deadly claws.

Kal closed his eyes as he shut the book. *They can't all be like Roolia.* He was pretty sure Lord Deleon and Sir Roland had been killed by a Lycanide. To protect himself and others, he needed to figure out how to kill one. He snorted. He'd add that to his list of things. Kal placed the book down and reached for the first letter from Master Evans.

Finished the evaluation of the box. It's a transfer box. There wasn't enough powder for two transfers since ours was not in a box, but shielded. Traced the powder remaining on the Rod of Trellium to a paired box in an empty warehouse. Have both boxes.

Kal swore. Jaxson must have funded the repair so they could replace it with a transfer box. When he pulled out his gloves to handle the rod, they must have been coated in powder. Closing the box had completed the transfer. It was a brilliant heist. The first thing he would have done was destroy those gloves. Without hard evidence, they couldn't prove a thing.

He opened the second letter from Master Evans. It was short and to the point.

Edward and his team are missing. The bond went dark a few days ago. He is still alive, but I cannot find him.

Kal grimaced. Was that where the children were? Somewhere in the caverns? If not, what's down there? A magical library? That wouldn't help him find the children. He needed to find out more about the Compact. They were clearly taking the children.

Kal groaned, then tore open the last letter from his transfer box, this one from Master Harram. Dread filled him seeing this one was in code. The hair stood up on the back of his arms as he translated.

Compiled info from various sites associated with the Compact:
Harvesting is almost complete.
Rod secured.
Sacrificial mage selected.
Soon, the invasion can begin.

Chapter 36

Pool of Light

C asi sat, head bowed, legs slowly swishing back and forth in the water as she surreptitiously studied the nearby guards. Two teenage siblings, Sarah and Jared Deleon, sat next to her. They had all shown up around the same time. She knew little about the Deleons, but their clothes were of high quality.

In here, social status didn't matter.

The bottom of Casi's blue maid's overdress dipped into the water of the pool, soaking up the moisture, staining it from repeated exposure to its high mineral content.

Casi, still eyeing the black-clad guards, frowned. It was the guards' job to keep the youth in the pool. The guards were always there unless the kids, ranging in age from nine to sixteen, were locked in the bunk room. When that happened, the children were so tired that all they did was sleep. The draw was harder on the younger kids.

When you first entered the cavern, it appeared cramped because the ceiling was so low, but where the pool was, it opened up into a giant hollow space. There were no stalagmites near the pool, but there were signs of them further out in the cave. The ceiling's dark rock reflected the shimmering light given off by the pool.

Casi could make out stalactites hanging down, and on occasion, she detected motion high up and was able to glimpse the bodies of the beasts that had brought them here. Casi shuddered, recalling the night she got captured.

Wrapping her arms around herself, Casi turned toward the doors. There was a large table where several mages sat working, distilling the pool water into a glowing fluid. From what Casi gathered, the pool acted as a conduit, siphoning magic from them. The mages filtered and extracted the magic in the liquid and stored it in barrels, reusing the remaining water in the pool. Each shift, the mages arrived with an empty barrel. At shift's end, they left with a barrel full of magically condensed liquid. From what Casi had learned, there were at least four shifts, which meant there were three other rooms full of sleeping youth while her room was on shift.

A dozen or so other children lined the pool's edge, legs bare from the knees down. Except for Casi, they were all showing signs of exhaustion. Casi had the highest tolerance to the drain of the pool, and sometimes, she pulled a double shift to allow one of the other children to rest. It had been many weeks since they arrived, and over that time, a handful of the children had gone missing.

The younglings were passing around a water pail and ladle when the doors opened, and three new youths were escorted in. One was slightly older and taller than the other two and wore formal garb that bore an official armband of the city. The other two wore matching blue pants and shirts, but Casi had never seen the design before. The eldest boy put himself between the other youths and the guards. The guards had them remove their shoes and led them to a spot near Casi.

When the guards turned and left, the tall young man stared at Casi.

"My name is Edward, and this," he said, gesturing to the other two teens, "is Aedan and Jon."

Casi introduced Jared, Sarah, and herself.

"What is this place?" Aedan asked, glancing around at the large pool with youths of various ages sitting on the edge.

"Hell," Jared said, shoulders slumped.

Edward was still staring at Casi, so she spoke.

"This is where they drain us of our magic. I think they are storing it for later use."

"Is there a way out of here?" Jon asked, looking around the cavern.

"Burnout," said Jared. "If you can't produce more energy, they get rid of you."

"Any other alternatives?" Edward asked with a sidelong glance at Jared.

"None that we've found," Sarah said.

Casi considered the problem again. Maybe if she tried sending more magic than the pool was taking? She had tried it before, but the pool had compensated, raising the amount it wanted, which had caused more issues with the other youth, as they only had so much to give. Besides, what good would it do? She suspected the guards wouldn't let them go because she powered it faster. In fact, she was pretty sure that if they didn't need the others, they would just get rid of them.

Casi sighed.

"Don't worry, we'll think of something," Edward said, glancing down at her again. Casi almost laughed. She, too, had once been optimistic like that. The best she could offer was a nod.

"What news from the city? Are they searching for us?" Casi asked.

"They are," said Edward, his smile not quite reaching his eyes. "I'm sure they'll find us soon."

The mages came back into the cavern, and Edward groaned. Casi estimated it had been several days since Edward had arrived. His enthusiasm already taking a hit. The mages sat at a table near the doorway, and the children were further in the cavern, near its center.

Casi had been at this for what felt like weeks. During the last session, several children had passed out and were taken away by the guards. Edward's shoulders slumped in anticipation. Whatever this pool was, it forced them to call on their abilities, but their powers never manifested because the pool then consumed the raw force of them. It left them in what felt like a continuous state of exhaling, which was exhausting.

Casi didn't know why she held up the best. She thought it must be in how she manipulated the flow of magic. She always perceived magic as motes, swirls, or eddies. Some were stable, while others weren't. Through trial and error, she had learned how to tell which motes would collapse or stay stable if you siphoned energy from them.

Standing by herself, Casi glimpsed Edward staring at her. He often did when she worked magic during the draw.

"Casi?" he called, moving through the pool over to her.

She glanced over at him, then at the guards, whose attention flickered at the movement. They didn't care what you did as long as you stayed in the pool.

"Can we try something?" he asked softly.

She nodded hesitantly.

"I'm going to reach out to you with my magic. Can you grab hold of me and hang on?"

He reached out a tendril of magic towards her, and she grabbed hold of him.

"Now you, Aedan." He nodded at him, and he joined. "Jon? Sarah, Jared?"

They joined. The mages were just sitting down to start up the process. "Casi, while holding on to us, pull as you normally would. We will siphon from your pull instead of using our raw energy. Everyone else, follow my lead."

They all nodded.

"Casi," Edward said. "Whatever you do, don't let go of us. Everyone hold on tight to Casi."

The magical draw started up, pulling on the magic contained within the children. Casi felt the weight of the draw and started her pull.

Edward slowly stepped through the actions required to pull energy from Casi's flow instead of from themselves. He paused to make sure they all were with him. When they completed the last step, they became passive observers of the power flowing through them into the pool.

Jon and Aedan laughed while Sarah's and Jared's eyes misted up. Casi stood in concentration.

"Casi, are you all right?"

She nodded, chewing on her lip as she changed her draw to balance out each of their pulls through the link. "I can do this."

It had been several hours, and the five of them were still funneling magic from Casi instead of themselves. Casi was handling the extra load with no issues until, down the line, first one, then another of the children not connected to them passed out as their magic levels dipped too low and their bodies were not able to compensate.

While one guard came over and fished them out of the pool, the load shifted violently on all the children, bringing some to their knees. Casi's brow pinched in concentration as Edward and the others scrambled to maintain their hold on her. Since the other children were not part of the link, she couldn't manage their load. Casi understood that increasing her flow wouldn't work since the pool would increase its ask accordingly. She viewed the threads of magic she held representing Edward and the others as a new idea formed.

"Edward? Is there any reason why more children can't join us?"

Edward wrinkled his brow. "It depends on how much power you can pull. Do you see spots?"

"No."

"Feel dizzy?"

"No."

"When you look at me, does it feel like you are looking through someone else's eyes?"

"No." She smiled at the absurdity of the question.

"Then you have not reached your limit. If you feel any of those symptoms, we need to stop or risk burning you out."

She nodded.

"Can you show the other children?" Casi asked, realizing that to do this, he would have to drop his connection and walk them through it, plus he would have to repeat it multiple times.

Edward frowned.

"I can try," he said. "Be ready, because my load will shift out of the team."

"Okay," she said.

Edward dropped out of the link. She saw his shoulders bow under the pressure of the draw. He walked over to the nearest child and got their attention. Casi's grip on the others wobbled as she stabilized it. It took a moment before she heard the soft murmur of speech, then a long pause before the boy turned towards Casi and the others standing upright as if the weight of the pool was not on them. He nodded to Edward, and a short while later, he joined the link.

Water splashed as the boy fell to his knees, sobbing in relief. Casi overheard Edward. "Don't let go of Casi." Then he himself let go again.

This time, Casi stabilized faster. A few minutes later, another child joined, and another.

In the end, eighteen children linked with Casi, who was sweating profusely now, the edges of her hair plastered to the sides of her face. Edward sloshed over.

"That's the last of them. Casi, how do you feel?" he asked, staring at her sweat-soaked brow.

"Heavy," she managed to say.

Edward grabbed her as she was about to sit down in the pool. He held her tightly as the other children came closer, fear on their faces.

"Are you dizzy?" Edward asked.

"No."

Edward studied her, disbelieving.

"You can see me?" he asked

She reached out and placed her hand on his face. One of the children laughed, and the others hushed him.

"Yes," she said.

Edward stared into her intense brown eyes, sensing the power swirling behind them.

"When you say it's heavy, show me where the weight is."

She closed her eyes.

Edward did the same while reaching for his magic. He visualized the links of all the children twined together and wrapped around her. She showed him the single flow she was pulling from what can only be described as a well, then Casi showed him the individual flows she was pushing out to the children, and last, the flow the pool was drawing directly from her.

"Casi, you added additional flows to compensate for the missing children, right?"

She nodded.

"You're funneling that power directly from yourself, not drawing it from the well," he said with a bit of awe. "All that time, you weren't really using a well at all. I mean, you are, but with only one thread, and that's going to the pool. On top of that, you became our source. You should be pulling just as much from your well as you are pushing out to the threads and the pool. You're like a living battery. You're amazing, but you will eventually suffer like the rest of us. Instead of pulling from yourself, try pulling from the well you found."

He walked her through the steps of increasing her draw on the well and processing that power, so she used it properly. Casi stood a little straighter each time they boosted the power. When they finished the last link, Casi said, "Thanks, that really helped."

Chapter 37

King's Vow

Kal sat across the desk from the king in his private office. He had just finished filling the king in on what he had learned about the coming invasion.

"I will quietly increase the guards and standing army, using the missing children as the excuse." Corin stood up from his desk and began pacing. "What news from surrounding kingdoms? Are any of them behind this?"

"No, all news from them remains consistent. Something would have leaked by now if they were behind this."

Corin frowned. "I know you've found some children, but I need you to find the rest. I'm being flooded with petitions." Corin referenced the pile of paperwork on his desk. "Even the Bakers Guild submitted one. The Bakers Guild! Did you know that statistically most bakers are women? They are mothers, grandmothers, and aunts of the missing children. People want action, Kal."

Kal knew he had to find the children. But how? He'd tried everything. Except...

Kal closed his eyes for a moment, thinking back to the journal on Lycanides. *Never declare yourself alpha.* If he couldn't change things, he would have to own it. Just what could he do with a pack of Lycanides as alpha besides die? His mind sifted through possibilities. If he was already dead, why not take a chance?

Kal opened his eyes to find his brother standing before him.

"You've thought of something. What have you got planned?"

Kal hesitated. "It's dangerous, but I need to grow my pack."

That night, Kal went to the kitchens and found Roolia gnawing on a deer bone, which splintered under her powerful jaws. She lapped up the marrow.

"Roolia, walk with me."

Kal left the kitchens, and a few moments later, she followed, bone hanging from her mouth.

Kal frowned, choosing to ignore the bone. "I wish to increase the pack. Tell me about the other Lycanides in the city."

Roolia dropped her bone. "Roolia not worthy?"

"Roolia is worthy, but I need to find more children."

Roolia sat on her haunches, fur matted with bone shards. She said nothing.

Kal studied her and asked the question he'd needed to ask for a while. "When we first met, why did you choose to hide children in that location?"

"Lycanide already there, not come back."

Kal parsed the words. "Why are you in the city at all?"

Roolia froze, then lowered herself as if she expected him to hit her. "Roolia left pack."

"You ran away?" He saw her flinch. "Why, Roolia?"

"Pack hurt humans."

"Why would that matter to a Lycanide?" he asked before thinking better of it.

Roolia growled, sitting back up. "Not monster."

Kal chewed on that. "Are the other Lycanides in the city hurting humans? Other than the knights?"

She deflated. "No, only capture."

"What do they get from capturing the children?"

"Don't know."

"Would any of them be worthy? Would they follow me as alpha?"

Roolia whined. "Only if you strong. You defeat."

"And am I strong enough to defeat a Lycanide?"

"You alpha," she said, then picked up her bone and left.

Kal did not stop her.

The next morning, Kal stared out Abasi's window at the green garlands decorating the city below. Tomorrow was the beginning of King's Vow, where the king opened up the castle, and more importantly, its pantries, to the people. Travelers came from all over the surrounding lands to take part in the celebration. There were performances and dances. Marriage vows fell like leaves from trees.

The guardsmen would put on a show of power with the heightened presence in the streets and scheduled bouts ranking incoming recruits. The king would bring his hall out into the streets, with the city council publicly reviewing the latest changes to laws and giving citizens time to offer rebuttals or agreements.

Kal focused on the wagons of people and wares coming into the gates and frowned. If his information from the Compact was correct, war was coming. People kill in war, especially mages. Kal's gut churned as he thought about the vow he had required of Jenna. What if he was wrong? The feel of his father's heart stopping flashed before his eyes. Kal clenched his fist. He wasn't wrong.

"You want to do what?" Captain Abasi asked, bringing Kal back to the moment.

Kal repeated himself. "I want to mark the children."

"And what exactly does that entail?"

Kal reached into his pocket and gave the Captain a small bright red ribbon and a tattoo kit. "There is a children's section chosen for the events, correct?"

"Yes."

"Could we pin the ribbons on or stamp the children on entry?"

"We could, but what does that gain us?"

"Hidden in the ribbon and the ink are markers that can track the children."

"I thought you wanted to stop them from taking the children, not use them as bait."

"My goal is to save lives. What would you do?"

"What do you mean?" the captain asked guardedly.

"What is your plan to stop a Lycanide? You and I both know that there must be more than one of them out there, and they can't all be on our side. How would you classify stopping her—as easy or hard?"

His mouth opened and closed several times. "Hard."

"Roolia has been sneak attacking Doha since they met. The webbing and the capture tactics she uses are a game."

The captain adjusted the collar of his shirt.

"It's a game designed to teach the young. The only reason we got any of the children back is because she chose to save them. From what Roolia has said, we are facing a male of the species. They take over training only after the female has taught the young enough to stay alive. In Doha's case, he would only receive training after his trial period was up, and he agrees to join the pack."

"So they are paternal?"

Kal sifted through all the research he had been doing.

"Not in the way you think of it. When they take over training, it's to teach them to kill. These spider wolves, as the men have taken to calling them, do not view you as friends or as equals."

"How do they view us?" the captain asked.

"Generally? As food. But in this case, I suspect it is something else. In this case, they view us as chattel, which makes us very lucky indeed."

"Lucky? How?"

"If a spider wolf wants you gone, they can take out an entire town in less than twenty-four hours. We've lost what, ninety children? They don't appear to want to move in and claim this territory. Someone has mobilized them and sent them on a specific mission."

"You mean another alpha?"

Kal frowned. "Yes."

"What could we possibly have that they want?"

"All the children taken so far, with a few outliers, are mage-born."

The captain went silent for a moment, then said, "Yes."

"Do you understand what that means?"

"Someone is trying to take down the king."

Kal sighed. "Yes, but what else?"

"Someone has a different use for the children."

Kal nodded.

"You mentioned they think of us as chattel. If they think of us as goods, what do they want to trade us for?"

"That is a good question, but if we find out, we will be in a position to make our own bargains."

"Doesn't Roolia know?" Abasi demanded.

"No, she entered the city on a different quest."

"And what was that?"

Kal didn't want to tell the captain she ran away, so instead he said, "Exploration."

"And you believe her?"

Kal thought about the Lycanide. He didn't think she was very old, and the words "not monster" echoed back to him. "I do."

"I will allow it," Abasi said. "The ribbons and stamps."

"Thank you," Kal said.

He left Abasi's office and returned to his room. There, he sent summonses to Jenna, his team from Canticle Inn, and Doha asking that he bring Roolia. It was time they planned.

J enna worked the entrance to the children's section of the festivities. She used a tendril of magic to identify mage-born children as targets and gave them special ribbons with just a whisper of magic to encourage them to keep them. She arranged it so the ribbons gave them access to the games in the central hall and was careful to tell them to come back to her for a replacement if they got lost.

Jenna stood by the wall, watching the sea of children and parents laugh and play games. Flashes of Casi playing at previous fairs brought a tear to her eyes.

To distract herself, Jenna forced herself to glance up. Roolia was hiding above. Kal had added some magic to deter people from looking up and seeing her.

Jenna had been with Roolia earlier as she made sure that her scent was everywhere they didn't want the male spider wolf to go. She and Kal had worked to clear Roolia's scent from the path they wanted him to take using magic. Jenna caught a brief movement as Roolia waited over the massive crowd below.

Jenna's shoulders had just started to relax when she made out a scream that didn't sound joyful. Jenna and several sentries turned toward the cry as it came again. Some children and parents in the crowd were starting to give sidelong stares. Jenna stared up at Roolia through the lens of her magic as Roolia anchored herself and leaped off the ceiling, spinning silk as she moved.

Jenna set off in the same direction, the guards following. She drew on the magic lying dormant in the ribbons. Thin threads formed in the air from Jenna to the ribbons. One stretched outside of the enclosure. Jenna took off running after the thread as she called out instructions through the yanzu in her ear.

Teams of guards positioned around the area responded to her instructions, and the thread shifted its course in response. Jenna couldn't see the beast, but she knew it was headed in the right direction. She continued ordering guardsmen to make their presence known.

T he hall where they herded the spider wolf had large double doors on both ends, with four supporting pillars spread evenly throughout the room. Its table had been disassembled earlier and spread out along the sides of the room. The hall was roughly twenty feet tall, with beams crisscrossing along the upper part of the room. Five chandeliers hung from the ceiling—a small one in each corner and a large one tethered in the middle of the hall.

Kal, hidden with magic, studied the male spider wolf as it moved into the side hall they had roped off with "Do not enter" signs. Powerful muscles gathered and released as it stalked with the smooth glide of a predator. The Lycanide cautiously sniffed the air, checking the room for inhabitants.

The male was similar to Roolia, but more substantial and powerfully built. Doha and Kal's team was positioned up in one of the crawlways, shielded by a see-through wall that Kal had created. It gave them a clear view of the hall, and they used it now to keep an eye on the Lycanide below.

The large male paused, sniffing the air as he turned right and climbed, carrying a small bundle between him and the wall.

The beast climbed slowly, pausing every few feet to sniff the air currents, and it became clear the spider wolf sensed something was off about the room but couldn't place it. He slowed as he neared the ceiling, then anchored himself and his package before starting across the ceiling, heading for one of the airways that led outside of the building.

Kal had a clear view as Roolia cautiously approached the doorway that the Lycanide had entered and peered into the hall. She waited until she saw movement on the ceiling that placed him behind one of the pillars, then entered.

Kal studied Roolia as she stealthily closed the door behind her and twisted the lock, as Kal had shown her. The doors on the far side of the hall were already closed and locked. Earlier, Kal had his team block the larger airways except one, and that one they rigged. If her fellow Lycanide made it that far, he would be trapped in the room's airway and sealed off by Kal's magic.

Above, the male spider wolf, hearing the noise of the door sealing, made a small leap to remove the pillar from its view and swiveled his head toward her. Several of their eyes met in an unspoken challenge. He leaped toward the left front pillar. As he jumped for the pillar, he threw four hardened web darts at her, one after the other.

Roolia jumped to the left, up, and away from the doorway, spinning a web that she split into two different threads. She bounced on the wall, balancing with the agility he had seen her use when following him through city streets. After landing, she anchored one line and continued. When she reached the blind side of the pole, she released one thread, spun a new one attached to the ceiling, and pushed off, reeling the line in as she went. Her momentum brought her up and around to the central beam on a collision course with the male spider wolf.

The male, apparently unfazed, barked a challenge, bared his teeth, and leaped to meet her. The two beasts crashed together in midair. Their two front paws locked together before their other feet connected in a mirror image. Their teeth gnashed, snapping at each other as they fell.

Kal tore his eyes off of the battle and signaled. The team crawled out of their hiding places. Kelly and Donovan took up archery stances. Doha and Justin went for the child, and Gabe and Wyn assisted with their tethers.

Kal followed the trajectory of Doha's anchoring darts as they went into the ceiling attached to ropes. Doha and Justin stealthily moved above the growls and thrashing below. Roolia had broken off from the larger spider wolf. Both had taken damage. Doha quickly pulled the cords through so they could climb over to the child. Kal saw the flash of the dagger he had given Doha earlier to cut the binding web with, but Doha still had to get the child back without getting stuck to the sack himself, or he wouldn't be able to maneuver. Gabe and Wyn steadied the ropes as Doha and Justin moved steadily toward the wrapped child.

Kal leaned against the wall, cloaked in magic, as he studied the battle on the other side of the hall. From what he had learned in his studies,

Roolia would not appreciate his intervention too soon, so he watched and waited.

"Why play?" growled the male Lycanide. "Am I pup?!"

Roolia shot two webs, one hidden by the other. The male blocked one and took the other one in the side, letting out a puff of air. She leaped in, but Kal could tell he recovered faster than she anticipated, sending a double set of claws against her, throwing her off to the side and into the pillar, stunning her for a moment.

The male turned, taking in Doha, who was trying to cut loose the captive. Dread filled Kal. Ignoring Roolia, the Lycanide growled, bunched his hind legs, and leaped toward the captive.

As the male jumped over Roolia, she vaulted up, attaching herself to his belly. She dug her claws into him, spitting and hissing.

"Mine!" she screamed. "Not for you!"

He curled around her, and they fell to the ground, rolling. When they separated, Roolia rose on her hind legs and hissed. Surprised by her ferocity, the male took a step back, eyes darting to the human reeling in his prize.

"Is pup?"

"Trial pup. Mine!"

Kal grimaced as the male spider wolf's lips curled in contempt.

She was on him before he could speak. During his indecision, she had spun several darts, which she embedded into his left and right sides. The male roared. Time slowed as he battled her to a standstill. Awe filled Kal. Even injured, he was her match. Kal studied the male spider wolf as he risked a glance up at the ceiling, noticing his package was gone. The team had secured themselves and the child behind the shield.

The Lycanide turned his full attention back to Roolia, fur rising in what Kal knew to be fury. He tied off two of her legs, pinning them to her body. Rising up to deal her a death blow, he suddenly stiffened. Embedded in his left shoulder was an arrow bearing the fletched colors of Mendallon. Then he was slammed by a beam of light, which hurled him up into a pillar. He fell to the floor, not moving.

Kal released his cloaking magic and walked over to the downed Lycanide. His right hand glowed softly. The spider wolf rose slowly, the arrow shaft broken off on impact. He shook his massive head to clear it, muscles bunching as he brought the weight of his gaze to Kal. *The Three, he's big!* Sweat broke out at the base of Kal's back.

"You alpha?" the Lycanide snarled.

Show no fear raced through Kal's mind. "I am." Kal's heart pounded loudly in his ears.

The hound lunged.

Kal's right hand shot up in front of him, and the hound slammed into a shield, flying back. He repeated the action with the same results.

Kal's eyes narrowed as the hound rose again and circled him, looking for a way in.

"Are you alpha?" Kal asked.

The growling coalesced into the word "no".

Kal struggled to keep the surprise off his face. *Even he's not an alpha? Just how big do the males get?*

Both of them shifted when Roolia spoke. "You overstep."

"He alpha," the spider wolf growled. "I challenge him."

Kal had expected this. What he had not expected was the ferocity and sheer size. *Can I beat this beast?* His mind jumped to his brother, then Jenna and her missing sister. *I have to.* Kal took a deep breath, exhaling his doubts and fears. Cool determination settled over him as he drew his sword, then dropped his shield.

"I accept your challenge."

The Lycanide lunged. Sparks flared along the edges of Kal's sword as he pushed magic into it, taking a fighting stance.

The hound reared, and Kal struck, slicing into the hard skin of the creature's chest. The Lycanide howled. Blood spattered the ground as the Lycanide retreated, spinning darts and launching them. Kal's eyes flashed briefly as he barely managed to generate a soft shield that captured all but one of the darts inches from him. The one that got through drew a grunt from Kal as it embedded itself in his right shoulder. Kal released the shield, and the darts caught up in it fell to the ground. He ripped the dart from his shoulder and advanced on the spider wolf. He had to limit the Lycanide's range while also preventing him from grappling with him.

Kal concentrated, sweat beading his brow as he approached, creating another shield—this one over both of them. The Lycanide backed into the shield and growled low, then lunged at Kal.

Kal tied off the shield with relief and stepped aside, cutting off his claw just before it reached his throat. The spider wolf hissed.

"Yield," said Kal.

The creature reared, and Kal lunged forward, his sword piercing its shoulder. The beast jerked away, snarling.

"Yield!"

Limping, the creature paced the edge of the shield.

"Is she not worthy?" he reasoned.

The beast stopped, massive head swinging from Kal to Roolia and back.

"She worthy."

Roolia growled out the word "stupid" as if to say, of course, she was worthy. The corners of Kal's mouth twitched.

"Roolia?"

She glanced at him.

"Is he worthy?"

"He worthy," she replied after a short pause, then began muttering to herself.

"Am I worthy?" he said to her.

"You alpha," she replied instantly.

He repeated the question to the male, who stared at him a long moment before replying.

"You alpha," he ceded.

Kal gave a brief nod and listed the rules.

No hunting in the city. No stealing children. You will protect Mendallon.

The hound growled louder at each one. After speaking the last rule, Kal said, "Are you challenging me?"

The growling stopped.

Kal lowered his shield.

Chapter 38

Garwan

Doha and Justin hoisted the child down to Roolia, who began cutting the hardened webbing. Doha climbed down next to Roolia as she worked, standing on her injured side, offering what little protection he could. Kal studied the newest member of his pack as the male Lycanide approached Roolia, and Doha turned around, hands on his sheathed sword, to face him. The room went silent as the Lycanide spoke.

"You in my place, little one."

Doha did not move. Justin took a step closer to Doha, ready to back him up.

Swat. "Ouch!" Doha yelped, turning to Roolia in surprise, hand on the side of his head. "Roolia! What was that for?"

"You heard," she rumbled, expression pinched. Doha turned and glared at the male, who chittered until she continued. "Stupid place now."

Doha smoothed his face as the male hissed and clenched his large teeth. "Name Garwan, not stupid."

Gabe and Wyn shifted uncomfortably, and Kelly and Donovan never took their eyes off the male Lycanide. Roolia spoke to Doha again.

"You other side now."

She gently nosed Doha to her other side.

Once Roolia was ready, they opened the doors, and Jenna approached Kal with some of the additional guards.

"You're hurt," she said, eyes on the blood where the dart had punctured him. She raised her hand to send a short burst of healing into him.

"I'm fine." He grabbed her hand. He couldn't afford to show weakness in front of the Lycanides. Jenna's eyes fixated on his hand, and he realized he hadn't let her go.

Reluctantly, he dropped it, and he led their mixed party as they made their way through cleared halls to bring the young girl to the healers before waking her. After injecting the girl to awaken her, Roolia slipped out of the room, leaving all the drama for Kal.

The team followed Roolia, who had healed some but was still limping a bit, while the male appeared almost fully recovered, his paw beginning to regrow.

Kal left the Healerie and found them all waiting for him in the hall. He led them all to the captain's office, which barely had room for the two massive beasts with everyone else squeezed in.

As they filed in, the captain studied the new, much larger beast, identifying each wound. "Report," Captain Abasi said.

Doha stepped forward and summarized the operation. Kal's gaze tracked Roolia and Abasi as Doha spoke. The two had not taken their eyes off each other. He still didn't know what had happened between the two or how she had gotten Doha reassigned to the team. And he may never know.

Roolia's tail swished back and forth across the floor where she sat. When Doha finished speaking, the room went silent as others noticed the battle of wills.

Kal followed the byplay with a half-smile. According to his information on Lycanides, it was about time for the females to go into heat. Roolia would likely leave to find a mate.

Garwan growled low and long, raising the hairs on Kal's arms.

"Roolia?" Doha asked.

The captain didn't move a muscle.

"Is nothing," Roolia said.

"Choose me," Garwan rumbled.

Kal, who was leaning on the wall, turned toward her. *Was it her time?*

"Is fine," she said again, but this time to Kal, whose eyebrows rose. *Could it be? How would an alpha respond?* Curiosity getting the better of him, an idea came to mind.

"My family has an estate in the west. There are hills to run in surrounding a large lake," said Kal, eyes locked on Roolia.

Roolia yawned, then started to pant.

"Lots of fresh animals to hunt. There are even fish in the lake."

Roolia quivered as Kal spoke.

She got up and walked over to him. Standing on her hind legs, she put four paws on the walls on either side of his head and torso.

Kal's eyes twinkled.

"Good Alpha," she whispered. "Protect pups."

Kal reached up and scratched the soft fur around her neck.

She leaned in closer, licking the side of his face.

Kal laughed. "When, Roolia?"

"Soon."

Kal frowned while scratching her ears as possibilities, not all good, coursed through him.

"What is happening soon?" asked Doha in a hushed tone.

"Mate. Make pups," growled Garwan.

The captain's eyes went wide.

"I can make arrangements," Kal said. Roolia stared at him, evaluating, and shook her head no.

"Garwan hold answers," she almost growled.

Kal nodded, all traces of humor fleeing as he realized he'd gotten sidetracked. He had business to attend to.

Roolia backed down and repositioned herself at her previous location, eyes focused again on the captain.

Kal surveyed the people in the room with hard, unyielding eyes before settling on the captain. "It's time we begin. Captain Abasi, where Roolia is first, this is my second, Garwan." Kal waved a hand at the new Lycanide. The male turned an imposing gaze at the captain.

"Second," the captain said, greeting him with no trace of fear. He then turned his attention back to Kal, who nodded in approval.

"Garwan?"

"Yes, Alpha?"

"Where are the children?" Kal asked.

"In catacombs."

The captain frowned and glanced at Doha, nodding permission to speak.

"All reports from the catacomb checks were clear," Doha said.

"Who submitted those reports?" Kal asked.

"The guard," Doha replied, not liking where this was going.

"The Royal Guard or the regular guard?" Kal asked.

"The regular guard," Doha said.

"Did they view the site themselves?" Kal asked.

Doha frowned before answering. "Not likely. The building and structures team would have done it, so the Andrades."

Kal turned back to Garwan. "Why are the children being taken?"

"To power portal."

"What portal?" asked the captain.

Garwan did not answer.

"What portal?" Kal was sure he knew the answer but wanted to hear it confirmed.

"The portal they build," Garwan growled.

Oh no. Kal spoke softly. "According to my intel, the portal is a door between worlds. It was buried generations ago to protect this world from outside warring factions. They must be building a new one."

"Is in catacombs," Garwan hissed. He paused again before speaking. "Near pool of light."

"Where exactly is this pool of light?" asked Captain Abasi.

Garwan stared at the side of Kal's head for a moment, then chittered in annoyance. "In catacombs."

The captain ground his teeth in frustration.

"Who has taken the children?" Kal asked before anyone replied.

"Cardinas. Andrade."

The answer had the captain on his feet. "Impossible!"

The other voice in the room that Jenna heard must have been Cardinas. The color blue at the Compact site, which matched their house blue. The look he had received at the meeting was triumph.

He couldn't act on this now. It was a Lycanide's word against a noble. He needed ironclad proof. Kal held up a hand. "Before we take action on that front, I would recommend we get the children back first. Jenna, go work with the healers at the Royal Healerie to prepare for at least a dozen more children."

Jenna nodded and left the room.

"The rest of you. Let's plan."

Kal led his pack, his team, and over a dozen guards into the caverns below the city. The descent was long, and the need to be quiet was paramount. When they reached the bottom, they stopped and took a break.

"Stay here," Kal commanded.

Garwan led Doha and Kal ahead to the main entrance. They peered out from behind a large boulder as two guards came out of the door, carrying cloak-wrapped objects, which they bore over to a side cavern. They came back a few minutes later without their loads. Kal's eyes flashed in anger, and Garwan moved away from him. Doha put a hand on Kal's shoulder as they waited for the guards to reenter the facility. After it had been quiet for a few minutes, he spoke.

"I will investigate the side cavern," said Doha.

337

Kal nodded as Doha went off, returning a quarter candle mark later.

"There are six bodies in that cavern. Two are still alive, though I don't know for how much longer."

Kal made a signal with his hand, and Roolia came forward with his team and the rest of the guards. Doha spoke with them, sending two guards to collect the dead and take the living to the castle for help. Once they were off, they turned their concentration back to the door.

"Garwan, is there a way through that doorway?"

"Yes, is left open for Lycanides. Hall on other side narrow. Easy to guard."

"All right," Kal glanced at Doha. "Justin, Doha, you're with me. Kelly and Gabe, gather your teams and follow silently."

Nods of acknowledgment went around as the words were whispered back to the other men. Kelly, Donovan, and her team gathered to one side, as Gabe, Wyn, and several other guards moved to the other side.

Roolia went ahead with Doha, and Garwan stayed with Kal as the soldiers fanned out around the entrance.

Justin opened the door, and Doha rushed into the silence ahead, Roolia on his heels. Kal and Garwan were next, and the soldiers followed behind like small shadows. The last man to enter closed it.

Kal created several small orbs that floated above them, generating light. They set off silently down the corridor. After a while, Kal held up a hand, and they stopped. He sent Garwan ahead, and a few minutes later, there was a small bump then another, and Garwan returned, dragging two men down the corridor, which he dropped in front of

Doha and Kal. They studied the men, who were wearing boots and garb that Kal had never seen.

Doha stared at Kal. "These men are not native to Mendallon, nor the surrounding kingdoms."

Kal nodded. "Maybe a mercenary operation? This one"—he pointed to the one on the left—"is likely from Bendicci, and the other looks Karlarean. They are from cities far to the south."

Garwan spoke. "Corridor opens to mess hall, offices, quarters."

Doha nodded, signaling Kelly and Gabe to come forward. "Our goal is the quick and quiet recovery of the children at the pool. Your goal is to keep others from joining the fray if the alarms go off, and if possible, free the children in the dorms."

They nodded.

Doha glanced at Kal, and he nodded. Doha commanded, "Proceed." The well-disciplined teams moved off to their assigned areas. Garwan had identified chokehold areas where a small force could prevent a much larger group from coming through. Kal, Roolia, Doha, Justin, and Garwan remained behind until a light flashed up the corridor signalling all were in place.

Roolia shifted, and Doha reached out to ruffle her fur. She growled. "Sorry," Doha said, removing his hand.

"Let's go," Kal said.

They went down the corridor and followed it past the other targets in search of the children. Within a few steps, they made out the clash of arms behind them. They were out of time.

Chapter 39

Rescue

K al and his team followed Garwan as he led them to the cavern entrance. Their plan was that Garwan would enter first and take down the guards.

Kal nodded, and Garwan prowled forward toward the guards.

"What are you doing here?" the first guard barked. "You are not allowed near us during the draw."

Hearing the exchange, Kal followed Garwan into the cavern. He knew from the journals that an alpha gave orders and his pack implemented them, but he didn't fully trust Garwan yet.

Two guards stared at Garwan while two others, who seemed to be mages, worked at a table funneling magic into a barrel. Kal glanced to the left and saw children huddled together in a luminescent pool, their features hidden by the powerful glow of magic.

Kal shifted, drawing the guard's attention as Garwan spun two darts. He threw one, and it jabbed the first guard in the chest, who fell to the ground unconscious. He threw another dart, but the second guard raised a shield before it hit, causing it to bounce away. Garwan lunged at the second guard as the other two behind him turned around. One of them triggered an alarm.

As the alarm started to clang, the door flew open, and Roolia charged into the cavern, followed by Justin and Doha. She leaped over Garwan toward the table and took down the two mages there. After injecting them with venom to knock them out, she turned and flung a dart into the back of the man shielded from Garwan since his shield did not surround him, and he fell to the ground.

Garwan growled at Roolia in dissatisfaction as he stomped over to the glowing panel and placed his paw on one of the symbols. The alarm stopped.

Kal came over, leaving Doha and Justin guarding the door, and studied the panel. The magic symbols for up and down were universal. He started touching different symbols engraved into the table in rapid succession, pushing them to the down position. Sweat broke out on his brow, and he hoped he was doing the right thing. The intensity of magic in the pool went down as he shut down the process. Kal sighed in relief. The draw dwindled, and they could make out the children's features in the pool. Kal craned his head as he searched for Jenna's sister in the pool. The draw dropped off, and all the magical light dissipated, leaving the cavern feeling dark and cramped.

Kal turned back to the panel, searching. He could have sworn he saw it. *Ah! There it is.* Kal hit a button, and lights came on, brightening the lower portion of the cavern.

The hair on Kal's arms rose as the children, all linked, turned as one to peer at them.

"Casi?" Justin called, moving closer to the pool.

"Justin?" she said tentatively, eyes still adjusting.

Casi surged forward, clambering out of the pool, and ran toward her brother. Just as he stepped forward to meet her, she crumpled to the ground, a Lycanide dart in her back.

R oolia and Garwan launched themselves into the cavern, searching for the source of the attack.

Kal threw a giant shield around the pool, holding the remaining children while Casi started to rise into the air as her Lycanide attacker reeled her in from the wall above. Justin grabbed hold of her while Doha took hold of the gossamer threads one by one and used the knowledge he had gained from Roolia to cut them. After Doha cut the last thread, Casi's weight fell entirely on Justin.

Justin pulled the dart from Casi's shoulder, and Doha, seeing the dart, looked up. The ceiling of the cavern arched straight up near the shield wall. On that wall, a Lycanide descended toward them. Doha pulled his small throwing knives and hurled one of them at the eyes of the descending Lycanide.

Kal shifted his attention away from Doha as another Lycanide entered the cavern through the door behind them. This one was even larger than Garwan. Kal stepped away from the table and moved towards the large and ferocious Lycanide standing in the doorway.

Kal glanced around the cavern. The large Lycanide stood in the doorway, taking in the surrounding battles. Both Garwan and Roolia were engaged with their own Lycanide.

Kal approached the large Lycanide, unsure if this was the alpha. He decided to state his intentions.

"I am Alpha," he said calmly, but with authority.

The towering Lycanide shot a dart at Kal.

The dart impacted a small magic shield over Kal's chest, pushing him back a few feet.

Kal reached up and pulled the dart out, throwing it to the ground.

"I am Alpha," Kal said again, this time with steel in his voice.

All six of the Lycanide's eyes focused on Kal as he pulled his sword, sending swirling eddies of power down its edge.

The behemoth tipped his head back and howled in response to Kal's challenge. Kal stepped toward the Lycanide as the creature leaped to meet him. Kal drew in more nites as he called on more of his magic, straining as he also held the shield over the children. Energy rippled through his sword as he swung. The Lycanide threw one of its forelegs to meet it. The sword hit something hard, jarring him. Kal's eyes widened in shock as he saw the shield flicker over the monster's arm. The Lycanide was also a mage.

The creature clicked in laughter as he swiped at Kal with his other foreleg. Kal stumbled back as the monster's claws raked his side. Blood oozed from the three stinging wounds. Kal's breath whistled through his teeth as he tried to control his breathing. None of the books he had found on Lycanides had suggested they could be mages.

Both of the beast's forelegs shimmered. Kal cast a Seeming on his sheathed second sword, then he reached for and drew it. Like the Lycanide, he funneled magic into both swords. This had to work. If it didn't, he was as good as dead. Kal lunged at the Lycanide. They met and clashed, shields flaring on contact.

The beast's muscles bunched, but Kal anticipated the attack. Instead of leaping out of the way, he surged his magic and struck. Pain rippled through the same side, but he moved forward and plunged his sword into the beast's flesh. Kal could see the moment its chest shield flared to life, but it was too late. Kal dropped the Seeming, which made his sword appear shorter to see it embedded in the behemoth's chest. The Lycanide howled and shuddered. The shield gave way as Kal pushed the sword further into the beast. Claws wrapped around him, scratching his back as the Lycanide went to its knees.

"Yield," Kal said.

The beast hissed and spat at him.

"Join my pack!"

"Never!" howled the Lycanide as it lunged forward, further impaling itself on Kal's blade. Then it slid off and fell to the ground, dead.

Kal extricated himself from the dead creature. Blood ran down his side. His limbs quivered briefly before he focused on what needed to be done. He went over to Roolia, who lowered a thrashing spider wolf onto the ground. Doha lay crumpled next to a different lycanide. Kal didn't know if he was breathing, and Justin stood protectively over the unconscious Casi.

"Your alpha is dead. Yield," Kal said.

The spider wolf went still.

Roolia went to Doha and injected him with antivenom. He groaned, eyes fluttering open.

Garwan came around the shield, dragging another large spider wolf.

Justin put away his sword and bent down to get his sister as Roolia came over and injected her with antivenom as well. A few moments later, she too groaned as the antivenom worked.

"Casi?" Justin said, cradling her and staring down at her. Her eyes opened and focused on him.

She reached out and brushed his face. "Are you real?"

He smiled. "Yes, I'm real. We've been looking for you for weeks."

Casimira hugged him and started to cry.

After treating the three spider wolves who introduced themselves as Colby, Lukas, and Seth, Kal inducted them into his pack and lowered the shield around the children. They all came up and surrounded Casi, laughing and crying.

Kal's ear tingled with yanzu wax. "Team one, this is team two. We've freed the rest of the children."

"Very good, team two. Let's meet back at the rendezvous site."

Chapter 40

Here and Gone

On returning to the castle, Casi joined nearly one hundred children as they arrived at the Healerie. Hours passed as families were notified and all the children were checked and rechecked. Once done, the healers began allowing the families in.

Jenna burst into the room. She searched through the crowd, looking for her sister. She found Justin first, and her eyes trailed along his arm to his hand, holding another. Jenna stared at her sister from across the room.

"Casi..." She mouthed as no words came out. Casi looked up regardless, and then they were running towards each other, meeting in a tight embrace. Tears slid down Jenna's face as relief flooded her.

Jenna patted her sister's hair and face. "I'm so sorry, Casi. I never meant to hurt you."

"I know. I've always known," she replied.

They separated, and Casi asked, "Where's Rowen?"

"He couldn't come, but you will see him when we all go home."

"Truly?"

"Yes."

After some negotiations, the doctors allowed Casi to leave, since she was the healthiest of the children. They kept the others for observation. Justin and Jenna escorted Casi outside to wait for the carriage.

"We live at the Sandoval estate now. With our grandfather," Jenna said.

"We have a grandfather who works at the Sandoval estate?" asked Casi.

Jenna and Justin shared a look. "Our grandfather is Lord Sandoval," Jenna said.

"Wait, you're telling me we're noble?" Casi's eyes widened.

"Yes," Jenna said as the driver pulled up and opened the door to the carriage.

Casi stared at the driver as Justin helped her into the carriage.

"We're noble *and* we have a grandfather?" Casi said after settling into her seat. "Related to Mom or Dad?" she asked.

"Mom," said Jenna as she entered the carriage and settled into a seat next to Casi. Justin followed.

Casi blinked, gaze shifting between the two of them. "Are you being serious?"

"Yes, and he's anxious to meet you. Guess what his name is?" Justin asked, smiling.

"Hm, Justin?" Casi said as Justin settled in across from them.

"Nope. Oswen McCabe Sandoval," said Justin.

"Seriously?" she asked, giggling. The carriage started moving.

"Guess what grandmother's name was?" said Jenna.

"Casimira?"

"Close. It was Jenivieve Casimira Sandoval."

"Wow, I guess our names really came from somewhere." Casi looked out at the streets as they rode through the city. "Is he nice?" she asked.

"Very," said Jenna as they rounded the corner to the Sandoval estate.

Kal had been watching as Jenna reunited with her sister. He could feel relief and joy through the bond. He was happy they had found the children in time to stop the Compact. Kal turned to go when Master Evans and Edward approached him.

"Kal, you remember Edward? He is one of the people we sent into the caverns to investigate your cavern simulation."

Edward looked thinner than the last time Kal had seen him. His easy smile was gone.

"Sir, there is something in the caverns you should know about."

"Let's talk somewhere more private," said Kal.

Kal ushered Edward and Master Evans toward the king, who had just arrived, and Corin escorted them to his office.

"Tell us what you found," Kal said after everyone entered the room but before they sat down.

"Three of us went to the door marked in the simulation. It required a half-candle mark to get through it. Once we were in, we followed a spiral staircase down. We traveled for at least another half candle mark before coming to the bottom. In front of us was a large cavern. We followed the right side and came to a room embedded in the stone."

Kal slid a cup of water to the boy, whose voice was fading. Edward took a sip before continuing in a stronger voice.

"Upon entering, we found a sarcophagus covered in indecipherable symbols. It drew me forward, and before I knew it, I had my hand on its outer shell, which sent a jolt of magic through me."

Edward licked his lips. "I don't know how long I stood there, but I came back to the sound of one of the guards calling out to me."

Edward looked over at Kal as if unsure of his next words. "When I recovered, I could read the markings on the sarcophagus."

His eyes went to Master Evans, who smiled encouragingly. Edward took a deep breath. "The sarcophagus, it—well, there's no better way to describe it, but it marked me. Whatever it is, knows who I am. Not only that, but I know how to open it. I just don't know if we should."

Jenna stirred under a cool breeze coming from her window. She didn't remember leaving the window open. Her eyes snapped open, and she peered across the bed at her sleeping sister. Relief flooded her. It wasn't just a dream. Casi was back. Jenna shifted closer to her sister when a gossamer thread fell across her arm. Jenna spasmed, creeped out by the sensation as she brushed it away, sleep clearing from her mind. She glanced around the room, scanning with magic and not feeling anything. Relaxing, she scooted closer to her sister.

Casi breathed, slow and steady. Jenna lay there listening to it for nearly an hour before she, too, fell back asleep.

Jenna awoke with a start to the sound of soft tapping at her door. A chilly breeze swept through the room. She snuggled closer to Casi, who had stolen all the blankets.

The tapping came again. Jenna rose and answered the door. The butler stood there.

"My lady, Lord Darren Navarro is here to see you. I tried to send him away, but he said it was urgent."

Jenna sighed. "Tell him I'll be there momentarily." She closed the door and got dressed. Looking back at Casi, she frowned, not wanting to leave her alone.

Jenna went down the hall to Justin's room and knocked.

He answered quickly, dressed for duty.

"Can you sit with Casi while I take care of something?"

"Sure, I'll be right there."

Jenna returned to her room, and Justin followed a few minutes later. He had strapped on his sword.

"It won't take long," she said and hurried downstairs to the parlor.

"Lady Jenna," Darren said, a tension to his voice.

"Lord Darren," she said, then smiled. "I haven't seen you since the party. What brings you here at this hour of the morning?"

His shoulders relaxed at the softness in her voice, as though he had feared her anger. He kissed the back of the hand she extended and studied her searchingly for a moment. "Do you have one of the recovered children here?"

Her eyebrows went up, and she nodded.

He spoke in a hushed tone. "Are they still here?"

Her mouth tightened, thinking of her sister. "Why?" she demanded, fearing he had been called here by his powers.

He rubbed a hand over his face. "Some of the nobles were talking at a breakfast gathering. They were alight with tales of the rescue, but one group of boys wasn't happy about it. One of them, well, I kind of used my powers on one of them."

Jenna waited, and he continued.

"What I got was that they were taking back the most powerful child. After that, I went to the Healerie but couldn't get any information from them. I heard your sister was one of the returned children, so I came here."

Jenna called for the butler and sent him to check on her sister. He returned a few minutes later and gestured to her.

"Lord Darren, if you will excuse me?"

"Of course."

Jenna stepped out of the room and shut the door.

"Come with me, Lady Jenna," the butler said, his expression grim.

Round-eyed, Jenna followed.

The butler led her upstairs to her room. They entered the room, which still had its curtains drawn. She glanced around the room, not seeing anyone. Both Justin and her sister were gone. Jenna stepped further into the room, where she caught sight of Justin's sword lying on the floor.

She reached out through her bond and called Kal, sending him impressions of Lycanides. Once she was sure he was coming, she viewed the room again, this time using her magic. She saw nothing else out of order. Jenna gestured the butler out of the room.

"I want a guard on the door, and no one enters until Kal arrives. Once that's done, inform Grandfather. Did you check the restrooms and the kitchen?"

"Yes, my lady, no traces were found."

She nodded, eyes gleaming with tears. "I will see to Lord Darren."

The butler bowed and went to get the guard.

After a brief moment, Jenna set off for the parlor.

Jenna entered, and Darren turned to stare at her, taking in the expression on her face.

"I was right, wasn't I?" His sun-kissed face lost some of its color.

Jenna's jaw clenched. She had to consciously separate it to speak.

"Lord Darren," she began in measured tones. "I appreciate you coming to me with this, but this is vital. I need to know with whom you were speaking." Her eyes bore into him.

"I know," he said with a sad smile. "It was Joseph Cardinas and Cornelius Andrade." Anger welled up in Jenna. *Why were they still free?* "Start from the beginning," she said.

From the parlor, Jenna heard the doorbell ring. She rose and said, "Come with me, please."

They arrived in the entryway as Kal entered the house with Lady Roolia, Second Garwan, and Third Colby, one of three new additions to Kal's pack. Jenna caught a glimpse of the other two outside. Oswen came down the stairs and escorted the Lycanides up to Jenna's room while Rowen stood at the top of the stairs, taking them all in. Kal started to follow, but Jenna interrupted.

"Kal? I need you for a moment."

He glanced at her, then frowned at the young lord standing very close, almost protectively, behind her. Since the ball, rumors had circled the courts about Lady Jenna being the first person to lure Lord Darren into a dance. Kal approached them. Darren inhaled sharply upon seeing Kal's expression.

"Kal, this is Lord Darren Navarro."

"We've met," Kal spoke gruffly.

Something unspoken passed between the two men.

Jenna ignored it. "He knows who took Casi."

Darren gave the list of names again.

Kal nodded, relaxing, and asked him to review the conversation as he recalled it. Darren recounted everything.

"Good," Kal said. "I'm going to need you to stay here today. Having you come to the palace could arouse suspicion. I'll send some investigators here to take your statement."

Darren nodded. "Yes, sir."

"Kal, this news isn't exactly surprising. *Why* are they still free?" Jenna asked, hands clenched into fists.

"Taking down a noble requires a paper trail and a lot of testimony. If I capture the Compact before the nobles can be tied to them, they will get away. Also, I don't even know if the courts would take a Lycanide's word as evidence. We need something more concrete."

"Does Lord Darren's word help?" she asked.

"It's a start. Come on." Kal, Jenna, and Darren went upstairs.

"Roolia, was it a Lycanide?" Kal asked, surveying the room.

"Yes, found hiding spot."

Kal gestured to the Lycanides. "You all stay here and see what else you can find. I'll speak with the king." He turned to leave, then paused, glancing at Darren, frowning.

Oswen stepped forward. "I'll keep an eye on him."

Kal nodded, then turned to Jenna. "You're with me."

Chapter 41

The Palace

Corin sat, a stillness to him as he processed everything.

The door opened, and Rowen slipped in.

"Rowen, why are you here?" Kal growled. "Where are your guards? You're supposed to be under house arrest."

Rowen licked his lips. "I don't know. The last thing I remember, there was screaming..." He trailed off, face turning ashen. "'m losing time, aren't I?"

The king nodded. "I'm afraid so."

"What—" Rowen paused. Something moved behind his eyes as his aura flashed, and he visibly calmed. "Sire, I need you to free me."

The room went silent.

"What would you have me do?" the king asked in a severe tone.

Rowen glared at the king. "They are coming for you as we speak. You are in danger. The block you have keeps me out, but it prevents me from protecting you."

"Why would you protect him?" Kal asked.

"He holds the key to my freedom."

The king stared at him for a long moment and sighed. "I'm afraid I cannot do that."

Rowen's face turned into a visage of rage and anguish.

"You are not listening to me," he said, stepping toward the king.

Rowen flew up into the air and slammed into the wall. Jenna held her hand up, face hard and glaring.

"Who are you?" she asked.

"I cannot say," said Rowen.

"Cannot or will not?" Kal demanded.

Sweat broke out on Rowen's brow, and he spoke as if each word was a struggle.

"I am... keeper of..."

White hot light flared around Rowen. Jenna gasped, and the king stood up. Kal knew that light. Whatever was inside Rowen was skirting the edges of breaking a binding oath. Depending on the oath, doing so is said to be excruciatingly painful.

"The Orbis... Arcanum."

Rowen coughed up blood. His breath rasped in and out. How much more of this could Rowen take?

Dread filled Kal, but he knew the early stories of The Three. He had to be sure.

"Guardian..." Rowen's fingers gripped into fists, veins bulging at his neck. "Of the East."

"Enough," Kal said. He knew who that was. All children in the royal house were taught the lore. Kal's mouth went dry. Someone had captured a god. Guardian of the East. Keeper of the Orbis Arcanum. Drakothadam. Kal looked to his brother, who stood, eyes wide in recognition. This was one of The Three.

Rowen sagged in relief, as if someone had removed a tremendous pressure from him.

"Free me," he mumbled, blood dripping from the corner of his mouth.

Jenna moved to his side, and the soft glow of healing flowed from her to Rowen.

Boom!

The building rocked under an enormous impact. Dust fell from the ceiling, and a vase rocked before stabilizing. Kal's ears rang as he let go of the desk he had grabbed onto.

"Are we under attack?" asked Corin.

"Yes, they are here," Rowen said, wide-eyed, staring at the king. "Please, heir of Mendallon, you must free me. My duty, I swear to you and yours. I will swear a binding oath to safeguard you and your family for two hundred fifty years."

"How do we free you?" Kal asked.

Rowen went taut. The white light returned around him.

"Bring Edward... find my... underground chamber... insert the Seal of Kings." Rowen roared in pain. "It will free me from the trap set upon me." He screamed.

"Trap?" the king asked.

"I am trapped in a dream..." Rowen screamed again, his skin taking on an ashen gray hue. "My duty... was to stop them early before they got a foothold. If they are storming your keep now, then they are confident they will win."

Boom! Another impact hit the building. This time, they could hear yelling, and the smell of smoke wafted into the room.

The office door burst open, and a creature never before seen in Mendallon prowled into the room.

It had a large carapace that ended in a curving tail, giving it the appearance of an enormous desert scorpion. Black eyes swiveled and locked onto the king. Pulsing lights flowed around the edges of the creature, and its tail started to glow as it curled up in a flash of motion, arching over its head and ejecting a ball of crackling energy straight at Corin.

Kal caught a twinge of emotion from Jenna through the bond and watched in horror as she turned and, with a smooth flow, sent her magic at the beast. He could tell by its composition of nites that it had one purpose: to kill.

Kal reached out a hand, the word *no* dying on his lips as Jenna's eyes widened in shock, her bond mark igniting. She had sworn an oath not to kill with magic, and she had just broken it. She shuddered as all of that power turned back on her.

Light and sparks flew around her as she fell to the floor, screaming and writhing in pain.

Kal looked at Corin to see the king throw up his right hand to form a shield. The force of the glowing orb pushed him into the shelving behind his desk. The globe burned and crackled against his shield, burrowing into the layers, seeking a weak spot to break through. Corin held steady as the orb burned itself out. Hearing more noise from the next room, he dismissed the tatters of his shield and built a stronger one.

A cry to his right drew his eyes away from Corin as Rowen fell to the floor and lay still, aura flashing as he wrestled with a god for control of his body.

Kal cursed as his oath mark pulsed painfully, indicating Jenna's breach of contract. The apprentice bond he had with her flared to life with pain. Focusing, Kal hissed and flung an arrow of magic at the creature, which penetrated its hard outer shell, killing it.

Kal went to Jenna and dragged her still-writhing form behind the king's desk and shields. Corin gave him a questioning stare.

"I had her swear a binding oath prohibiting her from killing with magic."

"I thought she was a healer?" Corin asked.

"She is. One with little regard for killing, and it's just—"

"Magic is what you used to kill father," Corin said, nostrils flaring. "You do realize you just used it to kill these beasts! What would have happened to her if you hadn't been here?"

Kal flinched as Corin's words hit like a blow. He didn't mean for it to apply to nonhumans. His eyes flicked to the dead creatures as a hollow feeling poured into him. He tried to contain it, but it consumed him. *Fear*. Fear of losing Jenna. Fear of killing someone else through his actions. Jenna's back arched.

Kal grimaced. There were things he could do to help ease her pain, but not while they were under attack.

Kal glanced at the door as two more creatures stepped over the bodies of dead guards and entered the room. Kal ignored the image of killing his father, which was followed by his promise never to kill with magic. These beasts weren't sentient. Both targeted the king, took aim, and fired. Kal launched himself in front of the king, putting up a second shield. The two orbs hit his defenses so hard it made his eyesight dim. The outer wall of his shield cracked, then shattered. Pain rippled through Kal, and blood dripped from his nose, but the remaining spheres barely damaged the second layer held by the king. Backlash from the destruction of the ward wall flowed through Kal, taking down his net and leaving him dazed.

Rowen, flaring with the aura of Drakothadam, stood and stepped into the gap. As both creatures readied another round, a third creature entered the room.

Rowen formed a small ball of light and threw it toward the ceiling above the first beast. When the ball was overhead, it fanned out, forming a cage around the creature just as it fired. The energy of its burst shot around the inside of the cage, hitting the beast, killing it. The cage dissolved.

The second beast was readying a shot. Kal heaved the dregs of his strength and flung an arrow of light that rammed into the creature's tail, causing the energy to turn back on itself. The creature fell to its knees, thrashing as the power consumed it from within, leaving a burnt-out husk.

While the second one was still screaming, the third one fired off a round. The king adjusted his shield, and when the orb impacted it, instead of holding firm, it gave way, stretching backward until it stopped moving. It then returned the sphere to its maker, blasting off the beast's tail. A second, smaller arrow came from a tight-lipped Kal, finishing it off.

Kal pulled in more nites, refueling his powers.

Rowen turned to speak when another wave of creatures, this time four of them, came into the room. He turned back while forming an energy shield in one hand and an energy spear in the other. Relief flooded Kal as behind the creatures came Roolia and Garwan.

Roolia leaped up to the corner of the room, sending liquid cords at the tail of one creature, preventing it from firing. She then added more threads and reeled the monster in as Garwan targeted another.

Another blast of pulsing light flew toward Corin. It rebounded off the shield, incapacitating the creature.

Kal lashed out, using an energy arrow to finish it off just as Rowen drove a spear through the final beast.

Panting, Kal took another moment to draw nites into himself and translate that into magical energy. He took in Jenna's quivering form. She seemed to be stabilizing. Kal turned back towards the doorway. They weren't safe yet.

"Roolia, where are the other Lycanides?" Kal asked.

"Sandoval's attacked. Guard there," she said.

Kal turned towards the door when Captain Abasi strode in with five guards.

"Sire," he said as his disheveled soldiers fanned out protectively around the room.

"Report," the king said.

"The uprising has been quelled," said Abasi.

"Uprising?" he demanded.

"Yes, sire. The enemy launched several strategic attacks around the city. The compact hit the Sandoval's first, but the Lycanides were there to help. The palace was the next place hit. A false alarm pulled some guards away before the attack. I will investigate that personally as soon as time permits. Lesser attacks happened to the Beltines, the Navarros, and the Deleons. We cleared the halls as we came."

"What about the Andrades and Cardinases?" asked Corin.

"I received no reports of damage from those houses."

"Bring me the Andrade and the Cardinas house heads. Alive, if possible; dead, if they object to coming."

Captain Abasi nodded and left the room, taking his guards with him.

Kal moved to Jenna, picking her up and placing her on the couch. She twitched and spasmed in agony at his touch. Using the hand with the binding oath mark on it, he put it on hers and started the process of willing an end to the pain. A candle mark passed as slowly her tension eased, and Jenna stopped twitching. Her breathing evened out, but her face still contorted in pain, and she did not awaken. Kal knew there was nothing else anyone could do for her at the moment.

"I'll bring her to the Healerie so she can rest," Rowen said.

Kal looked up at him, and it was indeed Rowen, not a god, staring back at him. Nodding, Kal let him take her. He could do nothing for her until she woke up, and right now, he needed to guard his brother.

Several candle marks later, a guard came to report to the king.

"Sire." The guard bowed.

"Report," said Corin.

"Lord Sandoval survived the attack, and his estate is secure."

"What of the Beltines?" asked Corin.

"Both the Beltines and Navarros are also clear, but the Navarros sustained heavy casualties."

"What of the Cardinases and Andrades?" Corin asked, hands gripping the sides of his chair.

"Lord Cardinas refused the honor of your request and died evading capture. Lord Andrade is en route to the dungeons."

Corin's shoulders slumped, and Kal breathed a sigh of relief. It was over.

S everal candle marks before dawn, Kal headed over to the Healerie, where he found Jenna in a small room. He reached out through their bond. *She should be near waking.* He stared down at her sleeping form, features twisted with pain, and shame filled him.

His binding oath could have killed her. His feelings about killing with magic didn't seem to apply to him. Or perhaps it was nonhumans? No, that didn't feel right. If Compact soldiers had attacked them instead of beasts, he would have killed them the same way. He was a hypocrite. Nausea roiled in his stomach. He could have gotten Jenna killed. As it was, she'd dealt with this agonizing pain, for what? His stupidity?

A vision of her surrounded, fighting off superior foes, filled his mind. Her striking at them but unable to reduce their numbers by killing them. They block her nonfatal attacks. In his mind, she struggled as they wore her down. They were toying with her before killing her.

Jenna grunted, bringing Kal back to the moment, his breathing uneven, throat dry. He reduced his hold on the bond. The pain she was going through was excruciating. He did not want Jenna to suffer. Nor did he want her to die. He stared at her face, beautiful despite the twist of her lips. He wanted the impossible. The type of relationship he wanted was forbidden between masters and apprentices. Leaning down, he kissed her on the forehead—a light brush of his lips.

Jenna shuddered, then opened pain-glazed eyes. Now that she was awake, he could act.

"Jenna." He took her hand in his. "I, Hekallion Mendathalon, release you from your binding." He studied her hand, waiting for her to process the words and break the oath.

"My fault," she gasped. "I didn't think," she said with a grimace as another wave passed through her. Horror filled Kal. It takes two people to create a bond. It also takes two to remove it. She wasn't letting it go.

"Jenna, I was wrong. It's not the means that is the problem. It's the intention behind it. You acted to protect. You've always acted to protect." An image of Kal's father came to mind, and he let it pass through him as though seeing it for the first time. Just like he did. "You were right to do what you did. Please, Jenna, I need you to release the oath."

A long moment passed as Jenna studied him through clenched teeth before the diamond pattern disappeared from both their wrists. Jenna shuddered in relief as the last of the pain dissolved from her features. Kal inhaled deeply as relief washed through him and the bond.

Her eyes flickered.

"Rest," he said.

Jenna's eyelids closed, fluttering a couple of times as if she fought to stay awake. Kal held her hand, waiting until her breathing evened out before leaving to send a notification to Oswen that she and Rowen were alive and well.

Kal yawned, exhaustion rolling through him. They would have to head into the caverns in a couple of candle marks. He would nap until then.

Chapter 42

The Keeper

As the sun rose over Mendallon, Kal met with Roolia, Garwan, and Colby in the palace gardens.

"Any luck finding Casi or Justin?"

Roolia growled. "No."

"Would they have taken them back to the caverns?" Kal asked.

Garwan's chest rumbled. "We checked. Not find. Caverns large, many entrances and tunnels. Could have missed."

Kal grimaced. "Keep looking. They have to be in the city or the caverns somewhere. Let's meet back here after lunch."

The three Lycanides left. Kal hurried back into the palace. They had a god to free.

Edward led the king, Kal, Rowen, and two guards down to a different part of the catacombs, directly beneath the castle, to the chamber housing the god's sleeping body. An impatient air surrounded Rowen, who was currently inhabited by the entity.

Outside the chamber loomed two statues depicting warriors prepared for battle. They were exquisitely cut and eerily lifelike—a man with a shield poised to strike with his sword and a woman about to let fly an arrow. Edward opened the doors, leading them to the sarcophagus. Kal and Corin took some time to study the intricate carvings of dragons on the sarcophagus, noting the round opening Kal assumed was for the seal.

"Wait here," Edward said. He went to the wall at the base of the sarcophagus and placed his hand on it. Magic flared as a doorway formed, and he walked through the wall. A long moment passed, and a bright light appeared in the room, lighting up the sarcophagus. It hummed softly, occasionally clicking and whirring as intense magic flared and shimmered across its surface. Once the magic stabilized, Edward came out. "Sire, press your seal against the sarcophagus."

Corin did so, and the sound of latches unlocking reverberated through the room. Air vented out of the sarcophagus as its door swung upwards and to the left with a resounding thud.

Kal grabbed Rowen, preventing him from hitting his head as his body crumpled to the floor. After he made sure Rowen was breathing, he joined the others and peered into the coffin.

A shadowed male figure lay unmoving within. For a long moment, there was no motion, then the being opened black-on-black eyes and sat up, rubbing his well-built arms and legs. Kal's eyebrows rose, and his mouth went dry as waves of power rippled off the figure, each more powerful than the last. The being's body was covered in binding oath marks. *How can one bear so many?* Kal thought as one of the marks along his chest swirled and disappeared, the king's seal breaking its hold.

The being stared at each of them, eyes lingering on Kal. "Thank you." His voice was hoarse after decades of disuse.

Tension rippled through Kal. This being—this god—was the voice he had heard two years ago. This was the monster who had made him kill his father. Kal shuddered. This was also a majestically powerful being. Kal's hands clenched into fists as raw emotions rippled through him.

The words were, however, not what Kal expected to hear. Gods can be humble. Scowling, he nodded before seeing Corin's mouth snap closed and nod.

The king reached out a hand to help him stand. The god stared at it a moment before taking it and shifting to his feet. He was taller than the king and broad across the shoulders. Long black hair ran down his back. Aquiline eyebrows framed his black eyes. His face was narrow, his jaw sculpted. He had thin lips and a cleft chin.

The being spoke. "As agreed, I offer you a binding oath. I, Drakothadam Jormangang, swear to protect the Mendathalon line for two hundred fifty years." Light flared on his right shoulder as the Mendathalon tower, with light shining, appeared. Kal could feel the magic place a similar mark on him, and the way Corin shifted, it appeared he received the same.

"Step back, please," Drakothadam said, his voice louder this time.

They all did so.

He held out his hands to the sides, and they shimmered as thin black fibers covered his body, thickening into outer layers of armor. Once complete, Drakothadam appeared ready for a battlefield.

He spoke with authority. "Xolia, heed my call."

To the right of him, a small orange light appeared, pulsing and throbbing. "Master," the light said.

"Status," said Drakothadam.

"A group of Compact soldiers are in the western caverns. It appears they are preparing to open the portal between worlds," said Xolia.

"How long until they are ready?"

"Less than two hours."

"Can you stop them, Drakothadam?" Kal asked.

The entity turned, frowning. "Call me Adam, and not yet. I need time to recover my powers. *Scieldan*, you will have to stop them." Adam reached into a pouch hanging on a belt and pulled out a small, pill-sized black capsule. "Take this." Adam handed Kal the capsule. "If there comes a time when all seems lost, swallow it."

Unease rolled through Kal. "What is it?"

"Condensed liquid magic," Adam said. "Have you been trained in using nites?"

Kal thought of Lady Millaine. "Yes."

"Then you will find it useful," said Adam.

"What about you? What will you be doing?" Kal asked.

"I will awaken the citadel under the city. If you can get the Compact out of that cavern, I will seal it off to prevent reentry."

Kal blinked. He had so many questions and so little time. "Edward? Escort the king back to the palace." Corin opened his mouth to complain, but Kal continued. "Send Doha, my team, my pack, and a platoon of troops down to aid me."

Corin's mouth snapped shut, and then he nodded. They gathered up the unconscious Rowen and followed Edward out of the chambers. There was no way they would return in time to help him with this fight, but he needed his brother to survive.

Kal turned to Adam. "Is there a way to see what they are doing in the caverns?"

"This way," said Adam as he led Kal out of the sarcophagus chamber and to another enclosure further down in the caverns.

Kal paused as he entered the spacious room. His eyes first went to two identical magic symbols embedded into the floor, which flared to life, casting a soft white light as he entered, then, to the orange orb that floated in the air next to Adam. The room's outer walls held chairs and tables, and the far portion of the wall displayed six moving images. It took Kal a long moment to understand that these images were being captured right now in different parts of the caverns. *Is this what it meant to have the power of a god?*

Kal refocused on the images. In one, he could see four men guarding the hall's entrance. Another view showed two more men hauling iron-wreathed barrels over to the far wall. On a third, he saw two intricately carved marble-like statues of fighters, like those outside the sarcophagus room. A fourth showed Casi and Justin lying prone. The fifth showed a man holding the Rod of Inanis while speaking with two black-robed mages. The sixth showed the wall where several men drew a series of symbols shaped like an arch.

Adam came up beside him. "Beneath the arch is where the portal will open. The barrels likely contain the liquid magic stolen from the children. They will use it to power the portal. Under no circumstances should you blow up those barrels in an attempt to stop the Compact from using them. It could take down the whole city above."

Kal's mouth went dry at the thought. He studied the men guarding the hall. Like the other men in the caverns, these men wore body armor and swords. How long would it take them to get back with reinforcements? Those men drawing the symbols would meet at the top of the arch in less than a candle mark. That wasn't much time. Could he reach Casi before that? Kal chewed his lower lip. He had entered the caverns prepared to protect the king. But the volatile nature of the liquid magic limited what he could do.

Adam talked softly with Xolia as Kal studied the images.

"Adam? Is there another entrance to that room?" Kal asked.

"Yes," Adam replied.

"So, there could be more of them in there?" Kal asked the obvious question.

"Yes," Adam said, voice tight.

Kal exhaled. At least Corin and Jenna were safe. He would do what he could. They had probably reached the exit by now, but they would have to return to the castle.

"Please wait here," said Adam. "I need to awaken two members of my team. They will assist you."

Kal nodded as Adam strode off, the orange ball of light keeping pace with him. Two members? So not the other two gods. Were the other gods trapped like Adam? Just how many people did Adam have down here? The old stories never mentioned a team.

Kal focused on the images. One of the soldiers approached Casi and Justin. He waved a hand, and a Lycanide dropped from the ceiling and injected them with antivenom.

C asi slowly awakened, tensing as she realized she wasn't in bed with Jenna. Tears filled her eyes as she took in the familiar caverns around her and the two Lycanides on the ceiling. A groan next to her drew her attention, and her eyes widened as she took in Justin.

Casi sat up, head throbbing as Justin reached for a sword that wasn't at his waist.

It took her a moment to realize that one of the Compact soldiers stood over them. Dread filled her as he said, "You will open a portal. If you do not, your brother will die."

"I don't know how to open a portal," she said, eyes widening. A hollow pit formed in her stomach as the soldier continued.

"It's simple. You just pull the magic from the barrels behind you and push it through the Rod of Inanis."

Her mouth worked wordlessly for a moment. "What rod?"

He pulled a short metal rod out of his belt and tossed it to her. The rod landed in her lap, caught in the folds of her nightgown. Light glinted off the silver rod as it sat inert. There was something wrong with the metal. Eyebrows rising, she studied it before realizing what it was. The space the metal took up had no magic. It seemed lifeless to her. She recoiled from the rod, not wanting to touch it.

"Pick it up," the soldier said.

"No," Casi replied, looking away from it.

"Pick. It. Up." He drew his sword and pointed it at Justin.

Hands shaking, Casi reached for the rod, wrapping her fingers around it as its cold pull leached into her hands. Casi could feel her magic being drawn into the rod. Her hands went cold and numb. Without thinking, she released it, and it fell back into her lap.

Quicker than she could follow, the soldier stabbed Justin with his sword. Justin grunted, but continued staring at the soldier. Casi screamed. Hands fumbling for the rod, she picked it up again.

"Behind you is a magic source. When I tell you, you will draw magic from the source and feed it to the rod."

Casi panted as the rod once again numbed her hands, sucking the life from her.

"You will point the rod at the wall with the arch while feeding magic into it."

Prickles were radiating from her hands to her wrists now. "For how long?"

The soldier grinned. "Until the portal opens."

"Wh-what happens to us then?" she asked.

"Then you and your brother are free to go," he sneered.

Casi didn't believe him. She stared at the sword still in Justin's shoulder, licked her lips, and nodded in understanding.

"When do I start?" she asked.

"When they are done with the glyphs. For now, just get used to its draw."

Casi turned her head, taking in the two mages drawing glyphs from opposite sides of the arch. They were almost shoulder to shoulder on their ladders. At the rate they were going, it would be done in a quarter candle mark. Casi shuddered as cold started radiating up her arms. Time seemed to slow as they waited. She could hear the chittering of a Lycanide from above and the hum of conversations as they echoed around the cavern. Dread filled her as a small pool of blood formed under Justin. She closed her eyes briefly as she exhaled. She had to do this. Slowly, Casi got to her feet as someone pulled the lid off the barrel behind her. Her senses blazed with the power coming from the barrel. *Is that what we were all drained of?* she thought. *All that power just to open a portal? Can I use this power to attack the Compact? Can I turn it against them?*

The man frowned and grabbed the sword in Justin's shoulder. Justin grunted as panic swelled through Casi.

"If you try anything, his life is forfeit." The solder grinned.

Casi licked her lips, stomach dropping. She wouldn't risk her brother. She took a deep breath and nodded.

Chapter 43

The Caverns

Kal saw the sword go through Justin. It was not a fatal wound, but it had to hurt. His fists clenched, and he stepped closer to the scried vision. He had to get down there. Kal felt two other presences as Adam entered the cavern from another room, accompanied by two people, a young woman and a young man. Both had short dark hair and serious expressions.

"Kal, this is Star and Jay," Adam said, gesturing to them in turn. "Since I have not recovered yet, they will fight with you."

Kal blinked his surprise. The two looked like they had just woken up from a bad dream. Physically, they were fit, but neither looked combat-ready. They wore closed-toe shoes and black outfits that left little to the imagination.

Star gave him a brief smile. "Nice to meet you, Kal." Then she walked over to one of the two symbols on the floor. Jay nodded to Kal, flashed him a mischievous grin, and then he moved to the other one. Magic flared about them, forming a sphere around each one.

Right, I don" have time for this, Kal thought. *I have to go rescue Casi and Justin, and stop an invasion.* This was war. He would live or die by his actions—or inactions. Kal prepared himself to kill or be killed.

Kal turned to Adam. "How do I get to that cavern?"

"Xolia," he called, and the orange ball came over. "Lead him," Adam said.

The ball split in two, and one took up a position in front of Kal while the other stayed with Adam.

"If I don't make it back, take care of my brother," Kal said as he left the room, following the orb.

Kal's net tingled as two guards moved out from the shadows and approached him as he entered the mouth of the cavern. He pulled power into himself, and his mouth curved in a grim smile as he thought of Jenna. Two magic darts shot out toward the men, each entering an eye. The two men silently fell as he drew his sword and entered.

Jenna opened her eyes. The pain was gone. The last thing she remembered was Kal's presence amidst waves of agony. She had felt his steadying presence through the worst of it. Jenna raised her hand, looking for the binding oath mark. Unmarked skin greeted her. She realized she could kill with magic again. Why had he freed her? She remembered the beasts attacking the king and she'd reacted without thinking.

Jenna sat up to find a tray with food on the side table. Her stomach growled as she inched closer to it. Quickly, she ate, groaning in delight. As she took her last bite, she thought of Casi and Justin. Where was Kal? She reached for the bond and found nothing. She reached again. She was sure it was still there. It was just dormant. Was Kal unconscious? Had they taken Kal, too?

The food curdled in her stomach. What was wrong with the bond? Jenna rose and dressed, her need to find Kal overriding all else. She opened her senses, focusing on the nites invading her body. She had lost another shield layer while unconscious. After a long moment, they responded.

There he was. To the south. Relief flooded her as she realized he wasn't dead.

Putting on a Seeming, she began her hunt.

She exited the ward looking like one of the aides. They wore similar outfits with different colors. Making her way out to the street, she hailed a carriage.

When she caught the carriage, she looked like one of the mage apprentices. He didn't blink twice when she said she would direct him where to go. Plenty of mage students had scavenger hunts in the city. The driver followed her directions until she reached the older part of the city. This carriage was too big for these streets. Jenna paid the driver, got out, and continued on foot.

When he left, she became a messenger delivery apprentice. They went everywhere around the city.

Listening to the nites, she followed their pull. Jenna hurried, coming to a dark passageway. The trail led to an uninviting arched opening.

Shadows filled the narrow passage, and her heart thrummed in her chest. She had to find Kal.

She entered slowly, following the path until she came upon a solid wall. *No!* She ground her teeth. This was the way. Kal was down through this wall. There must be a way in.

Jenna placed a hand on the wall and gently pushed some of her magic into it. The wall shimmered like in the archives and disappeared. Jenna stepped through the door, and darkness surrounded her as the wall reappeared.

She created a globe of light, blinking rapidly as she took in her surroundings. Her heart thumped in her ears as she saw two lifelike statues of warriors, both holding swords and shields. She licked her lips, assuring herself that they were not alive. Between the statues were stairs going down. After another long look at the lifelike statues, Jenna followed her orb under the city.

Jenna paused at the bottom. Her light showed the outline of a large cavern. The nites tugged her to the right. She continued on, letting the nites lead her. As she moved, she passed doorways and more statues, all warriors. Some doorways felt of Kal, but the path showed him leaving those rooms. She followed for what felt like a candle mark but was probably shorter before she came upon another cave entrance. Here she found the dead bodies of two Compact soldiers. The cavern entrance was eerily quiet. Then she heard a faint clanging echo.

Without thinking, Jenna removed a sword from one of the soldiers and entered the cavern.

K al stood at the entrance to a series of caverns. His net detected the approach of four more soldiers. Warned by the cries of the first two men, they approached cautiously with their iron shields up and spread out, blocking him from moving further into the caverns. Rolling his shoulders, Kal engaged the soldier on the right.

The soldier cursed as Kal's reinforced blade removed a divot from his sword. Kal kicked the soldier away in time to dodge a blow from a second soldier, which left the first soldier overbalanced. Kal stepped in and cut his throat, then released one hand from his sword and spun the dying man between him and the third soldier's sword, the body shielding him as he stepped back and plunged his sword into the first soldier who was coming up behind him.

The fourth soldier attacked as Kal threaded the delicate needle between blocking and freeing his sword by extending his magic down his arms to create bracers. The fourth man stepped back after Kal's shield blocked him. Keeping the soldiers in sight, he used the bracers as a shield.

He had to finish this quickly. There was no telling how many more guards would come in the next wave. Gathering in nites, he sent a pulse of magic all around him. The two remaining soldiers were pushed back; one tripped over a fallen body. Kal was on him before he could recover, thrusting his sword through his side.

One left. Panting, they faced off as Kal's outer net tingled. Kal swung his sword, breaking an arrow in half. Then another, and another from further into the cavern. More were coming. Kal struck at the soldier but failed to land a lethal hit. Six more soldiers appeared, forming a circle around them. The soldier he had been fighting smirked in anticipation.

Kal frowned. This was bad. Most of his magic attacks required distance. The bracers and his sword didn't draw on his magic as he had tied off the threads as Lady Millaine taught him, but his nets were a constant draw, burning through nites in the vicinity. He couldn't afford to add more shielding around himself. Kal turned, trying to keep all the enemies in his sight. His inner net showed movement behind him. Using it as a guide, he blocked a swing just as several more breached his net, drawing his attention. He spun his blade, blocking and dodging the attacks as pain lanced through him. A sword had sliced across his back. Kal stumbled forward, teeth gritted against the pain as he frantically blocked several more attacks before regaining his balance.

Blood streaked down his back. He couldn't sustain much more of this. They would wear him down.

His net vibrated. Bracing himself, he turned as a sword came straight at him. It would enter his side before he could block it. He followed its path, awaiting impact, when it jerked away as though hit from the side.

As he finished his turn, he found Compact soldiers being cut down by the hulking form of a stone statue bearing a sword. The marbled warrior moved fluidly as it killed several soldiers. Light glistened off its surface as Kal realized this was one of the statues he saw in Adam's cavern.

Eyes locked on the scene in front of him, Kal almost missed the tingling of his net. Surprise ran through him as he spun again to find a second stone statue, this one female, taking down the rest of the men before him.

"We've got you covered, Kal." Star's voice came through the female statue in front of him. Kal thought back to the glyphs on the floor. They must be piloting the statues. His backup had arrived.

A shout rang out, echoing, as Kal and the statues stalked into the next chain of caverns. The ceiling naturally dipped, creating a choke point. There appeared to be an even larger cavern beyond this. Kal briefly extended his net and detected several dozen life forces in the next chamber. Six approached the opening.

Kal pulled nites from his surroundings. Arrows of magic shot from him, striking three of the men down. The other soldiers raised their shields, blocking his attack.

Star and Jay edged around the sides, looking to surround the soldiers, when a Lycanide dropped down in front of each of them. The cavern ceiling was too far away for his net to detect.

Star swung her massive blade, which crackled with magic as the Lycanide dodged it. Arcs of magic shot from Jay, and chittering filled the cavern. Kal turned his attention back to the soldiers as a retreat command rang out. The men withdrew through the cavern's choke point, leaving the Lycanides as Kal approached.

Two men wearing robes instead of fighting leathers stepped toward Kal. Eddies of magic swirled about them, solidifying into a mass of raw power. Kal paused, pulling magic to block the mass, but they didn't use it against him. Instead, it spread out three layers deep, forming a shield wall spanning the narrow cavern's width in front of him.

Kal realized his error. He'd assumed it was an attack. He threw everything he had gathered at the wall. White sparks flew, and the shield glowed brightly but did not break. Kal hissed. He had to take down that wall. He glanced around to find both Star and Jay still fighting. He had to do this on his own. He gathered his will and tried again; this time, with sharper focus, he poured energy into the wall, focusing on disrupting the shield.

This time, the first layer snapped and the second layer flickered, shredding where his power touched it. But his power burned out. Kal watched as the shield automatically repaired itself. The lead mage gestured, and the soldiers inside the shield turned away from Kal, dismissing him as a threat.

Kal glared at the mages on the ladders, drawing the glyphs that marked the edge of the portal. They were shoulder to shoulder. He didn't have much time. To break through the shields, he needed more power. Kal reached into the pocket holding the pill as his net tingled. Someone was behind him.

Spinning about, he found Jenna approaching. His mouth dropped open. How had she found him? He couldn't feel her at all through the bond.

She walked up to him and extended her hand. "Use my powers."

That could work. Nodding, he decided to give it one more shot. Kal pulled nites to him, harnessing the additional power pouring from Jenna. Focusing his intent on breaking all three layers of that shield, he blasted the wall.

The shield wall fractured and came crashing down as Kal and Jenna's magic consumed the shields. The two mages who had built the shields felt them shatter and spun around.

Drawing further on Jenna, Kal lashed out, attacking them both. One of the mages crumpled as an arrow of light pierced his throat. The other took one in the leg. He fell to one knee, cursing. With the mages down, the soldiers turned and headed back toward Kal and Jenna. Through the oncoming soldiers, they could make out the sight of Casi and Justin.

"Casi!" Jenna screamed, pulling away from Kal and running toward the opening as the soldiers surged, boxing her in. Jenna raised her sword, taking on a stance that mimicked Kal's earlier.

When was the last time I pulled nites from her inner shields? Frowning, Kal sent another arrow over the throng and into the downed mage as the man with Casi barked out a command, and more soldiers flooded into the cavern from a side passage.

The two mages on the ladders climbed down. The portal was complete. Waves of soldiers came toward Kal and Jenna as the two mages prepared to attack. The man barked another command, and dread filled Kal as Casi began drawing on the liquid magic. Waves of magic pulsed through the caverns as the portal started to glow. *No one can survive that much power.*

If he didn't stop that portal, Casi would be dead. Correction, if he didn't stop that portal, they were all dead.

And the quickest way to stop the portal is to kill Casi.

Chapter 44

Decision

K al couldn't kill Casi. Every fiber of his being rejected the thought. There must be another way. *Could I just shoot her arm with an arrow? Make her drop the rod?* Kal could hit a target, but at this distance? He was no marksman. What if he missed?

No, Kal rejected that also. He needed something foolproof.

"Kal," Jenna called out, voice cracking. Only two of her attackers remained. He knew she wanted him to save her sister and brother. She dodged a blow but didn't go in for the kill. Kal frowned. Was she still trying to live by the oath? His stomach twisted as he recalled his vision of her being toyed with until they killed her.

The soldiers approached cautiously as Kal stood frozen. How could he save Jenna? How could he save Casi? Casi stood, holding the rod up as it funneled magic into the glyphs. Kal stared first at the rod, then Casi, and then at the liquid magic before taking the capsule out of his pocket and swallowing it.

Jenna went down beneath a soldier, crying out in pain. Kal drew a bow of magic and shot an arrow into the man towering over her. The man screamed and careened away. Jenna, eyes wide, rose to her feet as waves of magic swirled around her. Their eyes met briefly, and Kal nodded. She struck out at the remaining man, and this time she struck with the intent to kill. More soldiers approached Jenna.

Kal's net warned him just before a barrage of arrows came at him. He twisted, avoiding two arrows as a third struck him in the shoulder. Kal stumbled back a step before bringing his still glowing bow around and fired several more shots into the approaching men. His shoulder spasmed violently, and blood ran down the front of his tunic. He needed to stop Casi from opening that portal. He also wasn't sure he could pull the bow again.

A pulse of magic echoed through the cavern as the gate solidified into the clear image of a field containing dozens—no, hundreds—of compact soldiers wearing black armor with red undercoats and just as many scorpion creatures in the distance. The first of the soldiers poured through the portal.

The Three! he cursed. He'd taken too long.

Rage poured from Kal—anger at himself, anger at the Compact. There must be a way to close that portal. *When will that pill take effect?* Kal's vision pulsed, and his left leg gave way, bringing him to one knee. A wave of nausea hit him, his eyesight constricted, and an upwelling of magic rose from deep within him. Nites surged towards him, and he flared brighter than ever as the high-powered nites flooded his system. Kal opened his eyes, and puffs of light leaked out. He barely held the magic in check. With this kind of power, he could do anything, *be* anything. He wallowed in it and then felt something watching him.

The hair on the back of his arms stood on end. A great predator lurked somewhere nearby, ready to pounce. Kal thought of the conversation he'd had with Lady Millaine. "As long as you don't use too much power," she had said. Kal blinked as nothing but power roared all around him. Panting, he tried to focus under the weight of that stare. The portal shimmered brightly to his enhanced gaze as a dozen more Compact soldiers streamed into the cavern. More soldiers headed toward Jenna. He had to do this now, even if his life was forfeit.

Ignoring the weight of that presence, Kal reached out with his hand, focused his intent, and cast. The soldiers in front of Jenna stopped, confusion showing on their faces as their armor fell from them, the metal holding it together gone. Their swords turned to dust in their hands.

The wave of magic pushed past Jenna, through the soldiers pouring through the gate until it reached Casi, who was herself aglow with magic. The rod in her hand crumpled, then fell away, vaporized. The barrels of liquid magic behind her ruptured as the metal hoops holding them together disappeared. There was a popping noise from the wall as the portal wavered for a moment before collapsing in on itself. Cries rung out as the soldiers in transit were torn apart.

Casi screamed as magic came from her eyes and mouth, then fell to the ground.

Justin knelt, skin graying as the soldier standing over him reached to pull the sword from him, but it, too, disintegrated. Groaning, he fell to the ground as a fresh well of blood gushed from his open wound.

The soldier standing over him turned away. "To me!" he yelled as he turned towards Kal. The mage and the remaining soldiers headed for their captain.

Kal's hands shook at the sudden loss of all that power. He'd done it. The gate was closed. His legs quivered as he tried to stand, and his shoulder and back throbbed. Kal reached up and pulled the arrow's shaft free, its head having dissolved. Off to his right, the Lycanides still fought with the statues. Jenna stood over newly dead soldiers, looking ready to fight her way to her sister. His heart twinged as she pulled magic to her. Strands of hair had come free from her braid, floating around her like a halo. She was beautiful and fierce, and at that moment, something powerful and full of hope rose in him. He would rise and follow her into that cavern. He would follow her anywhere. Though unarmed, the Compact soldiers were still warriors, and some were mages. There were only two of them. They likely wouldn't live, but they would make it count.

Kal got to his feet and stepped toward Jenna as his net tingled behind him. Glancing over his shoulder, he saw his team and his pack along with the Royal Guard enter the chamber.

Thank The Three.

Relief flooded Kal as the king's Guard charged forward. Kal's net tingled as the Lycanides fighting Star and Jay launched up into the cavern, climbing into hidden shafts to escape, his pack in pursuit.

Kal pulled nites to refuel his power, but he felt insignificant compared to what he had been moments earlier. It would have to be enough.

His team came up beside Kal as Star and Jay approached.

Kal thought about the missing children, of his brother, and of Jenna. He thought about Casi, and Justin, and Rowen. He thought about every citizen of Mendallon when he gave the order. "Kill them all." Several dozen guards charged forward, swords and shields at the ready. Kal's net detected even more soldiers behind them. An entire platoon had arrived.

Compact soldiers and mages clashed with the guards, but without swords, only the mages could put up a fight, and Jenna took advantage of their distraction to end their lives. One of the Compact mages avoided Jenna's darts and drew on the power of the liquid magic, launching a wall of arrows at the royal soldiers, killing those who didn't get their small shields up in time. Before Kal could act, Star and Jay were there. Jay threw a mage shield over Kal, his team, and the remaining guard as Star stepped through the shield and attacked. Kal's eyes widened. How did these statues work? It was like they generated their own magic. Even if the Compact had swords, they wouldn't have been a match for Star, who sent a volley of magic arrows, puncturing their unarmored bodies and impaling the last mage, who fell to the ground as their formation shattered. Enemy soldiers broke free, scattering through the various openings in the cavern wall, but not before Star killed their captain.

Jay dropped his shield, and Kal's team surged after the Compact soldiers, cutting down the main group while several squads pursued those who fled into the tunnels.

Jenna raced into the cavern with the guards, looking for her brother and sister. Kal followed, senses alight as waves of power soaked into the porous ground from the liquid magic. *So many nites wasted.* Kal sighed. They were fortunate nothing had ignited the liquid magic. The Compact mages had either been too busy defending themselves to think of it, or they were under orders to save the gate since blowing the liquid magic would have brought the caverns down and killed them all. Either way, the liquid was gone, absorbing into the cavern floor.

Kal went to Casi as Jenna rolled her brother over, who lay in a pool of blood. Nites swirled around Jenna as she pulled on the liquid magic and began healing Justin. Kal checked, and Casi was breathing. She was likely exhausted from the sheer power she had channeled, and the backlash from all that power disappearing was likely not pleasant either.

A wave of exhaustion washed over him. He used liquid magic to fend it off. He shifted Casi into a more comfortable position as the sounds in the cavern became more muted. The guards dispersed into the tunnels, searching for stragglers. Kal breathed a sigh of relief. The Compact invasion was over.

Chapter 45

Bitter Truth

Two days after the attack, Kal stared at Captain Abasi. Corin had not only sent men into the caverns to stop the invasion but also to raid all the known Compact locations.

"Report, Captain," Corin said.

Captain Abasi straightened.

"Sire, though the Andrades and Cardinases were working with the Compact, we believe they were unaware of the Compact's goal to invade. According to documents recovered from the houses, they were each promised the kingship in separate deals."

Abasi placed a folder on the king's desk before continuing.

"At the Cardinas' estate, we found documents showing payment proving they hired the assassins to kill Kal. We also found a promissory note for rights to exclusive trade agreements and support for their bid for the crown in return for the mage-born children."

Corin frowned. "So what made them act? Wouldn't it have made more sense for them to wait until things had settled and try again?"

"We believe that Kal's order and subsequent freeing of the children was the catalyst for the uprising. Without the children, the rebels had no choice but to speed up the takeover. They used the scorpion creatures granted by the Compact at the castle to guarantee success. The alternative was to risk the Compact showing themselves to the populace to reclaim the children, which would have turned the people against them."

Corin rubbed his temples. "You and I both know that the attack failed because of Kal and his pack protecting the Sandovals and the palace."

"Yes, sir," Abasi said, looking like he had a bad taste in his mouth.

"What is the latest news with the house heads?"

"The head of House Cardinas died while trying to evade capture, but the head of House Andrade was captured alive and is currently in the dungeon. The heirs of both houses are confined to their quarters."

"What of the Compact?" Kal asked.

"We have shut down all Compact locations provided by the knights, plus a few others we've discovered through the Shadow Weavers. Unfortunately, we did not find Baron Jaxson."

"So there is something we missed," Kal said, thinking back to his white gloves he wore and the Rod of Inanis. Jaxson wasn't leading the Compact in the caverns as Kal had expected. *So where was he? Just what had been more important?*

"We put up wanted posters. It should make it harder for him to interact with people. Unless he is a mage, we will find him."

"Thank you, Captain. You may go," Corin said.

Captain Abasi bowed and left Corin's study.

K al and the king headed down the narrow stairs leading to the dungeons. As they walked, the giant stones making up the base of the castle changed from a gleaming white to a pockmarked gray and finally to coal-like black. Alternating mage and oil lights lit the stairs, giving off an eerie glow. A dozen Royal Guards followed behind them. When they reached the landing, the prison master, a broad man with dark eyes and a salt-and-pepper beard, greeted them. He bowed and pulled the lever to raise the massive bars, blocking the only exit from the dungeons. Chains rattled as it lifted, showing the entrance was in good repair. The clinking stopped as the lattice of bars reached its highest point and locked into place.

Waiting on the other side was the warden. "Good afternoon, sire."

"To you as well, Warden."

"This way, sire," the warden said.

They all followed him through the gate, which closed behind them. Kal and the king grimaced at the wave of force that suppressed their magic. The guards shuffled as if feeling something, too. There was an old saying: In the dungeons, all men were equal.

The warden turned, leading them along a winding corridor through two more gates. The dungeon was built into the caverns below the palace. Some side passages were dark and foreboding, while others were well lit. The air was cool compared to the palace. Kal could make out cells down some corridors. Finally, the warden stopped at a door with bars at the top and the prison master pulled out a set of keys. The keys rattled as he unlocked the door and opened it.

"Please wait here a moment, my lords," he said.

The broad shoulders of the prison master disappeared into the darkness of the cell. There was the sound of chains dragging against stone and then silence. A few moments later, light illuminated the cell, which looked like a natural cavern. From the doorway, they could see the disgraced Lord Erick Andrade sitting in a chair with a lattice of chains holding him in place. Across from him was an empty chair. The prison master stood off to the left. He removed his hand from the lever that triggered the light and walked toward them. Nodding to the king and Kal, he gestured for them to enter.

Kal entered the room first and took up a position near the door. The king followed, glancing up to take in the mirror system reflecting light into the room from a small hand-sized opening in the ceiling. The remaining guards, the warden, and the prison master stayed in the hall. Corin sat opposite Erick, who squinted at Corin as his eyes adjusted to the light. When Erick recognized Corin, his expression went from guarded to hostile before clearing.

"I suppose you are here to kill me," Erick spoke casually.

Corin raised an eyebrow. "Is that what you want?"

Erick snorted. "It's what you promised me if I betrayed you."

Corin frowned. "When?"

"After you almost killed me in the arena."

Now it was Corin's turn to snort. "That wasn't me."

"Ah, you'll claim ignorance?" This time, Erick sounded bitter.

"Is that why you betrayed me?" Corin prodded.

Chains rustled as Erick shifted positions.

"I betrayed you because you are unfit to rule. I've spent years listening to you ask me to dig, order me to provide maps of the underground, and command me to keep watch for invaders—"

"So when you found the underground and the invaders, you made a deal with them instead of coming to me?"

Erick licked his lips.

"You were unstable."

Corin flinched at the truth in his words. "And what of my brother? Was he unstable?"

"He murdered the previous king."

Kal stirred as Corin's shoulders tensed. His brother had always been angry on his behalf.

"So, you gave them the one resource that could have protected the kingdom?" Corin demanded.

It was Erick's turn to flinch, turning away.

"What did they offer you?" Corin demanded.

Erick paused. "Everything," he whispered.

Corin ground his teeth, veins popping out on the back of his hands as he balled them into fists.

"Do you know the price if they had succeeded?" Corin waited for Erick to meet his eyes. "Everything."

Bitterness gave the word weight. Erick's head rocked back as though he'd been slapped. The king continued. "Your reign would have been short-lived. You see, they were using the children to power a giant portal that would have joined our kingdom with theirs." He waited a moment for the words to sink in. Erick's eyes went round in understanding. "Thousands of enemies would have flooded the city from the underground caverns you claimed didn't exist. Hundreds of scorpion creatures that I don't even have a name for would have attacked us."

The color drained from Erick's face, then he flushed red as he stared daggers at the king.

"You don't believe me. Fine," the king said and turned to Kal. "Tell Adam I require his presence," he commanded in clipped tones.

Kal left the cell and sent a message to Adam before returning to his position by the door. The three men sat in silence. A while later, Adam entered the room, his boots echoing on the cell floor. He stared down at Erick and spoke in a richly textured baritone voice.

"So, you didn't listen." Adam crossed his arms.

Erick Andrade's eyes met Adam's. His brows furrowed.

"I know that tone," he said, squinting up at him. "But I don't know you."

Erick's eyes flickered back and forth between the king and Adam.

"Who are you?" Erick asked, face flushing.

"I was the one who broke up your little rebellion meeting." Erick's eyes widened as Adam's eyes bore into him. "I was the one who beat you in the arena. I was the one who warned you that if you or yours betrayed the king, I would destroy you."

Erick's eyes flicked back and forth between the king and Adam. "H-how is this possible?" His voice was hoarse, raspy. "Who are you?"

"I am Drakothadam—one of The Three."

"But how?"

"He doesn't owe you an explanation," said Corin as Adam towered over Erick.

Erick flinched, then laughed bitterly. "So you're telling me I went against the will of the gods?" His hands were clenched into fists. "I have striven all my life to follow the path of The Three." Erick squared his shoulders, facing Adam. "So, you'll kill me now?"

"Oh, I have no intention of letting you off the hook just yet. You will go through the process. As per the law, you are stripped of your house and lands. You will be a warning to all future usurpers. You will live out your life here, in this dungeon."

Each word hit Erick like a blow, his knuckles white with strain.

Adam laughed. "Remind me not to make you angry. If that is all, I will take my leave. I feel the need to stand in the sun."

Rising, Corin led them out of the cell, and they followed him into the light.

Chapter 46

The Last Wall

A day later, Kal escorted Jenna to the estate of Corvald Dydimus. She had spent the time caring for Justin, who had barely survived his time in the caverns.

"Not you, sir," the guard said to Kal. "My lord requested Lady Sandoval only."

Jenna flinched, which caused her head to hurt. She had been getting headaches since sharing energy with Kal in the caverns. It was only with makeup that she could conceal the bags under her eyes. Before this meeting, Kal had siphoned off as many nites as possible, but Jenna still found herself sluggish.

Concern shaded Kal's features, so Jenna forced a smile. For a moment, Jenna sensed a protest, but he graciously bowed. Then he surprised her. He took her hand and kissed the back of it. Her heart fluttered in her chest. She breathed deeply, controlled her expression but allowed her brow to raise. She then turned and followed the guard from the room.

He took her upstairs, past two guards standing outside a door leading to what appeared to be a study. Sunlight filtered brightly into the room.

When she entered, Didymus sat at the desk, going through missives. He still wore the multilayered Seeming that made it impossible to tell who he was. She gracefully arranged herself in a chair opposite him. When she finished, he stared at her appreciatively.

"You learn quickly."

"Thank you, my lord."

"So, about your future, my lady. Have you considered what you will do when your training ends?"

Jenna flared her nostrils in surprise. She had been so caught up in her family that she hadn't put any thought into it. Corvald tilted his head slightly, watching.

"I thought not." He paused. "I want you to work for me."

This time, Jenna was careful not to flare her nostrils. She leaned back. She didn't know this man, and Kal seemed a little afraid of him.

"Just what does working for you entail, Master Didymus?"

The corner of his mouth quirked.

"Oh, nothing untoward, my lady. Kal is a great asset. Irreplaceable, one might say, and with his training, you have proven yourself to be a lady of no small skill. You obtained information vital to the coup. You followed Kal into the caverns and aided in preventing an invasion. Per Kal, if you hadn't done that, the city would have fallen. As a lady of the courts, you can go where men cannot. It does, however, mean that you may never cross paths except at cocktail parties. I couldn't have the two of you working that closely together."

Jenna didn't know what to say. Her head started to throb. The idea of leaving Kal made her blood run cold. She tried to imagine herself only seeing Kal casually at cocktail parties, and her stomach churned, uneasiness washing through her, causing beads of sweat to form on her upper lip. Why was she having this reaction? She discarded several negative replies, looking for one suitable for a man of Corvald's standing.

"Oh, no need to answer now, my lady. I will send you a formal contract with duties on it. You can have someone look it over and decide later."

She pasted on a neutral smile and nodded acceptance, ignoring her headache.

"Before I call Kal in, I would like you to play a game with me."

His topic shift startled her again. "My lord?"

He escorted her to a side table with a game board, which allowed her to gracefully dab some of the sweat off her brow.

"Here is the game board. It's called chess. Have you played it before?"

Jenna shook her head and stared at the intricately designed board and pieces. They were beautifully handcrafted stone, polished to a high gloss, and depicted soldiers in various states of battle. There was no dust on this board, so she presumed he played often.

"I have seen a board before, though. Grandfather has one."

Corvald explained the rules and graciously gave her the first move. They played to a standoff.

Jenna was quite proud, but Corvald studied her with hooded eyes.

"My lord?" Her pleasure withered under his emotionless stare. *What have I done wrong?*

"It appears we have a problem, Lady Sandoval." Not a muscle on his artificial face moved.

"A problem, my lord?" The lack of visual cues put an edge of panic in her tone.

"It appears Kal has not been completely honest with me." He frowned as he went to the door, opened it, and sent for Kal.

She sensed Kal approaching the room. He entered, eyes scanning until he found Jenna unharmed. Two guards followed him in.

"Guards, seal the room. No one comes in or out until I give the command."

"My lord." They bowed and shut the doors as they left.

Kal stared down at his shoes.

"Kal?" she asked.

Kal looked up, hands clasped into fists, and studied Corvald.

"Why didn't you tell me it was this bad?"

"We've been managing the symptoms," Kal mumbled. "She's fine."

Corvald walked behind his desk and placed his hands on it, clearly thinking about where to begin.

The layers of Seemings melted off of him. In place of Corvald Didymus stood King Corin. Jenna stared at him in open astonishment.

"How did you figure it out?" Kal asked.

"I offered her a job and then told her she wouldn't see you in any capacity other than social."

Kal drew an unsteady breath.

"That was my first hint. I then challenged her to a game of chess. She claimed to have never played before, yet she played me to a standoff. Only you have ever played me to a standoff."

Kal's eyes flicked to the board, where he took in the position of the pieces and paled.

"Exactly," said Corin.

Jenna stared back and forth between the brothers.

"She learned twice what you thought she could learn in half the time. Some of that is indeed her, but the rest of it is you, Kal."

"Anyone care to explain?" Jenna hazarded.

"The maghin, when she removed it..." Kal trailed off.

"I thought you dealt with her shields."

"I did, but I have to treat her more and more often to get the same results. We were looking for the traitors behind the missing children and running out of time."

"Why didn't you say something? You know this will eventually kill her, right?"

Kal flinched.

"Unless." The king turned to study her.

Jenna followed the byplay between them and paled under the king's gaze.

Kal's eyes went wide, understanding. "No! I won't do it."

"Oh, so she's to die, then? For what? Your pride?"

Jenna mentally substituted the word fear. She understood why he hadn't reached out for help. He was so sure that doing this would bind her to an unworthy person. What he wasn't aware of, and she had not been able to articulate, was that she had long since bound herself to him.

"Is she worth so little to you?" Corin said softly.

Kal started to shake. "Please, Cor—"

"No. Whether you accept this or not, you are worthy. Perhaps this will make you see it. You *will* bow to me on this, brother."

Jenna froze.

Kal stood there staring at the floor.

"Swear it! On Father's grave!"

Kal flinched. "I swear. On Father's grave."

For a moment, Jenna believed Corin would require an oath.

"Jenna?" The king spoke.

"Yes, sire?" The words popped out of her mouth before she could stop it.

"Come and sit on the couch."

She hurried across the room and sat where asked.

"Kal, you too."

He came over and sat down next to Jenna.

Corin pulled up a chair and stared back and forth at the two of them.

He formed a three-way link between them. "Let's see the damage, then."

Kal flinched.

Corin peeled back the first layer of shields. "Kal," he gasped. "How could you?"

"How could he what?" she asked.

A long beat of silence echoed from them before Corin said, "How could he leave you like this?"

Kal's face mottled in anger as he glared at his brother.

Jenna started to defend him when a headache raced through her. She gritted her teeth, knuckles flexing as her fists clenched. She groaned, and Kal and Corin, who had been in a staring contest, shifted their attention to Jenna.

Jenna struggled to sit still as Corin measured the damage in her mind. She could feel the nites digging through the shields as he studied the traps used to collect them.

"The traps were a good idea," he said. "They are being overwhelmed at a fast rate, though."

"The more she used her powers, the more they grew, and we were on a timeline." Kal continued. "The attack and backlash from breaking the oath pushed her to the edge."

Corin frowned.

"Okay, I have a plan," the king said, and they both stared at him. "It's dangerous, though."

Of course it is. She frowned.

"Jenna?"

"Oh, now I exist?" she said, unable to control the anger flashing through her.

"Don't be peevish," said Corin.

"You're poking around in my head and speaking as if I don't exist. I think I've earned the right to be a bit peevish."

"Hmm," he said, as if trying to suppress a smile. "Jenna, I will need you to drop your shields."

"What?" Both Jenna and Kal spoke at the same time and in the same tone.

"Not all at once, but in layers," the king placated.

"But won't that leave me wide open?" she asked.

"No. Well, yes, especially the first time—"

"The first time?" she prompted.

"Yes, we'll start with the innermost shell first."

They both stared at him with identical quizzical expressions. He chuckled and explained. "Kal will act as a decoy and set traps on the inward side only; this will draw them away from your core self. Then, you will drop and rebuild just that one layer as thickly as possible. I will work with Kal to draw out the nites that are trapped. We're similar enough that I should be able to coax some of them out."

She considered several questions and chose one.

"What will you do with them when you have them?" she asked curiously.

Corin smiled, and Kal smirked.

"I will build a construct." He grinned, and then both brothers laughed.

Brothers.

"What happens when someone drops their innermost shields?"

The laughter stopped.

"I will be on the outskirts, so it will not affect me, but for a brief while, you will have no secrets."

"Like the merge?" she asked, recalling their training session when he'd made her swear the oath not to kill with magic. "Where all your thoughts, fears, and past are exposed?"

"Ah, so he did tell you about that. This is the basis of it, but in this case, it will only last as long as it takes you to rebuild your shields. You may not realize it, but you understand Kal as well as or even better than I do at this point. It shouldn't affect you as much, but Kal will be exposed to you."

"I will be able to feel his reactions to me?"

Again, that silence.

She was aware they were having a side conversation, but didn't care. She resigned herself to losing him. *I should have just taken the job.*

"Ready?" Corin asked.

"Yes," Jenna said.

She brought them down the quickest path through her mauled shields and into her conscious mind. Avatars representing each of them accompanied her. They were close enough to her core that she sensed them talking without her and excluding her from the conversation. They arrived at the innermost layer. Her avatar self peered around. Her shield had pockmarks and was so thin at points that she was surprised it hadn't already collapsed. She considered what it would be like to die that way.

Would I even know that I had died? Perhaps I am already dead? Her innermost shield was regenerating itself from the inside in an attempt to protect itself, and she shivered, not sure why she didn't care more than she did. She sensed Corin leave as Kal's aura come up beside her.

"Jenna?"

"Master?"

"Please, Jenna." He closed his eyes.

Jenna turned to him. "Kal, I'm scared."

He cocked his head, listening. "I'll be here with you the whole time."

That's what scares me the most.

After a brief pause, he said, "It's time."

She turned toward the core and passed through it.

From the inside, she studied Kal's graceful lines as he flung a net of traps around the core. When all the nets made a sphere around the center, he stopped and stared at her. She saw the resolve on his face.

The last nite left the core's outer wall. She couldn't sense them building up, so Corin must be extracting them as promised.

She put her hand over her heart, gathered as much energy as possible, and dropped her shields.

All that she was, all that she had ever done, all the potential—both good and bad—lay exposed. It was then that she sensed it. Admiration, pride, sympathy, love, support. These emotions all flowed from Kal toward her. She was so shocked that her avatar fell to her knees, and the tide of battle changed. She sensed him getting overwhelmed, trying to siphon off the nites coming down from the other layers.

With pride in her heart, she rebuilt her innermost shields. In joy, she kept building, filling each layer with love and acceptance of Kal. Layers upon layers. His compassion for others. His quiet thoughtfulness. His amusements. His frustrations. His fears. His abilities and his flaws. Kal stood in shock as the shield enveloped him and pulled him gently into her core. She sensed him as he took down his shields and gave himself to her. Memories of his mother, brother, and the death of his father. He added his years under the maghin, their first meeting, the removal of the maghin, and everything through to today. The nites stopped attacking her, recognizing that there was no enemy.

Within her innermost shields, Jenna stared at Kal for a long moment. Out of all the memories he had shared, he stood, shoulders hunched, seeing his mother and her reaction to him. She touched his arm, bringing him away from the image. "You are worthy of love. I know this because I love you."

Kal studied her as if he wanted to fight, but the proof was all around him. Slowly, the tension eased out of him, and a boyish grin she had never seen before stretched across his face. "I love you, too."

Kal leaned down, pulling her close, and kissed her.

The End

Do you still want more? Want to know how Roolia convinced Captain Abasi to reassign Doha? I have a collection of deleted scenes you can access using the following QR code.

Or click the link bookfunnel link to access the deleted scenes. Note: You will automatically be subscribed to my newsletter, which will keep you up to date on other freebies and future release dates.

To read the prologue of book two, turn the page.

Jaxson

J axson sat at his desk on his air class frigate, still hidden outside of Mendallon, contemplating his choices. His communications globe flashed. It was time to make his report.

Jaxson put his hand on the globe, and the world went fuzzy. When it cleared, he was in the prince's court. The familiar black-and-red sash sat over the prince's shoulders.

Jaxson knew he was just as visible as the prince, right down to the sweat trail down the side of his face.

"Report."

"The invasion site has been lost," Jaxson said.

"Then why are you not dead?"

Jaxson gritted his teeth. "While the gate was being built, I was attaining a place suitable for the High Warden and checking the various locations set aside for us to house and hide our forces. My presence wasn't required at the gate until the initial formalities were done."

"Have you been able to ascertain what went wrong?"

"Several men escaped the caverns to find our hideouts overrun with Royal Guards. A runner was sent to me, and following protocol, we met on the ship." Jaxson grimaced. "According to the reports, they were attacked by the king's brother and golems."

"Golems? Are you sure?"

"Yes, my prince."

"That means Drakothadam is awake."

Jaxson flinched. "Which, according to the histories, means the rest of the city will soon follow. Including the towers."

The prince frowned. "Weren't the Lycanides able to handle the golems?"

"We lost several members of our pack to the king's brother. He is far more powerful than reported. Somehow, he was able to destroy the Rod of Inanis."

The prince's eyebrows rose. "So you are trapped there?"

"No, there is a backup rod that should allow us to open a new portal."

"The king's brother will have to be dealt with, as well as Drakothadam. It will take some time, but I will send a contingent of airships to help you subdue the city."

"What about the towers?"

"If we're lucky, we will get there before they are active again, but if not, there is risk in every conquest."

Jaxson kept the emotion off his face. So far, the prince had taken no risk. "Yes, my prince."

"Figure out how to stop their mages and kill the king's brother."

Jaxson hid his flinch. "Yes, my prince." He bowed and severed the connection.

He needed to learn more about the king's brother.

Thank You

Acknowledgements

When they say it takes a village, they aren't kidding. Many people helped me along the way. From kind words when I wanted to give up, research on large scale battles, to help writing a structured story. I couldn't have done it without you.

Here goes.

Alpha, Beta, and Super Readers (in no particular order) Michael Fitzgerald, Andy Wrobel, Jon Fitzgerald, Aedan Fitzgerald, Dorothy Kerr, Chris Kerr, Heather Hopp, Aviv Yaacobi, Ralph Kerr, Amy Newhall, Terri Mitchell, Vincent Eiler, Alex Kerr, Augusta Bracknell, Kellie Hurth, Karen Massey, Cardell Kerr, Nate Kerr.

The Fantasy Writers "Greater Good" critique group: Elizabeth Wilbraham, Dragana Munitić, Holly Bernabe, Susan Mansbridge, Jenna Priaulx, Amanda Atsiaris, Fern Nueno, Leah Boyer.

Local critique group: Leah Samuel, Steven Wooden

Women Writing Other Worlds writing group: https://womenwritingotherworlds.com

Editors: Lacey Braziel at On The Page Editorial, Oren Ashkenazi at Mythcreants, and Michael Fitzgerald

Proofreader: Lindsey Hinkel at Ink Rebel Editing

Map: Stardust Book Services. Cartographer: Fred Kroner https:/ /www.stardustbookservices.com/fred

Cover Art: https://miblart.com/

If I've missed you, my apologies, and know that I am deeply grateful to you.

About the Author

Lark Fitzgerald is an African American fantasy writer. She began writing to explore the realms of her imagination. When she is not writing, she can be found watching Korean dramas with her husband, reading manga, listening to books, or walking the dog.